MINDLESS

Also by Keith C. Blackmore

Mountain Man
Mountain Man
Safari
Hellifax
Well Fed
Make Me King
Mindless
Skull Road
Mountain Man Prequel
Mountain Man 2nd Prequel: Them Early Days
The Hospital: A Mountain Man Story
Mountain Man Omnibus: Books 1–3

131 Days
131 Days
House of Pain
Spikes and Edges
About the Blood
To Thunderous Applause
131 Days Omnibus: Books 1–3

Breeds
Breeds
Breeds 2
Breeds 3
Breeds: The Complete Trilogy

Isosceles Moon
Isosceles Moon
Isosceles Moon 2

The Bear That Fell from the Stars
Bones and Needles
Cauldron Gristle
Flight of the Cookie Dough Mansion
The Majestic 311
The Missing Boatman
Private Property
The Troll Hunter
White Sands, Red Steel

MOUNTAIN MAN

BOOK 6

MINDLESS

KEITH C. BLACKMORE

All rights reserved. No part of this publication may be reproduced, stored in a retrieval system, or transmitted in any form or by any means electronic, mechanical, photocopying, recording, or otherwise without prior written permission from Podium Publishing.

This is a work of fiction. Names, characters, places, and incidents are either products of the author's imagination or used fictitiously. Any resemblance to actual events, locales, or persons, living, dead, or undead, is entirely coincidental.

Copyright © 2021 Keith C. Blackmore

Cover design by Podium Publishing

ISBN: 978-1-0394-4989-3

Published in 2023 by Podium Publishing, ULC
www.podiumaudio.com

MINDLESS

1

A figure stopped before the cell door, dimming the light coming through the window.

Milo Trasher, once known as "Top Gun", looked up from his e-reader and frowned.

The door clicked and slid open. Collie Jones entered, dressed in fresh camouflage pants and jacket. A warm-looking balaclava covered her face all the way to her neck, where the jacket was open three buttons, revealing a black t-shirt underneath. Black gloves covered her hands while sunglasses hid her eyes. Not one inch of skin showed. To those who weren't acquainted with Collie, they'd think they were looking at the invisible man fully dressed.

The man called Gus walked in behind her, also dressed in fresh clothing, but projecting an unchecked vibe of raw contempt. Checked shirt, black leather coat, and a set of faded blue jeans. His bald head gleamed in the light, and the sides were buzzed clean. His beard, however, hung off his face like a trimmed slab of steel wool, and his eyes narrowed as they locked onto Milo. All Gus needed to complete the grungy biker look was a motorcycle, some shades, and a couple of strategically placed tattoos, maybe even a cigar glued to his furry lip.

Milo didn't meet his gaze—he knew how the guy felt about him. He'd made it clear before and he was making it clear now.

Their entrance caused the soldier to put aside his book and sit up on his bunk. He scratched the back of his neck, feeling the ends of his eighties-style mullet. It wasn't elastic band length yet, and he didn't think he would let it grow that long, anyway. The wind-burned, aging-hippy look wouldn't do for him. Milo noted the clothes his visitors wore. Someone had done a little shopping since they'd last visited.

"Morning, cowboy," Collie greeted, sounding as if a smile accompanied the words. Her balaclava hid her expression, but she nodded at him and the e-reader.

"Anything good?" she asked.

Milo hesitated. "Yeah. Not bad."

"Yeah? Like what?"

"Western thing. With two Texas rangers."

"Nice. I was into reading once. History, mostly. Loved history." She gestured to the only chair. "You mind?"

Collie didn't wait for an answer. She pulled the chair out from a mini-table extending from the wall. She sat down wearily, settled in, and scratched at the corner of an eye.

Milo watched her. "How you doing?"

That question darkened Gus's face, and his eyes flicked from the soldier to the special operator.

"Not bad, thanks," Collie replied, taking the time to tug on one glove and then the other. "Could be better, all things considered. Nothing that a few cotton swabs and some disinfectant can't fix. Sorry I haven't been by recently. We've been busy. Buying groceries. Paying bills. Cleaning house. That was the worst. Cleaning up all them dead Leather fuckers. There were a *lot* of them dead Leather fuckers lying around, weren't there Gus?"

"Mm-hm," Gus grunted, once again glaring at Milo and projecting a vibe of disdain as strong as gamma rays.

No one spoke then, and Milo looked from one to the other, imagining one of them shooting him in the face right there and then. His money was on the angry shitty-assed biker called Gus.

But Collie surprised him. "So, look," she started. "We need to talk about a few things." She aimed a finger at him. "Concerning you. And what you know about these Leather fuckers. Namely, the still *living* Leather fuckers. And your continued existence here."

Milo scratched at his sandy blonde hair. "All right."

"Referring to them as Leather fuckers doesn't bother you, right?"

"No."

"You sure?"

"I'm sure."

"Because," Collie went on, "really, it's better than what Gus wanted to call them. What was that again, Gus?"

Gus's scowl intensified, from open disdain to potential axe murderer. "Leather chicken fucks."

"Yeah," Collie said as if attempting to contain a smile behind her mask. "That's the one. Thanks. Anyway, about them. I've decided to go out west and kill the one they call Dog Dick."

Milo blinked at that. "Uh… You mean 'Dog Tongue'."

"That's what he calls himself?"

"Yeah."

"Not Dog Dick?"

"No, not… no."

"Oh," Collie said and thought for a moment. "Sorry."

"No need to apologize to me," Milo said. "Really. Like I said before, I'm not with those guys. I was strictly freelance. Well… *forced* into freelance, you understand. We covered all that."

"I know." Collie picked at the holster on her right thigh. The button came free with a little pop. "You explained all that. How you were looking to get free of them. Your crew, I mean. What did you call them? Gus? What did he call them?"

"Skin Pirates."

"Yeah. Skin Pirates."

"That's what Jolly Jake called us," Milo said, trying very hard to keep his tone cool.

"Right," Collie nodded. "And you were looking to get away from your *crew* at your earliest convenience. I've had time to think about that. Really think about that. And you know what—and this'll pull your taint tight and leave you squealin'—I don't think you tried hard enough to cut yourself loose of your gang. Or your employers."

Milo's face drooped just a little.

"Shhh, shhhh," Collie soothed, cutting him off before he could start. "No need to talk. I understand. Peer pressure is a real thing. A bitch. Like when the Leather fuckers got you to shoot me."

Milo rolled his eyes, shifted on the bunk, and swallowed.

Gus's axe-murdering glare intensified, impossibly so, now glass-melting. He zeroed in on Milo alone.

"I know," Collie carried on, her sunglasses fixed on him. She was oblivious to the sheer hatred being lasered in by her biker buddy. "Now, thing is…I *also* remember what you did for Carson back at the box. And for me, really. That *does* count for something. And you were pretty forthcoming with information about the Leather fuckers and the… Leather fucking towns?"

She directed the question at Gus, who nodded, his mouth a puckered-up pustule ready to spit acid.

"Leather fucking towns," Collie said. "Let's just call them Leather towns. Keep it simple. Yeah. So, anyway, we were talking. Gus and I. We've decided to head out west. You're gonna come along with us. Way I see it, you're military, and I don't feel comfortable with leaving you here with a bunch of civilians. Too much could happen back here in case I'm wrong about you. See where I'm going with this?"

Milo stared. "Maybe."

Collie drew her sidearm, pointing it at the soldier and stiffening his spine as she did so.

"Relax," she said. "I'm not going to pop you. Not yet, anyway. Right now, you're sorta valuable to us. In an advisory role. As I was saying. We're heading out west, me and this meathead."

She indicated Gus, who frowned at the designation.

"We're going to go to these Leather towns," Collie explained. "See what's what. You're going to come with us and help out in every way possible. Let us know everything you know about these Leather whackjobs and the Dick Tongue."

Milo's face almost broke into a smile. Almost. Having a gun pointed at you made you think twice about chuckling at a joke, but the angry biker Gus was staring at him again, and somehow that made the gun look like the more painless way to go.

"Dick Dog," Gus growled, part of his eyebrow twitching when he spoke.

"Dog. Tongue," Milo corrected and smiled anyway. "That's what he calls himself."

"I like to think of him as…" Collie paused in thought. "An old-fashioned fuckwit."

"An overfull shitpouch," Gus offered.

Collie nodded at that one. "With delusions of grandeur. Y'know?"

Milo refrained from commenting.

"Anyway," she continued. "You're gonna come along and help us kill them. One by one, if we have to. By hand, knife, bullet, or boot. Just… kill 'em. Like the fucked-up cockroaches they are. That way you can prove to me—to us—that your heart is indeed in the right place. Understand?"

"Sure," Milo swallowed. The resulting click sounded like a pistol being readied.

"There's an upside," Collie said. "So don't think you're being forced to do anything you don't want to do. Do everything we ask and you'll be considered one of the new townsfolk of Whitecap. You'll be a citizen. In good standing.

Believe you me. You see the shit they got to do here on the weekends? You'll be happy. Sound good?"

It did indeed sound good, but Milo was trying very hard not to look at the gun pointed in his direction, all the while very mindful of the stone-cold Gus still watching him. "Yeah. Sounds great."

"So you'll come with us?"

"Oh, yeah. I'm... I'm in."

"Excellent. Get a good night's sleep. We leave in the morning."

"Huh?"

"You heard me, cowboy. Bright and early, too. Full on battle rattle. Nothing you're not used to."

That dimmed Milo's expression.

"You don't look too happy," Collie noted.

"No, I'll help. Said I'll help. It's just... I know what's out there. I've said it before—you got a good thing here. This bunker. It's remote enough that he'll probably never find you."

"But then he'll find the others," Collie countered. "Even the ones we don't know about."

Milo gnawed on the inside of his cheek. "Yeah."

"Then it's ball gags for everyone."

If they're lucky, Milo thought, but what he said was, "Yeah."

"That's fucked up," Gus whispered.

"Real fucked up," Collie agreed. "I mean... really. You're not actually *fine* with all of that?"

Milo lowered his eyes.

"Milo," Collie said. "You're Patricia's. A member of the 'vicious princesses' themselves. Joking aside, you are part of a decorated regiment. I say you 'are' because we both know, once in, you're never really out. Even if the PPCLI is gone and you're all that remains, well, that means you. Are. The. Regiment. You're it. And you represent it. You say you fell in with the wrong crew? Well, I believe you. These are wild times. Shit happens. Every day. To anyone. But you made a conscious choice to break away. When you helped us back at the box. And you've been very reasonable up to this point. You remember your regiment? Your regiment's *training*? The smoking ass *history*? Huh? Remember *Kap'yong*? South Korea? You remember that? What you owe to the *memory* of those soldiers? The *legacy*?"

A stunned Milo slowly nodded, totally *not* expecting that angle of persuasion.

"See?" Collie said. "I knew you did. Just forgot is all. Easy to do this day and age. In any case, you're still one of Patricia's ballbreakers. And these civilians *need* you. More than ever. Think of it this way—helping us washes your hands of whatever you might've done out there on the road. Well... most of it. I can see it's bothering you. I can smell it."

Milo didn't say anything.

Nor did Gus appear convinced.

"And that thing with you and me?" Collie pointed out. "As one professional to another, you were forced to do that. So, look... I believe you. And... I forgive you."

That widened the biker's eyes in disbelief before he stared at her.

Collie didn't seem to notice, however. She holstered her weapon and made a show of adjusting the strap. "We got some policing to do. Some people have been very, very bad. And we're going to stop them from doing any more very bad things. Help us and maybe that'll clear your conscience... if you're feeling guilty, that is."

Milo sighed and nodded again.

"And, like I mentioned. Help us and you'll get brownie points. You'll get a fresh start. Here. And here is pretty good. Isn't it, Gus?"

Gus frowned, looking more than unhappy with the proceedings. "The front yard still needs to be cleaned up."

"Hey, that's on you. *You* drove the truck up on the front lawn. But otherwise, it's good, right?"

"Yeah, it's good." But he didn't sound convinced.

Collie swung her attention back to Milo, who stared at the black sunglasses hiding her eyes.

"Said I'm in," Milo said. "So... I'm in."

"Excellent." She gripped the back of the chair. "In the morning then."

"One question, though," Milo said.

That stopped her.

"What about you?" he asked. "How is it you're still alive?"

She rose from the chair. "Sheer fuckin' force of will, cowboy. Sheer fuckin' force of will."

But Milo wasn't finished. "I mean... are *you* able to do this? I mean, with your... condition and all?"

She didn't respond right away, then, "Good point. Right now, I'm good to go."

With that, she nodded at Gus, who shut down the hate aimed at Milo and went to the door.

"Until the morning," she said.

Milo nodded.

The door closed.

Collie walked down a corridor with only half its overhead lights switched on, unconcerned with the rest of Whitecap's confinement wing. She'd gone only a few steps before realizing Gus wasn't with her. She stopped, turned around, and studied him. He was lingering around Milo's door.

"Second thoughts?" she asked.

Gus regarded the cell. He walked towards her, shaking his head all the while. "You're sure about this?" he asked.

"I'm sure. You don't look it, though."

He buttoned his lips, and the action emphasized his lack of front teeth. "He shot you, Collie."

"Straight through the heart."

That stopped him for a few seconds before he reset himself. "Through the heart. Yeah."

"And I forgave him for doing it. Maybe you should, too."

"Forgive him?" His disbelieving head rolled on his shoulders, winding up for an argument.

But then all fight left him. "Look. I'm just not sure about him. Matter of fact…"

"You feel like shooting him?"

Gus simmered with dark thoughts and didn't answer.

"You feel like doing *more* than just shooting him." A statement that time.

And no response to that either, but even though she was technically undead and reanimated by forces unknown to her, she *swore* she could feel the heat radiating off him, like a boiler on the verge of bursting.

"Well, don't," she warned. "He's useful. And it's better bringing him along than leaving him here, in a cell, with a bunch of civvies. As tough as the civvies might be."

Gus looked away.

"There something else?" she prodded.

Silence. Then, "I'm…"

"Scared?"

Gus glanced at her and didn't answer.

"You don't have to go," she said, lowering her voice. "Just stay here. Really, it's best you don't go."

"I'm going."

"Look, Gus," Collie said. "At risk of sounding like I'm stuck in a loop, you do *not* have to go. Seriously. Look…I'm dead. Long dead. And yet, I'm still here. Just two days ago I… I had to make cuts in my ankles. Just above the bone, where I squeezed the blood out. Congealed blood. Because it was all pooling down there. You know how that blood looked coming out? You wanna know? There's no saving me. No cure. Rogan wasn't able to find one. And the only thing keeping me walking is the same fucking virus that killed off everyone else."

Gus didn't break his stare.

"This—" Collie tapped her chest, the sound both plastic and hollow— "is where the bullet blew out my heart. Straight out my back. There's nothing there now but a softball-sized hole that needed to be filled. The only reason my chest isn't a shifting wreck of bone splinters is… you really want to hear this?"

Gus sighed and, ever so gently, shook his head.

And that extinguished any remaining argument in Collie.

"I'm going with you," he said quietly. He surprised her by stepping in to hug her, pressing the side of his face to hers, feeling the cotton of her mask against his skin. She let him, her posture a rigid thing, her body cold underneath her layers of clothing. That didn't stop him, however, and he held on, expecting to be pushed away any moment.

Collie did nothing of the sort.

"I'm going with you, babe," he whispered. "For better or for worse."

"It's all for worse, Gus. The only happy ending to this will be me putting down a delusional whackjob. That's it."

He imagined it was. And would be. That got him to hold onto her even tighter, nuzzling her head, then her neck. Smelling her very strong deodorant and not caring in the least.

A second later, the iceberg that was Collie relaxed, melting under him. She slowly hugged him back. "You meathead," she whispered.

"Yeah."

"This is… all bad, Gus."

"We're badder."

Her soft chuckle eased off into a sigh. "Don't kiss me," she warned.

Gus squinted his eyes shut. "You're wearing your mask."

"Best be careful. From here on end."

"Yeah. Well, then, I'm going to hold onto you for a few more seconds. That okay, babe?"

"Fine," she relented, her voice a defeated whisper. "Just don't call me 'babe', okay? Or 'baby girl'. Wallace called me those. That was sorta his thing."

"Sorry."

"No, it's… just… call me anything else."

"How about hardass?"

That got a giggle, and her arms tightened around him. Even with her layers of clothing and his, he felt the cold of her lifeless, reanimated body, but he held on anyway.

"Hardass is fine," she whispered.

2

"So what's up?" Collie asked as she and Gus entered the laboratory.

It was Gus's first time in the lab, and he slowed down to take in all the sterile whiteness covered in shade. Only a quarter of the ceiling lights were on, and Josh Rogan, the resident science guy, was sitting in his motorized wheelchair at a notably darker end of the room. Most of the computer terminals remained powered down, but there were a few steady lights, suggesting the machines were in sleep mode. It was a big room, perhaps over five thousand square feet. Mysterious equipment cluttered the area, leaving walkways just narrow enough to operate a wheelchair. Shelving units lined walls and were ceiling-high. Scientific texts and journals filled those shelves, as well as beakers and jars containing God only knew what. The air smelled clinical, as if doubly filtered and regularly spritzed with a sanitizing agent.

"You got a shitload of beakers in here, Josh," Gus remarked.

The smiling, jaw-shivering Rogan beckoned them closer. He faced a glass containment unit filled with blue light which might've been ultra-violet. The color shaded Rogan's otherwise patchy red complexion to a morbid maroon, brightened only by his twitchy, mad doctor grin. The research assistant had somehow managed to slip himself into a new pair of black pants and a sweater.

"Yes," Rogan said in that twitchy voice of his. "I suppose I do. Are you… all ready… for tomorrow's departure?"

"Just about," Collie answered. "Making a few last-minute requests."

"Is he going?" Rogan asked. "The prisoner?"

Gus forced down a snarl. The very mention of the man fired up a very dangerous, very personal anger.

"He is," Collie answered. "Milo's in. It'll be just the three of us."

"It might be safer... to shoot him," Rogan said.

"Harsh, coming from you," she said. "Gus didn't shoot you when he first met you. That turned out to be a very wise choice."

Rogan's jaw quivered. "He didn't... have a weapon... at the time."

"Let's not quibble over the particulars. Point is, he took a gamble and it paid off. I'm doing the same for Milo. It's not like I'm setting off a homemade bomb in the house. I'm taking it way out into the cornfield."

The research assistant winced, as if biting back a reply.

"You okay?" Gus asked him.

"As well as I'm going to be, I'm afraid." The man in the chair gave him a broad, amber-toothed smile. "I suspect... my time will come. Shortly. Perhaps while you're gone."

That left Gus speechless for a heartbeat. "Sorry to hear that."

"I'm... not," Rogan said. "I've lived. Only to turn over... the keys... to this place. To you. That being done. There's really not much more. For me. To do. I can pass on... in relative peace."

That silenced Gus and Collie.

Smiling, and trembling as if his ass were connected to live wires, Rogan pointed to the blue containment box. There, placed exactly in the middle of a crystal plate, was the decapitated head of a zombie. Its facial features were mostly intact, but desiccated and colored a morbid blue. The eyes were long reduced to dribbles of yellow crusts, and most of its scalp had been ripped from its skull. A speckled smear of rotting skin tags garnished the fixed sneer of its mouth, as if it were very much aware of being captured and didn't approve in the least. There was very little neck, yet the head remained upright without any external support.

Rogan cleared his throat. "Just wanted... to inform you. Of the results... of my study. Of this."

"And?" Collie asked.

"The tissue samples suggest... it's a year old. That is... it's been decomposing for a year."

"And it's still alive?" Gus asked.

"Well..." Rogan said with an amused wheeze. "As much as it's going to be."

His wheezing reached a frenzied peak for a second before settling back. Though Josh Rogan had been ever the consummate professional and, dare Gus say it, a scholar and a gentleman in regard to answering questions and explaining Whitecap's numerous features, the truth was... the assistant still creeped him out. Gus tried very hard not to show his unease, however, and that in itself, probably gave him away.

Josh Rogan, however, took no notice of him. Or at least maintained a much better poker face than Gus.

"Just wondering," Rogan said once he'd gotten himself under control. "Did you happen to... find... any more containers?"

The 'container' he was referring to was a small meat cooler discovered by Rich Trinidad. Rich and Gus, as well as a few others, had searched the Leather's vehicles for anything salvageable. Not that they needed to, not with Whitecap's vast stores at their backs, but old habits were hard to ignore. There were containers, filled with plastic baggies and jars of ready-to-use urine, since it was probably hard to piss in a bottle during a siege or any other offensive action. Or so they'd figured.

In one of those containers was a decomposing but very much reanimated head.

"No," Gus replied, staring at the bodiless thing behind the glass. "Just that."

"Well," Rogan said. "This specimen... was probably kept for... transforming undesirables... into more zombies. That's my best guess."

"All right," Collie said. "And the one we shot in the main entrance tunnel?"

That was the very corpse Gus and Collie had discovered *didn't* need a head shot to be put down. They were only partially wrong, as not a day later, the fully animated corpse had risen and followed its nose, haunting the mound of debris where Gus had taken a full piss bag to the face. Rich Trinidad had discovered the dead thing and shortly dispatched it with one shot to the brain. That had killed the creature and kept it dead.

"No doubt one of the spore zombies."

"So..." Gus drew out, "there's really no difference here."

"Not much. They become infected one way or the other. The spore zombies can be... temporarily killed. By being shot in the body. But they will rise again. Whereupon a head shot... is needed to permanently put them down. And keep them down. Just keep that in mind."

"So, really, we're back where we started," Collie said. "Head shots all the way."

"I believe that's... a fair assumption. Further testing would be necessary. For... clarification, but... I believe that is the case."

"So don't worry about whether they're first generation or second or even a third..." Gus rumbled. "Just keep shooting the head? Is that it?"

"Yes," Rogan said. "The horror movies were right, after all."

"Nothing we're not used to," Collie said. "Anything else?"

"No, not really," Rogan admitted, his smile shivering. "The… scent… the Leather were using… to direct the zombies."

"The pissbags," Gus clarified.

Rogan paused. "Yes. Those. Interesting discovery. Quite devious. The way the Leather… use it. In conjunction. With the zombies. But… from what you tell me. Water dilutes it. Weakens its potency. Keep that… in mind. For the future. If you encounter them again. Well, then."

The research assistant studied one and then the other. He slowly turned himself to a computer terminal next to the containment box. His fingers slid and scribbled over a wireless mouse, failing to grip it. The fingers shook so fiercely that Collie stepped in to help, taking control of the peripheral device.

"Thank you," Rogan whispered.

"You're welcome. Where to?" she asked, directing the cursor on the screen.

"The… green box. With… 'Initiate'… on it."

Collie placed the cursor on the button.

"One click… please," Rogan instructed.

She did exactly that, and flames puffed into existence inside the containment box, engulfing the zombie head. The flash and burn startled Gus, but what really bothered him were the orange curls exploring and feasting upon the eye cavities, while the remaining skin charred upon the skull in a grisly time lapse, revealing teeth.

"You are both…" Rogan said, "very brave. To do… what you are… proposing to do."

Neither of them spoke, while the containment box *pinged* from the intense heat of the incineration.

"You have everything you need?" the research assistant eventually asked.

Collie nodded. "Pretty much."

"Then… I'll say goodbye… to you both," Rogan said. "I probably won't be seeing you again. Then again, I might. It's hard to say… just how long I might last. I do wish to… speak with you in private, Captain Jones."

"About my condition?"

"Yes."

"Then shoot."

Rogan looked to Gus.

"Don't worry about him. He's a big boy. And he should know. Give it to us straight. You might convince him to stay."

Gus frowned at that.

"Very well," Rogan said. "Your situation… isn't much different from mine. Except I have no idea… how long you might last. Captain Wallace's condition… might resemble yours… with its symptoms… but in truth… the TI strain has proven to be… if anything… predictably *un*predictable. You may last… as long as Captain Wallace. Or you may… convert much faster. You may retain… your sense of self. And you may not. Your symptoms may be unnoticeable. And they may erupt. With a rage. I wish… I could provide more insight, but…"

"But I want to get on the road," Collie finished. "Yeah. My fault."

"Entirely your fault," Rogan added with a ghoulish smile.

"Any idea if—" Collie hesitated, then tossed her head in a gesture of *what the hell*—"if I'll start eating deodorant sticks?"

Rogan's amused chuffing and wheezing sounded like a steam engine riddled with bullets. When he settled down, he wiped at an eye. "I'm sorry. You caught me. Off guard. To answer you. I have no idea. The deodorant sticks. Were a surprise to me. My nose… led me to them. But for you… no idea. It could be deodorant. It could be something else. Are you hungry?"

Collie shook her head.

"When did you eat last?"

"Lunch. Had lasagna."

Gus nodded that she did indeed. Or at least *tried* to eat it.

"Oh my, yes," Rogan agreed. "One of the… freeze-dried ones?"

"Those are the ones."

"Oh, I used to love those…"

"I had one, too," Gus said. "It was tasty. Surprised the hell out of me."

"Only the best… for Whitecap. It is the government. And its supporting staff. And its serving military."

"I would've figured lasagna would've been the first thing you ran out of here," Gus said. "If… you know. People were still here."

"One might think," Rogan said. "Whitecap does have sufficient stores, however."

"Sufficient?" Gus smirked. "You kidding, Josh? From what I saw, you got *stores* the size of a couple of *Costcos* here. Or three or four Mollymarts. At least."

"They prepared for a twenty-year stay," Collie added. "In case some of the indoor farming failed. Or some shit."

"Or someone figured they could eat lasagna twenty-four seven for the next couple of decades," Gus remarked. "Seriously. What I saw down there? And what was on the menu? Who the hell ordered all that processed food anyway?"

"The resident psychiatrists," Rogan answered.

Gus shook his head in astonishment. "Who the hell was *that*? Doctor Rotten Ronnie? I mean, I thought *I* was a hoarder, but *man*."

"Studies have indicated that some… treats… were necessary. In one's daily diet. When living inside the bunker. To maintain mental health. And stability."

"Hey." Gus held up his hands. "I had five fucking *calzone* for breakfast. *Five*. I had two more of them shit bricks for lunch *with* the lasagna, just because there's an entire walk-in freezer full of calzone. Wall-to-wall calzone. There's another freezer stocked to the gills with freeze dried *cheeseburgers*, for Christ's sake. *Cheeseburgers*. And I can guarantee you I'm taking a couple dozen of those with me out on the road. So, for me? Foodwise? Mentally? I'm at a fucking all time high."

Rogan blinked and directed his attention at Collie. "The lasagna. How did you react to it? Any cramping? Nausea?"

"No, none," Collie answered, then looked at Gus. "*He* should've, though, the way he was eating."

"I'm fine," Gus said. "Right now, anyway. Hey, I know what I did. No illusions here. All bets are off tomorrow morning, though. Definitely a couple of calzone torpedoes gonna be launched into the harbor."

"Well," Rogan said, choosing to move along. "I can't comment on how your… diet will be affected. All I can say is… monitor yourself. And act accordingly… if there are any significant changes."

"Like wanting to chew someone's face off?" Collie asked.

Gus didn't like the sound of that. He remembered Wallace.

"Potentially," Rogan allowed.

"Don't you worry," Collie said. "Not gonna happen. I'm not gonna let myself do that. And if I do," she indicated Gus again. "He has my permission to shoot me."

Gus exhaled sadly, not bothering to hide it. If Rogan noticed the display, he didn't react.

"Well… that's all," the research assistant said. "You have… everything you need?"

"Pretty much," Collie said. "You take care of those codes? For the nukes?"

"Taken… care of."

"Excellent."

A look of stern focus overtook Rogan's face then, as he reached for something tucked between his thigh and his chair. He shook the material out, revealing a pair of blue latex gloves. His hands trembled as he pulled them on, snapping the elastic each time. Having done that, Rogan's smile brightened, and he extended a hand to Collie.

She gently shook it with both of her own.

"Oh," he said. "You're already wearing gloves. I didn't… notice."

"Always prepared."

They smiled at each other then.

"Safe… travels," Rogan said, his facial muscles twitching.

"Thank you, Josh," Collie said. "For everything."

"You're very welcome, Captain Jones. Thank you. For your service. Your… *continued*…service."

They broke their grip, and Rogan studied Gus for a few seconds before offering his blue gloved hand. Gus knew the gloves were for his benefit alone, but he didn't think there was a risk. Gus took the hand without hesitation and gave it a firm squeeze.

"And thank you," Rogan said. "Safe travels… Gus."

Gus felt that annoying welt of sadness in his throat. "Thank you *more*, Josh. For saving me. When you did. And for everything since. Safe travels… right back at you."

He held onto the infected man's hand for a very long time.

3

There was a knock on Gus's door.

He looked up and checked his digital clock.

5:30 am.

Thank you, God, he thought as he swung himself off the bed. He was already dressed. The bedroom was warm, so wonderfully warm, the corner lit up by nightlights resembling autumn branches. He'd woken up at 4:30 am, actually, and long completed his morning routine, minus breakfast. The knots in his stomach wouldn't allow him to eat. He was uneasy, wondering if Collie really would come and get him, despite her saying she would. He feared she might just up and leave without him, and that anxiety resulted in a poor sleep.

He would've chased after her if she'd left without him, and in the end she knew it.

The front door to his quarters was an opaque rectangle, with a glowing touchpad on the right, outlined in a wire-thin red light. Gus thumbed a key and the door slid open.

"Morning, Moonbeam," a shadowy Collie greeted, wearing her mask and sunglasses.

"Morning, Sunshine," Gus frowned. "You can see with those things on?"

"The shades? Yes, I can. All set?"

"Yeah."

She gestured for him to follow. Before he did, he reached for the aluminum bat he'd acquired from the batting cages. The same bat that he'd used to knock back a thrown grenade and end the fight for Whitecap. Despite praise from Collie and others for his reflexive act of bravery, Gus didn't feel one lucky swing amounted to much of anything. He did, however, recognize that it *was* a lucky swing, and if there was anything he'd need plenty of in the coming weeks, it would be luck. Not just *any* luck, mind you, but the top-shelf, triple-A grade, leprechaun level of good fortune. A *shit*-ton of it.

So what better charm to ensure he got exactly that?

Lucky bat in hand, Gus exited his home of only a short week and the door closed behind him. He didn't bother locking it as the door would do that by itself. The six-digit number he had to remember to unlock it had been a chore. His mind had been occupied with other matters.

Collie led him back to Main Street, an underground thoroughfare divided into four lanes all aglow with miniature sets of runway lights built into the floor's surface. She wore camos, but the addition of tactical webbing drew Gus's eye. The area's overhead lights were off, and the ceiling screens displayed a glowing October moon set against a prominent starfield.

An EV waited and in the front passenger seat, without any restraints at all, was the man who had killed her. The soldier who had blown her heart out of her back.

Gus had, for the last week, wrestled a losing battle with that knowledge. Collie had reminded him that she was dead anyway because of her TI injection—it just hadn't caught up to her. Gus countered that Milo had *still* shot her, and that if he *hadn't* shot her, perhaps there would've been a chance of Josh Rogan discovering some last-minute cure for her. At the very least, she still would have been *intact*, with a still-beating heart. Now, there was no chance of that since the TI was the only thing keeping her alive.

Gus winced. Technically she wasn't alive. More like 'functionally reanimated'. To a point. As far as he could tell, she was moving with the same speed and grace as before. And she talked normally. Memories of Wallace had haunted Gus, however, knowing what had happened to the operator.

Gus stopped and stared at Milo, who met his gaze dead on.

"Morning," the soldier muttered.

"Fuck off."

That turned Collie around, her sunglasses gleaming in the nightscape of the thoroughfare.

Gus momentarily felt bad for that slip, which broke his promise from the evening before, but he didn't apologize. *Good morning*, he glared back, wounded yet defiant. His frizzy *ass* whiskers *good morning*.

"I'll talk to you later," she warned him. "Get in."

Gus went for the rear, sitting directly behind a silent Milo. Collie pulled herself into the driver's seat. She checked on Gus, and he knew she wasn't happy with him. That was fine. He wasn't happy, either. Matter of fact, sitting as he was, *armed* as he was, he thought there was a very good chance he would just start swinging and bludgeon Milo to death.

"Glad you picked me up," Gus finally muttered.

Collie put the machine in gear. "Had to. Otherwise I'd be worried about where and when you'd catch up with us."

Milo cleared his throat. "Should I be worried about him?"

Collie regarded the soldier. "Cowboy, in all seriousness, you should be worried about *me*."

"Already have your word."

"You might have my word, but if anything happens to me, there's nothing between you and him. Then, you have my permission to be worried."

She hit the accelerator, ending the conversation. The EV shot along the street, exceeding whatever speed limits were usually observed in Whitecap. They whizzed past several residential doors, all with little displays of flowers in precise beds right below unlit windows. Opposite that was a multitude of wall-sized screens, interconnected to display a panoramic beach scene, complete with a quiet surf and patches of tall grass that swayed in an unfelt breeze.

The EV buzzed by it all.

All the while, Gus glared at the back of Milo's head, picking out the right spot for one grand slam swing.

"Wow," Milo said, studying the overhead night screens.

"Like it?" Collie asked.

"Yeah. Never got a good look at the place before. I mean, you know."

Gus knew. They had locked Milo up shortly after clearing Whitecap of the Leather invaders.

"I mean," Milo continued, "there's real, and then there's this."

"All paid for by your tax dollars," Collie said. "Nothing but the best. Gotta keep everyone living here from going bugshit nuts."

"All fake."

"Well, it's real enough. *Artificial* is a better choice of words. And it *was* home for hundreds."

Collie flicked on an indicator and drove left, into another residential area where the lanes were outlined by more lights.

"We're crazy for doing this, you know," Milo said as stars flashed overhead.

Collie didn't respond.

Gus wanted to say they were crazy bringing *Milo* along, but he figured the earlier *fuck you* made his feelings known.

Some ten minutes later, they drove into the vast complex that was Whitecap's garage. The area had been cleared of bodies and the parking arrangements rearranged just a little. One of the backhoes was parked near the main entrance, across from the box. There were several pieces of heavy, industrial-scale equipment within Whitecap, in case the main access tunnel suffered a cave-in for whatever reason. Jane Wong took to the big machines the best, quickly learning the finer points of operating a backhoe, and within a day, she had cleared the partial blockage in the tunnel where Collie and Gus had delayed the advancing Leather. The armored truck that had been pinned underneath the debris was pulled away, creating a wide passage to the outside world.

The main doors to the bunker, the ones meant to seal off the decontamination zone, remained open and would not close for reasons unknown. Efforts to shut them resulted in doglike whines and stressed cable creaks, before finishing in a series of ominous pings that echoed through the garage. Carson, still recovering from injuries inflicted upon him by the Leather, said he would figure out the doors when he was well enough to do so. Until then, the figurative drawbridge to the castle would remain lowered.

A harsh, starry light basked the equipment and vehicles. The thing that drew Gus's attention, however, was the mode of transportation Collie had chosen for their expedition into the Leather-controlled west. The very machine she had teased them about all the way to Whitecap.

A limousine.

Not just any limousine, but a *monster* of a limousine.

There were three such vehicles parked within Whitecap's garage. Two were obviously suited to more civilized times, being smaller and torpedo-sleek, resembling stretched-out eight-cylinder hearses loaded with all the necessary features due to a leader of a nation. The third machine, however, was different. That one wasn't meant for ordinary transportation within an urban setting. It was a motorized ogre, a mechanized behemoth, and only a tank would offer a superior level of protection.

And offensive power.

"Jesus," Milo whispered as he beheld the thing. "We're going out in that?"

"We are, indeed," Collie answered.

The soldier released his breath in a slow whistle.

Under the garage lights, the limo resembled a prickly SUV, black with chrome-trim highlights, elongated to well over a sixty-foot length. Black tinted windows gleamed. The limo was incredible, Collie had explained to Gus. She'd gleaned that from conversations with individuals assigned to protect the Prime Minister back in the day, as well as her own recent investigations. It wasn't intended for diplomatic functions of state. It would never see a parade. This machine was designed and manufactured for *after* the fall of civilization, which, admittedly, perplexed the hell out of both Collie and Gus.

Seriously, who the hell would want to drive around an armored *limo*…in a post-apocalyptic setting?

More to the point, who the hell would actually see the *need* for such a transport and sign off on it?

Obviously, the Prime Minister thought he might. And his advisors had gone along with the idea.

Advanced body armor, a futuristic mix of steel, aluminum, titanium, and ceramic plating, totalling almost ten inches thick in places. The windows were six inches thick and consisted of layers of polycarbonate glass and, like the main body, built to withstand the most punishing of sustained gunfire. Steel-sheeted wheel guards were fixed over the tires for extra protection. The tires were solid, reinforced with Kevlar, and impervious to punctures. Not only were the tires bulletproof, but thermoelectric fibers woven into the surface generated extra power from the friction with the road and energized rechargeable batteries. A hulking electric powerplant lurked underneath the hood, providing plenty of juice and capable of supplying short, intense bursts of speed when needed. The powerplant could keep the machine running for hours at a top speed of a hundred kilometers an hour.

A thick shell of steel protected the chassis underneath, rending it practically impervious to land mines, grenades, and improvised explosive devices. The interior was air-tight, in case of gas or biochemical attacks, and Collie even mentioned air tanks located somewhere in the back. The door handles could be electrified at a flick of a switch. Smoke bombs could be launched.

Those were the primary defensive features of the rig, but equally as impressive were the vehicle's *offensive* capabilities that might've been inspired by a super spy movie. Gas bombs. Spikespitters. Flamers. Machine guns. Missile launchers. *Grenade* launchers. And the crowning piece of it all, a steel jolly roger of a ram plate affixed to the front of the vehicle. The black skull had been painted onto the plate shortly after the limo had arrived at the bunker, and oddly enough, the PM didn't order anyone to remove it. Gus could see why. That smiling skull-face belonged there.

In short, the thing was a twelve-ton tank, perhaps even a match for the dead Komatsu truck laid to rest outside of Whitecap's halls.

And this beast—this... *monster*—would take them into the west.

Two familiar figures leaned against an EV parked nearby. They stood up when they saw the new arrivals. Bruno wasn't wearing his trademark pirate's cap this morning. His blonde hair seemed longer, thinner, and his beard looked a tad wilder. Rich Trinidad was the other man, his somber expression dark and made even darker by his own respectable beard. The man had ditched his own sombrero for a winter cap. Both were wearing warm jackets, as the temperature in the garage was several degrees colder than in the residential area of the bunker.

Collie stopped the EV in front of them.

"Morning," Bruno said, unfolding his arms.

"Morning," Collie said, watching the two men. "Kinda surprised to see you here."

"Well, it's a great morning for a drive."

"Think so?"

Bruno shrugged. "Any morning when you're able to go out for a drive is a good one. Since you guys are heading out in that," he nodded at the limo, "I'd say, yeah. Great morning."

"She is something," Collie agreed, getting out of her ride. Gus did the same, greeting the two men with nods.

"You look bright-eyed," Bruno noted.

Gus didn't answer.

"He's a little cranky," Collie said. "'Cause of this guy, right here."

Milo froze and wisely didn't say a word.

Rich Trinidad stared at the ex-soldier-of-fortune. His dark disposition expressed just how Gus felt about the sniper—just a breath away from taking a swing. Matter of fact, the extra bit of curl around Rich's lips made Gus realize that the man's usual scowl wasn't so bad at all.

"Yeah," Collie said, breaking the silence. "Anyway. We'll keep an eye on him. Make sure he's good. He's got a lot at stake."

Bruno didn't comment. His eyes darted from the special operator to the soldier, then to Gus. He and Gus had talked about including Milo in a war party, and how much of a risk he'd be. Milo was, as far as they knew, just one man now... but what if he had more merry maniacs waiting somewhere out there on the highways? What was to stop him from killing Collie and Gus once he was well away from Whitecap, reconnecting with another pack of killers, and then leading them back to the bunker to claim it?

That was all Gus's line of thinking. Bruno had countered it with his own thoughts; namely, if Milo had wanted to, he could've already betrayed Collie during the fight within Whitecap's garage. Right when he was being a footstool for the crippled Carson. Gus conceded that this much was true, but Milo still had shot Collie through the heart.

And he wasn't about to forget it.

"Soooo…" Collie said, studying Bruno. "Didn't we say our goodbyes last night?"

Bruno smiled. "Yeah, we did, but something happened last night. Figured I'd let you know."

"All right. Out with it."

"Monica started talking."

That surprised them all. Gus said it first. "No way."

"She did," Bruno said. "Around midnight. Damnedest thing. Little squirt woke me up on the couch. Said her name is *Sandy*, of all things. Sandy Garber. And that she was with her mother and father, who were—get this—heading *east* to look for other survivors. Just like what you were doing, Collie. Like I was doing."

"Huh," she deadpanned, in a 'That so?' tone.

Bruno became serious. "She stowed away in the back of her parents' ride. They didn't know. She was supposed to hang back with her aunt. Didn't happen. While on the road, her folks found out about her. Turns out she was covered up in the box bed of their truck, underneath a pile of sleeping bags. It was late so they decided to take her back the very next day. Except that night, they camped outside and were overrun by, of all things, a pack of zombies. Fresh ones. Her parents died, buying time for her to run."

Bruno paused then. "So she did. And was picked up by those guys."

They looked at Milo then, who cleared his throat. "We just found her on the side of the road. Jake spotted her. He just held out a hand and led her into the back to the cargo hold. I remember her. She was shellshocked. Traumatized. He didn't care. And I… didn't ask."

Milo glanced at the limousine then, as if wondering if he would ever leave Whitecap. Or perhaps he was just unable to meet the gazes of those around him.

"Why the hell would her mom and dad camp outside?" Gus asked.

"Yeah, really," Bruno agreed. "Not me. Not with all the nice hotels around."

"The meatbags were all gone," Collie said. "Or so we thought. No reason not to. Not now. Out on the road, in the middle of nowhere, if folks were used to camping outside, they just might be tempted. And shit happens."

"Shit always happens," Gus muttered.

"Always," Collie agreed.

"And when it did, she ran for it," Bruno said. "All through the night. A ten-year-old kid. Without knowing where she was or where she was going."

The garage felt a touch colder after that.

"So, that means they're not all gone," Gus said. "There are zombies running through the countryside."

"Some are, anyway," Collie said.

"Great."

She faced the limousine, showing no indication of having heard.

"How's the little one doing?" Gus asked.

"She's a little shaken up, obviously," Bruno replied. "But at least now she's talking. She knew you guys were leaving, and that unlocked whatever was blocking her. She wanted you to deliver a message if you can. So if you're on your way out west, you might want to make a detour to Fort Jay, Manitoba. Maybe… let her aunt know she's okay?"

Collie considered the request. "That a Leather town?" she asked Milo.

"No."

She regarded a frowning Gus, who nodded.

"We'll do that," she said. "What's a little detour? It's for a good cause, and it'll open relations between us and them. Thanks, Bruno."

"You're welcome. You know where Fort Jay is?"

"No."

Bruno supplied directions. The names and numbers of the highways went over Gus's head, though he knew Lake Winnipeg. Collie sucked up the information. In the end, she looked to Milo.

"Any Leather towns around there?"

"Just Winnipeg."

"All right, *the Peg*. We'll talk later." She studied Gus. "All set for this?"

"As much as I'm gonna be," Gus answered, tapping his bat on the concrete floor. The sound briefly echoed.

Collie considered Bruno then the limo. "You checked out the ride?"

Bruno cocked his head. "As much as I wanted to. That thing scares me."

"Didn't push any buttons?" she asked.

"Nope. Like I said. It scares me. You'll notice we were standing over here, away from the thing. I was scared just starting it up, afraid I might accidentally touch something and fry old Rich here."

Old Rich didn't move a facial muscle at the remark. The man was colder than stone.

"Smart," Collie said. "You're a smart man, Bruno. You take care. All the best with… whatever you do."

"So this is it, then?"

"This was it last night. This *now* is just a replay."

Bruno nodded and tugged at an ear. He appeared as if he might say more but didn't and got out of Collie's way.

"Keep watch over this place, sheriff," Collie said to Rich.

"I will," he answered.

"Try not to shoot anyone you like."

Rich didn't comment on that.

Collie opened the door on the driver's side. The interior lit up, softly, showing off a steering wheel and rich leather seating for two.

"Can't tell you how much I've wanted to drive this thing," she said to them all. "You hear stories from the PM's security spooks, but, well… Get in, you two. Milo, you're up front with me."

The soldier hopped to it. Gus lost sight of him on the passenger side, as the limo's height was equal to a full-sized SUV. Except the damn thing was nearly sixty feet long. And about a foot-and-a-half wider. Gus opened the door just behind the driver's seat, allowing him entry to what Collie called the business class section, separated by a well-designed partition that was just as tough as the exterior. He'd seen it a few times already, when Collie had first shown it to him. They had fun stretching out and wallowing in all that luxury. A post-apocalyptic ball cruncher it might be on the *outside*, but it was all billionaire love on the inside. Two first-class, beige leather seats and an opposite love couch fit for royalty filled the interior. Tinted windows. Starlight mirrored ceiling. Fold-out tables and cup holders. An opulent mini-island rose from the center of the cabin, with flat screens facing the passengers. Keyboards and controls were there, for things Gus dare not touch, but knew were for security and comfort. The whole business class section was fifteen feet long, with an inner door to the left of the loveseat. Behind that door (which was totally soundproofed when closed) was… heaven.

Gus didn't want to think about heaven. They had pretty much jammed all their supplies in there, from weaponry to even a secret supply of All-Dressed potato chips and Crunchie candy bars, taken from Whitecap's considerable stores.

Gus hesitated at the open door and glanced over at Bruno. "Seeya later."

"Seeya," Bruno said.

"Seeya Rich," Gus said.

"Seeya Gus," came the somber reply.

Gus did a double take at that, realizing he didn't imagine it. He got in and closed the door. He sat right behind the driver, where an opening in the partition allowed him clear sight of Milo's profile. Gus couldn't see Collie … but he could if he stuck his face through the slot.

He tossed his bat into the next seat, where it landed against a duffle bag. Just below, a suitcase lay on the floor. Gus fastened his seatbelt and angled himself so he could keep an eye on Milo. There was plenty of legroom inside business class. Containers for food and other supplies filled three quarters of the space, but he could still camp out on the floor if the tables weren't extended. He probably would, seeing as they packed in three sleeping bags and extra blankets. That was on top of everything else they'd crammed into the vehicle. The limo could potentially hold two dozen people if they were packed in, and that didn't include the driver up front.

When Gus closed the door, the cabin lights dimmed—only to be replaced by another starfield overhead. It wasn't the same celestial might of Whitecap's corridors at nighttime, but more of a Science-Fiction jazz lounge. Not that he minded in the least.

"All aboard?" Collie asked, having settled in up front.

"I'm good," Milo said.

"Gus?"

"Give me a minute. I only just got in."

Granting his request, Collie lowered a window and started talking to Bruno.

Eying Milo's profile, Gus popped open the armrest, revealing the compartment underneath. He pulled out a Glock. After sizing up the sidearm and checking on the extra magazines, he placed it barrel-down in a cup holder, not giving a shit. He then turned sideways in his seat, facing the passenger side. If Milo decided to try something, if he lunged for the steering wheel or whatever, Gus had it in his head to draw, shoot, and clean up the mess with a roll of *Mighty Ones* paper towels, *the big ones*.

Hell, in such close quarters, Gus wondered if he would make it to lunchtime without shooting the prick. Just on principle.

"Okay, I'm good," Gus finally said.

"Excellent," Collie replied and switched on the headlights.

Light bathed the garage.

Beneath the finely sculpted brow of the dashboard, instrument panels flared to full electronic life, transforming the driver's seat into the cockpit of a starship.

"Look after the kid, Bruno," Collie said through her open window. "You're her unofficial guardian, now."

"I am?"

"You are. Until you can get her back to her aunt."

"I will. Don't worry."

She nodded at him then, and he waved as he backed away from the transport.

"See you on the other side, bitches," Collie yelled out, and pumped the accelerator, producing a soft, synthesized blend of engine notes. To Gus's ears, it didn't sound like an ordinary motor being revved—more like the warp drive of an intergalactic star cruiser powering up.

The car started to move, and the headlights swung from the wall to that of the gaping mouth of Whitecap's decontamination zone. LED lights swept over the limo's bulk as the car rolled towards the exit. They scrolled past the bus-sized box, where Collie had activated the decontamination box's flamers and roasted several of the Leather. There was a muffled bump as the limo went over an open seam in the concrete floor. Then another, but Gus hardly felt it. The monster limo possessed superior suspension in addition to its other stately features.

Then they were plunging through the tunnel.

"Like a dream, boys," Collie said. "She handles like a dream."

"How do you know the thing's a girl?" Milo asked, glancing at her profile.

"I looked. And if you sneak a peek, I'll know. So don't fucking dare."

Milo got quiet after that. He noticed Gus glaring at him from the backseat. The soldier frowned and returned his attention to the tunnel.

The black ribs that rose from the floor all the way to the ceiling sped by. Collie increased speed. Overhead, white moons flashed to life at the limo's approach, shining huge cones of light and exposing masses of gray piping. Black knobs, strings, and intricate webbings of wire were also visible, extending in various directions from the pipework.

"Oh yeah," Collie said. She adjusted her grip on the steering wheel and, again, increased her speed.

Milo sank a little further back into his seat.

Gus felt the acceleration. "You know where you're going there, leadfoot?"

Collie squealed in answer.

That didn't make him feel any better as Gus nervously smoothed out his beard. He reminded himself that they were in a tunnel, with no oncoming traffic, and that if she could handle a bus-sized recreational vehicle, then a stretched-out limousine wouldn't be a problem.

The vehicle sped up even faster.

Gus glanced at Milo's frozen profile before leaning forward and seeking out the dashboard.

A hundred kilometers an hour.

"Collie," a nervous Gus started.

"Only seeing what she can do," Collie cut him off, her eyes on the confines of the tunnel rushing by. "It's practically a straight run, anyway."

It practically was.

Then the limo slowed down. Gus leaned forward to see why.

The bottleneck. Where he and Collie had made their stand. The limo slipped through the widened lane like a luxury liner navigating a channel.

Whereupon Collie hit the non-existing gas again. The engine jumped in response, releasing that artificial growl that marked a surge in power, and they charged forward once more. Vehicles flashed by. Machines of war belonging to the Leather, left parked along the wall in a ragged line. There were a couple of fuel tankers there as well, containing roughly half their capacity. A curious ethanol blend that would be utilized by Whitecap's people. Collie and her team had cleared the tunnel right up to the mountain entrance, and as they moved or shoved vehicles aside, whatever was deemed useful had been taken. Not that they needed much, as Whitecap had provided all in greater and newer quantities.

Milo glanced over at her, then back at Gus.

"Collie," Gus protested, glaring back at the soldier, and sending his own message.

"Relax," she said. "Straight on 'til dawn from here. Or close enough at least. I've only driven this thing in the garage. Gotta get the feel of her. And she's silky smooth, boys. Silky smooth."

She turned the wheel ever so slightly, ignoring her companions' unease.

A hundred wasn't fast, but in that level silo of a passage, Gus understood what a launched missile might feel like.

"Don't you worry," Collie assured them both. "I can handle this hog. It's not so different from other rigs. Better in some cases. The only thing I need to test, the thing I need to *know*... is the turbo boost."

Collie took her right hand off the wheel. She tapped at a huge touchscreen beside her leg. Bright red characters winked into existence.

"Turbo boost?" Gus lurched, bracing himself. He was no longer concerned with Milo. The soldier had braced for impact.

"That's my name for the boost of speed the engine can pump out. Regular limos got a tank of Nitrous Oxide strapped in if, say, someone needed to catch a plane. Or haul ass from an ambush. This thing doesn't have that, *but*, it does have a mule kick."

Ahead, the tunnel morphed into a whitened drag strip, and the finish line was an open maw of predawn darkness.

Collie returned her hand to the steering wheel. Her thumb moved to a button.

"Hold onto your shit boys," she advised, excitement in her voice.

Wide-eyed and borderline terrified, Gus squeezed his ass back into his seat.

Collie screamed pure joy and thumbed the button.

The dashboard blazed red.

And the limo blasted free of Whitecap's mouth like a horizontal rocket.

4

There was a brief sensation of leaving the ground before the entire limo crashed and bounced. Collie's scream of joy ended when the tires hit the ramp. Gus's seatbelt kept him in place, but his chin rebounded off his chest while his ass skidded across leather.

"Goddamn Collie," he barked with half a laugh. "That why you wanted the ramp all cleared?"

"'Course not," she yelled back. "That had to be done. Can't have bodies lying all over the place. Ain't sanitary."

Gus supposed so and peered outside at the tinted world. The outer buildings of Whitecap flashed by as dark husks and not-so ancient ruins that no longer held any surprises.

He wished he could say the same for what lay ahead.

"I overheard guys—drivers—talk about the handling of this thing," Collie said as she drove, towards Whitecap's outer security checkpoint. "I can hear them now. Like a dream, they'd say. Not like I knew what they meant. I could only imagine. Now I know. God*damn* I know. Like a dream indeed. A well-lubricated dream, and I dearly love my lube."

She chuckled, her signature laugh that sounded so much like bells on Christmas morning.

"Hey, you guys know this is Halloween?" she asked.

"Is it?" Milo asked, looking as if he'd just taken a boot straight to the chicken tenders and was only now feeling the pain subside.

"Mm-hm," Collie said. "Halloween. Honest to god. So, anyway, while you weren't looking, Gus, I took the liberty of transferring a few music files to the limo's stereo system. Whitecap's libraries are *stacked*."

With that, she turned on the sound system.

And the regal guitar opening of AC/DC's *Highway to Hell* poured through the speakers.

Perhaps because it had been a while since he'd heard it last. Perhaps it was the setting they drove through, or maybe it was just the company. In any case, the music surprised Gus, before his face slipped into happy approval.

Up front, even Milo kept pace with slight nods.

That bothered Gus, seeing the man enjoy something. Matter of fact, it outright pissed him off.

"Man," the soldier said in subdued wonder. "I don't even like AC/DC, but that's some sugar right there."

"I don't think AC/DC would call their music sugar," Collie said. "Maybe whiskey. Or whiskey bullets. Not sugar."

"Whiskey bullets sounds good to me. Anything like that on board this flight?"

"Nope. We are sans alcohol."

"Too bad."

I got a whiskey bullet for you, Gus thought grimly, his guts offended at how chummy their conversation was going. If Milo made one move he didn't like, he'd pour it into the bastard's ear with his Glock.

"Plenty of that back at Whitecap," Collie pointed out, oblivious to the murderous thoughts brewing out back. "You just focus on being a good boy scout and earn yourself some badges. Do that and I'm sure there's enough back at the bunker to keep you happy. Hell, there's even a Laser Lettuce dispensary."

That got Milo's attention. "Laser Lettuce?"

"Herbal jazz. Funky fern. The electric green."

"Whitecap has *marijuana*?"

"Purely medicinal, of course," Collie said and gently applied the brakes. They reached the outer checkpoint and she drove the limo straight on through.

"Funky fern," Gus rumbled. "Haven't heard it called that in years."

"Helps individuals cope with the PTSD of the apocalypse. Pain management, too. Y'know, that was one place I didn't think of visiting. I bet the greenhouse is a friggin' jungle right about now. Funny how Josh didn't mention it. You'd think that guy would need a hit or two."

Milo looked as if he'd just taken a shot to the jaw. "Whitecap—a super-secret underground government bunker—has a *grow-op*?"

"You better believe it, princess. Vegetables in there, too, of course. Food gets priority, but they got some whoop-ass grass in there. All under the loving care of professional agriculturalists, who are definitely all dead now, utilizing state-of-the art indoor greenhouse tech. All legally regulated to the nines and set up row by row, flower bed by flower bed. Not that anyone really enforced regulations. Funny how a zombie outbreak can change one's morals. But then, you probably know all about that."

Gus smirked as the soldier's jawline clenched shut, which was goddamn satisfying.

"Say goodbye to home base, boys," Collie announced, jabbing a thumb in the mountain's direction. "Lord knows you'll see it sooner than I will."

An awkward silence then, as the full weight of what she'd just said hit Gus and robbed him of speech. How many people had she known in Whitecap when he was living in his mountain retreat? How many friendships? Gus had no clue, but he could relate. He knew he had to say something, but had no idea where to start.

Even Milo lowered his chin, wisely keeping his mouth shut.

Collie spared them both, however, as she dabbled at the dashboard's touchscreen.

A rearview camera winked into existence, providing a cinematic black and white image of the landscape racing away from them. A stark, ghostly rendering of the military base filled the screen and, above it all, was the crown girth of Whitecap. The mountaintop couldn't be seen, however, as it was lost to both the predawn dark and the limits of the rearview camera.

Collie turned the wheel and the whole image swung out of view as if greased and left to slide. A few seconds later, she switched the camera off and just drove. Gus shifted, adjusting his shoulder against the seat, and scowled again at Milo. The song ended, and Collie decided not to play a follow-up.

"So, Milo," she said. "You remember anything more about the Dog Dick?"

"Better hope he doesn't hear you call him that," he said.

"Yeah? Whyiszat? You know him personally or something?"

The question took him off guard. "Well, no."

"Then relax."

"Yeah, fuckin' relax," Gus added. "What do you care what she fuckin' calls him?"

Milo shifted his jaw as if testing a tooth. "I don't know anything more about the guy."

"Nothing?" Collie asked. "No background at all?"

The man stared ahead, the dashboard light glazing the thick stubble growing upon his face.

"Never overhead anything while you were one of them?" Collie probed.

"Nothing. They kept me on my knees most of the time. In a trailer with about a dozen more just like me. That was a nightmare. Thank god I didn't have to suck any dick, but I'm sure it was coming."

That surprised Gus, considering the way the Leather had been dressed. He remembered the bodies they had to clear away, the ones he didn't blow to hell with one swing of his bat, and the leather outfits straight out of some weird submissive-bondage flick. But then there was the straight-up horror show. Masks and straps with seams both crude and triple-stitched for strength. Spike-studded jackets, pants, shirts, and full-length leather dusters. Half-masks consisting of grinning, oversized jaws or the empty eye sockets of skulls. There were toothy smirks, skeletal screams, and solid casts with nothing at all upon them. Plague masks. Traditional Greek and Roman masks, smiling, snarling, or simply stoic, not out-of-place at all but even more frightening. There were collars with buckles, rivets, and even fishhooks. Vests and one-pieces that buttoned up or zipped right down the middle. They'd even discovered hockey masks, with alien designs etched upon their surfaces. And the freaky thing was, upon further search of the Leather's vehicles, was that there were *spares*, as if the owners might need a *change* of freakiness. Or if their current costume (Gus had a hard time calling that outerwear clothing) needed to be aired out. Or whatever the hell they did to clean it.

He had to admit, as perverse as all that was, there was also an alien beauty about it. A disturbing yet alluring sophistication that escaped description. A deviant elegance that was both offensive and yet... oddly tempting, as if whoever wore the outfits was transformed into something else entirely. Into the order known as the Leather.

At least, those were the vibes Gus got at first, anyway. Collie showed him the error of his thinking, however, when she pulled a squid mask off one individual and revealed the pallid face of the dead man underneath. There was an equal number of women amongst the corpses as well, and every mask removed dispelled just a little more of the Leather's menacing aura and their post-apocalyptic hubris.

Underneath all those fearsome guises and accessories, they were still only people.

Gus remembered a whole chest of orange and black ball gags just right for Halloween, as well as handcuffs and straps for bondage. Or so he thought they were all for bondage. The sheer scope of outfits and accompanying paraphernalia shocked and unnerved him, as if the Leather had raided a warehouse full of the getups.

"Just wondering if you remembered anything," Collie said, staring straight ahead.

"I told you everything," Milo answered.

"Too bad you didn't hear anything about how they got their fuel."

"We didn't ask," Milo admitted. "You saw them. You just didn't … start up a conversation with those guys."

"Just saying," Collie said. "That and where they're getting their zombies."

"No idea."

"Think on it. Even a best guess."

Milo didn't answer, and Gus heard the soft warp drive hum of the engine fill the interior.

"That doesn't sound like a motor at all," he said.

"Well," Collie said. "Back in the day, electric engines didn't make all that much noise. And people couldn't hear them coming up from behind. Lots of folks stepped right out in front of electric cars and got bounced off the hood. So, engineers developed and simulated real car noises. 'Course, that was just the start of customizing your ride, right down to how it sounded. And that's what we have here today. Could be worse."

"How do you see out of those things?" Milo abruptly asked, referring to her sunglasses.

"Why don't you just shut the fuck up and speak when spoken to?" Gus erupted, glaring at the soldier.

Milo glanced his way and wisely kept his mouth shut.

More awkward silence then.

"Thank you, Gus," Collie said. "But no need for hostility. We're a team on this one. And to answer your question, Milo. I see just fine. Anything else you want to know?"

Milo shook his head.

"We still going to Winnipeg?" Gus grumped.

She fiddled with something on the steering wheel before checking the dashboard. "Not right away, no."

"No?"

"We'll go to Fort Jay first. Find Sandy's aunt. Let her know that we have her niece. Let them know what happened to Sandy's folks. And why we didn't bring her with us. With a little luck, we can deliver that message, establish relations, and then continue on to Winnipeg. See what's what. Start up a little urban warfare. How's that sound?"

"Yeah. Okay."

"Milo?"

The soldier regarded her. "I get a say?"

"You're on the payroll now, so yeah."

Milo fired off a glare in Gus's direction. "Sure. Sounds good."

"We can get exactly—" she checked a set of numbers, not seeing that executioner stare-off—"seven hundred kilometers out of this monster before she has to stop and recharge. At present speed." Then she noticed it. "All right. Settle down, the both of you. And Gus? Don't make me adjust my mirror."

And, as ordered, both men broke their stare and returned to neutral corners.

Collie exhaled, leaving it unsaid that she knew she was going to have her hands full keeping the two of them apart. Especially Gus.

"How does it recharge?" Milo finally asked.

"What's that?" she asked.

"How does it recharge?"

"Ah. Combination of everything. Direct plug in. Solar, gathered from panels on the hood, roof, and trunk. We'll use the EV stations if their solar panels are still functional. And the tires will collect energy, so there's that."

"How long does it take to recharge?" Gus asked.

"Full recharge depends on the source. So thirty minutes to an hour. An hour in direct sunlight."

"So," Milo began, deciding to test the waters. "If I got a say in things like where we're going, do I get a gun too?"

"One thing at a time, princess," Collie cautioned.

That wiped away the soldier's smile, and caused Gus to sprout one of his own.

That's right, he thought blackly. *GI fuck you.*

*

The sun broke over the horizon as they cleared the maze surrounding Whitecap. The limo hit the edge of the pavement with a light thump, and the ride smoothed out considerably. The tinted windows softened the dawn as they drove along, and the landscape outside was a gray but discernable mess of forest and cleared highway. Gus stared at the tree line blurring past his window, watching for wildlife and seeing none. No deer. No moose. Not even a squirrel. He wrinkled his nose in a question.

"Hey," he said, getting Collie's attention. "Look familiar?"

"Yeah."

"What?" Milo wanted to know.

"Nothing," Gus blurted.

"We camped out here a while back," Collie said. "Little place off the grid. Back there."

"That before or after you shot up my crew?" Milo asked.

"You keep calling them your crew," Collie said with interest. "Were you in charge?"

"No. Not really."

"You're sounding a little misty about them, which makes me wonder why."

Milo stared straight ahead. "Well, I'm not. That was just a slip. Really. They would've dropped me in a flash, if the situation asked for it. Well, maybe not the Jipman."

"Who was he?"

"Real name was Eric. Can't remember his last name. He was…" Milo thought about it. "Ran a motel once. Said to me, 'Always see the room first before you check in, and when you do, always check under the bed. And never sleep on the duvets.'"

Gus screwed up his face at that.

"He was the only one I really got along with," Milo said. "Doesn't matter now."

Collie dropped the questioning and Gus went back to watching the trees. And that was it for the conversation. The great white ball that was the sun lit up the interior. Collie kept the speed constant, her head turning now and again. The classic rock music was replaced by softer, more reflective, ambient tunes, heavy on the strings and piano, but nice. And relaxing. Considering what they were doing.

Gus dozed, the warm interior finally getting to him. He lurched awake and pawed at his mouth. One of the business class screens facing him had a clock in the corner. He saw the time was 7:45 am. He stretched his back and let his breath out slowly, forcing himself to stay awake.

"You seepy?" Collie asked from the front seat.

Seepy. He smiled. There was no point in lying. "Yeah."

"Want to pull over for a bit? Get some fresh air?"

"Yeah. That would be all right."

Collie flicked on the indicator out of habit and pulled over. "Man, I fuckin' love this thing. Smooth. Not a hitch in the brakes." She looked over at Milo. "You're not going to be a problem, right?"

"Huh? What? *No.*"

"Good. We're getting along so well. I'd hate to have to shoot you."

Milo cringed, indicating he'd hate to be shot.

"Excellent," she said. "Get out."

The order ended with a pop of the door lock. He got out.

Gus grabbed the nearby Glock and exited on the other side. The blast of fresh, cold air slapped his cheeks, woke him to the fact that it was indeed Halloween, and that winter snow could fall any day after that. He stood, taking the hot pins and needles in his fucked-up foot. Collie got out and shook her shoulders. Sunlight reflected off her sunglasses, and she adjusted the neckline of her balaclava.

"Cold?" she asked.

"Crisp," Gus asked. "Y'know, you look like the invisible man these days."

"Invisible and fuckin' *invincible*, babe," she said.

That snappy reply resulted in a flare-up of affection, which waned into a lingering sadness Gus had to hide by looking away. He walked over to the limo's hood and rested his elbows on it, eyeing Milo on the other side.

The soldier turned away, rubbing his face as if waking himself up.

Gus let him be and smelled the air. He enjoyed the cooler temperatures after the long, sweltering heat of the summer, but he wasn't looking forward to winter. Didn't even want to think about winter, or where he would be when the snow started falling.

Or where Collie might be. And in what condition.

"Crisp," Collie repeated, taking in the once fiery scenery. "The choice descriptor of fall mornings. *Crisp*, I say."

She walked to the front of the limo, hands on her hips, her sidearm holstered and within easy reach. If Milo noticed, he didn't show it. He was inspecting the patches of wild grass and the forest some thirty feet away. It was quiet. Real quiet, causing Gus to miss the metallic pings, whistles, and chirps of Whitecap's geothermal heating systems firing up in the morning. A sound that he very much found comforting. It was, he thought, the sound of the way things used to be.

"Any of you guys need to take a leak, do it now," Collie said. "I'm going to take a walk that way."

She started for the trees.

"You need to use the can?" Milo asked as she walked away.

"Mind your own business," Collie said. "Y'pervert."

Milo met Gus's unapproving glare, and noticed the Glock not quite aimed at him but just off to the side. The soldier rolled his eyes and looked at the sky.

Collie stopped at the edge of the pavement. "Y'know something, princess? I'm sorta torn between nicknames for you. Can't decide on whether to call you cowboy or just straight up princess."

"Nice to have a choice," Milo said.

"Yeah it is," she agreed and resumed walking. She trudged down the soft shoulder of the highway, where the grass reached past her knees. The ground was uneven, as hinted by a few wobbles in her step, but she marched onwards for the forest.

The sound of Milo taking a leak on the other side of the limo distracted Gus. He adjusted his grip on the Glock against his thigh and glanced over at Collie, almost to the trees. He checked his hikers (taken from Whitecap's impressive hoard of fashionable footwear) and heard the soldier stop pissing, restart, and stop again.

"Any more than two shakes and you're jacking off," Gus muttered.

Milo finished his business, zipped, and regarded Gus. "Where's she going?" he asked.

"I think that's obvious."

"She gonna be gone long?"

"You got someplace to be?"

The right side of Milo's face hitched up into a grimace from the brightening sun. "You don't like me much, do you?"

"You have to ask? You shot... my friend."

"Hey, look," Milo said. "If you want. I'm right here. And I'm not going anywhere. Shoot me and get it over with. Double tap. Save me the trouble. And save you putting up with me."

Gus snarled at the soldier. "I don't do that sorta thing. Only if I got a damn good reason to."

"You said it yourself. I shot your friend. That would be reason enough for me."

"You're not me."

"Obviously. Just sayin'."

Thing was, he wasn't wrong.

"*Well, don't,*" Collie's voice replayed in his head. "*He's useful. And it's better bringing him along than leaving him here, in a cell, with a bunch of civvies.*"

Gus took a breath and released it through his nose. Collie had disappeared into the woods.

"No?" Milo asked. "Then look. I'm gonna stay out of your way. You saw the Leather. How fucked up they are. Honestly? I'd much rather be back at Whitecap, but the only way I'm going to get back there is by helping you two out. I ain't looking forward to it, but a deal is a deal. And I owe her. For what I did. Even though it was… trying circumstances. And she's SF. Cool that she's around. Really cool, actually. I… I don't want to disappoint her."

"Because she's army?"

"Because she's an *operator*," Milo stressed. "That's enough for me. I knew my crew was bad, but that was… choice. A bad one, but, there it is. I knew the Leather was bad, but that was *survival*. They had me. I had to do what I was told. I didn't like it, but… when you got a pack of psychos standing around you, and one of them's holding a hammer to your head, you do whatever they tell you to do."

That set Gus's senses tingling. "Like now?"

Milo hesitated. "Yeah, like now. But it's different now."

"Not so different," Gus countered. "Matter of fact, way I see it, you're almost free, but here we are, bringing you back. Back to the same psychos who had a hammer to your head. After what I've seen, I wonder if you really mean all your 'a deal is a deal' shit. I wonder if you won't try and bolt at first chance and… and go back to Whitecap. Say anything you want. Maybe before you do, you'll pop me and Collie. Just to make sure. Tie up the loose ends, then you're home free to say whatever you like."

Milo's expression darkened. "Except for one thing."

"Yeah? What's that?"

"The Leather. They'd still be out there. Still on the highways, coming this way. And we'd be living with the fear that they might find us. Just show up one day. Hell, they might be looking for us right now. You might have missed a couple at Whitecap. There could've been a few who were in the rear and ran for it. Maybe headed back to one of the Leather towns, where they'd tell whoever's in charge about what they found."

That thought made Gus's guts go cold.

"If *that* happened," Milo continued, "then all of this might be for nothing. Who knows what we'll meet out here. At the Leather towns. We might come face to face with a whole other army of them fuckers. You heard me say you got half, but I could be wrong. And I doubt *this* rig—" he nodded at the limo—"will save us."

Gus thought about it. "Yeah, well, I'll take that bet."

"That's not a bet. Just making a statement."

"Well, if it *was* a bet, I'd take it."

"I wouldn't."

"I would," Gus said.

"Well, that's you."

"Well, *yeah*, that is me."

"That's what I said."

"This rig is bulletproof," Gus stated and tapped the hood with the barrel of his Glock. "Fuckin' *grenade*-proof even. Before they got their mitts on Whitecap guns, your Leather shits were all carrying around bow and arrows and fuckin' axes."

"Mostly crossbows," Milo corrected.

"Whatever."

"There's a difference."

"I don't give a shit. My point is, they had nothing except a trailer load of fresh dead people. If that's the best they got…"

He didn't finish the sentence, because the thought of having a trailer full of animated corpses was bad enough, truth be told. He'd thought zombies were done and gone and in the past. The fact that the Leather were carrying them around, *transporting* them…

"They might have something in reserve," Milo said quietly, unconsciously tugging at the back of his hair. "I wouldn't put it past them. Guns. *Big* guns. With big shells."

"You ever see any of these big guns?" Gus asked, realizing this fucker played with his hair a *lot*.

"No."

"Well, there you go."

"Just saying they might." Milo pointed at the limo. "Just for shit like *that*. That's all I'm saying. Pays to keep things like that in the back of your mind."

Gus squinted. "You always this fun to talk to?"

"Depends on the person. And whether or not I got a gun pointed at me."

"I'm not pointing a gun at you."

Milo scowled at him. "You got that piece right there. What am I, blind?"

"Big difference from pointing at you and holding it at the ready."

"All right, you got it at the ready, Mister Fucking Particular. Ready to shoot if you got to."

"Yeah. *No.* Well... *Yeah.*" Gus waved as if fending off mosquitos. "Quit fuckin' arguing, okay?"

"Guess I better. Wouldn't want to piss you off enough to shoot me. I'd fuckin' miss all the fun I'm sure we're going to have later."

Milo spread his hands and turned around, sizing up the nearby wilderness.

"Fuckin' princess," Gus muttered and stared off in the direction Collie had gone.

*

Sunlight filtered through the dense foliage. Branches clawed at Collie as she pushed her way through the woods. A soft layer of leaves, twigs, and moss covered the ground while exposed roots, worn away by years of elemental scrubbing, rose and twisted and demanded her attention to where she was placing her feet down. The men were yammering at each other back at the limo. She could hear them, but damned if she could understand what they were saying. She'd have to remind them to keep their voices down on the five-percent chance there were others afoot.

Five percent. That was Wallace's number. No matter how low the chance of something bad happening, however small the chance, if something *did* happen, five percent was suddenly as good as a hundred. It was silly reasoning, but there had been times when it simply worked out that way, much to Collie's annoyance.

A branch snapped underfoot. She stopped and crouched without difficulty. It was only a day earlier when her knees crackled like Gus's, which both amused and bothered her. It had been a week since being killed in action, officially KIA'ed, before rising again some fifteen minutes later and joining the ranks of the undead.

Undead.

Collie couldn't believe it.

She had become a goddamn undead creature of the night. Wallace would joke about it, as he'd joked about his own deteriorating condition. She would smile to go along with it, to bring about some much needed levity, but in his quiet moments, she could see it bothered him.

It bothered her.

Which was one of the reasons she had to get out of the limo for a bit. The drive wasn't a long one, but in that post-dawn silence, when morning stares replaced conversation, a maggot of doubt wiggled to life at the back of her mind. There, that little white grub bore into her thoughts, creating a microscopic fissure big enough to allow more doubt to leak inside. The limo, for all its luxury, slowly became a coffin. A damn *fine* coffin, but a long black box all the same, and she needed to get out of it. Not for the fresh air, however. Collie literally couldn't breathe, but for some damn reason, she could still smell. Her taste was practically gone, her last meal (lasagna) had tasted overpoweringly sweet. The only reason she tried to eat was because Gus was enjoying his so much, and she knew she had to ingest something to keep appearances up. The food did nothing for her, however. Her energy levels were the same, as far as she could tell, even without sleep. Collie hadn't slept since she'd risen from the dead, but she still excused herself at the appropriate time just to appear normal to the others. To keep up morale. Not that it helped a lot. They knew what was going on, especially the islanders, who were visibly wary around her.

That insistent feeling of being inside a coffin was just the latest bit of weirdness assaulting her, and she knew from experience there would be more. She remembered how Wallace felt in his remaining days. She knew exactly why he was telling her he was fine, when in reality there was some serious inner turmoil churning underneath his stoic exterior. She understood all of that now, especially the part about projecting an air of *all is well* to those around her.

Especially to Gus.

Conflicted feelings welled up and ached around the cavity where her heart once resided. She touched her chest, pressing the fabric of her jacket, and felt the plastic container lid just underneath. The shattered ends of her ribs, where they were smashed by Milo's bullet, rubbed unpleasantly against the container she'd jammed into her chest cavity. She needed something to fill the hole, however, something to brace her ribs against, to strengthen the foundation. Rogan had suggested Tupperware, simply because there wasn't much else to fit the killing wound. A round container worked best. Every now and again, however, the sensation of splintered bones rubbing against that plastic shell disturbed Collie. Unnerved her. It felt like the last scrabbling of a dying crab. Or crumbling fragments of a failing tooth filling, caught between the gumline and the side of one's mouth. Minuscule pebbles that you knew were there but couldn't remove.

Knowing she shouldn't but also not quite giving a damn, she pressed the plastic lid in her chest. The container moved. Slightly, but enough for her to ease off and stop. The thing was still lodged in her chest with lengths of duct tape, and there it would stay.

Bird song erupted from deeper within the forest. An old tree, broken off at the base by age and wind and covered in moss, was a few feet off to Collie's left. She threaded her way over to the fallen timber and planted herself on its green trunk. Her shoulders sagged. Her chin dropped to her chest. She stayed that way for a few moments, allowing herself a pinch of self-pity.

Then her willpower kicked in.

Collie straightened, looked around and, deeming herself alone, bent over and unlaced her left combat boot. She pulled her foot free and stripped off the sock, exposing a wad of duct tape wrapped around her ankle. The flesh above and below the joint was noticeably swollen and colored a sickly purplish blue. Bloated veins formed a pattern of black lace. Those veins disappeared into the meat of her foot, towards her toes.

There was another reason for getting clear of the limo.

Very much aware of the extra weight in her legs, she needed privacy for what she had to do next, having already dealt with it two days earlier. Collie didn't concern herself with the condition of her feet. She peeled back the tape, revealing the slit she'd made before. A positively *fugly* little mouth that showed no signs of healing, right above the knob of her ankle. She wavered on making a new cut or using the old.

"Pitter patter," she whispered. She grasped her ankle and squeezed.

That horrible little mouth opened in a breathless spurt, and a black, infected-looking seepage as thick as toothpaste oozed forth and fell in clumps.

That sight alone would have broken anyone else.

Collie massaged her ankle for almost two minutes, coaxing the last few annoying ounces of blood that had pooled around her lower leg, releasing it from her system. That dense jelly plopped onto the ground like rotten teardrops. She ignored the sight and smell and continued to juice the lower part of her leg until nothing else came forth. When she finished, she leaned back and flexed her foot, deeming it functional, but bloated. She couldn't have that, so she pulled her foot up and milked that as well, getting out whatever dead blood had collected there.

She worked it until a tongue of dark meat appeared in the mouth, whereupon she stopped with a breathless *fuck me*. It occurred to her that she had forgotten the extra duct tape, that it was back in the limo. The memory slip annoyed her, which was something an after-supper soldier might do. She'd have to wrap her ankle up when she got back to the car, which meant she'd have to seal herself in the lounge section, away from the others. That would raise suspicion.

Eyeing that self-inflicted cut above her ankle, Collie decided to leave it until night, when the men would be asleep. That sounded like a plan. It wasn't like it was going to get infected any time soon. And she didn't have to worry about dying.

Positive points, she told herself. *Keep it that way.*

She just had to put a seal over it, to make everything watertight.

"Overcome and adapt," she whispered.

Without another thought, she pulled on her sock and boot, laced everything up, and got started on removing her right boot…

5

Some time later, Collie returned from the forest. She checked east-to-west and tugged at her neck, where her balaclava was tucked into her camo jacket. Both men watched as she marched towards them, but Gus's eye strayed to Milo.

"I know you're watching me," Milo said.

"Fuck if I care," Gus muttered. "At least I'm not pointing my gun at you."

Milo didn't reply, and ran fingers through that thinning blonde top of his.

"And quit fucking teasing your hair, Jesus Christ," Gus said.

Milo squinted. "Want some?"

The comeback was so quick, the gears of Gus's head snagged to a stop before starting up again.

But then Collie chugged up onto the road. "You girls getting along?"

Neither man answered, and Milo directed his gaze at the forest.

"How come you were gone so long?" Gus asked, resetting himself and forgetting about the hairdresser he was left to guard.

Collie approached the rig. "Take a guess."

"Oh. Sorry."

"I mean, I can tell you all about my bodily functions if you like."

"No. No, that's okay. I just didn't think… you could…"

Collie stopped not two steps away from the driver's seat. "What? Go to the can?"

Gus wisely didn't answer.

"Thought so. Listen. You didn't answer me earlier. You guys okay?"

Neither man answered her then, either. In fact, both looked guilty as sin, mindful of each other, as if someone had already shit the bed and was wondering when she would smell the chocolate.

"Like that, huh?" Collie again checked on the highway. "Well, anyway, fair trade winds. Let's see where it takes us. All aboard, you two. And you're still up front with me, cowboy."

Milo didn't appear to like that, but he got in the limo all the same.

Collie held back. "He give you any trouble?"

"No," Gus said. "He just... no."

"He just what?"

"We straightened out a few things, is all."

"Like what?"

"Guy shit."

"*Guy* shit? You know how that sounds?"

Gus did but didn't want to talk about it, so he changed tactics. "He plays with his hair, Collie."

She stared at him.

"A lot."

"And you feel threatened by that?"

Gus frowned, refusing to go any further.

Collie studied the limo's tinted windows. "Look. We talked about this. Watch him, but don't give him a hard time. Okay?"

"What if he gives me a hard time?"

"Then tell me and I'll slap him. Hard. Right across the nutsack if needed."

Gus wavered, on the cusp of protesting, but then settled back down.

"Let me hear you say it," Collie said.

"Okay," he let out. "We're good."

"Acceptable. Get in. We got a lot of driving to do. And not a lot of time."

That didn't sound good, but Gus did as told. When he was inside and buckled down, he turned as much as the seatbelt would allow to get eyes on Milo. The soldier knew he was being watched, but stared ahead all the same.

"You hear any of that?" Collie asked the man.

"Only the part about slapping me across the ballsack."

"'Nutsack', but yeah. Better believe it. Take that to the bank of 'keep my shit in line' and watch your savings grow."

Milo frowned at the weird analogy, inhaled through his nose, but smartly kept his mouth shut.

"All right then," Collie said. "We're off, bitches."

The limo's engines kicked in with that space warp sound.

In short time, they linked up with Highway Eleven and continued west. The road wasn't anything special, just a two-lane strip right down the throat of the surrounding wild. The sun beamed down on cracked pavement, attempting to split it further, but there was nothing on the road or blocking the way. No movement along the edges and nothing flew. Gus figured he'd see at least a crow but not even that.

"All right," Collie announced. "We're on the slippery Eleven and heading northwest, which will take us all the way to the Seventeen."

"How long will that be?" Gus asked.

"This speed? Nine or ten hours. With stops."

Silence followed that.

"Why do you call it the slippery Eleven?" Milo put to Collie.

"Because shit happens on it."

"You been this way before?" Gus finally asked, forcing himself to sound civil.

"Yeah."

"Me too," Milo said.

That stuck in Gus's craw. "With your crew?"

"Yeah."

"Have anyone with you then?" Gus probed, an edge creeping in his voice.

Milo sighed. "Might've."

Silence again, and Collie didn't turn on any music to fill it.

"Tell you one thing," she said finally, glancing to her left. "I like this traffic."

They sped through that paling landscape where end-of-October clouds darkened old asphalt. An hour went by with no conversation. A weariness seeped into the cabin, and before long, Milo got comfortable and leaned against his window. The hum of tires on pavement worked its magic on Gus as well, lulling him to the point of struggling to stay awake.

Then he drifted off.

And dreamed. At some point, a polar bear appeared outside his window. Biggest bear he'd ever seen, and it was right *there*, black nose sniffing, peering inside the limo. Then it was gone, and Gus was once again drifting, the seatbelt keeping him in place.

At some point Collie said, "Wake up, bitches."

Gus cracked open his eyes and saw houses zip by. He looked the other way, where a broad band of wild grass ended in an autumn tree line. Two houses and their barns sprang up alongside the road, and that was it.

"We in Cochrane?" Milo asked, wiping at his mouth.

"Negative," Collie answered, fingers flexing on the steering wheel. "Past that."

"What's after Cochrane?"

"Whole buncha places. Coming up on a place called Moonbeam."

"Oh yeah," Milo said, remembering. "I know this place."

"Yeah?"

"Kill anyone here?" Gus asked.

That earned him an exceptionally dark look.

"Did you?" Collie asked, neutralizing Milo's expression.

"No," he finally replied. "Not that I can remember, anyway."

"You both passed out almost two hours ago," she said, changing the subject. "Thought I might wake you by running over some potholes, but the angel in me decided not to. You bitches lucked out. I did notice that he drools." She nodded at Milo. "Which was starting to gross me out."

Milo wiped his face again before cleaning his hand on his jeans.

"You guys hungry?" Collie asked.

"Not so much," Gus said.

"Yeah, I'm not either," Milo added.

"You're awful quiet back there, Gus," Collie said.

"It's the company," he answered.

"Hear that, cowboy? He means you. I'm pretty sure he loves me, but you… nope. You're going to have to work on that."

Milo kept his mouth shut.

Gus, however, felt staked to the core. *I'm pretty sure he loves me.* The quip was so well placed, so laser accurate, that it left him speechless.

"All right," Collie said, oblivious to what was happening behind her. She pointed at the clock. "We stop in Moonbeam."

"Moonbeam," Milo said. "Nice place."

Gus didn't give a shit about what Milo thought was nice or not.

The little town was no more than a collection of houses strung out along the highway. Rural to the core, large, empty lots divided the properties, and more than one farm tractor had been abandoned to the unchecked advance of Mother Nature. Some of the front doors to the houses were open. A small convenience shop with its window smashed out passed by. There were three abandoned transport trailers alongside the road, as well as a few cars and trucks. A few side streets came into view on the right, leading deeper into town, but there was no point exploring them since the limo was already packing a full load of supplies and time was of the essence.

The scavenger part of Gus's mind, however, wondered what might lay inside.

"Keep watch now," Collie advised. "Just in case."

A short time later, a large flying saucer came into view on the right.

"The hell is that?" Gus asked.

"It's a UFO," Milo answered with a touch of snark.

"The hell is it doing here?" Gus asked, not appreciating the snark.

"Roadside attraction," Collie said and slowed just a bit. The metallic UFO was a fabrication that had seen better days. Silver paint peeled in several places, and a windstorm might've bent the antennae. Tall grass tickled its undercarriage, and almost concealed its support legs.

"Early settlers either saw stars falling from the sky or reflecting off the water of a creek," Milo explained. "Something like that."

Gus didn't give a shit about the history lesson. Watching Milo's weary profile and his shitty hairdo made his trigger finger itch. He had the urge to shoot the man in the ear. Just pop him and clean up the slop afterwards. Make up any story for Collie.

I was checking my gun and my finger slipped.

My gun slipped and I made a grab and the thing went off.

Fuck it, Collie. He was trouble anyway. I told you he was trouble.

Except all those sounded like shitty excuses to him, especially with the safety feature. He just wanted to shoot the guy and be done with it. To exact revenge for Collie, and to avoid the inevitable double-cross before it happened.

Because that's who Milo was. A shitty-assed, dick-biting snake with its tail rattle snapped off.

Collie kept on driving.

Milo turned to study her and Gus checked on his gun—still in the cupholder.

"So, uh, there was nothing at Whitecap to help you?" the soldier quietly asked her.

"Help me with what?"

"… Your condition."

"This? Nope. I'm done like dinner."

"All the doctors or scientists were dead?"

"Most all. There was a research assistant, but he couldn't do much." She checked her side mirror out of habit. "He was in hard shape himself."

"Infected?"

"Yeah, but not like a zombie. Zombi*fied*, maybe, but still human."

"Was he all fucked up?" Milo asked.

"He was indeed all fucked up. Still *is*."

Gus listened, staring at the grip of his pistol, going through the mental movie playing through his head. Somewhere along this part Milo would make his move for the steering wheel. Collie would resist while maintaining control of the limo, and Gus would switch him off with one, maybe two bullets to the head, plastering the nearby window with brain jam.

A part of him hoped the soldier would make his move.

"And he couldn't help you?" Milo asked.

"Couldn't help himself," Collie replied. "He gave himself whatever antidotes they were working on at the time and more. He became his own test subject. Not that it helped. He's eating deodorant sticks now."

"What?"

Collie nodded.

That quieted the soldier. "Goddamn," he eventually whispered and returned to watching the road.

"And there's that thing about my heart being blown out my back," Collie said. "So what I got now is the only thing keeping me going."

Milo remained quiet.

Keeping his movements nice and easy, Gus placed his fingers around the gun grip. Up front, Milo leaned forward, shifted his weight, and settled back to watch the procession of little houses outside his window.

Gus waited. And waited. Feeling the agonizing drip of seconds, waiting for the soldier to spring into action. One look, and Gus would end this nonsense. Collie was wrong about bringing the soldier along. It wasn't about trust, it was about history, and in Milo's case it was all bad.

Gus watched him.

Milo didn't move, however. Milo did squat. He sat and stared, blinking in a world-weary fashion, as if Atlas himself had tricked him into cleaning out his shithouse.

"You okay back there, Gus?" Collie asked.

The question startled him. His mind fluttered like a TV in need of a shake before picking up a signal. "Yeah. I'm fine."

"Kinda quiet back there."

"Just keeping a look-out on things." And that sounded like fresh horseshit if ever there was a load.

"Well, join in, whenever you feel like it."

"Join in what?"

"The conversation."

The conversation? Holy chunky peanut butter.

"Gonna be a long trip," Collie explained. "Relax, is all I'm saying. Not like we got a trunk load of nukes or anything."

Nukes.

That distracted Gus, got him thinking about that *other* surprise. The country possessed and maintained a small nuclear arsenal, just as a deterrent against foreign aggression.

Milo turned away from the window. "That's something I wanted to ask you about."

"Yeah?" Collie said. "Go ahead."

"Whitecap has nukes?"

"Where'd you hear that?"

"From you guys. Outside my cell door."

"You rascal, you."

You piece of shit, you, Gus projected.

"Yeah, we got a half dozen," Collie admitted, causing Gus's eyes to bulge. "No secret now. Not like anyone can use them. Not in their current state. That was taken care of."

"News to me," Milo said. "How'd we get them in the first place?"

"Short story, we traded for them. You remember your history? Back in the late fifties? We were developing the Avro? A fighter aircraft capable of reaching Mach two. Interceptors to counter the Soviet bomber threat, right?"

"I don't remember."

"That's okay. I do. The Avro was scrapped in favor of an American-produced interceptor, which was previously *not* accepted. We got the first nukes along with them. Little added bonus to soften the deal. One or two more as years went on."

Gus cleared his throat. "Should you be telling him about the nukes, Collie?"

"I told you," she pointed out.

"Yeah, but—"

"And he's military," Collie continued. "Matter of fact, after me, this guy's the only military Whitecap's got. When I'm gone, he's going to be the warden of those things."

That stunned both Gus and Milo.

"You're shittin' me," was all Gus could say.

"Nope."

Milo stared at her. "You *must* be shittin' me."

"Nuh-uh. Not in the least. You remember our little pep talk not so long ago? All those regimental flashbacks? Me reminding you who you are *still?*"

"Yeah. I remember."

"There you go. You're it, princess. The task of keeping an eye on those things falls on your shoulders. I mean, if you get back in one piece that is. No pressure."

Milo cupped his forehead and gazed at the road.

"Not that you gotta do much. The launch codes have been disposed of. So, all Whitecap has now are a handful of missiles about as dangerous as sharpened pencils. So don't worry about it."

She kept on driving.

Gus couldn't believe his ears, and from Milo's reaction, the soldier couldn't believe his either.

"Tell me more about Dick Dick," Collie finally asked.

Milo glanced her way. "Like I already said, I don't know much. He's the leader of the Leather. That's about it. Well, wait. He likes to put… dog skulls outside his towns. Let everyone know it's his. Not that he has any worries. There's no one to go up against him."

"We're going up against him," Gus said.

Milo continued as if not hearing. "They worship him, did I mention that?"

"Yes, you did," Collie replied.

"I don't know why that is, but they talk about him like… yeah. A priest. Or a god. It's pretty fucked up if you ever talk to one of these guys. Not that they talk much, you understand, but when they do, it's all for the Dog Tongue. The Dog Tongue wishes it to be. The Dog Tongue will be pleased. The Dog Tongue will *not* be pleased. Like something from a bad movie, but the scary thing is… they say that shit like they believe it. Really believe it. Fanatical. Like the Dog Tongue is the one who saved them all. Jolly Jake and the rest of us? We wouldn't say shit about the Leather until we were well and truly gone, you understand? And we wouldn't even *think* shit about the Dog Tongue when we *were* around the Leather. It was that kinda vibe with them. One look, one hint of a *smile*, and we would've been… fucked. Tortured. I mean made to suffer. Until death."

The chills returned to Gus.

"You said he was from out west?" Collie asked.

"West of the Rockies, yeah. But moving this way."

"No idea of numbers?"

Milo shook his head. "Not definite, no. Like I said, I think you wiped out a lot of them."

"But there's more."

"Yeah. Maybe. I've heard talk."

"Any idea where they get their fuel?"

"No," Milo answered.

"And no idea how they do their communications?"

"None. We figure straight-up messenger."

"Are they military?"

Milo took a sharp breath through his nose. "No. I mean, they *move* like they might be, but no."

"All right," Collie said, fingers flexing on the steering wheel. "That's a good thing. Tell me more about the Leather towns."

"Already told you what I know."

"Tell me again."

"Cities, really," Milo said, sounding bored. "Sections of cities."

"Which ones?"

"The big ones."

"Ottawa?"

The mention of the capital put Gus on alert. He remembered Collie's aversion about heading into any city and staying north of the border.

"Not Ottawa," Milo replied. "Not yet. But it's probably on the list. Toronto, too. Not there yet, but making their way. The ones you knocked off? They just might've been the advance force but got distracted with everything else that happened."

"What cities then?"

"Ah…" Milo thought about it. "Regina. That's one. Calgary. Maybe Banff."

"Banff?"

"Yeah."

"That's not a city."

"Well, the Leather talked about it. That's all I know."

Collie spared him a glance. "Anywhere else?"

"Vancouver. I think that's the main place."

"Figures," she muttered. "Goddamn it. Not Edmonton?"

Milo thought about it. "No, I don't think."

"All right, we'll find out the hard way. One of them will talk. Vancouver. Shit."

"Don't like the cities?"

"No, I don't like the cities," Collie answered.

The landscape sped past their windows.

"I don't like them either," Milo said under his breath.

6

They drove on in silence, preferring the quiet rather than talking about events to come. Just after one in the afternoon, they cut through the little town of Mattice, and Collie decided to pull over at the outer limits.

"See something?" Gus asked.

"No," Collie answered. "Just going to stretch my legs."

"Not a bad idea," Milo said and opened his door, prompting Gus to reach for his gun. Milo was already out by the time he had a hand around his Glock.

Irritated, Gus got out on the other side.

As for most of the trip, the majority of the houses and businesses were on the right side of the highway, while the railbed continued on the left. Just up ahead was a Super Eight hotel with a parking lot half-filled with vehicles. Gus only spared the place a second before locking onto Milo. The soldier had his eyes on Collie as she walked away from the limo. She had her Sig Saur out, which she tapped against her leg. Ahead of her, on her right and across a ditch, was a little bungalow. Collie walked across a short, crushed stone bridge with an exposed culvert and proceeded up the driveway. She stopped at the open door, placed a hand against the frame, and entered.

Milo glanced back at Gus. "She okay?"

"'Course not."

"I mean, why'd she go in there? There's nothing in there."

The man had a point. Gus didn't really know why she'd gone in there either. "She wanted to stretch her legs. So…she's stretching 'em."

Milo returned to watching the house. Gus moved a few steps along the limo, but kept watch.

Something occurred to him.

"About these Leather guys," he started.

Milo looked back at him.

"How many you think they have in each town?"

Milo shook his head.

"Who's leading them? In each town?"

"No idea," the soldier said. "Probably a designated whistle head. The Leather equivalent of an officer, I mean. A valued henchman. Someone who's demonstrated qualities that set him above the others."

"What kind of qualities?"

"Who knows? Viciousness. A capacity for violence. Maybe physical strength or skill with a weapon. Or willingness to *use* a weapon without hesitation. Or a conscience. Maybe all that. Intelligence is probably in there. Along with loyalty."

Gus sampled the inside of his cheek and regarded the bungalow's front door.

"Just don't get caught," Milo warned.

That brought him back. "What?"

"Don't let them capture you. That's all. Remember what they did to that Carson guy? How they smashed his toes? And knees? They'll do that and that's *kind*. I don't know if Jake was joking, but once he said they disemboweled some poor asswipe, stretched his guts out, and dumped burning coals into his abdominal cavity."

"What?" a disbelieving Gus whispered, one hand drifting to his own belly. "No way."

"Way. Don't know how Jake knew about it, but frankly, it's in the Leather's wheelhouse. Jake talked with them the most, and one of them probably let that slip, just to keep him in line. We should've just nodded then and gotten the fuck outta Dodge."

"Can't get any worse than that," Gus said, his hatred for Milo momentarily blotted out by that very thought.

"They do have zombies," Milo reminded him.

"Thanks," he said sarcastically.

Milo resumed looking at the house.

"Fucking zombies," Gus fumed. "Y'know, I thought we were done with those things. I really did. I'd *hoped* we were done."

A short time later, Collie came out of the house and walked back to the limo. She sized up the lay of the land as she moved, her balaclava hiding her expression completely.

"Find anything?" Gus asked when she got close enough.

"No, nothing."

"Stretch them legs?" Milo asked her.

Collie stopped at the driver's door. "Don't you worry about me, cowboy. I'm fine."

"I'm not worried," Milo said. "Sir."

She paused at that. "Get in," she finally ordered.

Which he did.

Gus got close to her. "Everything okay?" he asked in a low tone.

"As okay as they're going to be," Collie said and got aboard.

Gus did the same.

Minutes later they passed a construction site ringed by a metal fence. A couple of heavy rigs and trailers were parked inside. Then it was more houses, which were a little nicer. One home had a pickup truck embedded halfway through the main window, and when they slowed to appreciate the scene, Milo pointed out the human bones in the ditches. No skulls, however. Gus had seen plenty of wreckages in the last few years, so size or scale did little to move him. The uneventful drive and starship engine sound of the limo made him sleepy again, so he settled in and stared at the window across from him. Yellow grass. Trees losing their leaves. The limo's soft humming, working just fine. An early winter fog floated into existence, hiding the sun. The landscape faded into gray. Gus sighed, struggling to stay awake.

More houses breezed by, then a hardware store. A car rental place. Dentist's office. Liquor store…

Gus's eyes snapped open. He lurched forward only to be restrained by his seatbelt. His fingers clawed at the release button as his knee jostled the Glock in the cupholder. He got loose of the seatbelt in a buzz of rushing fibers and pitched to the opposite window, cracking his knee off his aluminum bat and sending it tumbling to the floor.

"See something, Gus?" Collie answered, already hitting the brakes.

"Some*one*. In front of the liquor store."

She reversed, the limo's starship engines changing their tune, now a low grind. Gus snatched up his Glock. The shop fronts whisked by, as did parking meters. Then the liquor store was before him, its wine-colored overhang just above a pair of automated doors that were open. Bottles and cans littered the threshold and a turnstile stood just inside the building.

"Right here," Gus said, sizing up the entrance.

Collie hit the brakes.

Gus placed a hand on the door. The lock popped as Collie released it for him.

"I can't see anyone," Milo said, but Gus was already gone. He hurried from the vehicle, bringing up his sidearm in a two-handed grip, mindful of the cans and bottles covering the ground. He stepped over the clutter and proceeded inside. Ravaged aisles. Emptied cash registers. Signs hung in disarray. A few bottles remained upon the shelves but not much. It was quiet, the air winter dry. Gus turned right, then left, aiming as he went.

And stopped.

Right there, tucked against the wall as if waiting for him, was the Captain.

Not *the* Captain, but the retail one. A full-sized cardboard cutout of a dashing Captain Morgan dressed in his finest attire. He stood in a permanent toast, with one arm outstretched and a fabricated glass in hand. His other hand gripped the edge of his coat, which was adorned with gold buttons. The character smiled at Gus, a great beaming beacon that reflected a powerful fondness. A thin coating of dust dimmed the character's bearded face, but only a touch. The expression was otherwise unblemished. Pristine, even.

Gus did a double take of the display. His spirits rose at the sight of his old friend, but then sank when he realized he'd released the Captain—*his* Captain—back into the sea, months earlier. Perhaps months too soon. And the display wasn't the shadowy figure he'd spotted from the road. Of that he was certain. His mind seized upon the present, realizing he'd forgotten the vast unlit cavern of the store and its numerous places to hide. The aisles weren't straight, rather a collection of shelving units that blocked Gus's line of sight. Studying the cuts and angles of the store's innards, he realized his phantom could be hiding anywhere within that maze.

"Hello?" he asked. And waited.

Nothing.

"Anyone in here?" he asked. "I, uh, saw you when we drove by. It's okay. Come on out. I won't hurt you. Or anyone."

No answer.

"Aww, c'mon," Gus said. "Look. My nerves aren't up for this shit, okay? We're not going to hurt you. Just come on out so we can talk."

No reply.

"Goddammit," he swore, scanning the darker recesses, straining to catch a telltale tinkle of movement. Bottles and cans littered much of the floor, as if whoever had gone through had cleared the shelves with a shovel and a shopping cart—and missed most of the shopping cart.

Jagged edges of broken glass lurked in between the intact bottles, and Gus swore at the sight, wondering why all the bottles couldn't be made of plastic.

"All right," he whispered and inched forward. He puzzled over where to place his boots at times, before realizing he didn't have to be careful. He'd already asked whoever was in the place to come on out, thus alerting them to his presence.

"So what the hell am I creeping around for?" he asked himself and rubbed at his temple with the heel of his gun hand, the weapon pointed at the ceiling.

No one answered, so he shrugged and kicked aside the garbage on the floor, sending a few bottles spinning. He marched into the rear, gun lowered, and stopped to look around. The shelving displays were pushed back in places, as if whoever had done it was in a hurry. That got Gus thinking about dead things. The rest of the shop was empty. He found the office area, a hexagonal room three steps up from the main floor. By this time, the angry accordion that was his troubled foot was starting to warm up, as if warning him about taking so damn long. Two computer terminals, one with two screens. A tension ball was beside a keyboard. Gus went through the drawers and found nothing except folders full of inventory receipts.

Only the storage area remained.

Gus went to those swinging doors and stood before them, sizing them up as if they were the retail version of the gates of hell. Senses tingling, he put a shoulder to one and pushed through.

Darkness. Pitch black and as deep as a galactic void.

Gus listened for breathing, for whispering. For anything. And heard nothing.

The nearest shelves were looted, and he felt less inclined to explore any further. At this point, he knew from experience when the undead was present. One thing about the gimps. If they were nearby, they wouldn't fuck around. They'd come at you.

And, God help him, Gus didn't feel like going through the motions of trying to earn the trust of anyone potentially hiding from him.

"Hey, you know what?" he announced to the dark. "I don't care anymore. I don't give a sweet, swinging dingleberry of a shit. I came in here in peace and I'm walking out in peace. If there's anyone in here, sorry if I freaked you out. Have a good one. Stay safe."

He eyed the empty shelves. "You probably already had a good one. Or a couple of good ones."

Having vented, Gus returned to the entrance. The limo was out there, waiting for his return.

As was the Captain. The *new* Captain.

Gus stopped before that great cardboard display, hoisting a rum-filled glass into the air as if toasting life and all its goodness. The smile was a beacon of good times and good friends, perhaps lounging around a driftwood fire somewhere, enjoying the Caribbean heat of the day. Or the blazing star fields of the night.

"The hell you so happy for?" Gus asked the Captain.

And, not surprisingly—and a little thankfully—the character didn't answer.

"Keep an eye on the place," he smirked and walked by.

He stopped, however, as if he'd just stepped into dog shit. There he stood, thinking and internally debating.

"You can't come along," he finally whispered, not looking at the cardboard character behind him. "You understand that. You can't."

No reply.

Gus turned around. "It's going to be dangerous. Real dangerous. And... Collie's sick. She doesn't have much time left. Worse, we got a ride-along who I don't trust in the fucking least. Then there's a guy somewhere out west... whole buncha guys, in fact, who... I mean..."

He sighed again. "It's just bad all around."

The display didn't say a word.

He chewed on the inside of his cheek. "I... I poured you into the sea, remember?" he said as a final argument.

He waited for an answer, but silence ruled. Gus's shoulders trembled, and he released a great defeated sigh.

"God... damn." He croaked, gazing upon that smiling face.

*

"What's keeping him?" Milo asked Collie.

"Don't you worry about that one."

"Why? Is he good or something?"

"That one has lived through more undead shit than you and I combined," Collie informed him, her fingers flexing on the steering wheel. "*Without* any training. Just getting by on sheer guts alone. And industrial-sized horseshoe luck."

Milo absorbed that without comment before eventually looking out his window.

A large shape flattened against the liquor store's front window as if tackled full-on from the inside. It rose in a funky lurch, stayed there for a second, and then got yanked to the right in a series of skidding stops—just before disappearing entirely.

Milo didn't know what he'd just seen, and he was about to say as much to Collie, when Gus came out of the shop.

With something under his arm.

Something big. And flat.

Gus stopped, thinking matters over, before striding forward. He knocked on the limo's window. Collie pushed a button and the door swung open. Without a word, Gus peered inside, sized up the business class section, and withdrew.

Only to stuff the cardboard display of the Captain through the door.

The rapscallion officer slipped inside without a hitch, smiling roguishly all the way. The display kept on beaming, even when Gus got aboard and made room for the guy amongst the supplies and seats. Gus stopped only long enough to glare at those in the front, warning them to say not one goddamn word.

Then he went back to work, positioning the Captain just right against the seats, ensuring the officer was comfortable.

Milo shot a questioning look at Collie.

She shook her head.

Gus closed the door, thrashed around until he was situated in his own seat, and sat back with a weary sigh.

"Okay," he huffed. "Place is clean. Let's go."

Without a word, Collie put the limo in drive, checked her mirrors out of habit, and drove out of town.

The scenery drifted by at a good clip, but Milo squirmed. His fingers drummed on the armrest. He glanced outside at the passing houses, then he glanced at Collie's profile twice before twisting side-on and studying Gus with serious intent.

"What?" Gus asked.

As an answer, Milo made side-eyes at him, then the carboard display... and then back again. "The hell is that?" he quietly asked.

Gus cleared his throat. "Captain Morgan display."

"Yeah, I can see it's a Captain Morgan display."

"Don't worry about the display, cowboy," Collie said.

"Yeah *cowboy*," Gus took up. "Don't worry about the display."

"My question is," Milo pressed on, ignoring the warnings, "is why'd you take it?"

"Souvenir."

"Souvenir."

"Yeah."

"That's a souvenir?"

"What'd I just say?"

Milo stared for a few passing heartbeats before shaking his head. "Whatever."

"Not like it's taking up room," Gus grumped and waved at the cardboard character. "It makes me feel good. He's like, you know, morale-lifting."

An approving Captain stared right back.

"And, oh yeah, before I forget," Gus said to Milo. "Fuck off. Cock taster."

Milo scowled. "The hell's a cock taster?"

"Like a professional wine taster, where you spit instead of swallow. If you'd ever seen a professional wine taster in action, you know what I'm talkin' about."

"I'll power up YouTube when I get a chance," Milo shot back.

"Yeah? Well, when you do, refer to my previous memo, the one that says *fuck off*."

The soldier fumed and settled back into his seat. "If he gets to pick up a souvenir, that mean I can too?"

"Sure," Collie said. "Fair's fair. But not another display. Try something smaller."

Milo waved a hand in a flourish of *why not?*

*

Daylight took on that familiar wane around three-thirty in the afternoon. Potholes and sunken sections became pitfalls in the two-lane highway, and Collie adjusted her driving accordingly. Grass sprouted from cracks in the pavement, and she noted that if the vegetation was standing tall like it was, then no one had driven through the area in a long time.

She flicked on her indicator, checked her mirrors, and slowed down to turn off the road.

"We're gonna stop here for the night," Collie said, aiming the limo for a bare patch of pavement, one that might've once been the foundation for a roadside gas station long since removed.

"Here?" Milo asked.

Collie nodded.

"Why not in town? Get ourselves a nice hotel somewhere? Or a house?"

Collie scanned the parking area and pointed to a back road almost lost in the overgrowth. "I can't be bothered with checking out a place. That's all."

"But out in the open is fine with you?"

"Right now, it is." She swung the limo around and backed the massive machine onto the roadside parking area. Once it was parked, she switched off the engine, checked the power levels, and then the position of the sun.

"We're down to twenty-two percent here," she told them. "But we're hauling a lot of weight. We'll need to stay put and soak up some rays to fully recharge."

"How much can we recharge?" Milo said, checking on the sun.

"Before nightfall?" Collie asked and shrugged. "Close to full, I hope." She examined the dashboard interface for a flicker of light and said, "All right, it's recharging. Says so right there." She tapped her finger on a flashing lightning bolt symbol.

Satisfied, Collie faced Milo and then Gus. "Looks like we're here for the night. Off the highway. When it gets dark, anyone who might be driving by will do exactly that. And before either of you start talking, remember what our limo is made of. We're better off in this thing than anywhere else."

"I'm good," Gus said.

"'Course you are," Milo said. "You got your life-sized souvenir from the pop-shop back there with you."

"We still talking about that?"

"That thing won't blow you."

"That your professional opinion?"

Milo shook his head and sighed.

"Relax, Milo," Collie advised before he could fire off another shot.

"Just saying," the soldier directed at her. "I've been driving around with some pretty unstable people. Maybe I'm a little sensitive right about now—"

"*You're* a little sensitive?" Gus interrupted.

"But dragging *that* thing along," Milo pointed for emphasis, "strikes me that someone's nuttier than squirrel shit."

Collie stared at the soldier. "All right, I'll address this right now. To hopefully alleviate your concern. Gus?"

"Yeah, Collie?"

"You okay?"

"Jesus Christ, I'm fine. It's just a good luck charm, is all. We all have them. We all need them. And he's the best one I've ever had."

He pointed at the Captain.

"Then I'm good," Collie said and reclined her seat just a touch. "Put up your feet and relax, Milo. The man says he's good and I believe him. And that's coming from a secret squirrel."

Milo had nothing to say to that.

"We eating?" Gus asked.

"Why not?" Collie said. "Cowboy? Guess I'm settling on 'Cowboy' as your nickname."

Milo's expression said *Guess so.*

"I'll take orders," Gus said.

"Nothing for me," Collie told him.

"You sure?"

"I'm sure."

"You haven't eaten in a while."

"I know. No appetite. What can you do?"

He studied her. "Okay. If you change your mind, just holler."

"You'll hear me."

"What about me?" Milo asked.

"You can go eat—"

"Gus," Collie cut him off. "Fix him up a sandwich, please. I'll keep him company."

Gus didn't particularly want to, but what he said was, "Fine."

"With any of that processed meat I heard you talking about," Milo said. "Two sandwiches if you can spare it."

"'Course we can fucking spare it," Gus snarled back. With a nod and a wink at the Captain (who beamed right back at him), he eased around the cutout and the gear, toward the jazz lounge door.

Or what he *thought* was a jazz lounge. From the fucking future.

While the business class was sinfully opulent, the *lounge* area, designed with total billionaire slobbery in mind (or at least in Gus's mind), was entirely next level. When Collie had initially shown it to him, his jaw dropped, and his eyes dried out from a lack of blinking. An ultra-comfortable wraparound sofa took up most of its space. Black and gray square cushions matched a dark blue upholstery designed to not only soak up a person's ass, but to suck it down and leave them breathless. Overhead, an artificial starfield shone prominently, enticing one to stretch out and gaze at the fabricated heavens. Across from the sofa was a large-screen TV that seemed much too large, in Gus's mind. If that wasn't enough, the designers decided to place a complete bar right below that, with soft back lighting in case anyone missed it. Glasses filled cupholders cut from a sheet of extravagant granite, while other dining materials were tucked away in a cabinet. There was an onboard water tank as well as a refrigerator, and even a frigging microwave because why the fuck not? A moonroof was situated just near the back, in case four or five people wanted to pop up and wave at the nonexistent masses. Storage closets were located at the front and back. A single door, which only opened from the inside, was to the right of the bar setup.

The lounge was stunning, a Lamborghini-level of breath-stealing extravagance.

And so incredibly out of place at the end of a zombie apocalypse.

Provisions taken from Whitecap now filled most of the lounge. Stacks of bottled water and coolers containing food were crammed into the space, covering half of the huge sofa and dribbling over onto half of the bar. They had brought enough food and water for two weeks on the road, in addition to weapons and other gear Collie deemed necessary, and items of interest Gus very much wanted to bring along. Just in case.

The designated armory was to his immediate right. Gus left that alone. He cut a line to the fridge and opened it.

Whitecap had surprised him with its immense stores of freeze-dried food of just about every kind imaginable. One of the little eye-poppers was a shockingly wide selection of processed meats. Pepperoni, salami, honey ham, pastrami, roast beef, and turkey, and the cheese and crackers to go with them. A part of Gus wanted to place a portion of those treasures in a museum of some sort, but that part immediately had the living shit kicked out of it by his stomach. Art, the short order cook from New Brunswick, actually produced some spicy pepperoni and salami from deer meat and beef, and it wasn't half bad, but it was a work in progress.

This, however, was the real shit.

And as good as all that was, the true delicacy… were the cheeseburgers and the calzone. That rare-seen culinary staple from an age now gone was an attention grabber at the back of the fridge. Individually wrapped and stacked in the back in columns of *mm-mmm* goodness.

To go along with all that, real processed ketchup, mustard, and mayo. Even a jar of salad dressing spread, whose tangy goodness had to be brought along.

Stooped over, Gus inspected the fridge's contents and faced the toughest decision of the day—right behind whether or not to shoot Milo in the balls. He spotted the resealable plastic bags containing all those meaty, colon-clenching delights. Cheeseburger. Or calzone. Or a straight up deli sandwich.

God love it all, what a way to end a day.

He went with the sandwich, deciding to save the cheeseburgers and calzone for later. The activity of putting together a few sandwiches—with a plate of assorted cheese cuts and crackers—made him feel better. He'd been… staring at the Captain for much of the drive since stuffing the display into the back seat. The Captain didn't talk to him, which was a good thing, since the very presence of the eternally dandy bastard both lifted and troubled Gus.

He *had* seen someone moving underneath the liquor store's canopy. He was certain he didn't imagine it. Gus stopped making sandwiches and planted himself on the nearby edge of the sofa. He stared at the open fridge and thought, then thought some more, replaying the episode in his head.

He'd seen someone. Some *thing*. And now the Captain was onboard, grinning his rosy ass off.

In the end, Gus figured it was a good omen. He resumed preparing what would be the first and last meal of the day.

Then he stopped and examined the sandwich he was preparing for that treacherous piece of shit riding with them. Salad dressing, heaps of meat, along with dashes of mustard and a few cuts of honest-to-god cheddar. It almost seemed a waste to be feeding the guy. A very petty feeling of nastiness welled up within Gus's chest then, one that urged him to add a little extra gourmet flavoring to the food.

He stared at the sandwich, holding one slab of white bread slathered in salad dressing and mustard and took a deep, considering breath…

Only Gus and Milo ate. Collie excused herself to step outside and to scout the area. The two men sat and dined alone, the partition separating them. Which was unquestionably a good thing.

The sandwiches weren't as good as pub-served prime rib with a side order of home fries and a hill of buttered giblets, but all things considered, it was mighty fine. They devoured the food. Milo took down the first sandwich, chased it with bottled water, and went to work on the second one.

He was halfway through it when he stopped and glanced over his shoulder.

Gus was watching him, not bothering to hide a dirty smile.

Milo stared back. In time, he resumed eating, taking wary bites, and not looking in the other's direction.

Then, with a pinch of sandwich remaining, he looked at Gus. "You didn't fuck around with these, did you?"

"Me?" Gus said, sipping off a bottled water as if it were uncorked champagne. "'Course not. Why do you ask?"

"Because you got that guilty-monkey smirk on your face."

"I look like this all the time."

"Be pretty fucking low to fuck around with a man's food."

"Agreed," Gus said, wiping at his whiskers. "Pretty fucking low."

"Especially when it's a good couple of sandwiches."

"They were a good couple of sandwiches, weren't they?"

"You fucked with them, didn't you?"

"I did not."

"Goddammit."

"I said I didn't."

"I don't believe you."

Gus half-shrugged. "Fuck if I care."

Milo regarded the last of his supper. In the end, he gobbled it down and then sat and fumed and waited for whatever was going happen.

"Thanks," he said, glaring at Gus.

"Don't mention it."

They nursed their water bottles then, looking anywhere but at each other, the tension palpable.

*

Collie walked some twenty feet back behind the limo, her pistol at the ready. Supper didn't appeal to her. Nothing in the way of food appealed to her, really. What she wanted, what her brain was trying to tell her it *needed*, was the very thing she once dreaded to think about. To remember. When Wallace was undergoing his own transformation. The nights he would be on guard duty, without anything to eat, yet… there were hints that he was consuming *something*. A strand of hair on his chin that he'd missed. A flicker of blood on his collar. Or his sleeve.

She asked him about those telltale crumbs, and god help her, Wallace told her. Told her everything, leaving nothing out. So she understood.

She wondered if Gus would understand. He probably would. He was with Wallace just as much as she was in his final days.

She just needed a little more time, to analyze what was happening to her. That afternoon, while the two rug rats snored away in the limo as she drove, she became aware of an odd sensation at the back of her mind. At the rear wall of her brain, almost, like the skin of a peach just beginning to show a hint of rot. There, biological matter was breaking down into withering curls and strands that flickered and popped like a lit fuse, except when that fuse reached its end there would be no explosion.

Collie figured there wouldn't be much of anything.

Or at least she hoped there wouldn't be much of anything.

Like anyone else who'd survived this long, she'd seen scenes of horror and heart stabbing sorrow. She'd witnessed friends turning and had even shot a few. She didn't think Gus would be capable of ending her. Didn't want him to be left with the task, in fact, because she knew it would severely damage him. Break him. That was the last thing she wanted.

That was all beside the point, however, which was that weird sensation at the back of her brain, coming to life, twitching, droning, *emerging*, like the cancerous welt it was, festering on the inside of the vault that was her mind. She knew the infection for what it was, and she strove to seek dominance over it, imposing her considerable will upon it like a five-hundred-pound weight squishing a bug.

Except this bug would not die.

Even though she'd subdued those disturbing feelings, they were still there. Radiating. Triggering a need. A craving. Not for anything sweet or spicy, mind you, or any weird combinations of flavors. No, what *she* wanted…

Collie mentally stomped on that, drubbing it into the dirt of her mind as if snuffing out a cigarette. She stopped and saw an old road where four-wheel quads had left their prints years ago. She was cold, always cold, and unknown to the boys traveling with her, she'd switched on the heating coils within the driver's seat in an attempt to get warm. She'd put it on the highest setting, in fact. It didn't work. She'd turned it off after an hour, for fear of either cooking her undead ass or setting it on fire.

The day was ending, and the autumn hue of the surrounding wild was pleasing, thought-clearing. She used those sights and smells to quiet the sinister mewling of worms chewing away at the fabric of her mind.

As if squeezing her own jellifying blood out of her ankles wasn't bad enough. Collie wondered briefly if things couldn't get any worse.

She shut that thought down as well, knowing better.

7

Built in the early 1700s to protect the nearby glistening waters and sandy beaches of Lake Winnipeg, as well as the fur interests of the Northwest Company, Fort Jay was an enormous fortification of the day, firmly situated on a stubby toe of a peninsula. It lorded over nearby sand dunes while waters lapped at its white bedrock base. At its height of power, Fort Jay possessed seventy-two guns, ranging from cast iron thirty-two-pounder cannons, to the bigger sixty-eights. Forty of those guns faced the calm waters of the lake, while the others were aimed at the cleared farmland to the south. The fort's walls, originally built of earth and logs, had been replaced over time by stone, brick, and concrete. Its star-shaped design had been devised to impede attackers, establish kill zones, and provide the widest field of fire for the fort's defenders.

So, naturally, when the zombie apocalypse first broke out, the fort was an ideal choice to seek refuge.

The hillside leading up to the main gates was grass-covered and sloped, providing nowhere to hide. A drained moat cut across the front of the fort, nearly spanning the width of the peninsula itself. Narrow bridges were sluiced at the ends of the land mass and could be easily defended if the enemy attempted to cross. The moat itself was both twenty-feet wide and deep, and filled with all manner of pointy objects designed to impale the enemy and keep them there. Overlooking the moat were the mighty stone walls themselves, high enough for any attacking force to have a very bad day. The main entrance was accessed by crossing a single bridge, well within the striking range of a southern pair of triangular fortifications called ravelins. Those outworks boasted a half-dozen cannons which were aimed at the sluices at either end of the moat as well as the central bridge to the fort. Anyone crossing those points would find themselves in a devastating bottleneck.

All these features had been dutifully maintained over the years, reconstructed where necessary, and in an overall solid state of affairs.

Regular tents dotted the courtyard, over a dozen in all, arranged side by side some fifteen feet apart. Cars and pickup trucks occupied the spaces in front of these homes. One mighty building occupied the center of the courtyard. Some three stories tall, perhaps a hundred feet wide, and three hundred feet long, the architecture was a no-nonsense eighteenth-century British military design. Three stone wells rose from various points around the parade ground, as well as a pair of open brick firepits. Figures strode around the area, clad entirely in leather and carrying an assortment of medieval weapons.

Within that main building, in a room designated for the commander of the fort, a single man stood with his hands clasped behind his back. He was slim, just above average height, and went by the name of Reid. Reid Harrison. And unlike the dozen or so leather-clad individuals also present, Harrison wore an olive-green army coat, with the rest of his attire perhaps taken from an army surplus store. His hair, both long and prematurely gray, was tied at the back of his head. His beard had gone into a state of grizzly-man wild. Several scars covered his features, as if he'd been whipped repeatedly across the face. He still had all his teeth, however, and in this day and age, he believed that to be admirable, if not beguiling to some. When he was on the road, his smile was as good a weapon as the two sidearms he openly carried in thigh holsters.

This moment, however, he was not smiling.

In fact, he kept his face positively neutral as he watched the leather-clad officer rise from behind the impressive desk meant for the fort's commander. His mask was of a Venetian design, aristocratic in concept, but with a red spiderweb festering around the edges. An intricate inlay of lace ringed the eyes in a raccoon's mask, while dust and grime dimmed the rest of the face. At a glance, the mask appeared to be made of papier-mâché, but this was untrue. The mâché ended around the mouth, where a cloth material was seamlessly attached to the cheeks. A zipper ran up the middle of the neck to the nose, splitting an otherwise benign smile.

On the forehead of the masked Leather, stamped into that grime-shadowed scalp, was a spider. Huge and eight-legged, the tips of the lower legs stretched down along the profiles.

Opaque eyes stared at Reid Harrison.

"Say that again," the Spider asked in a neutral tone, standing and showing off a swimmer's broad-shouldered physique. A black shirt covered his upper frame, and suspenders were latched onto his similarly colored jeans, giving him the air of a post-apocalyptic gangster. The Spider was just a few fingers taller than Harrison, but his limbs were freakishly gangly, his hands well past his hips.

Harrison resisted the urge to clear his throat. "I'm just the messenger," he rumbled, raising his own hands in a gesture of *take it easy*.

"You're a prick, Reid Harrison," the Spider said simply in that same toneless voice. "A little prick."

Not many could call Reid Harrison a prick and get away with it. Not in this day and age. Not even the Spider. Reid Harrison could smile and keep it on high beam for a long time, but call him a prick, call him *anything*, and he'd end your day with a kick to the balls and a pair of bullets to the face. But seeing as these fetish-crazies greatly outnumbered Harrison, he decided silence was the best response.

And the one before him, the one called the Spider, wasn't a prick, but he *was* one of the creepiest sonsabitches taking orders from the Dog Tongue. Harrison considered all of the Leather to be mentally unstable—some more so than others—but the Spider was a piece of work. He moved with an economy of motion that, quite frankly, made Harrison think of English theatre. Harrison had never seen the Spider in a fight, but there was a spring-loaded lethality there, ready to be switched on.

The fucking mask the guy wore had to have been stolen from a museum. It freaked Harrison out just a touch, and he supposed that was the point of it.

"You go find them," the Spider continued. "I'll stay here. Entertain myself with the prisoners. I like to ... entertain guests."

I bet you do, you fucking nut, was Harrison's first thought, but what he said was, "The Bear Trap was specific."

The Bear Trap was the designated commander of the little army the Dog Tongue had sent east. He remained in Winnipeg, lording over the city in the Dog Tongue's name, while he sent out the Spider and the other gob of nutbutter called the Vulture to scout and conquer any and all leftovers that might be found.

One of those leftovers had been Fort Jay, a target that Reid Harrison had ferreted out.

It wasn't hard. Just put on a friendly face, perhaps do a small job or two to win over the community's trust, then infiltrate the place, stay friendly, and once you had a good idea of the strengths and weakness of the town, slip away and notify the Leather. Harrison had checked off all those to-do things on his list and, upon informing the Bear Trap, received orders to return to Fort Jay. Return, stay cool, keep an eye on things, and open the gates when the time came.

Which Harrison dutifully did.

Except, the residents of Fort Jay had initiated plans of their own without Harrison's knowledge. Namely, sending out scouts to make contact with whatever leftover pockets of humanity remained. Harrison learned of this when he returned to barter discovered goods for supplies and safe harbor— his usual cover when on a mission. He also learned that the scouts who had gone were, in fact, a husband and wife team related to the *leader* of the fort— one Collette Garber—who had been entrusted with taking care of their daughter while they undertook their scouting adventure.

A kid who had, presumably, stowed away in her parents' rig in order to go with them, because, as Harrison knew all too well, there was no sight nor sound of the little bitch anywhere in the fort. That missing kid sent her aunt and the rest of Fort Jay's residents into one massive kerfuffle of a search-and-find effort, where a few even suspected Harrison of foul deeds. Having no part of any such mischief, it was easy for Harrison to deny the accusations. An undercover piece of shit he might be, but he wasn't into child abductions. Not yet, anyway.

He even helped look for the kid.

And while he had been looking, he realized how to take the fort without firing a single shot. Notify the Leather that the family had gone east, then find the family, capture them, return to Fort Jay en masse, and threaten to kill all three unless Auntie Garber opens the gates.

Which, in Harrison's mind, they would. Oh, there would be a few nippleheads screaming *no don't do it*, but the aunt would open the gates in the end, because it was family.

And because the Leather would take the fort eventually, one way or the other.

So, Harrison eventually offered to drive out into the countryside, to search for the mom and dad duo, and to determine if the kid had indeed stowed away with them. Harrison, however, did no such thing. Instead, he drove to Winnipeg, where he met the Dog Tongue's army on the move. Knowing the strength of the fort, the Vulture—in all of his dick-nose wisdom—decided to leave a small force behind to keep an eye on Fort Jay, while he took the rest of them east. The Vulture intended to not only find the family and return, but gather up any and all little groups of survivors along the way.

The person neither Harrison nor the Vulture counted on was the Spider, and his sizeable pair of balls.

After learning about the fort's numbers, the Spider decided to conduct a midnight strike, taking a small group of wall-climbing Leather into the defensive structure. Their plan? Climb the walls, subdue the guards, and take the fort while its inhabitants were sleeping.

Long story short, the long-armed, moose-knuckle fucker pulled it off, and pulled it off perfectly. The fort's people were all captured alive. There were no shouts of alarm. No metallic shrieks of bullets. All done at the price of two Leather being killed in the assault.

The victory greatly increased the Spider's stock as a leader, which was exactly what he wanted. And he dispatched Harrison and his small pack of goons to relate the news to the Bear Trap, still back in Winnipeg and minding the Leather's interests there. The Spider would remain at Fort Jay and wait for the Vulture to return, whereupon Harrison figured the twatwaffle would rub his nearly bloodless victory into the leader's nose.

Except the Vulture did not return.

Nor did any messengers arrive in Winnipeg, to provide updates on the Vulture's whereabouts.

That was all a week ago, and that prompted the Bear Trap to send Harrison back to Fort Jay. And Harrison didn't enjoy his current role as messenger boy. Or the current discussion of who was going to search for the missing army.

"*I'm* not going to look for the Vulture," Harrison argued. "I got other things to do. The Bear Trap wanted *you* to look for them. And he wants to regroup. You have to send back everything except a dozen or so. Enough to hold this fort."

"Everything?" the Spider whispered in unchecked surprise.

"That's what he said," Harrison repeated. "That's all I'm saying. I mean, really, the fort isn't that big a deal. The people were the main prize and you have them all, so pull everyone back and use them, regroup, and leave Winnipeg for the next target."

The Spider's fingers did a nervous river dance upon the desk's surface, which went on for a long time, and really got on Harrison's nerves. The fingers eventually stopped, and those long dangly arms rested at the Spider's sides, as if he were lying inside an invisible coffin.

"You'll go," the Spider said. "Or you'll stay here with me."

Half a slab of artic ice against his spine wouldn't have given Harrison the same chill upon hearing that. There was no mistaking the hidden message within those words. Harrison and his crew had done plenty of work for the Leather while remaining independent of the entire clan. There were talks amongst Harrison's gang that perhaps it was time to get away from the Leather, before they were assimilated and either forced into ball-gagged servitude, or transformed into the mindless to be used as cannon fodder. In secret, Harrison had hoped his work might result in simply becoming one of the Leather, bypassing ball-gagged servitude entirely. That would've been fine. In reality, however, no one really knew what the masked bastards would do when the time came, which fueled the conversation even more about getting the hell away. No one wanted to be trussed up like the meat.

So Harrison held up his hands. "Fine. Fuck it. Whatever. I'll go. You just send someone back explaining things to the Bear Trap. If me and my boys are heading out after the Vulture, then I'd best leave today. That okay with you?"

The Spider thought about it, and his fingers wiggled.

"So be it," the masked leader said.

"You'll outfit us?"

"Of course."

Harrison relaxed as much as he could in their presence. "All right then. I'll do it. No trouble. And thank you for all that."

It was always best to leave the Spider with a thank you.

And the leader actually nodded at the words. "When can you leave?"

"ASAP. Soon as we're loaded up. Which way they go, again?"

"Head south. Find Highway Seventeen. Follow it to Thunderbay."

"And you'll take those prisoners to the Bear Trap?"

"Of course."

"Because he's been *waiting* for them, you know. You been up here for a week and some change now. He's tapping a toe wondering what the holdup is."

The Spider didn't speak. He stood with his hands at his sides.

Harrison sensed a lie, but he didn't care. He'd done his bit. "Okay. Great. I'll leave you to it, then."

He backed away, palms up, knowing the door was somewhere behind him. Two rigid columns appeared at the corner of his vision, two stock-still Leather minions, much closer than he'd expected. One wore the mask of a goblin, while the other was a straight-up ninja with silver around the eyes. Harrison didn't make eye contact.

The door opened for him, and he turned to ensure he wouldn't back into the wall.

Then he was gone.

The Spider watched his minions close the door behind the mercenary, fully aware of the tension that remained in the room. The Spider knew he would have to watch the man, anticipating a defection. *Defection.* More like a *defect.* Reid Harrison would never be one of the Leather, and he was no longer a mere civilian.

The Spider looked to a green cooler resting on a table set against the nearby wall. Report to the Bear Trap. He would report to that offensive shitbag, but at his own time. Fort Jay was the Spider's now, and he recognized its defensive worth for what it was. He'd been long searching for a place to call his web, and the fort suited that need *perfectly.* It would be his, and the select few Leather secretly faithful only to him would become his own private army.

The Dog Tongue could have the rest of the world. The Spider wanted *this* place as his own personal kingdom, where he could entertain himself without interruption.

As he was about to do.

The Spider went to the table with the cooler. There was another box there. A plastic container with air holes punched into it. Inside was a ceramic green skull with a tangle of webbing about its face. The Spider picked up the container with care, inspected it, and returned it to the box. He then looked to the minion standing next to a closed doorway.

The minion nodded and removed the padlocks.

The staircase within had once been lit by electric lanterns, but the Spider preferred the old ways and had ordered these lanterns to be replaced with torches. One of the lessers lit the first torch and held it aloft, revealing gray brickwork and a set of stone steps leading into the fort's secret depths. Sacks of provisions and stacked barrels were placed against the walls, as decorative ambience to amuse tourists once upon a time, but the cell block below was of particular interest to the Leather.

The Spider descended the staircase, carrying the box with the green skull. A handful of lessers followed. Two of them were the Goblin and the Ninja. The torch bearer led the way until they stopped at a formidable door of iron and wood.

The Goblin opened the door and bade the Spider to enter.

Inside was a connected line of six iron cells. Ten by ten by ten, with a single cot to each. And a single bucket to serve as a toilet. People filled those cages, dirty and beaten, grimy faces colored a Halloween orange under the offered torchlight. The Spider knew a brig was for a military vessel, but he wasn't sure of the proper term for a jail within a fort. Not that it mattered. He considered the cages his personal dungeon, with a few additions.

One of those additions was a gurney, with a few more straps involved.

The Spider inspected the four dozen men, women, and children jammed into those six cells. They were clearly exhausted and weakened from being barely fed. A stink of body odor and excrement flowered the air, as buckets obviously needed to be emptied. That would happen later. Maybe.

Distrustful eyes watched him, but when he stared back, they quickly darted elsewhere. That pleased the Spider greatly. That was power in its rawest form. The ability to cower a foe with a single look. He intended to break them in the days to come, singling out individuals when the whim took him. In his mind, that was power on a level rivaling Caesar's.

The Spider focused on perhaps the biggest of the prisoners. A bearded man who stood over six feet tall, with broad shoulders and a ponytail at the back of his blonde head. The Spider stared at the prisoner and the man didn't flinch.

That was his mistake. He would be the day's entertainment.

The Spider nodded at his minions.

Black garbed figures pulled swords and spears and went to the prisoner's cell, making it clear that if the tall prisoner resisted, blood would flow. The door was opened and the Goblin and Ninja wrestled the prisoner outside, to the gurney. The people still in the cell remained, watchful of the other minions brandishing weapons.

The Spider removed himself from the selection process and waited at a nearby table, where he accepted a medical bag from another. The Spider fussed with both the box and the bag, while his lessers strapped the prisoner down. A minute later, the Spider stepped over to the gurney's side, where the tall man had been secured. Thick bands of leather held the prisoner's arms and legs. A similar strap stretched across his forehead, keeping his head in place.

Mutters and horrified moans erupted from the prisoners in their cells. The Spider silenced them all with a single look. Then he raised a finger.

Metal encased the digit, and its tip ended in a scalpel. The Spider opened the rest of his hand, revealing a crude glove where each finger ended in an identical surgical instrument.

There were gasps of disbelief. Someone whimpered.

The Spider turned back to the gurney. Torchlight crept over the benign smile of the Venetian mask.

The tall man became very still.

The Spider stepped in close, taking care to hide the tall man's face with his own body. He didn't want his captive audience to see what was about to happen. That would only lessen the fear. He knew that when one was deprived of sight, the mind did very wicked things.

The Spider gazed down at his prisoner, studying him, basking in the dread slowly seizing him.

The Spider reached up to his smiling mask and pinched the zipper between the bottom of his nose and upper lip. He pulled the zipper down, the popping distinct in the dungeon's forced silence, slowly revealing the second mouth. That mouth was red and scorched and scarred, and had missing sections where black teeth shone through. It was twisted into a puckered-up button of hate and loathing, and as the Spider leaned over the prisoner, as he drew closer, sweat glistened upon the tall man's features.

The gloved hand with the scalpel fingertips rose as if ready to take a swipe out of the prisoner's face. But then the Spider opened his mouth.

A *real* spider the size of a quarter darted forth and crept across his cheek.

Which was right about when the screaming began.

8

At 7:45 am, under brightening skies, Gus woke up.

Milo was snoring away, reclined in the front seat and curled up under a gray blanket. The sight and sound of him disappointed Gus, who'd hoped the blonde bastard would up and die in his sleep. Heart attack. Stroke. Exploding aneurism. Or just fucking choke on his own tongue. Gus didn't care how, just croak, and save him the misery of the soldier's untrustworthy company for the rest of his days. But *no*. Milo was alive and snoring, attempting to piss him off in his *sleep* no less, with an annoying rattle that sounded like a flooded chainsaw.

A rapping on the window zapped the living squirts out of him.

"You up?" Collie asked, her sunglasses staring and her outline darker outside the tinted window. She was bundled up, showing no skin.

Gus placed a hand to his trembling heart. "I'm up."

"Get your shit on, then."

Milo stirred in his seat, but Gus let him be. Maybe God would do him a favor by shorting out the coils in his heated seat and frying him right there in the next few seconds. That actually made him pause and watch, to no avail. Grumbling, already in a miserable funk, he still reminded himself to hide his hatred of the guy from Collie. Resigning himself to do just that, he got out and took a snort of cold air.

"Jesus," he shivered. "Fuckin' *cold*, man."

"It's November first," Collie informed him. "Practically winter."

"Think my ballsack just froze to my leg."

Collie chose not to respond to that one.

"You sleep good?" Gus asked, changing the subject.

"Yeah. A little. I'm good."

"Wait—" he held up a hand. "A little? What's that mean? One hour? Two?"

"About four hours."

"Not in the car, though."

Collie shook her head. "I was just over there, camped out at the base of a tree. Not far. Figured you and Milo would be fine."

On cue, the limo door on the far side opened. Milo slid out and straightened, stretching with a grunt.

"B and B, boys," Collie informed them. "That's breakfast and bowel movements, but not necessarily in that order. Get 'er done in thirty and we hit the highway. I want to be in or past Thunderbay by the day's end."

Gus kept his eyes on her. "You camped outside?"

"Yeah. Over there."

"Alone?"

She nodded and looked at Milo. "Where are you going?"

The soldier held up both hands. "Just taking a leak. That all right?"

"Leak away. With a smile. No more than two shakes, though."

Milo walked off for the nearest clump of bushes and unzipped.

"Don't think about running off anywhere," Gus warned him.

The soldier didn't answer.

"Nowhere to go, anyway," Collie said. "We're pretty much in back country out here."

She tugged at her mask, flashing a sliver of skin around her wrist and neckline. Skin that was blue-gray.

Gus's heart skipped a beat.

Collie quickly covered up, tucking her mask into her collar and then her glove into her sleeve as if not noticing what Gus had seen.

"Collie," he asked.

"Yeah?"

He glanced over at Milo before asking, "You okay?"

The sunglasses stared at him. "I'm fine."

He didn't believe her. "All right, what do you want to eat?"

"I'm good. You guys go ahead."

"You haven't eaten in a while."

"Nope."

"You should get something in you."

"Gus," Collie said gently. "I'm dead. Actually, I'm *un*dead. As fucking undead as anyone can be, so I don't need to eat anymore. The good news is

I'm not craving brains and shit. So, when I say I'm fine, just leave it at that and move on. Let's just be glad I still have the capacity for thought."

Milo half-turned from his business, detecting some heat in the exchange.

Gus, however, only nodded at the soft scolding.

"Okay," he finally said.

*

Twenty-six minutes later, after a quick breakfast of more sandwiches, they boarded the limo and got moving. This time, Collie ordered Milo behind the wheel while she rode shotgun. Gus sat behind him, his Glock within easy reach if needed, but he wasn't thinking about Milo this morning. He was thinking about Collie and her refusal to eat anything, and the little tongue lashing he'd received. Collie kept all conversation to the point after that, and Gus figured he'd keep his own mouth shut. Until he could get a minute alone with her.

The morning drive felt tense as a result, so Collie switched on some music. The collection of seventies and eighties classic rock did little to lessen the mood.

Two hours into the drive, she cricked her neck. "See that old Esso station up ahead there?"

"Yeah," Milo answered. "Pull in?"

"Yeah."

So he did.

"Going for a walk," Collie announced and got out without waiting for an answer. She slammed the door and marched off towards what appeared to be a crumbling foundation almost obscured by tall grass. The ESSO logo had fallen off a signpost, its lettering barely hanging on.

Gus watched her until she was around the station.

"She okay?" Milo asked.

"Huh?"

The soldier leaned forward so that his head was visible. "I asked if she's okay."

"You ask that a lot."

"Well, I worry, okay?"

Gus sighed. "No idea. Probably not."

"You don't know?"

"No, not for certain."

"I thought you two were buddies."

"We are…"

"But you don't know what's going on with her?"

"No."

"Jesus, man," Milo swore softly. "You best figure out what's going on. We're going up against some very bad hombres out there. And as far as I'm concerned, *she's* the best chance we got making it back alive."

Gus scowled. "Look, just sit back and drive. Do whatever she tells you to do. She'll be fine."

"You listening to yourself?"

Gus was.

"We need to know if she's about to *turn* or not. We need to know. She ever go for this many walks before while on the road?"

"No. Not that I noticed."

"Well, she's sure as hell fond of them now."

Milo wasn't wrong.

"Just leave her be," Gus said. "God only knows what she's going through."

"All the more reason for you to talk to her."

"Yeah."

"Yeah what?" Milo pressed.

"I'll talk to her."

"Okay, when?"

"When?" Gus snarled. "Listen, Sally, you're not in fuckin' charge here so fuck off. Leave it to me."

"Just wanting to know you'll get it done."

"Oh I'll get it done. Don't worry about that."

"You don't seem to be the get-it-done type, honestly."

Gus narrowed his eyes. "Yeah? Well, you don't seem to be the *honest* type. To join up with a bunch of fucking slave hunters and then stay with them as long as you did."

That took Milo off guard. "That was different."

"Oh yeah, right, that was different. A *lot* fucking different, I bet. Before you shoot your mouth off again about what I'm doing, you think about those people you tried to pass off to the Leather. Sandy included."

"Sandy?" Milo asked dubiously.

"The little girl, remember?"

The soldier winced and looked away.

"Yeah, thought that one might sting," Gus said.

Milo let his breath out and sank back into the driver's seat. Silence ensued.

As Gus preferred. He won that round.

Collie returned a few minutes later. Fresh air flooded the interior when she got inside. Gus waited for her to settle down in her seat.

"Goddamn that was fine," she released. "You two wanna go? Get the blood moving? Winter is out there, boys. She's a'coming."

"Collie?" Gus asked.

She turned around.

"Why're you getting out and walking around so much? Everything okay?"

The sunglasses studied him for a second. "First, a little break is good to let the limo recharge itself. Not much, but it's there. And second…" she faltered. "I… get stiff."

That got Gus's attention.

"In my legs. And arms. Even my back. And… everything feels heavier. Like I'm attached to lead. But I find that when I get out and move around, things improve. They don't return to normal, but they get better."

"Well, shit," Gus let out. "Anything else?"

Collie looked down. "I'm constantly cold. That's to be expected, I suppose."

Silence then, as they all sat and absorbed the information.

"I'll keep you updated," she said. "I have to, from here on in. Anything I notice, I'll let you know. Same goes for you two. If you notice anything, if you notice me doing anything, let me know."

"You smell," Milo said quietly after a while. "Bad. I didn't want to say anything, and the limo's air circulator keeps the air in here fresh, but every now and again. It reaches out and hits me."

"Sorry," Collie said. "Body odor?"

"No," he replied and wavered. "Rot. Spoiling meat."

Gus pinched the bridge of his nose. Dreading what he was about to do, he leaned forward and took a whiff. *There*, faint but there, was the raw and unchecked stink of decay.

The news silenced Collie for a while. She sat there, staring at the soldier before taking a snort of one armpit, then the other. "Yeah. You're right. I'm starting to smell like dead ass, here. Sorry. Sorry, Gus."

As stunned as he was, Gus could only sit and nod.

"You got some unstink back there?" she asked. "That case of deodorant sticks?"

"Yeah," he answered. "We do. Somewhere. Straight from Josh himself."

"Get one for me."

"You think it'll work?" Milo asked.

"Can't hurt," she replied. "Can't have you two choking because I'm going bad. Shit. Should've realized. Wallace went the same way. He was hanging air fresheners all over the place. Shit, shit, shit."

Gus pawed his way through the back seats and started going through the duffel bags. Right on top was a box of deodorant sticks. Aluminum-free *Ocean Mist*.

"Here," he said and handed her the full case, minus the one he'd taken for himself.

"Thanks," Collie said. "Since we're past embarrassing each other, here." She gave one to Milo. "I might smell like dead ass, but you smell like straight-up unwashed balls. That's after one day on the road."

"Thanks."

"Don't mention it," Collie said. "All right. Excuse me for a minute while I freshen up a bit. And don't peek. I'm telling you, you won't like what you see."

With that she got out of the car again and walked towards the rear.

"You didn't shower back at Whitecap?" Gus asked him.

"Three, four days ago."

"Three, four days ago? You had hot water for Christ's sake."

"I don't shower every day."

"You should've."

"Wasn't doing anything, only reading in my room. No need to shower every day if you don't need to. Scientists proved it."

"Scientists proved it," Gus muttered, not believing what he was hearing.

Ten minutes later, they were back on the road, and the flat smell of *Ocean Mist* filled the limo.

"Christ Almighty," Gus said. "Whoever called that *Ocean Mist* sure as hell never went to any ocean I know of."

"Maybe it was the ocean around a waste management plant?" Milo suggested.

"Maybe. Or the end of a cracked off shit pipe."

"That bad?" Collie asked.

And he realized what he'd said. "No, it's not you anymore. It's the deodorant. It's pretty strong stuff for something called *Ocean Mist*. I can't smell you anymore. It's all *Ocean Mist*."

"I can taste the shit," Milo added. "But I'm not smelling you. So that's a good thing."

Collie stared ahead. "I swear, you two say the sweetest things sometimes."

That actually put a smile on Gus's face, perhaps the first one since they'd left Whitecap.

"What's that?" Milo said.

"What?" Collie asked back

Gus stretched out his neck to see what was going on.

There, perhaps a kilometer away, were three vehicles descending a low hill.

Coming straight at them.

"The hell is that?" Milo said, gripping the steering wheel.

"Company," Collie said. "Fellow travelers. Our first contact. Anyone want to bet they're friendly?"

Neither man responded.

"Figured," Collie said. "Slow down, Milo. Ease into a full stop."

Gus pointed. "Looks like they're slowing down too."

"Might as well. You don't see a rig like ours every day. All right, then." She flexed her fingers and tapped a code into the dashboard touchscreen. The back-light switched to red and blue.

"Battle stations," she said in a resigned voice.

9

Reid Harrison rode in the lead pickup with a snowplow fixed to the front end. The truck was on a high suspension that elevated the rig an extra foot off the ground. It was hard to get used to the height at first, since Harrison felt as if he were riding around in a motorized lighthouse, but like the old saying went, there was no going back. Everything else was deemed too low to the ground. As it was, Harrison spotted the approaching car in the distance just as they were rolling over the hill.

"The hell is that?" John Barlen asked, leaning into the steering wheel. "Young'un" John was fifty-seven and the oldest of Harrison's mercenary crew. The man didn't talk much, didn't fight much, but he'd run over a person's skull in the same space of time it took to stomp on the accelerator.

"See something?" "Rabid" Rob Madsen perked up from the back and immediately filled the gap between the front seats, peering ahead like a Saint Bernard that had been shaved to the quick, tattooed while drunk, and none too pleased about it.

"Yeah, I do," Harrison said, peering ahead. "Looks like… goddamn, I'm not sure what that looks like."

Like the rest of this particular stretch, the land leading to the two-lane pavement had been long cleared of trees some fifty feet back, and the remaining vegetation was fading fast with the cold. There was no mistaking a vehicle was on the road, but it was weird-looking.

"One of that Vulture's crew?"

"You mean *army*?" Harrison asked back. "And no, I don't think it's one of his. For one, it's too damn long to be a pickup. Or anything else for that matter."

"Let me see."

"Sit back you fuckin' lunatic," Harrison ordered, wincing at Madsen's extreme case of halitosis. They'd often joke—either around Rabid or not—that the mindless must take a shit in his mouth whenever he slept. Toothpaste might be history, but there were still plenty of toothbrushes and floss around. There was no excuse to not maintain oral health.

"Stop this thing, Johnny," Harrison said. He pulled on his lower lip and squinted at the approaching vehicle.

John Barlen complied. The two SUVs following behind did the same, one coming within a car length of the rear bumper.

Harrison stared at the machine ahead, which had also stopped about less than two hundred feet away.

"What is it?" Barlen asked, his wooly beard barely moving with the question.

Harrison leaned forward a little more and shook his head. "Well, fuck me. Is that a *limo*?"

"You asking me?" Barlen asked.

"Fuck no, I'm not asking you," Harrison muttered as Barlen's eyes were growing old fast. "Rabid? What does that look like to you?"

"Looks like a fuckin' limo."

"It *does* look like a fucking limo."

"A *super* fuckin' limo."

Harrison had to agree.

"That ain't no recreational vehicle, Reid," Rabid said. "She's got some jacked-up titties."

"I think you're right." Harrison agreed, twice now, with the Rabid one. He wasn't sure that had ever happened before.

"And a big ass," Rabid said, stretching out his unwashed arm to point. "You see that big ol' ass on it? I did, and from way back here. *Big* ass. That's a *limo*, Reid. One of them party rides where you could fit a couple dozen people inside."

"Sit back," Harrison ordered, absorbing not only the sound but the after-stink coming from Rabid's second, higher-placed asshole. Even as he thought it, Harrison cracked his window a few inches.

"A stretch limo," he whispered over the hum of the pickup's engine. "Out here. Heading west."

"Guaranteed a limo," Rabid said.

"Who the fuck drives a limo?" John Barlen grumped, seeing only a black fleck. "Especially out here. It would fucking drink gas. Or ethanol. Or diesel."

"You would think," Harrison thought aloud and drummed his fingers against a dashboard festooned with garbage. "You would think." He flicked a finger at the limo. "Drive on, Johnny. Take 'er in slow. Nice and friendly. Don't spook the rabbits."

John Barlen took his foot off the brake, and with a stare every bit as warm as a rattler, let the pickup creep ahead.

"Rabid?" Harrison asked.

"Yeah?"

"You get yourself outfitted. Keep everything out of sight until I say otherwise. Understood?"

Rabid started gathering up his tools in the back of the crew cab.

"Nice and easy, Johnny," Harrison said. "Just a creep. I'll let you know when to stop. We're all just travelers out here. On this big old highway. And a long way from home."

A sinister smile spread across Harrison's face. "And it's always nice to meet new friends."

10

"They're coming," Milo said.

Collie didn't speak, and Gus checked on her before watching the vehicles farther down the highway. Three of them, moving in single file, creeping along like dogs on their bellies, careful not to draw their ire. The one out front had an honest-to-god snowplow fixed to the front.

"Serves me right," Collie muttered. "Not wearing my vest."

"I can get it for you," Gus offered.

She shook her head. "No time." With that, she unholstered her Sig Saur and readied it. She sat back, her sunglasses staring at the approaching three-vehicle convoy. "But you can dig out that assault rifle. The big one. Not the little ones. You can grab your favorite, but if any shooting starts, let me handle it, okay? Stay inside this thing. Understood?"

"Yeah."

"What's his favorite?" Milo wanted to know.

"Shotgun," Collie answered, glancing over at him. "He's a shotgunner."

Gus frowned at that.

"Well, you are." She looked back to the road. "Might want to get a vest on, too."

Gus went to the seat behind Collie and reached down. He extracted the formidable German-made HK-H50Z assault rifle.

"I can support," Milo said.

"You can *drive*," she told him. "Keep your foot on the brake and be ready to roll. And Milo?"

He stared into her sunglasses, which almost resembled the bulbous, compound eyes of a fly.

"Moment of truth here, now," she said. "Don't disappoint me."

"I won't."

Gus fed her the assault rifle, butt-first through the opening. Collie guided the weapon to her feet, where she unintentionally angled the barrel at Milo's face.

Grimacing, Milo gently pushed the rifle away.

In a rush of cold air, Collie got out of the limo.

She put a hip to the door and stayed behind its shielding bulk, exposing only her feet and knees, and a few inches of her right side. She drifted a little more out into the open, so that the approaching driver could see her, but maintaining a good percentage of cover.

She raised her arm to signal them to stop.

The creeping motorcade halted in a squeal of brakes that only seemed to sharpen the chill in the air. Exhaust swirled around metallic edges. The lead pickup, a tall jacked-up critter, had its headlights smashed out. The windshield was tinted, and she couldn't see who was behind the wheel. The two rigs following the truck were SUVs, both black just like the leader.

No one got out from those machines, idling like thunder on the horizon.

The two opposing groups faced each other, only a couple hundred feet apart. A breeze rose and ruffled Collie's collar, but she ignored it. The sun overhead lit up her sunglasses, making the lens twinkle.

The passenger door of the pickup opened and swung wide. A pair of brown work boots slid out and made contact with the pavement. The person stayed behind the door, being careful. A head bobbed, peeking around the frame and locating her. He stayed motionless for a few considering seconds, before stepping into clear sight.

"Brave fucker, ain'tcha," Collie muttered.

The newcomer slowly raised his hands, presenting them as empty, and smiled. Collie guesstimated they were less than a hockey rink away from each other, but the smile that came over the guy's face seemed like a lighthouse powering up. He wore what might've been an army surplus coat, but Collie couldn't be sure.

"How you doing?" he bellowed, breaking the morning silence.

She shrugged. "Not bad. You?"

"Good, thanks. Good. Don't see too many cars like yours on the road."

Again the smile, as bright and polished as a sliver of porcelain chipped away from a brand-new toilet bowl. If she could see it from here, there was a damn good chance that smile could blind a person up close. Not that it impressed her. In her experience, it was wise to be wary of folks trying too damn hard to be friendly.

"Don't see many motorcades on the road these days," she shouted back weakly, considering she no longer drew breath.

That turned the Smiler around as he checked on the other rigs. He flinched in a *Holy shit, you're right!* kinda way. He then shrugged and, as impossible as it seemed, turned up the volume on that sunny crocodile grin until it blazed.

"You know how it is out here," he yelled. "Dangerous. Gotta be careful. Strength in numbers and all that."

"All that," Collie whispered thoughtfully, checking on Milo and Gus. Milo had both hands on the wheel and stared ahead, clearly thinking hard on something. Gus's lack of teeth was on display in a grimace, suggesting he was straining to hear.

"Where you guys from?" the Smiler asked.

Collie didn't answer right away. "Back that way," and pointed a thumb over her shoulder. "You?" she asked.

"From Winnipeg, actually."

Interesting. "Winnipeg?" Collie blurted. "The hell you doing in a city?"

"Cities are fine now," the Smiler said. "Just mass graves. Once you get over that, there's nothing really to worry about. It's pretty quiet. No dogs or cats. No neighbors beating the drums at two in the morning. We stay at the Royal Bentley downtown. Five-star hotel. Could never afford to use the toilet in a place like that, but now, well, we got it all to ourselves. Great set-up, too. Big fuckin' rooms. Killer views. Awesome comfort. Cool in the summer and warm in the winter."

"Yeah?" Collie said, letting the guy ramble. He certainly liked to talk, that much was obvious.

"Oh yeah. Everything we want. Just barricade the main lobby and it's like a downtown fortress. Great spot. About three dozen of us. Everyone has an awesome room. Fit for a king, really. Makes my old place look like a broom closet. And the view? On the upper levels? Su-*perb*. I go up on the ninth and just stare out over the city, wishin' I had a dart. Beauty. Just beauty. How about you?"

"Nothing as nice as that," Collie answered.

"No? You in a hotel? Or…?"

She smiled beneath her mask. "How many folks you traveling with?"

"Me? Half a dozen. We… we're searching for others. Y'know? Looking for people. Gathering up the last few pieces of humanity. All that. Doctors. Mechanics. Carpenters. That sorta thing. Trained professionals are hard to come by these days. How about you?"

"Doing the same."

"Yeah?" the Smiler let out. "Well, shit. Maybe we should talk? See if we can't come to an agreement of some sort."

"Maybe we should," Collie said.

"How many are you?" he asked, stretching while lifting a hand to the back of his head.

*

"Holy shit," Milo let out, catching Gus off guard.

"What?" he asked.

"That guy."

"Yeah?"

"Collie," Milo said in a suppressed yet urgent tone, ignoring Gus.

Collie waved him off.

"*Collie*," Milo insisted, glancing at the distant pickups.

To her credit, she raised a hand at the Smiler, signaling a time out. She pulled herself back behind the door and met Milo's anxious face.

"That guy," he said. "I *know* that guy."

"You do?"

Through the windshield, the Smiler folded his arms and appeared to consult with someone inside his own pickup.

"Yeah," Milo stressed. "The Leather didn't use just my crew to find survivors. There were *others*. I never met the guy, but I saw him from a distance once, and he… he *stretched* like he did just now."

Collie's mask stared at him. Gus rolled his eyes.

"I'm serious," Milo whispered harshly. "That guy, Jake knew him. Knew *of* him. He'd go into a place, make friends, and then disappear, only to show up a few days later with the Leather. He's fucking rotten to the core. A pure shit snake if there ever was one. Jake said he had a smile on him that was trying way too hard. Like he was wearing dentures that were bleached snow white and much too big for his mouth. Said he was on scary good terms with the Leather for some reason, like he was trying to become a permanent member."

"What was his name?" Collie asked.

"His name?" Milo frowned.

"You didn't forget his *name*," Gus said in disgust.

"Give me a minute. It'll come to me."

"We don't *have* a minute here," Gus told him.

"*Hey whatchoo guys talking about over there?*" the Smiler blasted.

Collie didn't answer right away. When she saw that Milo wasn't about to produce a name, she withdrew and faced the question.

"Just talking," she strained, noting her voice wasn't as loud anymore. "Discussing whether or not we should trust you."

The Smiler arched his back and threw his hands wide, in a gesture of *who me?* "Well," he said after composing himself. "No trouble at all. I understand completely. Hell, if you feel that way, we can pull over here and let you go on by if you like. Or, if you want, you can pull over and let us roll along. Whichever way you want to go. You go your way, we go ours. Full disclosure. I don't want any trouble. Don't *need* any trouble. Just trying to show you that we're, y'know, good people."

"Thanks," Collie yelled back.

"Hey," the Smiler resumed. "Take all the time you want. Hell, we're open for trade, too, if you like. We got food and water. Got some Peach schnapps over here, too, if you're into that. Even some quality grass."

"Quality grass?" she asked.

"Quality grass?" Gus repeated from inside.

"Where'd you get that?" Collie asked.

"From a private grower," the Smiler answered. "Can't say any more. That's a secret. Ha! You might be cops. What's your name, anyway?"

"Olga," Collie answered. "You?"

"Olga?" the Smiler echoed. "Your name's Olga?"

"Right here. All day. You?"

The Smiler laughed. "You have to be the first Olga I've ever met. *Ever.*"

"I bet," Collie muttered and checked on Milo, still trying to remember a name.

"So where you from, Olga?" the Smiler asked again.

"He's fuckin' dying to know that," Gus said.

"That's what he does," Milo said, watching the distant figure. "Pumps people for information."

"No, no," Collie shouted to the Smiler. "I've been asking *you* for *your* name for the last ten seconds here. What is it?"

That backed the Smiler up. "Sorry. Didn't mean to be nosy."

From inside the limo, Milo shook his head. "Oh, it's his job to be nosy."

"I'm Reid. Harrison," Harrison finally produced. "From out west. Around Banff. That way."

"Reid Harrison," Collie tried the name. "How you doing, Reid?"

Harrison waved, pleased to be making acquaintances.

Collie glanced at Milo.

"That's him," the soldier said. "Shoot me now if it's not."

"So, Olga," Reid started in all seriousness. "Just wondering, if we *do* go our separate ways here, anything dangerous on the road behind you?"

"No."

"Any mindless?"

"What's that?"

"Mindless. See any mindless?"

Her hand hidden by the door, Collie motioned for the assault rifle. Milo pushed it her way, butt-first. Gus brought up the Glock, aiming it directly at the soldier's profile, ensuring he didn't make any moves.

"Did you say mindless?" Collie asked.

"Yeah, I did," Harrison replied.

"Those are…?"

"Zombies. Our nickname for zombies."

"You call them mindless?"

"Yep. Why?"

"That's interesting."

"Yeah?"

"Just seems like, everywhere I go, someone's got a different name for them. Besides zombies, I mean. Moes, gimps, meatbags. MBs. Undead fuckers. One dear old soul even called them walking sacks of shit. Always different."

Harrison suddenly wasn't smiling so much anymore.

"But," Collie said, wrapping her fingers around the HK-H50Z, "seems like every group I've encountered, each one stuck to the one generic term for the dead. The most *used* nickname. Last bunch I came across also called them mindless. One little girl, in particular, who lost her parents while trying to escape those carnivorous shitbags."

Across the way, Harrison's smile disappeared entirely.

"And those things, those *mindless*, were actually *controlled* by another group. Craziest bunch of nutbags calling themselves the Leather."

Harrison ducked inside his pickup and slammed the door. Not a second later the machine catapulted forward in a scream of tires and smoke.

Collie dove into the limo, hauling the door shut behind her. She tapped the touchscreen, bringing up smaller windows. Her fingers did a drunken jig over the bright interface. The screen flashed red. Collie bent over a little lower and repeated the sequence.

The charging truck was less than a hundred feet away.

Something clattered to life over Gus's head, distracting him from the developing scene.

A joystick emerged from the center armrest next to Collie, one with a red button on the tip. She grabbed the control and fired.

The unmistakable chatter of a heavy machine gun erupted from overhead. Tracers resembling laser beams shot forth from the limo's roof, lancing out in long fine streaks and bouncing off the snowplow of the oncoming pickup in bright sparkling blooms.

Collie manipulated the stick and that punishing scalpel of gunfire rose over the snowplow. Bullets dappled the hood in a series of explosive holes until punching its full might into the vehicle's windshield in a spurt of bullseyes.

The pickup swerved right, and an angry line of bullet holes zipped across the passenger's side. The side mirror blew apart like an overloaded lightbulb. The passenger window shattered. The pickup bounced over a low embankment in a spray of rocks and dust and rattled towards the tree line.

Collie diverted her fire toward the other two SUVs on the road, the murderous stream loud and stinging. Bullets raked the front of the oncoming vehicle, forcing the driver to bank hard to the right. The SUV tipped, and the continuing gunfire shredded its roof and windows in flashes of silver teeth. The SUV toppled onto its side just as its cousin bashed into the vehicle's undercarriage, spinning the wreckage before veering off to the left.

Collie lit it up, strafing the machine as it departed the road in a jaw-clapping jump. It charged down the embankment and stormed up the far side, all the while having its sizeable ass shot off. The rig slowed as it closed distance with the impassable forest, as if wondering where to go next.

Under that devastating onslaught from the limo, however, those two or three seconds of indecision ended the fight.

The SUV trickled forward, rising and falling over unseen ruts, until its front pushed against that wall of trees. There the rig stopped with a loud pop of metal and a cloud of smoke.

Collie ceased firing long enough to aim again at the SUV still on its side, now blocking the road. She released three seconds' worth of gunfire before pausing, whereupon she released another three seconds. Sparks flared as aluminum parts crimpled and popped free from the undercarriage. When it was over, nothing moved from the smoking block.

"Christ almighty," Gus breathed, beholding the destruction. He no longer pointed his gun at Milo.

Collie grabbed the key fob. "Everyone out. We gotta check those rigs."

"Do I get a gun?" Milo asked.

"Fuck no, now get out *now*."

Neither man needed to be told again.

Collie was out and bringing up her assault rifle into firing position. Gus followed, his Glock raised with two hands and wondering where to aim. He finally settled on Milo, who watched the two dead SUVs.

Collie stopped and fired three quick shots into her target.

Harrison the Smiler.

The first round caught him as he struggled free of his ride. The second and third shots slammed him against the vehicle and pinned him there for a second, rattling him against the machine. Collie fired once more, nailing Harrison dead center, whereupon he slumped to the ground.

"Milo," Collie said, swinging her rifle towards him. "Get to that SUV and check it out. Double time."

Milo hesitated before scrambling for the wreck taking up the middle of the road.

"Gus," Collie said.

"Yeah?"

"Get out there and check on that dead fuck I just rang up. I'll cover."

Orders received, he jogged to the edge of the pavement, keeping his gun pointed at the truck. Nothing moved, but the engine block smoked thin curls that suggested it wouldn't be moving anytime soon.

Not wearing a vest, Gus thought, feeling naked as he scrambled down and up a small embankment, approaching the truck at an angle. The tires cut two narrow paths through the tall grass, which he followed, keeping sight of the one called Harrison. Collie's shots were placed in the upper chest and neck, where the man's body armor couldn't protect him. Thing was, the guy wasn't *wearing* any body armor, not by the way he was bleeding. Gus stopped and stared for a second, inspecting the dead man's pallid face, the lightless stare, and the amount of blood leaking onto the ground. Then he remembered himself and went for the passenger door.

He swung it open.

The driver was an old guy, with the back of his skull spattered against the destroyed head rest. His chest lay against the steering wheel while his missing face dripped over the dashboard and column. Blood colored the inside of the windshield, highlighting the bullet holes in gruesome starbursts. The smell alone was something out of an overflowing septic tank.

Hinges creaked and Gus flinched at the sound. The rear door opened on the other side and a figure sloughed into daylight.

Shit, Gus mentally huffed. He hurried around the front of the truck, gun raised and pointed. The truck was flush against a series of tree trunks, snapping off several boughs. He backed up, whereupon his bad foot slid out from under him. He went down, cracking his left elbow on the truck's hood. Nerve pain enveloped his arm. Through that sickening jolt, Gus heard someone moan and realized it wasn't him.

"Other side, Gus, other side!" Collie screamed, straining to be heard.

"Then shoot him!" Gus hollered back.

"*I got no shot!*"

That made him move. He staggered to the rear, hunkering down just enough to keep his head from being blown off. He peeked out around the corner and spotted one man, face down and making fists in the grass he lay upon. His head was shaved and Celtic lines covered pale skin.

Gus moved in and when he did, a face that might've been hosed down with blood turned in his direction.

"Muh," the face said.

And collapsed.

Gus stopped, composed himself, and aimed his Glock not two inches away from the guy's head.

11

Gus dragged the figure away from the truck, just enough to get him clear of the mess.

"Milo?" Collie asked at her best volume.

"All clear, Collie. All dead."

"Gus?"

Gus stopped pulling on the guy and let him drop. Unlike the others in the truck, the unconscious one wore an armored vest. And that vest must've had a lead plate or something as it made the guy heavy as hell.

"Yeah," Gus panted, realizing once again his heart was close to flaming out. He stood back from the lump at his feet and nodded. "Yeah. Good over here. Got a... got a live one."

"A live one?" Collie asked.

"Unconscious."

"On our way."

Two minutes later, the three of them stood around the unmoving prisoner.

"God almighty," Collie said under her breath. "What's wrong with this guy?"

No one answered.

"They skin him or something?" she asked.

"If they did," Gus said, "they realized they fucked up and gave him a quick paint job. Fancy, though."

"That's Celtic war paint," Milo said.

Gus looked at the soldier. "How do you know?"

"Studied that shit. Used to, anyway."

Gus glanced over at the machine gun that had lifted itself from the compartment on the limo's roof. The weapon had stopped smoking, but he could still hear that monstrous chatter in his head, could still feel the shuddering of the limo as the weapon kicked.

"Christ almighty," he said, studying the mounted weapon. "That was… fucking *awesome*, Collie. I gotta say. Thought that thick roof was just for extra luggage."

"Nope," Collie informed him. "Where'd you think the big gun was?"

"Dunno. Behind the headlights?"

"Not a bad guess. Needed to do a test fire, anyway," Collie said. "Forgot to do it back at base. Not that it was really needed. The bullet heads at Whitecap would've made sure all was functioning and ready to roll."

"How much ammo you have for that gorilla?" Milo asked.

"Two-thousand-round capacity. Chewed through a third of it in that exchange. As impressive as she is, the limo's not a full-scale battle wagon. It's an armored VIP transport with offensive capabilities if needed. The stinger's there to scare the shit out of anyone with the balls to try and jack it."

"No extra ammo for it?"

"Sure we got some," Collie said. With a boot toe, she nudged the tattooed prisoner. "Wakey, wakey."

No response.

"How long we gonna be here?" Gus asked. "It's getting cold."

Collie kept watching the unconscious man at their feet, the sunlight reflecting off her shades. She eventually dropped to one knee, alongside the guy's head. Without warning, she extracted her service pistol and jammed it in the nearest ear.

"Hey," she repeated. "You. With the fucked-up lipstick. You faking? 'Cause I don't have time or patience to deal with an actor."

The prisoner's eyes cracked open.

"Excellent," Collie said, keeping the weapon in place. "What's your name?"

"Huh?"

She dug the barrel a little deeper into the ear, producing a whiny-ass peal of pain. She grabbed his jaw and held it, squishing lips and exposing teeth outlined in scarlet.

"Rabid," he said through a mashed-up mouth.

"What?"

"Name's Rabid."

"Rabbit?"

"Like the animal?" Gus asked.

The guy's eyes widened. "No, Rabid. Ra-*bid. Bid.* Like… *rabid*, man!"

"You mean like rabies?"

Rabid nodded as much as he could with a gun sticking in his ear.

"I'm not fucking calling you *Rabid*," Collie said. "Fuck me gently. What's your civilian name?"

Rabid rolled his eyes and exhaled with disgust. "Rob. Madsen."

"Better," Collie approved. "Now, Billy. I've got questions. And you're going to answer them. Okay?"

Rabid's face and forehead were bleeding from several lipless cuts, the kind you get when being hit by extreme force. As Collie spoke, those cuts continued to ooze a deep berry red, as if squeezed straight from the liver.

"Yuh," the tattooed man got out.

"How many are with you?"

Rabid squinted as a line of red reached his eye.

"Leave it," Collie warned. "Now answer me."

"Eight," he said, the words all mushed together. "No. Nine. Nine of us."

There were eight bodies accounted for in the other vehicles.

"Are you working with the Leather?"

Gus glanced at Milo, who had his poker face in place.

"Yeah," Rabid sighed.

"And what do you do for them?" Collie asked.

Those pained eyes regarded her, and for a split second, Gus thought the man had up and died.

"We collect people," Rabid finally replied.

"Collect people?"

"Yeah."

"And then what?"

Rabid squeezed his eyes shut. "We hand them over. To the Leather. We get paid for them. Food. Gas. Shit like that."

"Gas?" Collie asked.

"Whatever the fuck these things run on today. Fuel. Whatever. Call it whatever you want."

"What happens to the people you collect?"

Rabid scrunched up his face in distaste, knowing full well he knew he'd come to the end of his run in this new world. "Fuck if I know. The Leather takes them. They do what they want with them."

"Where did you come from?"

Winnipeg, Gus figured, but got a surprise when Rabid said, "Fort Jay."

Collie remained all business. "You came from Fort Jay. What's there?"

"Leather."

"The Leather's there?"

"Yeah."

"Anything else?"

"Just Leather. And prisoners."

"People?" Collie asked.

"Yeah. Couple of dozen or so. Leather has them."

"How many Leather are at the fort?"

"A lot," Rabid answered, still cringing from the blood in his eye and perhaps some unseen pain.

"Numbers?"

"Three. Four dozen. Maybe five."

"Weapons?"

"Just axes. Bats. Crossbows."

Collie soaked it all in. "Anything else you want to tell me?"

Rabid thought about it. He glanced at the other faces before returning to that grim ski mask. "No," he said quietly, sounding contrite.

Collie didn't say anything for seconds. She stayed on one knee, with her gun jammed into Rabid's ear.

Gus wondered what they were going to do with this guy.

"Thanks," Collie said and shot Rabid dead right there, his head jerking free of her hand.

The unexpected killing startled both Gus and Milo, causing both to back up a step. Collie straightened and aimed at the corpse's chest. She dropped the pose a second later, deeming the bullet to the head was more than enough, and smartly holstered her weapon.

"All right," she said. "Let's get out of here."

She marched away from the corpse.

Milo promptly followed her.

Gus hung back for a second, taking in the unmoving carcass at his feet before reality sank in. He hurried after his two companions, suffering a savage burn crisping his forever damaged foot.

"Collie?" he called out.

"Yeah?"

"Stop for a minute, will ya?"

She stopped, and Milo stopped with her.

"What was that?" Gus asked.

"What?" she asked back. "Him?"

"Yeah, him."

"That was a piece of shit, Gus. That was a piece of shit realizing Justice had finally caught up with him. For his crimes, that was the quickest punishment I was willing to dole out, because we have a group of people being held against their will at our destination. Believe you me, he got off fucking lucky."

Collie faced him, waiting for an argument, a scolding, or even a comeback.

All Gus did was shrug, sigh, and mumble, "All right."

Milo and Gus searched the vehicles while Collie stood guard at the front of the limo. There was a blood-stained sawed-off shotgun in the back seat of the pickup. Gus checked the magazine and took the two remaining shells. Other weapons included assorted knives, a handheld crossbow with a dozen quarrels or so, a pair of hatchets, and bats.

The SUVs had nothing better.

"Anything?" Collie asked when Gus and Milo returned to the limo. She was leaning against the ram plate, her holster undone and her hand dangling beside it.

"Nothing," Milo reported, very much aware of the gunfighter stance.

"No firearms?"

"There was a sawed-off shotgun, but he left it."

"I took the shells," Gus said with a little heat.

"You didn't let me finish," Milo countered without looking at him. "He did take the shells."

Gus rolled his shoulders, to reinforce the point.

"Though that was a perfectly good shotgun," Milo said to himself.

"My gun's better," Gus said.

"Yeah, how so?"

"Never the fuck mind, how so. *That's* how's so."

"You watched him?" Collie asked Gus, referring to Milo.

The two men regarded each other.

"Yeah," Gus answered.

"He didn't slip anything on him?"

Good question, and Gus was suddenly very uncertain of the man beside him.

"Pat him down. Just to be sure."

That disturbed Gus a little. "I've never patted anyone down before."

"I'll give you directions," she said.

"Why don't you do it?"

"You need the practice," she said. "Go on. He's not going to try anything. If he does, I'll shoot him."

Milo became quite still. Gus didn't want any part of touching the guy, but he could see there was no way out of it. He rubbed his hands together as if they were coated in glue, wondering where to start.

"Go up and down his sides," Collie instructed.

Gus did so, patting him down quickly, as if Milo's legs were scalding to the touch.

"Run your hands up and down there," Collie corrected. "Put pressure on there. Feel everything."

Feel everything. Gus's mouth became an unpleasant knot, but he did as ordered, sliding his palms up Milo's frame to his back.

"Check the pockets," Collie said. "Stick your hands in there. That's it. Do his chest, too. Good. Now, for the nasty you knew was coming. Check the crotch."

That stopped Gus on the spot. Milo wasn't the happiest about it either.

"Maybe you should," Gus said.

"Go on. You know what's there."

"I'm pretty sure he—"

"Check that ball hammock, Gus."

The quiet edge to her voice compelled him, so he did, reluctantly. Milo grimaced, telegraphing he wasn't keen on Gus's handling of precious goods either.

"Take it easy, man," he warned. "Not like you don't have a pair."

"Shut the fuck up," Gus shot back. When he finished, he looked as if he'd dunked his hands into a vat of shit.

"All good?" Collie asked.

Gus wasn't good in the least, not after feeling up another guy's junk, but he nodded all the same.

"Good job," Collie said. "Never doubted you, Milo."

The soldier wouldn't meet her gaze.

"Ah, those awkward silences," she remarked and checked on the sky. "Let's get moving. Leave this mess here."

Neither man commented.

"Look," Collie addressed them. "Get over it. Both of you. We're building trust here. Trust. And what better way to do that than having another guy hold your nuts for you? Think of it as locker room initiation."

Neither man made eye contact.

"Fine," Collie said. "All right, *boys*. Let's get out of here. Milo, you're driving again."

Without a word, the men got aboard the limo. Gus settled into the back seat, his hands still remembering the contact of Milo's crotch candy. He shook them out and looked around, hoping that *maybe*, somewhere amongst the goods they'd packed away, there was some hand sanitizer.

He met the gaze of the Captain.

Not a fuckin' word, he mentally warned the cardboard display.

And not a word was spoken.

12

The one-note shriek announced the opening of the dungeon door, silencing the screaming from the imprisoned audience and the naked man strapped to the gurney. The Spider straightened from his administrations and whirled around, as if caught doing something incredibly naughty.

And he was.

Blood pattered upon the floor from the gurney. An ominous speckling of red marred the lace adorning the edges of the Spider's Venetian mask, while the namesake upon his forehead appeared to have had a recent scrubbing, perhaps by a balled-up fist while pausing for thought. The Spider placed his back to his latest victim, as if attempting to hide his work and failing miserably.

In the lamplight, the few Leather, including the Goblin, also ceased whatever they'd been doing.

The Ninja stood in the door.

"Yes?" the Spider asked with feigned innocence.

"Visitors."

That cocked the leader's head.

"From Winnipeg," the black garbed figure announced dourly.

That got the Spider's attention. He remained motionless for a few heartbeats before remembering his most recent work behind him. He turned slightly, inspecting the damage done to his latest meat toy before his shoulders heaved in annoyance. A clearing rumble left his throat, one of guilty admittance.

The man on the table moaned.

One of the Leather stepped out of the shadows and smashed a padded fist into the prisoner's face, silencing him.

The Spider faced the Ninja. After a reflective thought, the leader nodded as if remembering his duty and stripped off his bladed gloves. Tossing them onto the gurney as if just emerging from surgery, the Spider headed for the door and beckoned the Goblin to follow.

The remaining Leather proceeded to clear the gurney of the evening's entertainment.

The Ninja got out of the Spider's way and fell into step with the Goblin. The three of them ascended from Fort Jay's cellars and marched towards the commander's office. The Spider's fingers twitched and wiggled all the while.

Five newcomers waited for them within the officer's chambers. Form-fitting leather clothed their brutish exteriors, while bats and axes were held at the ready. Two of the visiting five, however, were much more startling compared to the others.

The visiting leader drew the room's attention, dressed in a long leather duster and a shiny golden vest. A pair of katanas—their sheaths hanging low from the waist—parted the folds of the heavy coat. A golden helmet and the unhappy faceplate of a samurai warrior shrouded the figure's head. Black eyes sparkled within that mask.

Though the Samurai was bad, the wasteland executioner *behind* the Samurai was even worse.

He was the tallest in the room, with an ogre's physique. Leather straps covered meaty shoulders and thickets of hair sprouted from whatever skin was left exposed. Black bands roped around the torso from the nipple line to the waist. The biceps were bare, to better display the muscular meat. Spiked bracers armored the forearms from elbow to wrist, while matching gloves protected the hands. Two-inch nails crusted the knuckles. The mask hiding the brute's face resembled a mosh pit mummy burned at a stake, while a polished set of aviator's goggles covered his eyes.

The presence of the Inflictor meant the most serious of affairs—the highest priority given. The Inflictor demanded action to be taken... or immediate *punishment* would be doled out.

The Spider stopped behind his desk as his henchmen spread out behind him. There, he folded his arms and stared back at the unexpected guests. The Inflictor towered over the Samurai, and that was even with the ogre's bandaged brow lowered.

The Spider bowed.

The Samurai bowed back.

The Inflictor's goggles gawked at the Spider, clenching his nail-studded hands like a hairy, freakish strongman from a horrific sideshow.

"I have questions from the Bear Trap," the Samurai asked, his unsmiling face gleaming.

The Spider waited.

"Why haven't you returned with your minions?" the Samurai asked.

The Spider took his time in answering. "I'm making preparations to do so."

"Where are the prisoners?"

Again a pause. "I have them here."

"Why?"

"I'm… enjoying them. For the moment."

"The Bear Trap wants them brought to him."

"Which I'll do once I'm done breaking them."

The Samurai became silent, then, "The Bear Trap will break them."

"Breaking them here will make them easier to transport," the Spider countered.

The Goblin flanked him on the right. The Ninja stood on his left. Though they would not do anything without a command first, the Spider sensed an eagerness in both to challenge the Inflictor. The Spider did not *want* to challenge the Inflictor, however. He'd seen those giants fight before. There was a reason the Dog Tongue kept them close. Of all the Leather, the Inflictors were fanatical. They were the Dog Tongue's private police force, a small but exceptionally terrifying death squad.

The Samurai was merely a lieutenant for the Bear Trap. A mouthpiece.

The Inflictor was the right hand of the Dog Tongue himself.

Anyone else might have begun sweating or shaking under their mask. Perhaps the Spider would, later on, when he was out of the Inflictor's sight, when he realized what could've happened upon one wrong word. For now, however, he did the impossible, standing his ground even though part of his brain urged him to get out of there and run.

"Where is Reid Harrison?" the Samurai asked, assuming a stance where he might leap into a spinning side kick.

"I sent him to look for the Vulture."

"That was supposed to be your task."

"I was too busy here."

"Breaking the prisoners."

A bead of sweat slid down the inside of the Spider's mask. "Yes."

The Samurai stared. The Inflictor hefted his beastly shoulders but otherwise kept on clenching his hands.

"This is the word of the Bear Trap," the Samurai said. "Do you acknowledge him?"

There it was. *Fuck no*, the Spider thought, but what he said was, "Of course I do."

"You will return to the Bear Trap today, bearing whatever it is you've taken here. You will bring him the prisoners for breaking, and, if need be, converting. You will do so, because he demands it."

The Spider nodded. "I apologize for being late. I will do as you ask, for the Bear Trap. For the Dog Tongue. I will do all that and more, tomorrow, however."

The Samurai mask stared, as if not believing what he'd just heard.

The Inflictor's hands balled into fists and stayed that way. The aviator's goggles stared, those black lenses wide and monstrous.

"You will do so today," the Samurai repeated. "It's the Bear Trap's will."

"I can't move this day. Tomorrow. I'll be in the city before nightfall, with everything and more."

"Why tomorrow?"

"I have sent scouts out into the smaller towns surrounding the fort," the Spider lied, as easily as flinging out a strand of webbing. "They are looking for more of the fort's people who might have escaped. Perhaps nine or ten. One of them is supposed to be… a doctor."

"A doctor?"

"Yes."

The Samurai considered that. "You're sure?"

"I would have returned to the Bear Trap days ago if I wasn't."

No one spoke.

"A doctor," the Samurai finally repeated.

"Yes."

"A GP?"

"A surgeon, perhaps."

The Samurai nodded as if waiting for more.

"A general surgeon," the Spider added.

"What's that?"

"Mostly trauma."

The Samurai straightened. "Battlefield?"

"I'm not sure. But a certified licensed practitioner. Which is why I'm still here. When my people determine if there's anyone to bring back, they will do so. And that's when I planned on returning to the Bear Trap."

The Samurai folded his arms. "He wishes to regroup."

"Understood."

"Immediately."

The Spider nodded.

"He believes we are stretched too thin."

"I hold the Vulture responsible. I stayed while he pursued the family. I took the fort at night while he scours the countryside. I'm here... I don't know where the Vulture is."

With that, the Samurai did a most unsettling thing. He strode forward, purposefully, and stopped at the desk. The Samurai leaned toward the Spider as if smelling for fear.

"Tomorrow, then," he whispered. "Or face the Bear Trap's wrath."

Sweat slid in the Spider's eyes, and he blinked. "Tomorrow. I promise."

A promise he had no intention of keeping.

The Samurai didn't move, didn't flinch, searching the Spider's mask for traces of untruth.

In the end, the Bear Trap's lieutenant backed away. He retraced his steps to his followers, where he turned and walked around the baleful Inflictor and headed for the door. The rest of his pack followed. The Inflictor, however, with his stoic demeanor and Steampunk goggles did no such thing.

It was said that the Inflictors could *smell* lies. Could somehow detect them, like the Dog Tongue. It was said that the Dog Tongue actually trained the Inflictors on how to detect untruths, in addition to how to extract information. Once you knew one skill, the other was easier to ply.

And as God above was the Spider's witness, the Inflictor standing within the room sensed the Spider's lie.

"Inflictor," the Samurai said, and that summons broke the brute's spell of concentration. The big minion turned and stomped to the door, which was opened by a lesser posted there. Daylight marked the bare floorboards.

The Samurai looked back before leaving, one unhappy look filled with meaning that the Spider knew exactly.

Tomorrow.

Then the frightening little group left, the doorway framing their exit until they were gone from sight.

The lesser closed the door.

As badly as the Spider wanted to gasp for breath, he did not. Instead, he let it out in a shuddering hiss, knowing how close he had come to a fight. A fight he doubted he would win.

He'd bought himself and his followers some time. Even if the broken ones revealed there was *never* a doctor among them, it didn't matter. The Spider had already been following that line of questioning, merely for show. He'd already committed to his plan of breaking away from the Leather and forming his own kingdom.

He had no intentions of traveling to Winnipeg tomorrow.

Fuck that noise.

The guards at the main entrance only allowed the Samurai inside for appearances, because the Spider hadn't executed his plan just yet. He would change that. If the Bear Trap wanted to talk, he could come to the fort and shout from the fields below. And with the Bear Trap on the outside of the fort, the Spider was quite confident of his chances. He'd *convinced* himself of his chances. As the Samurai had said. The Leather was strung out. Divided and weakened because of the Vulture's leaving.

The Spider wanted his own kingdom. His own private web.

Fort Jay and all of its considerable defenses were *his*, and he would kill any more messengers from his former clan who ventured into his web.

And yet, even as this urge of rebellion surged within him, a part of him wondered how long he might hold the fort.

When it came to that time, he would find out.

13

There were no further encounters on the way to Fort Jay, yet Gus's unease grew with every passing kilometer. He sat in the back, oblivious to the once scenic sights passing by his window. Collie stopped the limo twice to get out and stretch her legs, and when she did, she switched up driving with Milo. Their conversations grew longer, as they recalled their time serving in the forces. Gus listened but couldn't relate. As much as he'd disliked the label, the truth was, he *was* a civilian. A survivor, sure, but still a civilian.

And a damn lucky one.

Gus scowled with sour humor at that, trying to stop his mind from uncovering memories he'd suppressed, of family and friends lost. The horrific sights of undead carnage and the nightmares they induced. Scenes that were only smothered by generous medicinal shots of alcohol back in the day. He wondered if the heroes in all the action and horror movies he'd watched ever got nightmares about what they'd seen. What they'd done.

Probably not.

Then there were the physical scars he'd sustained. The burns. The parts missing or constantly short-circuiting. The day-to-day reminders that he'd taken as good as he'd given. Lucky? Maybe. He was still alive and able to carry on, but it seemed to him that every time he got into a fight, another piece of him got chipped away. Only a matter of time before an important piece got hacked off, and every minute on the road increased those odds.

Of course, his brain pointed out that the final fight in Whitecap didn't take *anything* away from him, and that not only did he survive, but he survived without injury.

Goddamn fucking brain, Gus fumed. He glanced at Collie's masked profile. *You forget something?*

His brain shut up.

The military types continued to converse, warming up to each other, at least on a professional level. That quietly dumbfounded Gus, how Collie could sit and chat up the guy who had shot her dead. A part of him still hoped that some unnatural event would take Milo out of the picture for shooting her. Something utterly freakish, like him having a brain-frying stroke while taking a dump, or slipping out of the car and breaking his head open on the pavement. One of those completely unbelievable "shit happens" moments that would end the bastard's worthless existence.

Nothing of the sort happened, of course, but Gus still hoped. He idly listened to the two professional soldiers. Or at least one professional. Milo obviously knew the lingo, keeping up with Collie's army talk, or what Gus thought of as army talk, which was an artform onto itself. He refrained from asking the obvious, for fear of further revealing his civvy upbringing to Milo, and offering openings for sarcasm.

That didn't stop him from puzzling over one nugget after another.

Ammo trees. The fuck was an ammo tree?

Anchor cranker? Shitter fitters?

Awaiting parts? That one he got. Maybe. Sort of. *That cheesie was awaiting parts*, Milo had said… but… the fuck was a *cheesie?*

Boot fucked. That one Gus liked and would save for later.

Then there were other question marks, the acronyms, which further mystified him.

POC.

PONTI.

SISOL.

FIGMO.

That last one broke Gus's silence.

"All right, I'll bite. What's a 'figmo'?" he asked at the first break in the conversation.

The two military members up front shared a look, and even that little buddy-buddy, secret code moment kinda got on Gus's nerves.

"Stands for 'fuck it, got my orders'," Collie informed him.

"Oh."

"Any other questions?"

Gus shook his head and said, "No."

"Not the first time you heard military talk shop," she pointed out. "You heard me and Wallace chat before."

"Yeah." But Gus had been equally discombobulated then as well.

Collie kept her shades pointed at the road. "I know it sounds like we're talking in tongues, but you pick up on it real fast."

Gus didn't know about that. He felt he would need another year.

To his credit, Milo didn't say a word. The soldier didn't even look back at Gus, which was smart. Real smart.

Road signs pointed the way to Fort Jay. Late afternoon sunlight spilled through a clump of trees crowding a two-lane road where previous winters had crackled and popped the pavement. A house came into sight, its garden overgrown and near jungle status. A long driveway curved behind the bungalow, where the mighty waters of Lake Winnipeg could be glimpsed.

Collie pulled in behind the house and stopped the car. All heads turned towards the lake, where a northerly wind rustled the waters and the surrounding forest. There was even a small car shed next to the place, with a set of steps leading down an escarpment to a little dock. No one spoke, appreciating the scene.

"All right," Collie eventually said, breaking the moment. "Everybody out."

Cold air hit them, reminding them that winter was coming. A huge summer deck defined the back of the house, where twigs and small limbs littered a faded, wood-stained surface, blown off the trees by windstorms. Those same gales rearranged the outdoor furniture, shoving them up against a rose-painted deck railing that had lasted longer than the wood-stain. Stain, Gus knew, had to be reapplied every two years. Three years at best. Whoever owned the place had a nice setup, and he figured in normal times, the outdoor furniture all faced the lake to appreciate the evenings. The back door of the house was open, so he left the others to check out the interior.

Empty. No one had retired to their bedrooms and departed their lives by pills, guns, or hangings. The place was small, with an open living room, kitchen, and two bedrooms. A cottage on the lake.

When Gus returned, Milo was leaning against the limo.

"Anything?" the soldier asked.

"Fuck off."

"That's getting old, y'know."

Gus ignored him, not caring in the least what was old. He didn't see Collie, so he went to the open limo door on his side.

"You in there, Collie?"

"Yeah," she answered, moving things around inside. "House all good?"

"All good."

Amongst the numerous supplies packed into the limo was the cache of weapons taken from Whitecap's bountiful armories. All of Collie's favorites which included the German-made rifles, as well as muscular submachine guns that were no longer than Gus's forearm and hand. There were pistols and knives and explosives—mostly grenades, but there was a suspicious suitcase which Collie had tucked away in the back. There were backups for each rifle, and they had taken three complete sets of body armor, which further roused Gus's suspicions that she intended to outfit Milo at some point. If the soldier convinced her that his interests were in sync with her own.

Collie emerged from the limo outfitted for war. Tactical webbing covered her black body armor and helmet. Slung around her back was an assault rifle, in her holster a sidearm. At least one knife looped in her belt. And those were only the things Gus could see. The sight of all that paralyzed him.

"Thinking deep thoughts again?" she asked.

"Yeah."

"Well, stop it."

He nodded he would, but figured she knew he was lying.

She hefted a backpack and looked at the sky. "Last road sign I saw said nine klicks to the fort. It'll be dark before I get there."

"Wait, what?" Gus said.

"I'm going alone. Best that way."

"But what about him?"

Collie and Milo exchanged looks. "What about him? He'll stay with you."

"Alone?"

"I know," she said in a sympathetic voice. "He looks scary. But you have your special friend. And your Glock. Don't be scared to use them if you got to. Otherwise, just babysit. That's all I'm asking."

"But what are you going to do?"

"Kill 'em all. Sometime tomorrow morning. Depending on how alert they are. Don't you worry. I do this for a living." She paused. "Sorry. I winked just then. Forgot about the sunglasses."

"You're going to kill them all?" Milo asked.

"All."

That silenced both men.

"I'll try and link up with you in the morning," she explained. "Say around oh-six hundred. If I'm not here by then, something's gone wrong. They either have me or I'm just tits up dead. So, if you take it into your heads to come looking, just be careful when you get to the fort. If you see guards on the wall and a heightened state of alert, chances are I didn't make it."

"We could drive up there," Milo offered, appearing every bit as excited about spending time alone with Gus as Gus did with him.

"Negative. Who knows who they got stashed away on the road for lookouts. Or booby traps. I'll hike in. Off road. Got my special ninja boots on. No noise. No tread. Besides. They're a bunch of civvies playing dress-up. Don't you worry about me."

That last comment she directed at Gus. She stepped into his personal space and placed a hand around his neck. With gentle pressure, she pulled him in until her helmet was against his head.

"Don't worry," she told him. "About anything."

"Yeah," he managed to get out.

She patted the back of his skull and retreated a step, taking a moment to look upon the waters of Lake Winnipeg. Getting her bearings, she walked around the house and disappeared from sight, without any further goodbyes.

Leaving the men alone.

Until Milo looked over at Gus.

Who already had his Glock out. "Where's the duct tape?" he asked.

Not an hour later, Milo was lashed to a wooden lawn chair on the deck, facing the lake. The soldier had taped up his ankles and left hand by himself, and when that was done, Gus did the rest, doubling up on the ankles and a couple loops around the upper arms and chest.

"I can't fucking believe you're doing this," the soldier muttered.

"I can't fucking believe you didn't think I would," Gus countered, standing back and inspecting his work. "What did you think I was gonna do? Let you choose a bedroom in the house there? Huh? Have you kill me in my sleep?"

"I…" Milo wearily shook his head. "I wouldn't have done that."

"Yeah, I bet you wouldn't. I'll nap better knowing you're strapped to that chair."

"For all night."

Gus scratched at his nose, then dipped at the knees as he adjusted his balls. "Looks that way."

"I'll freeze out here."

"Freeze my ass. Been there, done that. You're wearing a lot more than me when I was strung up by the giblets. And I was stripped down to a pair of shit-stained Fruit of the Looms."

Milo sighed and took in the darkening sky. "How long you gonna hold this thing against me?"

"Dunno. Best not bring it up."

"Look. *Listen*. When I shot her…"

"Killed her."

Milo bit back a reply. "When I did that *thing*… the Leather was right *there* on *top* of me. Okay? Right there. I could see the fucking *hammer* one of them had. And they would've used it. They'd have done it in a flash. I couldn't shoot them. They would've been right on me. They would've *smashed* me within an inch of my fucking life and kept me alive *ALAP*, as an example to the rest of them."

"The fuck does that mean?" Gus growled.

"What mean?"

"'A-lap'."

"As-long-as-possible."

"*A-lap*," Gus scoffed. "Here's one for you. You're going to stay right there, '*a-lap*'. All *night* a-lap." He settled down in a nearby deck chair and watched the lake. He squirmed a bit, adjusting his crotch, and glanced in the direction Collie had gone, in case she returned. She didn't however, so he fixed his attention upon the soldier. "Tell me again why you joined up with them?"

"Who?"

"Them Leather bitches."

"I didn't join up with them," Milo replied.

"You said you did earlier."

"I… I was working for them. With part of a crew."

"Delivering people to the Leather."

"Yeah."

"People who would be either become slaves or more of the mindless."

Milo's expression twisted up as if he'd just bitten into an unpleasant knob of fat.

"Because that's what the Leather did, right?" Gus prodded.

"Yeah."

"A fucking bunch of nutbags who you just said that, if you *didn't* do what they wanted you to do, they would've made you an example. To others."

Milo sighed and nodded in defeat.

"So why were you *willingly* bringing them people?"

"We'd get paid shit," Milo almost moaned. "Food and fuel, mostly. And to stay out of their ranks. To stay clear of them. It's deadly out here. Murderous. You got better chances to stay alive in a group. You won't believe this either, but I was… I was planning to break away. There was this one shitpouch who was already fried upstairs. He was a…, well, damn. I forget what he was. Used bookstore, that's it. He worked in a used bookstore. Back then. Before the zombies. But after, he called himself a cosmetic surgeon."

"A cosmetic surgeon?" a doubtful Gus asked.

"Yeah," Milo nodded. "Rhinoplasty."

"What's that?"

"Doesn't matter," Milo said. "You didn't want him working on you. Like I said, his sanity had long gone south. You watched yourself around him, or even better, stayed clear entirely. Now, the others weren't much better, but we all knew—well, with the exception of O'Leary. He was the crazy one— everyone besides him knew that it was better to be together than apart. Especially with the Leather on the move."

Gus waved the Glock at him, indicating he continue.

"They're like ants," Milo went on. "Sending out feelers. Scouts. Find whatever it is to find then report back. We were camping out in a hotel one morning when we met one of them scouts. Jake, he was the leader. Our leader. He already knew about the Leather. Knew they had access to fuel. A blend of shit they ran all their machines on, all year round, and never lost any octane levels. They had fresh food, too, but the juice was the commodity. That shit's important on the road, and the Leather had plenty of it. So…"

Silence then, as Milo remembered, long and deep, until Gus tapped a boot off the deck.

"Jake thought we could work for them for a while," Milo resumed. "Do a few jobs and get what we could. Then get clear. But after the first job, it became clear to me and the Jipman…"

"The who?"

"Don't ask. That's what he told us to call him. Anyway, it became obvious that the Leather were fucked up. That what we were *doing* was fucked up. But Jake was all in with them. And the Jipman and me knew we needed a crew. So… we did what the Leather told us to do."

Milo looked to his boots.

"Sounds pretty damn easy to me," Gus quietly remarked. "How quick you went along with it."

"At first, I…" Milo shook his head. "I didn't think the Leather were that bad. Even with the meat puppets. We just thought they *wanted* to be like that.

All that shit was a barrier to whatever virus might be still on the go. But by the second job, we saw what they did to whoever we brought in. We knew."

"And you kept doing it?"

"We only did three."

"And you kept doing it?"

Milo glared. "Remember, I was part of a crew. For only a few months, but I was part of them. We hooked up on the road and they kept me on because I had some training. And I was good with guns. But with regards to what we were doing for the Leather? Jake didn't care. The Jipman didn't care. And O'Leary sure as fuck would've shot me for even suggesting wanting to get out. That was the group I was with."

Gus glared back. "You could've left them."

"Coulda, shoulda. I was getting around to that. Really. I was."

They stopped talking then, aware of the vast emptiness of the lakeshore.

"I'm not… guiltless," Milo finally confessed. "Not by a long shot. But I bet if it was you sitting here, and I was doing the questioning? Well, I bet I'd find things about you and whatever shit you did in the past. Since all this happened. Things you knew were bad but you went through with, anyway. Hating yourself. Or not."

Gus blinked at that, not meaning to, but Milo's words stabbed home all the same.

"All I could think about was going west," the soldier continued. "After you killed Jake and the others. You did me a favor then, y'know. Or she did. I was out, and the only thing in my head was getting away. Slipping by the Leather. Hiding somewhere up north. Some little hole where it would take ages for them to find me, if ever. But I drove right into them. And here I am. Duct taped to a chair on a fucking porch."

Gus stared at the lake. It truly was a nice spot. There were old pictures inside the house, of parents and kids, capturing a time when all that was going on with the world was climate change and capturing super cybercriminals targeting world banks. Back then, all he'd been was a schmuck with a paint brush, working for a small company with a shitty name.

Brushit.

Got some painting to do? Brushit off! Call us!

That put a smirk on his face.

"Something funny?" Milo asked.

Gus got serious. "No."

"Look. Really. How am I gonna take a leak now?"

"Take a leak, I don't care."

Milo frowned. "What if I have to take a dump?"

"Hold it."

"You can't hold back pipe."

"Sure, you can," Gus said, before remembering his time in an attic with Scott. "For a while, anyway," he added.

Silence then.

"Do you haveta take a leak?" Gus finally asked.

"Not right now."

"Then shut up."

More silence.

"She forgave me, remember?" Milo reminded him. "You were there. You heard it."

Gus remembered, but he chose not to comment.

Silence again.

"Dicksmack," Milo finally said under his breath.

"Fuckwit," Gus sent back, and studied the guy's head with squinty-eye disdain. "And seriously? A shit-dried *mullet*? Who's your fuckin barber?"

"Who's your fuckin' dentist?" Milo replied.

That melted the contempt off Gus's face and replaced it with pure, unchecked surprise. The soldier might be many things, but Gus had to admit, the sandy-haired cock gobbler was sharp. Or particularly scared, considering how he was wrapped up.

They settled down after that last exchange.

"You ever kill anyone?" Milo asked after a while.

The evening set the lake waters aglow. Far too picturesque for such a question, yet Gus answered. "I put down one or two."

"And I bet there was a reason behind it, right?"

"Sure there was a reason."

"I mean, you did it in self-defense, right? And not because you were getting a taste for it?"

Gus was a little slower on that one. "Yeah. Self-defense."

"Any of them a mistake?"

"Maybe."

"Say one of them was a mistake," Milo continued. "You ever regret it?"

Gus sighed.

"Well?" Milo pressed.

But Gus didn't answer him.

14

Collie stayed off the main road, hiking along an old trail that was once used for all-terrain vehicles. She'd long since pocketed her sunglasses, as her sight was much better at night. The woods were thin and stunted, and a number of houses were on her left, while the embankment and lake were on her right. As long as she kept the shore on her right, she'd be seeing the fort eventually. Probably well after nightfall.

And she was right.

Three hours later, under a clear night sky, the fort came into view on a distant hillside. She stayed low in the surrounding forest and studied the fortification. Whoever had chosen the site knew their business. The place appeared as a dark outline against the night sky. Lightless. Solemn. Abandoned. Situated perfectly on a high point of rock overlooking the lake. A field of wild grass, cleared of trees, lay before the historical site, running all the way up to the stone walls. Or so it appeared. Collie wondered if the walls were the only things she had to worry about.

She unslung her rifle and dropped to the ground. Lying on her belly, she checked out the fort with her scope's improved night vision. The stone became a light gray and green with varying degrees of shading. She located the top of the walls and gently swung right, recognizing several of the fort's cast iron, thirty-two-pounder cannons aimed at the slope. The thought that the guns might be loaded occurred to her, and she filed that away for later.

There were no guards, however, and after a few minutes, she decided to get moving.

Upon creeping closer to the fort, she dropped to the grass again. She examined the main gates. A pair of closed doors set within an archway, just wide enough to get a pickup through. There was a small guardhouse outside the gates, just a one-man closet really, but unattended. The shadows appeared deeper near the base of the walls, and when Collie chanced lifting her head she saw why.

A moat. A wide one, a short hike away. And probably quite deep.

Shit, she thought and sank into the grass. After a moment, she used her rifle's scope again. She scanned the top of the wall and swept left, studying the crenellated stonework. Nothing moved, however. Not a—

A gray figure passed between two merlons—the stone pieces making up the crenellations—and strolled out of sight.

Collie trained her scope upon the next opening, and Mister Nightwatch Leather sauntered past that as well, rather unconcerned with his designated duty. She tracked him until he reached the upper section of the main gates, where he stopped and leaned, perhaps admiring the slope leading up to Fort Jay.

Just the one guard.

But where there was *one*...

For the next hour, Collie watched.

Her patience was rewarded when she spotted three of the Leather pacing about the battlements. They were slow, as if bored or fighting off sleep, and certainly not expecting anyone to be watching them so late at night.

When the moon was nearly overhead, Collie wormed her way through the tall grass, towards the lake, taking her time, careful not to draw attention. Within minutes, she reached a drop off. Below her some fifteen feet or so was the lake's shoreline.

Fine.

Collie had all night, not that she intended to use it. She dropped to her chest once again and crawled through grass and shadows. She moved only inches before pausing, waiting a few seconds, then repeating, keeping her rifle alongside her body. There was barely any sound as she crawled upslope, but such a stealthy approach ate up time. A sluice finally came into sight, as well as the narrow walkway spanning the moat. She slunk towards the walkway, sliding over stiff, stabbing grass. There was a chance someone might spot her wake from up above, but no alarm was raised.

No one shouted.

She eventually crossed the walkway, dropped on the other side of the moat, and continued crawling. In short time, she placed her back against a reconstructed wall of stone, brick, and concrete. There were no spotlights, no cries of alarm. The main gates were far and away to her right, cut off by angular juts. The walls were sheer, some twenty feet high. Scaling them wasn't out of the question but would be difficult. Her arms and legs buzzed with a numbness she didn't recognize but attributed to her condition. She didn't remember Wallace talking about experiencing any numbness. And as unstable as TI was, she had no idea what her symptoms might be or how they would compare to his.

She slung the rifle and secured her weapons to ensure nothing swung loosely. Then she peered upward, taking in the stark contrast of the starfield overhead and the line of the fortifications. Twenty feet at least.

Well, goddamn, Collie thought, and ran a hand over the brickwork.

Coarse, somewhat irregular, and minimal handholds.

She had an aluminum grappling hook and nylon rope in her backpack, but upon feeling the wall, she didn't think she'd need one. Seeking out a handhold, she fixed one boot toe onto the narrowest edge of a brick.

And hoisted herself up.

There was no pain, but there was that numbness in her limbs, a feeling that eased when she really pressed down on the brick.

Going up, she thought. And started to climb.

Just after midnight, she hauled herself up and through a battlement opening. She pulled herself into the gap, adjusting her rifle. The crenels were wide for gun placements, and tall grass covered the upper sections for camouflage as well as the look. God bless Parks Canada for keeping with tradition in their restoration efforts.

A wide walkway behind the battlements ended in a low partition of brick and mortar that overlooked the courtyard. Collie crouched and assessed the battlement heights. No one patrolled the wall she'd just breached. In fact, there wasn't a soul in sight. Seeing as it was near midnight, she supposed the guards were either struggling to stay awake or already sleeping. She crept to the low wall and peeked over its height. Small tents and parked vehicles filled the courtyard below, set up around a main building some three stories tall built in the fort's center. Chimneys smoked lightly but were in need of wood. Far back from the main gates and within the cluster of tents, a pair of brick firepits burned. Four figures stood around one of those firepits.

Only four.

No doubt enjoying the heat on a cold November night.

The guards coaxed the fire to greater heights, feeding cut wood to the pit they attended. Sparks flew briefly, but nowhere near the tents to endanger them. Collie wondered how cold it actually was, as she didn't feel anything at all and not because of her exertions. She wondered if the Leather would be inside those tents on such a cold night, and suspected they weren't. Not the brass, anyway. Not with the smoke coming from the chimneys of the main building. She would have to prove herself right, however.

She gathered up her rifle. The rear of the fortress, facing the lake, wasn't patrolled either, and she spotted what she knew to be an enclosed stairwell leading down into the courtyard, far away from the guards and their firepits.

Three. Four dozen. Maybe five. The one called Rabid reminded her. *Just axes. Bats. Crossbows.*

She'd take care of them all.

Her weapons were all outfitted with suppressors, the professional kind, which rendered a gunshot to nothing more than a soft cough. Such a feat was a modern engineering marvel, but there were drawbacks. The compatible ammunition was standard issue only. No hollow points.

Collie composed herself before visualizing her objective.

Then she was low and all no-noise, becoming a shadow, racing toward the stairwell on silent feet. She aimed her assault rifle ahead of her, reached the stairwell, and descended in a whisper of fabric. At the bottom, she melded into the darkness and faced an open archway. Seeing her moment, she kept one shoulder to the wall and aimed her sights on the archway as she ninja-scurried to the corner and froze. There were no firepits behind the fort, leaving that side of the building in complete darkness. Shouldering her weapon, she speed-crept for the nearest corner, pushing, pushing, every bootfall a whisper, and reached the building.

There she paused, waiting for a cry of alarm.

Nothing of the sort.

She peeked back towards the main gates. The outline of tents and the glow from the firepits was out of sight around the distant corner.

No one was between her and that far corner. It was a straight run along the building. Overhead, the starfield blazed.

Rifle firm against her shoulder, Collie stayed low and rushed ahead in silence, staying within the shadow of the towering building. She reached the corner and placed her shoulder to the wall. She lowered her rifle and peeked out, spotting the four Leather sentries still around the firepit. They talked in low voices, with either their arms folded or hands stuffed into their pockets.

All four were well within her kill zone.

Thank you, Lord, Collie silently sent off, *for making my life a little easier.*

She took aim under the cover of darkness, marking her targets at around twenty meters away. Her finger left the guard and stopped on the trigger.

The sentries remained in place, like points on a square.

Collie fired, expertly shifting her aim after each shot. Two targets dropped within a second of each other, their heads whipping back as they fell. The third target tensed an instant before his skull burst apart underneath his leather mask. The fourth was too stunned to squeak, let alone squeal, paralyzed by the unexpected deaths of his companions.

Collie put a single bullet into the side of his head.

Two seconds. Four sentries down.

She pulled back and hugged the corner, waiting for a response, eyeing the tents and the surrounding battlements. Nothing moved. No snores either, confirming what she suspected. No one slept in the tents. It was too cold for the boogeyman clan known as the Leather. They were inside the main building, no doubt taking advantage of the bunks there and whatever eighteenth-century heating system was still in place. A road tribe they might be, they were still only civilians, taking civilian comforts when needed.

Collie slipped around the corner to the front, her right shoulder grazing the wall. She ducked under the windows as she passed.

No one shot at her. No one shouted.

A clacking of metal from ahead and a door opened. Flashlight flared over stone tiles before centering on a tent wall some thirty feet away—and some ten feet from the corpses around the firepit. A figure stepped outside, poised as if he'd heard something and decided to check on it.

Collie shot him through the ear.

The doorman collapsed in a death-rattle of leather and buckles upon crushed stone. That prompted Collie to charge the main entrance. She reached the threshold of a set of double doors, arched and reinforced with black iron. One of those doors was opened.

Collie pushed through, rifle first, aiming where she looked.

She entered an eighteenth-century British office setting, and a prominent board with a message that read "FORT JAY WELCOMES YOU." That greeting seemed familiar, but she couldn't grasp why. Historic military banners with raging lions hung from the walls. Underneath a sign that read "INFORMATION CENTRE" were billboards covered in brochures. A pair of bagpipes rested on the nearby desk, perhaps being given a go before discarded. White paint covered the interior, while black beams of hardwood outlined and framed it all, suggesting more of a Dutch influence than English.

There were four doors in the place. Two on the right. Two on the left.

The left one had been opened, and a cot and meager army kit was within. A rechargeable lantern sat upon a night table, the only source of light in the room, and a magazine had been tossed on the ruffled blankets, as if the sentry had gotten up after hearing an odd thumping outside his window.

Collie withdrew to the main room and spotted a white sign with black lettering.

"TO BARRACKS."

Complete with a little arrow pointing the way up a set of drawn steps.

The tour guide labeling made her job easier.

Five down, she thought and proceeded to the barracks' door. The hinges worked without a sound as she opened it and peered up a staircase. Scant light glowed two flights up. Adjusting her rifle again, Collie ascended, swinging her weapon around, searching for targets. She reached the next level, where a lantern burned on a small table, marking the midway point of a hall that ran the width of the building. Dark windows were just visible at either end of an unlit corridor, where snores ripped and echoed through the walls.

She edged along to a closed door. More snores. Her hand gripped a wrought iron doorknob and gave it a turn. The door swung inward, releasing a wave of heat. A square stove occupied the center of the floor, its toothy grate grimaced fire, as if pained or overworked. The light illuminated gray cotton blankets hanging from a bare timber ceiling, as well as a figure sitting next to the stove, its legs propped up on a pile of cut wood. Leather encased the person's features. The figure turned, as if roused from dozing off—and stared as if confused by what he was seeing.

Collie shot him twice, and two crisp tinkles of metal rang out in the room. The impacts blasted the figure from his seat, whipping his legs off the wood pile and sending cut logs rolling across the floor.

A few snores choked to a stop. Someone moaned. Another swore.

Then a voice. "The hell you doing out there, Beagle?"

It was strange hearing the Leather speak, but Collie supposed they didn't communicate with each other by telepathy. That would require a brain. The barracks was a huge dark thing filled with wood heat. The blankets hanging from the rafters suggested some wanted privacy. All those makeshift berths were filled with people that wore the Leather.

A few of which were awakening.

There was no doubt in her mind she could shoot them all, but she wasn't about to waste the ammunition. Collie lowered her rifle and reached for a dimpled golf ball of a grenade. She pulled the pin on that ornamental-sized egg of destructive fury and tossed it into the middle of the room.

The thing bounced and rattled along, weaving a drunken line up the middle of the berths, beyond the stove with the grimacing mouth.

Collie was already out of the room and closing the door.

The explosion, however, blew the slab of wood off its hinges. The door slammed against the opposite wall in a gush of fiery smoke and a brief cymbal crash of shattering glass.

15

Gus woke with a choked-off snort that rattled the back of his throat and left him gasping. He jerked his head up and sleepy-stared for seconds. He realized he was gazing at the unmoving sheet of glass that was the lake, lit up by the moon. The wind had died out, taking the edge off the cold night air. Nothing rustled, nothing moved, except the soft expulsion of breath from across the way. *Milo*. Still duct taped to the deck chair—ass-planted, head down, and dead to the world.

Gus watched the soldier, wondering how Collie might be doing at the fort. He should've gone with her. He should've made a better *argument* for going, not that she would've let him. She wouldn't have. Not her, and there was no arguing with a specialist. With that, he rubbed his mouth and beard and realized how cold it had become. Although the wind had dropped out, the temperature felt five degrees lower since he'd fallen asleep. That prompted him to stand and stretch, mindful of making a racket. Not for dickhead strapped down to the chair, but just out of habit.

Gus shook his head at his absolute shit job of staying awake and gave his crotch a tug. Another glance at Milo and he left the soldier to go to the limousine.

The sleeping man didn't wake.

Which was fine. Gus didn't want to talk to him, anyway. He opened the limo's door and peered inside before pulling himself aboard. There, he shuffled through the various items until he located a sleeping bag, black with a fluffy checked pattern inside. He foraged a little more and grabbed a second one. His hands full, Gus backed out of the limo and closed the door, careful not to slam it. All he needed was to give away his position and have some crazy skidmark jump him at night.

He lumbered back to his lawn chair, watchful of Milo, wondering if the man might be pretending to be asleep. Chin down like he was, however, Gus doubted it. The soldier was obviously a person who didn't mind sleeping upright. Gus returned to his chair and threw one of the bags over it. After a moment's adjustment, he'd covered it completely. He sat down with a little groan and felt his ass smile into the cushion. A little extra cushion always made life that much better.

He shook out the second sleeping bag, unzipped it down the side, and pulled it apart. With a sniff, he tossed the thing over himself and tucked it in tight around his neckline, fidgeting with the full thigh holster underneath. Not happy with the sleeping bag's coverage, he pulled the edge of the thing up to his eyes. Nose sticking out, he glared at the lake.

Glass. Just like a sheet of glass. Or silver.

Cold, Gus thought. He reached up to adjust his winter cap, pulling it further down over his ears. That was better. Too bad he didn't have something like Collie's ski mask. Or *balaclava* or whatever. That made him smirk. All things considered, however, he was doing okay. He was doing just fine, in fact. He settled back with a sigh and stared.

Until he glanced over at Milo.

Head down and unmoving, Gus watched until he saw the sleeping man's chest rise before relaxing. Milo was still dressed in his outdoor clothing, winter jacket and a cap like Gus himself, and nothing more. Milo was supposed to be a soldier, however, so he was probably used to sleeping in harsh conditions. No doubt had winter training or something like that, not only sleeping outside in the cold, but extreme cold. Gus wondered if that might've included sleeping at the top of a mountain somewhere in January, or just crashing in a deep freeze for a couple of hours. Whatever, the three-finger taint-pinch probably had to sleep in some cold shit somewhere. *Real* cold.

That conjured up a memory Gus really didn't want to recall, but like most memories, it just materialized. And that memory was the one with the gang of highway killers. The unstable shit buckets who'd shot him off the road, captured him, stripped him down, and then strung him up from a tow truck. He remembered how he was left out overnight—perhaps two nights—he couldn't recall exactly the length of that miserable time—but he remembered only wearing his Fruit of the Looms. And that cottony nut hammock was feeling fairly crusty after one night. He remembered dangling from the tow truck's boom, arm sockets screaming, bare feet lashed together with rope and anchored to a rusty tire rim. The cold feasted on his bare skin, torturing him with potential frostbite, which thankfully didn't happen. It was cold, though. So very cold, perhaps only a degree or two from zero. Then there were the cockburgers that strung him up there in the first place, and how they played with him.

Gus stared at the lake. Bad time. *Real* bad time. He remembered the one called Boll putting a knife to his eye and threatening to hook it out. Hook it out with one flick of his wrist. Boll never did it, but he did cut Gus down the side of his ribs and left him to bleed. Then there was the terrible burn in his arms from the lack of circulation. He remembered pissing himself, and the laughter of those who'd watched and delighted in his misery.

Gus frowned.

In fact, he was almost scowling.

He looked over at Milo.

You got it easy, buddy, he projected. *You got it fucking easy. I only duct taped your shitty ass to a chair. A chair. I wished for a chair when I was trussed up. I wished for death, too, for that matter. Goddamn right I did. I'm no fucking Comeau or caveman Boll, or whatever the name of that fuckwit was, and you can be goddamn thankful that I'm not, because I could make your life pretty fucking miserable if I wanted to. Pretty fucking miserable. You bet your shitty ass drawers, I could.*

And he could, if he really put his mind to it. He'd been in Comeau's possession for a couple of days, taking everything they had. When they got bored of torturing him, they hauled him out to the middle of nowhere and left him hanging like a bloody piñata. Just waiting for a gimp to walk by and start chowing down on his half-frozen ass.

Gus's eyes narrowed to slits, watching the sleeping soldier.

I could do anything to you right now. Any-fucking-thing. And there's no one around to stop me. Not even Collie. I could do it. I could. Got plenty of reason to. I could do all sorts of revenge shit on you. All sorts. Make up any story I want. And get away with it, too. Damn straight.

Gus sighed, knowing that he could. Easily.

But he wouldn't.

Not like this. To do so would make him no better than Comeau and his pack of nut-bars. He just wasn't that person. And that realization kept Gus in his chair, underneath the comfortable warmth of the sleeping bag.

Milo twitched. Perhaps the cold finally affected him.

Gus watched, his mind drawing a flat line of thought, his memories playing out like a spool emptying of thread. A frustrated sigh left him then and he threw off the sleeping bag. He stood and the cold sank into him.

"Fuck," he swore.

Shaking his head, he went for the limo.

"Fuck, fuck, fuck," he whispered to himself as he located a third sleeping bag.

"Fuckity, fuck, fuck, *fuck*," he muttered on the way back, putting a little extra meat on that last swear.

And even though he hated himself for doing it, he unzipped the sleeping bag, spread it wide, and tossed it over the sleeping soldier. It didn't cover him right, so Gus stepped behind the man, got ahold of the cushiony edges, and hoisted it up around his neck, effectively tucking him in.

Whereupon Milo woke.

Gus stood back as the guy checked himself over.

"Shit," Milo said. "Thought I was being smothered there for a second."

Without a word, Gus returned to his chair.

"Thanks for the blanket," Milo said.

Gus muttered something.

"What was that?"

"I said don't fuckin' mention it." He paused before adding, "Dickhead."

Milo chose not to comment.

"Don't say I never did nothin' for you," Gus warned as he got comfortable underneath his own sleeping bag.

All became quiet then for a few fleeting seconds.

"She should be at the fort by now," Milo said, easily heard over the polished stillness of the lake.

Gus didn't say a word.

16

Collie moved.

She hoofed it along the hallway, her rifle poised to kill. Smoke filled the historic confines of the hall. One door opened ahead and a wraith emerged, waving to clear the air.

She lit him up with three quick shots, the bullets striking and bouncing the Leather off the doorframe and back into the room. Blood spattered the wall. Screams and shouts of alarm went up, prompting Collie to advance to the entrance. She peeked inside and spotted a dozen or so more Leather pushing aside their blanket partitions and going for weapons. Some of the Leather weren't wearing any leather at all and seemed almost alien without their costumes.

Not that she cared.

Collie pulled out another grenade, yanked the pin, and lobbed that destructive nugget into the midst of the room. She withdrew and an orange blast of flame raged against the opposite wall, scorching it black.

On impulse, she whirled to check her six.

There, behind her, a black head appeared in the stairwell, swiveling in the direction of the first blasted barracks.

Collie put a bullet into that skull. The collapsing figure rattled off the stairs as he dropped from sight. She turned and motored back, past the second blasted nest. Fire crackled as she spared a quick glance inside the room. Flames consumed the bunks and lit up the hanging blankets. Nothing stood on two legs.

Then she was charging past, seeking the window at the end of the hall.

A figure materialized before her, a smoky golem swinging an axe at her face.

Collie ducked and felt the blade miss by hairs. She rammed the butt of her rifle into a bare knee, buckling the owner. The naked minion went down, one hand clawing at her. Collie whipped her rifle across the man's head. He collapsed and she retreated a step before placing a single round into his face.

Then she was rushing for the window.

The framed glass appeared through the smoke, and she bashed her way through. Glass exploded outward as Collie landed on an outer walkway above the main courtyard. She forced herself to rise, surprised by the weight of her limbs, and willed them to obey. Bright stars hung overhead as she swung one way then the other, now at the rear of the main building. She faced the dark ramparts and she hurried towards the end of the walkway, her footfalls creaking the wood. Windows flashed by, offering glimpses of the fires burning within.

She reached one window that didn't have a fire burning behind it.

Collie smashed it out and entered. She aimed inside the room as she scissored her legs over the jagged sill. Empty beds filled the room, their upturned sheets and blankets suggesting the Leather weren't a mindless road clan at all. Civilians, perhaps, but there was order within the masked savages. A closed door appeared at the far end.

She sped by the empty beds and an unlit stove in the middle of the room. She stopped at the closed door, paused, and jerked it open.

Two of the Leather stood in the hallway, spinning at the sound.

A short eruption of stars blew out the back of the first target, splattering him against a wall. The second burst lifted the other Leather off his feet and painted the corridor. A *third* Leather charged Collie from the right, sprinting from the flickering dark. An axe flashed down, but the operator was faster, darting, spinning, and firing, destroying the Leather's head.

*

The first muted blast sounded like a great barrel falling and bursting upon a wooden floor. One bladed finger shivered over the wide and staring eye of a young woman, whose breath caught in her throat. The Spider held that pose, every bit as surprised as his captive, and scanned the bare timbers of the cell block. He wasn't exactly sure what he'd heard. The prisoners also studied the ceiling, but the half-dozen minions with the Spider, including the Goblin and the Ninja, looked to their leader.

The Spider drew back from the woman strapped down upon the gurney. He was at a loss, wondering what that noise had been.

A second muted blast then, landing not so far from the first. The Spider flinched at the noise, his bladed hands going up to shield himself. He glanced at his minions and beckoned the Goblin, showing him his gloves and needing help to remove them.

"Go," the leader ordered the Ninja and others.

The Leather grabbed nearby weapons and scrambled out of the dungeon.

*

Collie discovered a second stairwell and descended, leaving the level overhead to burn. She reached the ground floor and made her way through a series of halls, approaching the front of the structure. A number of dark portals came into view, spaced apart in measured white-painted intervals. She checked every door, throwing them open, finding mostly bedrooms containing cots, old-fashioned dressers, and actual bed pans. Then she located the museum, where a single window allowed night into the room. Glass cabinets were arranged in wide aisles, containing medals and regal uniforms standing at full attention. In between those were old maps of England along with numerous, ancient-looking photographs of unrecognizable figures. Swords, flags, and various other historical military items either hung from walls or on display racks, tastefully arranged throughout the place. An old Vickers machine gun had been set up upon a table. The weapon didn't quite fit the timeline of the fort but was present anyway.

Collie threaded her way past the machine gun, searching for another door and discovering more historic treasures. A twinge of regret sparked within her. The fire would destroy everything if left to burn, and there wasn't much to prevent it from happening. She entered a short corridor, swinging her HK around, and entered a larger room dominated by a formidable desk. Windows lined the wall, glowing with faint firelight from the courtyard.

A door on the far side of the desk got her attention.

Collie sped around the desk in her hyper-stealth mode and stopped at the wall. She leaned against the wood as fire crackled overhead. Timbers groaned and orange lines glowed and flickered between the floorboards. Despite all that, Collie concentrated on the door before her, believing she heard movement behind it—when a freezing spike of static split her thoughts, stabbing her mind from her forehead to the back of her skull. That spike swelled into a great twisting spearhead of craving, becoming a cancerous knot right behind her ears. There it stuck and bloomed, expanding into a wormhole that threatened to suck her consciousness into a web of corrupted neurons sparkling and festering beneath it all. An orange and black bolt of insanity struck Collie as hard as a hammer, and her knees buckled. She slumped against the wall while her rifle drooped. She grabbed her masked face, cringing under that pulsating onslaught.

Before her, the door opened and a black figure stepped out.

The shadow recoiled upon seeing Collie, before a white hand grabbed for her rifle barrel.

That was all the distraction she needed. With a surge of urgency, she mentally slammed that invader crawling through her head back in its place and focused on her physical attacker. The Leather twisted the rifle to one side and lunged for her. Collie drove an open palm into her attacker's throat. He *gurked* and stumbled to his knees, a knife clattering to the floor.

Collie fired, three quick squeezes of the trigger that plied the Leather back. Her mind returned, she straightened in time to see a towering shadow erupt from the darkened doorway. The figure grabbed the rifle by the barrel, forcing it away. Collie pulled back on the weapon, but the new attacker was not only bigger but much stronger. He pushed forward, wrestling for the rifle, as a third Leather entered the room.

Collie twisted her weapon up, lifting it, exposing the Leather's black legs. She snapped a side kick into a knee. The figure crumpled.

But he did not release the rifle.

More figures entered the room in a spidery gush and converged on her. One stabbed for her chest, but her Kevlar vest deflected the attack. Collie released the rifle and retreated, pulling her sidearm as the shadows coalesced into a mass of bodies. They charged, obscuring the minion holding her rifle. Boots clattered off the wooden floor. Knives gleamed.

Collie shot the first one in the face. A spray of oil spurted from the back of the dead man's head, but it didn't slow the onslaught. She fired as she backed up, putting bullets into that attacking mass. Light flashed and men and women tumbled. The charge faltered. Through the confusion, she sighted the Leather aiming at her with her own rifle.

Another figure on the floor, not quite dead, reached out and clutched at her ankle.

Collie put two bullets in the chest of the potential shooter. The rifle clattered to the floor. Before metal hit wood, she altered her aim and snapped off a third bullet, into the skull of the one holding her. No sooner was he dead when she immediately brought up her sidearm and dispatched her remaining attackers. Light flared, punching into bodies, shoving them backwards. Shadows crashed to the floor, until the final two actually *leaped* over the fallen.

One wore what looked like a goblin's mask.

Collie slammed up against an unseen pot-bellied stove just waiting for her. She tumbled over that cast-iron pitfall, yet managed to keep a hold of her gun. She hit the floor. The Goblin kicked one of her legs, crunching a boot-toe into the meat of her thigh. On her back, Collie clutched her Sig in both hands and fired. The bullet shattered the Goblin's chin, driving the skull back and dropping him in a messy puddle of torsos and limbs.

He fell just as the last shadow kicked the gun out of her hand.

The Sig clattered across the floor, but Collie was already twisting onto her side, kicking—*sweeping*—the Leather's leg out from under him. He crashed amongst the stew of bodies covering the planks. Her kick had been solid enough, but not enough to do any real damage, as the final Leather scrambled to regain his feet.

Collie got to hers.

They stood and squared off against each other in that dark room. She faced what appeared to be a goddamn *ninja*, holding a throwing axe and a thick knife. The sight triggered a memory, of the killer called Sick, and the fight that almost ended her in the rear of a transport trailer. The similarity between Sick and this current foe was close enough to give her pause.

The ninja attacked, loading up on his throwing axe and chopping for all his might, looking to bury the blade in her face.

Collie blocked the arm and straight punched the ninja's throat, hearing, *feeling* that organic crinkle of a dented windpipe. There was a sputtered hiss and all fight left the man. She grabbed the ninja's knife before he dropped it, righted the blade, and sank it deep up under his chin.

The man flopped to the floor, ripping the weapon from her hand as he fell.

Careful about where she stepped, Collie stood over him. The idiot might have worn the pajamas, but he possessed no training. Just another civvie.

"Just proof," she said, "the look doesn't mean shit."

A presence prompted her to look up.

To the open doorway, where they'd all come through.

There, on the threshold and watching her, was a final masked figure. He froze there, half visible against a black backdrop. An axe was in his right hand, an honest to Christ battle axe stolen from some museum. A white face with a fancy design around the edges studied her with a hint of bemusement, but what really caught Collie's attention was the spider print stamped upon the forehead.

For a full two seconds, they stared, sizing each other up as the raging fire overhead produced an increasing party of pops, creaks, and increasing smoke, all to the tune of a nerve-eating roar. Something heavy crashed into the ceiling, and the Spider flinched at the sound.

In that instant, Collie knew he was scared.

"You're fucking next," she quietly informed him.

And the Spider ran.

17

Collie scooped up her Sig Saur and holstered the weapon. She then snatched up the rifle.

Whereupon she launched herself through the door, pursuing the fleeing figure.

She stood on a wooden landing, where sacks of provisions and barrels lined a gray brick wall. A staircase led below. Collie descended, aware of the growing weight in her feet. She reached a lower level and spun towards a single torch, rolling and sputtering across the stone-tiled floor. The runner tried dousing the light and failed even that. Collie hurried to a corner, whirled around it, and aimed.

Open door. More torchlight within.

She edged into the room, filled with a connected line of iron cells time-warped in from an earlier century. People filled those cages. No, people were *crammed* into those cages to a point where they couldn't even lie down to sleep. Dirty, stinking, and beaten, a single torch burned on the wall and colored the nearest grimy faces a Halloween orange.

Those frightened expressions watched her, ready to scream, when the next sight stopped the operator. There were two tables in the room, their surfaces covered with an evil assortment of picks and hooks and knives only seen in horror movies. There was a medical bag as well, but the thing that grabbed her attention was the pair of gloves with scalpels fixed to the fingertips.

That, and the woman strapped down tight to a nearby gurney.

"Holy... shit," Collie whispered, processing everything at once.

"The keys are over there," a woman said, thrusting a skinny arm through the bars to point at the wall.

Well out of reach from the prisoners and hanging from a peg was an iron ringlet with a set of keys.

"What the medieval fuck has been going on here?" Collie asked.

"He went that way," one of the men said and pointed, his face practically mashed against the cell bars.

That sent a rumble of alarm through her. There was only one way *into* the dungeon and the prisoner was pointing at it.

Which was when the door slammed shut.

*

Mine, bitch! the Spider mentally shrieked, his fingers clawing at the top and bottom bolts and locking them in place.

A split instant before a weight slammed into the door.

Jesus Christ! the Spider's mind ejected as he backed away, his shuffling now a full-on scamper. That soldier had a rifle and more than enough firepower to convince him to get his ass topside. The door would keep her there long enough for him to rally his troops and return, and he was thinking of stuffing the whole place with combustibles and then tossing a match at it. Which was unquestionably the best way to deal with the soldier.

And where the hell did she come from anyway? his brain demanded as he hurried back to the steps, where he stopped and stared in the direction of the dungeon.

His gloves. His prized gloves. And his *spiders*. All locked away with the rest of the meat. That stabbed him through the peehole. He clenched a fist to his heart at the thought of losing his possessions. Especially the spiders. They were *precious*, and he'd taken great pains to keep his collection alive and warm during the colder weather. The gloves could be replaced but not his pets.

Shaking his head, the Spider climbed the stairs and returned to the commander's office above. The rumbling of fire slowed him to a stop upon the landing, while the smell of smoke worried him even more.

The hell was that?

The Spider stepped into the office, waving at gauzy coils and failing to clear the air. Figures littered the floor, his minions dead and gone, and he gave them no further thought. The windows and the sight outside caught his attention. An orange glow drew him across that spillage of bodies and soaked planks.

Fire.

Somehow, the blaze roaring overhead had escaped the building, perhaps in the form of embers riding the air currents, and pitched on the tents in the courtyard. The resulting conflagrations had quickly consumed the structures and would soon reduce them to scorch marks.

The Spider gazed at the ceiling, hearing the inferno chewing its way through the upper levels. He didn't hear anyone cry out, which drew him out of the office and to the main entrance.

The Spider went outside and looked up. He flinched at the sight.

Fort Jay was on fire.

Black intestinal coils of smoke spewed from broken windows while flames thrashed the interior, destroying the historic site. The snap and crackle of an uncontained blaze mesmerized the Spider as he drew in a full load of smoke. That got him choking, and he bent over and barked out a few good notes to clear the pipes, all the while looking around to see if anyone was still alive.

No one approached him. No one tried to shoot him, and he didn't see *any* of his pack screaming for help or calling out to survivors.

That straightened his back.

"No fucking *way*," he whispered in awe, an orange hue coloring the porcelain cheeks of his mask.

That bitch soldier didn't kill them. She couldn't have kill them. Not *all* of them.

Something let go within the upper reaches of the fort's main building. The Spider didn't know what it was, but the fire was clearly working its way to the foundation. A solemn lump of despair dropped into his gullet and he actually whined. His fort was gone. His crew was gone, and with them his dreams of having his own little kingdom in a very big and empty world.

That pissed him off.

A groan of timbers warned him away from the main entrance, whereupon he almost tripped up in the dead guards all gunned down by a fucking female *Rambo*. The Spider stomped a boot and glanced around, wondering if there might be others lurking atop the outer battlements. No, he'd be dead by now if there were. He composed himself and decided on a course of action.

The fort was gone and he had no idea what the protocol might be for a commander losing his command. He sure as shit wasn't going to hang around and get cooked with the thing, that was for certain.

Keys.

He charged inside, heading for the officer's room. Smoke filled the quarters, turning the place into a murderous haze. He stumbled twice over the limbs of the dead and almost fell flat. Pawing his way through that choking fog, he located the desk and pulled open the top right drawer. *Keys.*

He snatched them up and damn near shit himself when he heard an explosion from the direction of the dungeon. Thick smoke wafted from the open doorway, and the Spider's guts suddenly cramped and twisted, as if a pair of icy hands had grabbed hold with a message of *looky here*.

Keys clutched in his fist, the Spider decided this was the part of the movie where the villain escapes for the sequel.

18

Collie tried the door and couldn't open it, not that it surprised her. She recalled the two empty slots for bolts on the frame before she entered the basement jail... the sight of the prisoners stuffed into all those cells had distracted her. And now, the skidmark with the fancy spider mask had snuck up behind her and slammed the door shut.

Where the hell was your brain, Collie? She felt the bitter burn of knowing she should've done better.

The prisoners yelled and screamed for her to free them while two other things popped into her mind. The first one concerned the fire raging overhead, unleashed by her own hand, no less. The other thing was the very door before her, closed and barred shut from the other side. That thing was a slab of iron, and to make matters worse, the hinges were on the outside. The framework was concrete and stone.

We're fucked, her brain informed her.

"Can you open the door?" a little boy asked, his voice somehow the only one she picked up through the rest of the crowd.

"Sure I can," Collie lied.

"He'll be back with guards," someone else yelled at her. "So if you're gonna do something..."

Collie ignored that and concentrated on the door. The hinges couldn't be shot out. The ricochets would clip someone in the cell, and no doubt an eye. *All fun and games until someone loses an eye.*

"GET ME OFF THIS FUCKING TABLE!" screamed the woman strapped to the gurney. She thrashed against the leather bindings as if both her feet were being fed into an industrial woodchipper.

Collie realized it was time for super-spy shit. She didn't know if what she was considering would work, but since the fire would eventually bring the fort down on them all, she didn't like their chances. Not when she remembered all those sacks and barrels stored along the wall leading to the dungeon. Little spider fucker had to have hidden amongst all that shit somewhere.

"I'll get you out," Collie promised. "All of you."

On impulse, she grabbed the set of keys from the wall and tossed them onto the woman strapped to the gurney.

"Hurry the fuck up then, bitch!" one of the men yelled.

That froze her, and when she turned in the direction of the voice, the room got quiet real fast.

Fuckin' civvies, she thought.

"Get us out first!" someone chirped.

"We can help!" yelled another.

"Just let us *out*!"

Collie turned her back on them all and faced the door. Dealing with frightened civilians was the *worst*, but she wasn't going to let them out of their cages just yet.

Then she did what needed to be done.

She removed her vest, which took a few seconds, and dropped it onto the floor. Once the vest was off, Collie unbuttoned her jacket. Then her shirt. She pulled up the undershirt and nipped the hem under her chin, exposing her sports bra… and the plastic container wedged solidly in between her blue-gray breasts, right where Milo's point-on bullet had passed through.

The plastic container was a small one, but it fit damn near perfectly. She needed *something* there to fill the cavity in her ruined chest. And since it *was* a container, she'd filled it with a few last-ditch items.

She clawed at the thing and pulled it out in slippery jerks, ignoring the congealed slop around the top, and that drag against her ribs that didn't feel right at all. When she extracted enough of the container, she pulled off the top. Inside were a few surprises of the explosive kind, packed in tight with sweat socks. She pawed through a couple of grenades until she found what she was looking for.

A small stick of C-4, along with the tiniest detonators perhaps in existence.

Collie pulled out the C-4, dispensed with the plastic wrap, and separated the plastique into two portions. These she jammed into the door seams where she guessed the hinges to be. Once stuck, she stabbed a pin-sized detonator into each, and readied the remote no bigger than half-a-cracker. When that was all done, she scrambled everything back into the container and shoved it into her chest, all the while keeping her back to the people. Thirty seconds later, she had her coat buttoned and vest strapped back in place.

She glanced over at the gurney. The explosives were small, but powerful.

Two seconds later, she was undoing the straps holding down the woman. Seeing that she was being released, the lady changed her tone considerably.

"Oh, thank you," she blurted. *"Thank you.* God *Almighty,* thank you."

Once freed, the woman slid off the gurney and went for the cells. Collie took the gurney and rolled it towards the door. She flipped it and, with some effort, placed it upright against the door itself.

"There's going to be a bang," she warned everyone. "Stay in your cells until it goes off."

"You'll kill us!" a negative-thinking idiot screamed—the same one who had called her a bitch.

Collie didn't bother replying. She placed her back to the stone wall and thumbed in the code. A single button flared red, then green.

"Here we go," she warned everyone. "On the count of three."

She pushed the button on two.

19

The Spider ran for the far side of the courtyard, towards a cluster of parked vehicles. In particular, an old 2025 Ford Mustang. The Mustang was the Spider's ride.

He waved the key fob and the machine flared to life in a growl of red and white lights. The Spider reached the driver's side and almost ripped his fingernails off opening the door. He got in, fingers buzzing, and slammed the door shut.

Before him, the fort's main building might have been a full-scale effigy in remembrance of Guy Fawkes. He spared a second to marvel at the fire, then he buckled up. He might be many things, but when it came to personal safety he didn't fuck around.

The Spider hit the gas and the Mustang shot forward with all the force of a Cape Canaveral launch. He turned the wheel hard, thumped over a few meaty speed bumps, and almost clipped the still-burning firepit. He straightened the Mustang's path before stomping on the brakes and lurching forward, causing the seatbelt to pull tight across his chest.

The headlights lit up the fort's gates. Closed. Barred by a single timber.

"Piece of *shit*," the Spider squealed as he struggled to free himself of the car.

*

The dungeon door popped open as if kicked in by a giant. Hinges tinkled off concrete, while more smoke swamped the interior. Collie pushed the gurney out of the way.

"Get your people clear," she yelled at the woman she'd freed, and didn't wait for an answer. She had to get moving. There was one little shit that was trying to escape.

She peeked around the corner and charged the stairs. Collie ascended, very much aware that she wasn't clearing two steps at a time but rather one, and she was dangerously close to tripping. It wasn't a lack of energy, but more an issue of weight. And diminished strength.

Christ, she thought, *I've aged ten years.*

And at the worst possible time.

She reached the top landing and spun into the officer's room. Half a dozen corpses remained right where she'd killed them. All that carnage got her attention, but she was too much in a hurry to fathom why. She rushed past it all and eventually zeroed in on an open doorway leading to the courtyard. A familiar firepit burned beyond, surrounded by burning tents.

Past all that, across the courtyard and right in front of the fort's gates, was a car, its brake lights a bright red.

A shadow pulled open the gates, revealing the tunnel beyond.

"Oh no you don't," Collie vowed and sprinted for the doorway.

The figure rounded the car for the driver's side, and climbed in.

Clearing the burning building, Collie stopped and raised her rifle. She sighted the Mustang's rear window and fired. A spider hole popped in the surface of the glass, causing the entire sheet to tremble.

The driver stomped on the accelerator, propelling the car through the tunnel.

Collie continued to fire slugs into the machine's rear. The narrow confines of the tunnel scraped the side mirrors off the escaping car and sent them flying. Stone continued to claw at metal in a flurry of sparks as the car shot through that stone channel.

All the while Collie fired, hoping to splatter the driver's head across the dashboard.

The car cleared the tunnel and raced off into the night, the sound of the engine receding and the brake lights dipping out of sight.

Collie lowered her rifle. "You lucky bastard," she whispered.

The burning building reached her then, and she turned around and beheld that flaming structure.

The prisoners were still in there.

Collie raced back inside.

*

When the first bullet punched through his rear window, the Spider ducked in reflex. His headrest was reduced to shreds of black and white. He crushed the gas pedal a split second later and the tunnel became a launch tube. Sparks flared from the sides. The interior flickered with tracer fire and glass pebbles. The Spider peeked over the dashboard, trying to see through the only clear spot in his windshield. A follow-up bullet twisted the passenger-side headrest off its metal post, while two more shots destroyed the cushion completely. More bullets smashed through the front windshield, creating black suns and keeping the Spider low. The Mustang blasted free of the tunnel, but the shooter continued firing at its escaping ass, each round scaring the living shit out of the driver. The headlights flashed over tall grass and a paved road, and the Spider remembered the straight run to the forest. By then, the bullet storm had ceased, and he lifted his head to check his rearview mirror—which was no longer there. The crumpled remains of the mirror laid on the passenger seat in a pool of glass pebbles.

The side mirrors no longer existed, having been shorn off the car in his escape through the stone tunnel.

The Spider hunkered down over the steering wheel, to better see the road through the wreckage of his windshield. He was alive, but he feared he would need a new car. That pissed him off. He loved this rig. His hands tightened on the wheel, realizing the fort—*his* fort—had just fallen. His followers dead and gone, and with it all, his plans for his own little private kingdom effectively kicked into the shitter.

And him racing off into the night.

The Spider knew the road, however. The highways were familiar to him, and his car, damaged as it might be, seemed to be running fine. The fuel gauge indicated he had a full tank. Plenty to get his ass to Winnipeg. Winnipeg it had to be, as much as he loathed to go there and once again become a pretender to the cause. He had to. He would need the Bear Trap and his minions to take back the fort. Or what was left of it.

And then find and punish that bitch responsible for it all.

20

The roar of an approaching vehicle pulled Gus from his sleep.

"Someone's coming," Milo said from underneath his sleeping bag.

Gus didn't bother responding. He tossed off his covers, stood, and stretched, feeling a chill through his layers. He frowned and rubbed an eye, realizing he'd passed out on the lawn chair and then realizing he *could* have been sleeping in the limo with the door locked.

Dummy, he scolded himself.

The car drew closer.

"What time is it?" Milo asked.

"No idea," Gus said, listening to the vehicle. Whoever it was, was in a hurry.

"You could check the clock in the limo."

"Yeah, I could," Gus said, but ignored the suggestion. He wandered past Milo's scowl of puzzlement and headed for the driveway.

The car was getting closer, and it wasn't slowing down.

"That's not Collie," Milo said.

Gus realized he was right. That wasn't Collie. Feeling a stab of fear, Gus went back to his limo and quickly located his military shotgun. He picked up the weapon and held it at the ready. It wasn't the old Benelli he had while living on the fringes of Annapolis. This one resembled an ass kicker of an assault rifle, except it was shorter and meaner looking. The logo *Ram Fist* and the faded picture of one pissed-off looking goat covered the shoulder butt.

Collie informed him it was a bullpup-style military shotgun, much favored by the army. She went on about the specs of the weapon and comparisons to others in its class, but Gus didn't remember any of that shit. What he did remember was her taking him down to Whitecap's firing range to familiarize himself with the weapon, and how the thing absolutely *destroyed* wooden targets. There were ten shots to a banana magazine, and Gus carried three comfortably. The bullpup even had a twenty-five-round drum, but he found that weight awkward with his missing fingers, and so stuck with the magazines.

Cradling the shotgun, Gus hurried to the corner of the house and sighted the road.

The car continued to speed towards them.

"Gus," Milo called out.

He didn't answer. The car was coming, getting louder in the country quiet of the night.

"Gus!" Milo repeated, and Gus ignored him again as he stuck to the shadows of the house.

Upon the road, a glaring white set of LED headlights rapidly approached. The car veered to the left and right, as if the driver had downed a case of beer and decided to test the handling. That or the road was really shitty. In any case, Gus confirmed what he and Milo both already knew.

It wasn't Collie.

Which asked the question… who was driving that machine?

And were they friendly?

A shape became visible behind those bright headlights, then it was racing past the house, a sports car of some kind.

Ford Mustang, Gus thought, and, for a second, he believed he saw a *ghost* behind the wheel. A white-faced ghost. It certainly wasn't Collie. Which got him thinking about where she could be. A knob of ice formed in his core, and he hurried back to Milo.

"Who was it?" the soldier asked.

"Damn if I know," Gus replied. "But it wasn't Collie. Some fuck in a white mask was driving."

"A white mask?"

"Yeah, anyone you know?"

Milo shook his head. Gus went to the man's chair and pulled a knife from a sheath. "Watch your hands. I'm cutting you loose. We're heading for the fort."

"Forget the fort," Milo said as Gus sawed through the tape binding one hand. "We go after that car."

Gus drew back.

"You saw a mask?" Milo pressed. "A white one? Chances are that's one of the Leather. And if it *is*, chances are he's running. I don't think they travel much at night. And the speed he was going? He wanted to get clear of here in a hurry. I'm thinking he was running from Collie. And if he's running, the question becomes where? Winnipeg is a Leather town. I bet that bastard is driving back to his buddies looking for reinforcements."

The explanation left Gus staring. "And Collie?"

"She's probably still kicking around somewhere. Now listen…"

Gus did. The noise of the escaping car was diminishing and nothing replaced it.

"Hear that?" Milo asked.

"I don't hear anything."

"Exactly. One car. One shit-house rat fleeing the scene. To get back to his shit-house rat buddies. To let them know the exterminator's in town."

Milo held out his hand. Gus stared at it for a split second before handing over the blade.

"We gotta get back to the fort," Gus said, gripping his shotgun. "See what happened to Collie."

"We do that and that fucker is gone," Milo said, slashing his other hand free and then going for his ankles. "You got the keys. We go after that runner."

Gus looked in the direction of the escaping Mustang. "He's long gone."

"We can catch him. We catch him and if he's Leather we kill him. We *don't* let him reach his buddies. That could be another small army. We nail that driver and maintain our element of surprise. Don't worry about Collie. Worry about the chicken fucker with the head start."

Milo abruptly stood and faced Gus, who angled the shotgun in his direction. The soldier didn't flinch.

"That's my thinking, anyway," Milo said. "But it's your call. You're the guy with the gun."

Gus hesitated, knowing full well the soldier hadn't tried to rush him or use the knife.

As if sensing that very thought, Milo held out the blade handle first. "What do you say?" he asked.

As much as he didn't care to admit it, Gus didn't think the man was lying. He snatched the knife from Milo and stepped back, waiting for him to try something while considering the best course of action.

"Goddammit," he swore and backed up to the limo. "All right. You drive."

They were on the road thirty seconds later, gunning for the Mustang.

The night was clear and bright, so Milo kept the limo's headlights off and his boot on the accelerator. Darkened forest streaked by on either side. The surge of the engine, the steady increase in speed, and the empty highway caused Gus's anxiety to spike.

"You got the headlights off," he said from the passenger seat, the bullpup aimed at Milo's chest.

"Yeah," the soldier said.

"You gonna keep them off?"

"Yeah."

"You think that's wise?"

Milo glanced at the intimidating shotgun, then at Gus, before concentrating on the road ahead. "Don't want him to know we're after him. If he doesn't see our headlights, there's a chance he might slow down."

"What if we hit a moose?"

"Tough shit for the moose."

Suppose so, Gus figured, and divided his attention between the road and the driver. A sign that might've said "59" whisked by, but Gus wasn't entirely sure if that was the highway number or not. Over the glowing instrument panel of the dashboard, the road was only a two-lane affair, with a dark and fibrous screen of vegetation lining the shoulders.

"Don't worry about her," Milo said, absorbed in the driving. "She's fine. This is the smart play. And if we're wrong, if it's someone else who's driving, we'll turn around and head right back."

"Goddamn right we will."

"Hey, you're in charge here."

"That's right. I am."

But Gus didn't feel that way. He felt gut-punched, ball-tugged, and left sprawled out on a mat, waiting for the boot-fucking to begin. The only thing he wondered was if Milo would be the one doing the boot-fucking.

"I'm in charge," Gus repeated, but he sure as hell didn't want to be. Being in charge required critical thinking, and he knew firsthand he wasn't one for critical thinking. He was more than willing to hand that off to Collie and had gladly done so. This was her element. Not his. His was simply getting by on whatever he had in the tank and a shitload of fumes.

Thinking of Collie sank his spirits even more, until he forced himself to focus on the present. She wouldn't want him to worry about her. She would remind him that he got by just fine on his own before meeting up with her. But damn if it wasn't easy letting her do the thinking—especially when she *knew* what to do, the *right* thing to do. She'd been trained for and had experience in all manner of shitstorms, and Gus had confidence in her. That was the short and simple of it. He didn't have that confidence in himself anymore.

Then another thought hit him. "You know how to operate this thing?"

Milo frowned. "What do you mean?"

"The gadgets. The super-spy stuff."

"That requires codes. I wasn't briefed on those."

"No, you weren't," Gus said. "So how the hell are we supposed to stop the guy if we catch up to him?"

Something darted across the highway. The limo whumped over a solid mass, the impact hard enough to lift both men from their seats.

A second later, the smell caught up with them.

"Skunk," Gus said, making a face.

"Yeah." Milo nodded, taking a firmer grip on the wheel. "We're blacked out and we don't make much noise."

"Oh shit," Gus winced, getting a whiff of the dead animal. "Oh that's bad."

"Recirculate the air in here. Draw it out."

Gus studied the glowing interfaces and spotted the universal symbol for the control.

"Don't think it's doing anything," he said after a few seconds.

Milo checked the dashboard and took a deep breath.

"Hitting a moose doesn't seem so bad right about now," Gus added.

"Get used to it. 'Cause if I can, that's how we'll stop the bad guy when we catch up to him."

"Hit him? You mean *ram* him? With the limo?"

Milo nodded. "The Mustang will take the worst of it. We got greater mass."

Gus checked the glove compartment and that of the nearby armrest. "Must be an owner's manual in here somewhere. Something so we don't have to ram the guy. I don't like the sound of that at all. What if you fuck up the limo? How do we get back?"

"We'll figure out something."

Gus released his breath in a whistle. The stubborn lingering reminder of running over a skunk's shitbag was distracting him. They were buzzing along the highway, and only the moon was providing light. It was a straight run, apparently, and that would help them but also the driver of the Mustang.

He glanced at Milo. "What's the power like?"

"Fifteen percent."

That mortified Gus. "That can't be right." But he saw the number. "Holy shit."

"We drove hard yesterday and she didn't get a full charge in," Milo said. "The tires might give us back something. Otherwise, that's it."

"But there was sunlight."

"We parked behind the house. In the shade. Whoops."

Gus rubbed at his suddenly aching right temple. "And how far to Winnipeg?"

"At this speed? I dunno. Maybe less than an hour."

"Christ almighty."

"Hey," Milo smiled grimly. "Maybe we can coast for a klick if we have to."

Gus scowled at him. "Har-dee-fuckin' har. Just… drive."

They lapsed into silence then, focusing on the nighttime road and eyeing the wilderness for animals.

The dead skunk stink faded but didn't completely go away.

21

At roughly 5:45 in the morning, the road turned for the first time since the limo got on Highway 59. Gus and Milo raced over a small bridge where the waters shone under the clear night sky and sped past a couple of long-deserted recharging stations. Towering powerline structures rose above the land like old Japanese castles that had been gnawed down to the bone. The highway eventually split into divided lanes, and a speed limit sign with a "2" spray-painted over the "1" zipped by.

Tall, forbidding-looking columns that resembled oversized shotgun shells came into view.

"What are those?" Gus asked, pointing.

"Grain silos," Milo replied.

Gus eyed them until they drifted out of sight. "How we doing?"

"Nine percent."

Gus rubbed one side of his face. He was getting a very bad feeling about this highway gamble. "It's going down fast."

"We're driving fast," Milo said. "Hey, look ahead."

A kilometer or more out, glimpsed just before disappearing, was a set of red taillights.

"That him?" Gus asked, his morale suddenly lifting.

"That's our boy."

"Where'd he go?"

Milo increased speed and the limo gradually eased into a curve. A few seconds later, the distant taillights became visible again.

"Forest along here," Milo pointed out. "But we've caught up to him. He's not driving as fast as I'd thought, but there he is."

"Will he see us?"

"Possible, but I doubt it. Unless he's got super night vision."

"He'll see us sooner or later."

Milo pointed at the clock. "Sky starts to lighten around six-thirty. He'll spot us eventually. Especially on this road."

The highway remained a two-way expressway. The forest appeared as an impassable thicket, and Gus found himself looking one way and then the other. The woods soon fell away, and the limo eventually sailed under an overpass. Ahead, the taillights were visible, like a glowing lure trawling a vast dead sea.

Gus glanced over at the power indicator.

Seven percent, the number flashed in red.

He released his breath in a whistle. There was a long dawdling curve then, one that pressed Gus into his armrest. The divided highway merged into one, and traffic lights became more frequent. An orange filament of light crept along the horizon. The taillights of the Mustang became a set of evil eyes, growing larger by the second.

"You're getting close," Gus noted.

"We want to ram him, remember?" Milo said. "Can't do that from back there."

"Yeah, but... you're getting close."

"We don't have much time before there's enough light to see us."

Dead powerlines drooped in between skeleton towers of steel. More houses came into view. Some were huge sprawling pieces of properties no doubt belonging to farmers, while others were smaller and hiding behind screens of tall grass and trees. Two overpasses streaked by. Fences eventually appeared, still intact after all this time. Roofs materialized behind the fences, while more derelict cars cluttered the sides of the road or were stopped dead in the highway.

"Dammit," Milo said and reduced speed. "Gotta slow down. Shit's getting thicker on the highway the closer we get to the city."

The city.

A warning light flashed in Gus's mind, and he tried to understand what it was about the city that bothered him. Damn if he could recall what it was.

Shopping plazas coasted into sight, along with parking lots littered with cars. School and regular transit buses were stopped in the middle of grassy fields. Signs of various businesses popped up and went by, the posts disappearing in high grass. All the while, those red taillights slid in and out of view as the driver navigated the unmoving traffic.

"He's slowing down, too," Gus said excitedly.

"Yeah," Milo agreed. "One problem with that."

"We're not close enough?"

"We're not close enough. And we're running out of juice. *And*… we're driving one big ass bitch into a very cluttered highway. Hard to weave in and out of lanes."

"Like an asteroid field."

"Yeah, like an asteroid field."

That turned Gus's attention to Milo's driving. The soldier was concentrating on getting closer to their quarry while safely navigating the growing number of abandoned vehicles on the road. All under the fading night sky.

Gus pressed himself back into his seat and, as if it might make a difference, angled his shotgun away from the soldier.

A long, corrugated wall became visible on the side, displaying signage for *Hot Tubs! Pools! Baths!* That was replaced by more commercial sights. Shopping plazas. Factories.

A long train became visible, perhaps a hundred meters away on Milo's side. More fences ran parallel to the highway, sheltering rows of houses just beyond. A series of intersections clogged with unmoving traffic, followed by five- and six-story apartment complexes.

And not a soul in sight.

Not that Gus expected to see any. He would've been surprised if he did.

The Mustang kept right on rolling, perhaps only a hundred meters ahead of the limo.

Gus looked over at the power indicator.

"Five percent," Milo reported stoically.

"What happens if we get to zero?"

"Curious about that myself."

"Not fucking funny."

"Well, Gus, I don't know what to tell you. I've never driven a rig like this before. I'm guessing we'll stop dead in our tracks."

A church came into view on the right, and Gus took comfort in the timing of its appearance, but not too much.

"Six-ten," Milo reported, nodding at the clock.

The sky was that much lighter, becoming that familiar spun gold. More tall structures rose against the horizon, a huddle of rectangular blocks of varying sizes, marking what Gus suspected was the downtown area. They maneuvered through a thickening maze of derelict vehicles, threading their way toward the city's hub. Then the first rays of light broke the horizon, shooting across the asphalt and driving the last of the shadows from street level.

"That's it," Milo, said, fixated upon the car in the distance. "He'll see us any second, if he hasn't already."

"Then what?"

"He'll either run or he'll fight. I'm hoping he'll fight, but my luck's been kinda shitty lately."

"You hooked up with us, didn't you?"

Milo nodded that he did indeed.

"Then there you go."

Ahead, the Mustang turned right and sped along a westerly road, gunning for the downtown area.

"He's seen us," Milo said, still mindful of the dead traffic.

The red taillights winked in and out of sight as the Mustang passed numerous roadblocks and eventually disappeared entirely.

"Shit," Gus muttered, before Milo swung the limo hard to the right, getting around a transit bus displaying an ad for *Skittles*. He straightened his course and stayed on the pavement before driving up onto the wide sidewalk.

"What the hell, right?" Milo said, knocking aside a trashcan. "No one's walking their dog this morning."

He cut across one corner, shot between a pair of unmoving SUVs, and turned hard to get back in line.

Gus looked over at the power gauge and felt his balls draw up in fear.

One percent.

Jesus Christ, his mind shrieked. *The fuck happened to four-three-and two?* It only seemed a few seconds ago they were on *five*. They weren't moving that fast anymore.

Just then, the power indicator reached zero and the limo's engine stopped.

The end wasn't totally unexpected for Gus.

Milo pumped the accelerator and did a frantic check of the dashboard, but the limo had just used its last drop of juice. The monster drifted to a stop, dead center of the double yellow line.

The Mustang's taillights still flickered in the distance, but it had increased its lead to perhaps two hundred meters ahead, straight for downtown.

"Well, shit," Gus huffed in annoyance.

Milo gripped the steering wheel and checked his side mirrors.

"So what do we do now?" Gus asked.

"What are you asking me for? You're in charge."

"Well, what do you think we should do?"

"He's gone," Milo said, indicating the distant Mustang. "Long gone. We got maybe fifteen minutes before we can get a recharge going. Then a little longer until we got enough power to move."

"So… what are you saying?"

"I'm saying we're stuck here and he's gone. We lost him. He'll join up with the rest of his twisted nut buddies and… they'll probably wonder why he was in a hurry to begin with. Which *might* mean a group will be going back to the fort."

"Coming this way, you mean?"

"Exactly that. And we better be gone by then…"

Gus stared at the taillights, which were still in sight. "Well god*damn* it."

"We blew it," Milo said. "We best get back to the house when we can. Wait for Collie to get back. I wouldn't doubt she's there now, wondering where we are."

That probably was the case. Gus studied the dashboard, realizing they were inside a powerless tank and forced to wait. *Shit*, he mentally swore and stared at the Mustang's taillights, still in the distance. Any second and he would be gone. They'd been close. Maybe even real close.

It was right at that moment he realized the Mustang hadn't gone any farther.

"Milo," a squinting Gus said and pointed. "That car moving?"

The soldier studied the distant vehicle. "Y'know… doesn't look like it."

"I don't think that guy's moving."

"I think you're right."

No sooner did the words leave the soldier than the Mustang's taillights winked out.

22

"Holy shit," Gus exclaimed, shaking his finger at the car. "He just switched the car *off*."

Milo stared at the vehicle.

"He's not moving!" Gus blurted and looked at the soldier. "The fucker's not moving."

Milo frowned, unable to grasp why that might be.

"All right," Gus said. "Come on."

"What do you mean?" Milo asked.

"Get out. We're going after him."

"*We?*"

"You're not staying here," Gus said and grabbed the key fob. "Get out."

He kicked open his own door and a blast of cold air swamped the interior.

"Now!" Gus ordered, gesturing with his intimidating shotgun.

Not one to argue with a semi-automatic bullpup pointed at him, Milo raised his hands and got out. Gus did the same on the other side and they closed their doors at the same time. Gus pressed the key fob, and the limo battened down its hatches with an audible chirp.

Standing outside the impressive machine, Gus wavered with a moment's indecision, knowing his armored ride loaded with valuable supplies was stopped dead in the middle of the street. He met Milo's eyes a second before going for the nearby door leading to the business class section.

The door was locked.

"Goddammit," Gus blurted and fumbled with the key fob. "You stay right where you are, shithead."

"The hell am I gonna do?"

"Stop talking to me," Gus said, which Milo only half-heard as Gus lunged into the limo. He scrounged through the interior, locating the bat and extra magazines for the shotgun. His Glock was already on him, but the body armor… Gus sighted one of two remaining vests and suffered another moment's indecision.

The Captain smiled at him, but it was glossy and facile.

"You got any advice," Gus said, "now's the time to start talking."

No reply.

Figures, he thought, and he left the vest. No time to muck around with that. And the bat—he only had two hands, and they were both needed for the shotgun. The two extra magazines were strapped to some tactical webbing, which he grabbed. He also popped open a box of spare twelve-gauge shotgun shells and proceeded to stuff his pockets. He withdrew from the car and closed the door, careful not to slam it. Under brightening skies, the Mustang remained as dead as the rest of the city.

Milo remained standing on the driver's side, which surprised Gus a little.

"What's that look for?" the soldier asked. "You thought I'd run for it?"

Gus ignored the question and tossed the webbing at him.

Milo caught it. "What am I supposed to do with this?"

Gus locked up the limo. "Carry it."

"Where's *my* gun?"

"No gun for you."

"Jesus Christ, Gus."

"Shut up and get moving. You on ahead."

He waved the shotgun and Milo backed off a step.

"Double time," Gus said, and they started jogging, cutting down the distance to the Mustang. They hoofed it, darting in and around the vehicles between them and their quarry. The streets were wide, much wider that the ones in Annapolis, and the usual decaying litter jammed into corners and crevices had long since been reduced to ruins. Shop fronts flanked the road, built on large lots that allowed plenty of space around them.

Gus focused on the Mustang and Milo's back.

A hundred meters.

Seventy-five.

His foot started acting up, and Gus slowed to a stop. Milo, in considerably better shape, braked and looked back. Both his hands went wide in a gesture of *what?*

Gus shook the shotgun at him, urging him to continue on.

Not impressed, Milo hurried off towards the stopped car. Gus shuffled along at his best speed, swearing to Christ above that the oil patch reject better not decide to make a break for it. That would piss him off to no end.

Milo reached the driver's side of the Mustang. Gus increased his speed, limping down the last few dozen meters as Milo pulled open the door.

The soldier didn't seem impressed.

Now what? Gus moaned inwardly, hefting the menacing ten-round ass-shredder he carried.

Milo stepped back from the car. "Gone," he said.

"Gone?" Gus slowed to a stop and looked past the man, scanning the streets for a fugitive.

Like an untended garden that gradually developed into an urban jungle, the buildings grew closer together, forming a solid hedge of concrete, steel, and wire mesh that ran deep into the municipal mire known as Winnipeg. And as the sky continued to brighten, not a soul could be seen among the cars and trucks left upon the pavement. Nothing moved.

A knot of fear welled up within Gus.

"I know where he went," an unimpressed Milo stated.

"Yeah?"

"Yeah."

"Well don't make me fuckin' ask again," Gus snapped.

"Leather headquarters. That way." Milo nodded in the direction. "The Royal Bentley."

Gus remembered the guy Collie killed on the highway. *The Royal Bentley downtown. Five-star hotel.*

He reached the car and glanced inside, verifying for himself that their man had fled on foot.

"Don't believe me?" the soldier asked.

"Fuck off, Milo."

Thing was, he'd *hoped* the guy had lied. Would've been easier if the driver was still aboard, but he wasn't.

"Well, *shit*," Gus swore and slammed the door.

*

The door slam stopped the Spider in his tracks. He turned around, eyes narrowed behind his mask, and stared at the vehicular knots jamming the road and sidewalks. Nothing moved. The Spider tensed, straining to hear, gripping a battle axe with both hands.

Then he heard angry voices, barking at each other.

Someone was close, perhaps following him.

The Spider ran.

*

"The hell you do *that* for?" Milo grated.

Heat rose to Gus's cheeks. "Because I…" and he trailed off, unable to excuse his own momentary lapse of fucking up.

"Why don't you start screaming?" Milo asked. "Wake up the whole fucking neighborhood."

"I'm sorry, all right?"

"You're fucking sorry, all right. You just blew our stealth mode. There's no way he didn't hear that."

"I said I'm sorry!" Gus flared.

Milo ignored the apology and stared in the direction of downtown.

Gus shook the shotgun as if it were a witchdoctor's totem and stomped off a ways. He stopped, turned, and also gazed downtown.

"Goddamn civvies," Milo released under his breath.

The two men glared at each other.

"So what do we do?" Gus finally asked.

"We go after him," the soldier eventually answered.

"You still want to?"

"We're fucking here now, and the limo ain't going anywhere soon."

"He's got a head start."

"And he knows we're after him."

Gus sighed. "I'm sorry about the car door."

"I shouted. We both fucked up."

"I'm an idiot."

Milo shook his head. "Yeah, well, I've had to work with psychos before and you're a step up from that. And you haven't shot me yet, so that's a good thing."

Gus still felt like shit, despite the piss-warm compliment. "Come on, then," he said and started marching past the Mustang, shotgun at the ready.

Milo kept pace with him. "Watch the alleys," he advised. "Plenty of places to hide, but I think he's making a bee-line for downtown, which makes sense since most of the big hotel chains are there. Can't you move any faster?"

"No."

"How about giving me a gun?"

"Fuck that."

"Then we gotta double time it here," Milo said and quickened his step, his boots loud on the street. He eventually got ahead of Gus—who struggled to keep up. The city remained quiet, and if the Mustang's driver had heard them, he was doing an outstanding job staying low and out of sight. There were more than enough places for a person to duck and hide, especially if that person knew someone was after him. Next time Gus felt like slamming a car door just because he was angry, he would make sure to stick a finger inside first.

So they marched, double time, deeper into the city. Milo kept checking on him every now and again. The soldier was on point, moving some ten paces ahead and not straying any farther. The shotgun probably had something to do with that, but in reality, Gus wondered how easy it would be for the guy to try something in this dead parade. They hurried past a street sign that said *Nairn Avenue*. The street abruptly transformed into a residential area made up of squat, single-story houses with wire fences. Bare bushes and hedges pushed against the fences, and leaves covered the ground. The windows were opaque and forlorn, and, here and there, eavesdrops hung off roofs at a slant as if squirrels used them for playground slides.

A pink and white sign designating the *Paramount Hotel* was on the left with its main doors wide open. The hotel very much needed a paint job.

Gus winced, enduring that incessant buzzing in his fucked-up foot. The pavement made the aching worse.

Dropping back a bit, Milo sized him up. "Foot bothering you?"

"Yeah."

The soldier slowed down. That was a blessing right there, but Gus still felt like he was holding the bastard back, so he made an effort to pick up the pace.

"Nothing," Milo said, looking ahead. "No sight of him anywhere."

"Where are we?" Gus asked.

"The Red River is just over there," Milo swept his finger from northwest to south. "And that's also the downtown core. There's a couple of bridges heading over the river but…"

They continued on, until the road ahead split at a set of unlit traffic lights. Two lanes went to the right, into another section of town. To the left was a truss bridge. Steel girders rose up and over an empty two-lane crossing. To the left of that were a couple of broad, easy sloping embankments, where vehicles were shoved, bumper to bumper, onto an improvised parking lot.

The impressive width of the mighty Red River could be glimpsed just beyond that.

Milo stopped and inspected the bridge.

Gus stopped beside him. "What?" he asked.

"Bridge," Milo said.

"So it is. And a long one."

"Yeah. A long one."

Gus took a good gander at the thing, then at the cars. "The fuck's up with all the cars?"

"Someone wanted the bridge cleared," Milo replied. "And someone cleared it."

"The Leather."

"Yeah."

"Why? Easier to drive along?"

Milo nodded. "You got it. And I bet our driver has already gone across this thing."

Gus stared at the other side while the rising sun lit up the river's slow-moving waters.

"Well, let's go," Gus said.

Milo didn't move.

"Now what?"

"I don't like it," the soldier replied. "I think he's too far gone."

"How long we've been marching?"

"About an hour. Give or take ten minutes."

Gus didn't bother answering, and in the resulting silence he couldn't hear a damn thing. The city was ominous that way, as if very much aware the living walked across its asphalt back and was none too pleased about it.

"How about we cross this thing quick," Gus suggested, gesturing at the bridge. "See if he's any closer. And if not, we go back."

Milo stared across the river. "That's Leather territory over there. This is getting dangerous, now."

"I say we go."

The soldier cocked an eye at him. "You ordering me?"

Gus exhaled. "No, fuck no. I'm voting here. And yours counts as two, okay? To make up for slamming the door back there."

Milo sized up the bridge again. "All right," he let out. "Let's go."

*

Not fifty meters on the other side of the bridge, the Spider, breathing heavily, reached the front door of an office building nearly three stories high. It resembled a border crossing checkpoint, except much bulkier, built on a raised foundation, and part of a much larger structure that might've been a warehouse for building supplies. The entire place was painted beige, and, like most, in need of a touch-up that would never happen. Several of its windows, all intact, faced the bridge.

Chest heaving, the Spider hurried to the smaller section that resembled a guard house. He scrambled up a set of concrete steps, reached the front door, and knocked.

The door opened and a leather-bound guard lurked within, wearing a muzzle resembling a cartoonish set of curved teeth. The Leather's raccoon-shaded eyes narrowed in question, and he rolled his shoulders studded with two-inch nails.

"I'm being followed," the Spider said.

23

Gus and Milo hurried across the bridge, towards a row of city-planted trees grown tall and thick and facing the broadside of the river. A few buildings towered over the trees, and they were close enough for crossbows *if* the Leather guarded the bridge.

Which brought up a question in Gus's mind.

"So why don't they have guns?" he asked Milo, who was a few paces ahead, glancing about like a deer that had sucked down a bucket of reheated cappuccino.

"They have guns," he answered. "Just don't have any ammunition. That's why Whitecap would've been a jackpot for them. Still is, really. But I think they like the quiet gear, too. Gotten used to it. Bows. Arrows. Spears. That sorta shit. It's fucked up."

"Real fucked up."

"You have a bat. That's fucked up."

"That was for zombies."

"Never used that on a real person?"

Gus didn't answer. His foot continued to bother him, feeling like a prickly sponge jammed into his boot. Reaching the midway point of the bridge caused him to curse at the unfair width of the river.

"How wide's this thing?" he blurted.

"This? I dunno. Hundred meters. Hundred and ten."

"Goddammit."

"Problem?"

"Just my foot."

"You can still walk," Milo said.

"Yeah, I can."

"Then push through it."

"That's what I'm doing."

"Then do it *harder*."

"Fuck off, Milo."

They reached the other side, where the road sloped downward, into the shadow of an elevated railroad trestle, high enough to allow regular traffic to pass underneath. They walked underneath, deeming it safe. A scrapyard could be seen after that, on the right, filled with stacked lumber and a couple of white trucks. A building partially hidden behind a small copse of trees and bushes was beyond the scrapyard, standing right on the shoulder of the road and facing the river.

Milo stopped as if he'd just stepped on a landmine.

Gus stopped behind him. "What?"

The soldier slipped behind the nearby trees and Gus hobbled after him. Standing behind a couple of bare maples, Milo peeked out and watched that building.

"See that place?" he asked.

Gus saw. A two-story structure on top of a high concrete foundation, sticking off from a larger warehouse. A set of steps ran up the side to a gray door. The high foundation got his attention as it made the building almost three stories tall. He wondered who the hell would have designed such a place, but then realized the place was next to a river, one that might have a flooding problem in the spring.

"What about it?" he asked back.

"See the first-floor front window? Facing the river?"

"Yeah, so?"

"Someone's standing behind that window."

That got Gus's attention, so he moved around Milo to a better position amongst the trees and bushes. Once hidden, he focused on the window facing the river. The soldier was right. To the right of the stairway and door was the nearest corner of the building, and the east side which faced them. There was a window there, the large rectangular picture kind, and a figure stood behind it. Perhaps thinking he was back far enough from the glass to avoid detection.

Not that it mattered.

The front door opened and a half-dozen Leather scurried down the stairs. Three of them carried compound bows, while the others brandished aluminum bats and knives. The archers spread out across the pavement.

The others charged Gus and Milo.

"Jesus," Gus swore, just as an archer released an arrow.

The missile shot past the tree trunk, hissing as its broadhead split the very air. Gus ducked and pulled back. Milo pressed himself to the tree's base.

"Give me the gun," Milo held out a hand.

"Like fuck," Gus said and got clear of the bushes. He brought up the Ram Fist combat shotgun, jamming the butt firm against his right shoulder

The Leather-bound crazy he had lined up raised a bat.

Gus blew the guy back fifteen feet, the spent casing flying from the side of the shotgun, the blast sounding like a Norseman's twenty-pound war hammer whacking a leather punching bag next to a microphone. The dead man landed flat on his back, in a spray of his own blood, skidding another five feet or so before coming to a stop. Which was practically in front of the archers.

Though there was very little recoil, the blast and startling power of the weapon upon a *real* target rattled Gus for all of two seconds.

"Jesus *Christ*," he said.

The wooden targets at Whitecap's firing range simply blew apart in splinters. He'd thought at the time it was cheap-ass plywood, and remembering how Collie giggled at the assessment. Now, however... he understood. *Someone* had figured out how to put all the power of a speeding transport truck into a shotgun.

The two other Leather charging them had lurched to a complete stop upon seeing the effects of the powerful firearm.

One dove for the bushes. Milo went after him.

The other one bolted across the pavement, unlocking Gus's momentary shock.

"The fuck you goin'?" Gus asked and fired, winging the escaping man— but *winging* him with the bullpup called *Ram Fist* was something of an understatement. The shot didn't just hit the Leather—it *launched* him— off his feet and into a bloody skid that would leave one wicked case of road rash.

Arrows buzzed by Gus's face then, one close enough that it felt like a violent sneeze.

He'd been shot at by arrows before, remembering the villainous Donald back in Mortimer's mansion of horrors. Gus didn't like the memory, but he realized something—once gone, the archers had to reach for more arrows.

So he charged them, steaming forward from the trees and underbrush, running at best speed while his foot felt like it was being dissolved in acid. He fired at a Leather wearing a hockey mask. *Missed*, but the Leather he shot at flinched and dropped his arrow, while his two buddies visibly balked.

Ram Fist!

Fuck if Gus wasn't starting to like the name more and more.

His follow-up shell nailed the hockey mask Leather dead center with spectacular, if not horrifying, results. The impact didn't just heave the figure back, it slammed him against the building's foundation as if he were nailed by a rocket, spattering him in a water-balloon burst of color.

The surviving archers nocked their arrows.

Gus locked onto one target.

Ram Fist!

A shoulder disintegrated in an explosion of rawhide-covered meat, crumpling the man, and if he wasn't dead already, he'd be wiping his ass with his left hand forever more.

Ram Fist!

A hip blew apart in a grisly, fire-hydrant spray of organic matter, upending the guy face-first into the ground, where he stayed in a shiver of shocked nerves.

Ram Fist!

Boots rattling off pavement alerted Gus to see another Leather with a set of butcher knives rushing him. Not needing to pump the shotgun, Gus fired, pitching the figure backwards and bouncing him off a thick maple. A tangle of bushes swallowed everything except the boots.

Gus whirled again.

The two leather archers he shot weren't entirely dead, but whining and writhing on the road. One of them, the one with the destroyed hip, was attempting to pull a knife. Gus killed them both with follow-up shots, horrified and amazed by the killing force of the weapon, and kept clear of the messy results.

There was no hesitation, and certainly no remorse. Not from him.

The rattling of more casings brought Gus back, and he searched for other targets.

Milo emerged from the bushes holding a bloody metal bat and not looking happy in the least. The soldier stopped and stared at the mess upon the road before finally regarding the lone gunman.

"Got a bat, huh?" Gus asked.

Milo scowled and nodded.

"Keep it then."

"You okay?" he asked Gus.

Gus took his time answering. "Yeah. Nothing like shooting up a bunch of crazy folk to clear the sinuses."

"The wrong way to start the morning," Milo muttered and regarded the little guardhouse with the open door, where the Leather had stormed from.

"That guy still in the window?" Gus asked.

"Nope."

"Wanna go find him?"

"You sure you're all right?"

"Quit asking me that. I'm fine. Titties on Christ. You a priest or therapist or something?"

Milo didn't answer. Hefting his bat, he started for the front door.

Behind him, Gus released the magazine from the Ram Fist. He fumbled it a little before stuffing the thing away in his coat pocket.

"Hey," he said to Milo, "where's that tactical webbing with the extra ammo?"

"Back there." The soldier pointed at the tree where they first took cover.

Not pleased, Gus went back and snatched up the webbing, cursing at the handful he carried. He hurried to rejoin Milo at the front door. Bat in hand, the soldier peeked inside.

An overturned desk dominated a porch area, along with the lingering stink of unwashed skin. Beyond the desk was an open doorway leading into a hall quite dark despite the early morning. Screwing up his face at the smell, Gus reloaded the shotgun and had no clue what to do with the webbing. He placed the weapon against the wall and quickly attempted to put on the straps. He tangled and untangled one arm before he got it right and snapped the two buckles in place.

"Not bad," Milo said, not meaning it. "Got it the first time."

"Fuck off."

"We're back to that, again?"

"We never left." Gus snatched up the weapon. "I'm ready."

"You spent time training with that thing, I see."

"A few hours. Enough to get the basics. Lead on."

Milo went inside, to the open doorway, and peered into the dark hall.

Gus joined him. "Don't get any ideas with that," he warned, indicating the bat. Not waiting for an answer, he moved forward.

"We should've put on those vests," Milo whispered as he followed.

"Yeah," Gus muttered back.

Light from the main entrance filtered past them. Wire-thin lines of more light outlined two partially opened doors just ahead. Artificial ferns stood in the corners at the end of the hall. The combined stink of asscrack and armpit was borderline eye-watering and offensive to breathe, but breathed it in they did, polluting their mouths and throats.

Gus inched forward, hating how his boots sounded on the floor, and very much aware that anyone could be waiting for them. His heart was beating in overdrive as he tried to control his breathing. He checked on Milo, who stood poised and ready for the first pitch. Gus looked to the first door on the right, then what appeared to be the shadowy cavity of a stairway just past that. The other door—on the left wall and near the back—was open just a crack and bled the faintest gray light. Unlit bulbs resembling hornet nests hung from the ceiling, and a bare bulletin board was nailed to the wall between the first door and the stairs. What looked to be an honest-to-God scalp, hair and all, was stuck to the bulletin board with a survival knife.

As sure as Gus could still feel his missing fingers, he sensed someone waiting behind those doors. He flinched when Milo placed a hand on his shoulder. The soldier signaled to retreat when the door on the right whipped open and a chair lunged out legs first, hunting for a head. Gus turned and fired in pure reflex, obliterating the chair's seat in a burst of wood fragments and sponge confetti. The chair legs smashed into his chest, trapping his left arm a split second before he was slammed against a wall. Holding that wrecked chair was a ghoulish figure with spray painted eyes and a face-full of teeth.

Then total mayhem.

The ghoul's eyes flicked left just as Milo swung his bat, looking to belt a solo homerun. That length of bloody metal wickedness smacked into the ghoul's upraised bare arm with a slap of aluminum on meat. Those spray-painted eyes clenched shut as *more* attackers launched themselves into the hall, springing from the other doorway and the open stairs.

The chair frame dropped, and Gus was no longer pinned. He lurched into a fern-filled corner and attempted to bring up the shotgun, but a bat clipped him over the left eye, transforming his legs to rubber.

Gus went down in a heap he was only partially aware of—pulling the shotgun's trigger as he did so. In the close confines, the Ram Fist's blast was as loud as cannon fire. The single shell nailed the bat-wielding Leather pointblank, slamming him backwards, transforming him into a one-man wrecking ball that crashed into the charge behind him. Bodies hit the floor, either knocked off balance by the flying carcass or diving to get clear.

And in a split, ear-ringing second, only Milo had the sense enough to react and swing his bat.

The soldier smashed the ghoul's toothy face, bouncing him off a wall. He kicked the wrecked chair away, clearing a path to the slow-moving Leather. Into that stunned morass of uniform black he waded, bludgeoning faces as they lifted. One figure rose and Milo practically leapt two steps before hammering the Leather across the back, driving him to the floor. Far from finished, the soldier continued bashing anyone attempting to rise. He kicked a head, spun, and was tackled by a white-masked Leather. Both men slammed against a wall. They wrestled, pushing, clawing, punching, until they fell through the doorway at the far end. The noise replaced the diminishing ringing in Gus's ears. Across from him was the Leather with the half-mask displaying a set of cartoonish dragon's teeth. The Leather lifted himself from the floor, spray painted eyes narrowed as he also heard the wrestling match. He pulled a long blade from his side and advanced upon the two men fighting in the other room.

Gus realized he still had a hold of the bullpup.

Ram Fist!

Gus yanked the weapon into his lap as the ghoul's head jerked around. He fired, catching the ghoul broadside, the blast not just shoving him through the doorway behind him, but *propelling* him through, as if God himself were flicking away an ant. The Leather's head clacked off the solid doorframe in mid-flight and forcefully folded him in two. The dead man's unwanted trip came to a solid halt with a mighty clap, where an unseen mass stopped him cold.

Gus struggled to his knees.

Another Leather jumped him—springing forth from the inhuman tangle upon the floor. Gus unloaded a single shell into the attacker, shredding his chest and sending him backwards, fully airborne, before smashing him off another figure attempting to rise.

Both of the Leather ended up in a bloody heap in a corner.

Gus tried to stand but his brain said *unh-uh*, before whisking away all ankle support. The world tilted and spun, becoming a sloshing fishbowl. He slumped against a wall, his senses stretched and warped, his back skidding in an unlubricated slide until he sat with both legs splayed wide. The bullpup's hot barrel dropped in his lap, right on his boys, hot enough to yank his consciousness back where it was needed, but not quite in the right slot.

In the far corner, a still-living Leather fought with a dead man's weight, fighting to get clear of the corpse.

Christ Almighty, Gus realized in dreamy wonder. *Shitbucket Milo swings a bat like a ten-year old.*

"*Hey!*" Gus barked at the figure... who froze.

And pulled a knife.

"I said *hey!*" Gus bellowed

A jester's mask regarded him, a second before the Leather stood and slowly swayed.

Or maybe that was just the room, still tilting like a fucked-up amusement park ride.

Regardless, Gus put a shot square into the Leather's chest. The blast destroyed the material there and shoved him through the same doorway as the other Leather with the dragon's teeth mask. The door slapped a wall from the violent passage and only partially closed, stopped by a guy's boot. A gruesome splash of stew and fabric coated the door, which immediately made snail trails towards the floor.

Gus climbed to one knee, let his breath out as if about to puke, and managed to stand without barfing.

"Gus?" Milo asked from the open doorway at the end of the hall.

"Yeah?"

"You done out there?"

"Yeah. I'm done."

"I'm sticking my head out, okay?"

Gus frowned. "I'm not gonna shoot you, Milo."

"Just... making sure is all."

And with that, Milo peeked out from the doorway, inspected him for seconds, and then took in the dead cluttering the floor.

"Jesus Christ," he said under his breath. "You sure you're okay?"

The ringing in Gus's ears and the repeating hammer of pain where he got clipped by the bat made him want to say no, no he most certainly was not okay.

Instead, he said, "I'm good."

Milo didn't appear to believe it, but he was wise enough to let it go. "C'mere," he said.

Gus reluctantly did so, stepping over the wet jumble of bodies, and realizing not one goddamn fern had been knocked over during the whole melee. He stopped in the doorway of a large office area.

Just inside and laid out on his back was one of the Leather.

"Got one," Milo said, indicating the meat sack. "Just before your twelve-gauge cleaning spree."

The Leather bastard wore, of all things, a fancy white mask with a spider stamped on its forehead. Long legs went down either side of the mask. The man was broad-shouldered, dressed in full rawhide regalia, and…

Gus's frown deepened.

"What?" Milo asked.

"Is it just me or does that guy have really long arms?"

Milo inspected one arm and then the other. "You're right. He does have long arms."

"What did you do to him?"

"Choked him out. Figure we could use him for information. And this guy was holding back from the others, which makes me think he's either a real sack of shit, or someone used to giving orders."

"Think he's the driver?"

An unsure Milo shook his head. "No idea. Check the other room there."

Thankful for the task, Gus lumbered off for the first door, stopping for a peek up the stairs. Seeing it was clear, he stepped over the dead men sprawled out underfoot. He slipped on a bloody forearm and winced at the contact. Upon righting himself, he stood before the door covered in wet meaty bits. Sighing, knowing it was going to be a mess, Gus entered the room. It was a small conference area with only two windows—one overlooking the road to the right, and the other facing the railbed and distant river. More artificial flowers filled the corners, untouched and appearing dusted, as if someone had wiped them down recently. In the center of the room were chairs ringing a long conference table. The board game *Life* was spread out upon the surface, the game about halfway finished. The two Leather Gus had shot were inside, and he had to stretch his legs to step over their crumpled forms. Blood and bits coated everything, the thickest amounts plastering the door and the nearby walls, but a notable spray splattered the table, the gameboard, and even one of the windows.

Gus returned to the hall and climbed the stairs to the first landing. The door was open at the top, but nothing moved and nothing could be heard. Sensing no danger, Gus returned to Milo and his prisoner in the office. Two dark and narrow windows were located at the north wall, on either side of a door. Two more doors were located at the left and right walls, one being only a few steps away from where he'd just stepped through. A final door was to the south.

"Back already?" Milo asked, lugging the prisoner to a chair behind a desk.

"Yeah."

"Find anything?"

"All clear."

"You go upstairs?"

"Not yet."

Milo frowned. "You should've checked upstairs."

"I'll do it later."

That got Milo's eyes rolling. "All right, we'll do that in a bit. We probably got everyone, anyway. Find me something to tie up this prick."

Gus pulled open the nearest door, revealing heaps of stacked boxes and a single bookcase therein. It looked to be a storage room, but not the kind he was interested in. A washroom was across the way, complete with a small stack of individually wrapped, one-ply toilet paper. *One-ply*, Gus thought. *Savages.* Ignoring the lowly stockpile, he moved past Milo and the unconscious prisoner to the final door, just behind the desk.

Another office, perhaps the owner's or someone equally important. Fine panel wood walls. A metal filing cabinet near a much bigger desk. Pictures of sailboats and marinas hung throughout, daydream reminders for those hump days. Computer and peripheral devices and all other trappings of what appeared to be busy management with a longing to be on the water. The window in the back wall faced the street and the bodies outside. One corner of the frame was scuffed, as if that was where the shoes rested when the boss leaned back in his chair.

"Find anything?" Milo yelled.

"Not yet."

"Well find something!"

The urgency in the soldier's voice hurried Gus to the desk, where he started pulling open drawers. Folders. Pens and pencils. *Popular Mechanics* magazine. *National Geographic.* Scotch tape but nothing heavier. Not even a secret bottle of whiskey or rum or vodka to get a person through a long afternoon.

Then he saw the power cords, connecting all the computer equipment to the outlets, and the ringing in Gus's head didn't seem so bad anymore.

24

Gus stepped back and inspected the handiwork with the air of a job well done.

"Not bad," Milo said, finishing up on the ankles.

There was about seventy feet total of power cords and connecting cables, and the two men used it all to tie down the Leather in the chair. Wrists, ankles, and chest were all bound, though Gus didn't think the chest looked really secure. At one point the prisoner stirred and woke, whereupon Gus greeted him with a tap to the masked cheek.

With the barrel of the bullpup.

"Morning dickshit," Gus greeted without a smile. "Guess who's only a few words from being boot-fucked?"

The Spider made side-eyes enough to see the shotgun aimed at his face.

"That's right. *You*," Gus said. "Don't you move. Not until he's done wrapping you up. This hog barely kicks, so I have no worries about fucking up my arm. You? You'll have plenty of problems getting by without a goddamn head."

The Spider didn't move.

Milo finished using the cords and stood up. "That'll do for now. We'll just have to watch him."

"There was plenty of tape back there."

"Duct tape?"

"Scotch tape."

That visibly pained Milo. "You can't use *Scotch* tape."

"Why not? We can wrap it on thick."

That got the soldier thinking. "Why the fuck not?" he said in a defeated voice.

So Gus went off and retrieved the tape, leaving Milo to guard the Spider.

Ten minutes later, the ankles were reinforced by Scotch tape.

"That looks like shit," Milo said.

"It'll be a pain in the ass to tear off," Gus said. "It's stronger than it looks."

"It's fucking Scotch tape."

"It'll hold him."

"It'll barely rip the hair off his ass."

"He probably shaves his ass."

The two men glared at each other before, on some silent cue, they turned on the Spider.

"You drive a Mustang?" Milo asked.

The mask stared.

Gus reached out and ripped the spider mask from the guy's head. There was a leather hoodie underneath, but the uncovered face took a moment to process.

A wretched, scorched-earth expression regarded them both, snarling in disdain, hissing black and yellow nubs that might've once been teeth. The guy's fried flesh appeared cooked to a second-degree crispiness, and scarred, as if he'd been pulled face-first through a very dry carwash system. There was no facial hair to speak of, just that savage face and a hateful pucker of lips, which alternated into a grimace.

Even though it was years after everything had gone into the shitter, a few of the old world's social rules still bound Gus.

One of them was not to stare.

But damn if he couldn't help it.

"Uh," he started and clamped down on whatever it was he was going to say. Maybe a threat of violence, a promise of pain, but the man before him had clearly suffered already. And had suffered worse than anything Gus might threaten.

"Yeah," he finished with a glance at Milo.

The soldier, however, was unmoved. "I don't give a fuck what you look like. I'll torch you a second time unless you talk. You hear me?"

The trapped Spider flexed his fingers and his unnaturally long arms that might've been stretched in a tractor pull gone dreadfully wrong.

"Don't do that," Gus warned, moving the shotgun within an inch of the prisoner's profile.

The Spider stopped.

Milo studied the desk. There was a plastic organizer there filled with pens and pencils. He took one of the pencils and held it up.

"See this?" he asked their captive and tapped a finger off the tip. "It's real pointy. Now, I'm going to ask you some questions. You're going to answer them. If you don't, I'm going to stick this thing into your face and leave it there. Then I'll get another pencil, until they're all gone, which is when I'll start using the pens. They're gonna hurt more, because I'll have to use more force. To sink them deeper, you understand."

The Spider tensed, his eyes darting, scanning the floor, as if struggling to think.

"You might think that's cruel," Milo continued. "And honestly, you're right. The problem is, I've seen you guys work someone over in the same situation. I've seen the hammers. And the nails. And the blow torches. We haven't found any of that shit around here yet, but I'm sure we can use something else."

"Fuck, I'll find a toaster," Gus threw in.

"See?" Milo pointed out. "We'll improvise. So while I'll feel a little shitty about torturing you…" He let that hang in the air. "I'll do it anyway. Just 'cause. Now, back to the first question. Were you the shithead hauling ass in a Mustang?"

The Spider blinked. A prolonged and uncomfortable silence then, where the man bound to the chair refused to say a word.

Milo reached out and wrapped a hand around the back of the prisoner's head. He leveled the pencil to the guy's red and ruined cheek and readied himself as if about to plug in a power cord.

The Spider broke. "I drove a Mustang."

"Where were you coming from?"

Another few seconds of petulant silence. "North."

"Where, exactly."

"Fort Jay."

Milo arched his eyebrows at Gus, then returned to the questioning. "You were in a hurry. Why?"

The Spider narrowed his eyes. "Huh?"

"You heard me."

"How did you know I was in a hurry?"

"I'm asking the questions."

The Spider watched him, thinking, wondering, until Gus nudged the prisoner's cheek with the barrel of the shotgun.

"I was coming here," the Spider answered.

"Yeah? Why? What was going on in Fort Jay? For you to leave like you cut your ballsack while shaving it?"

"I was reporting in."

Milo twiddled with the pencil while studying the Spider's face. "I don't think so. See, I think you're a little more important than that."

"Just a little more," Gus added from the side.

"So what is it?" Milo asked. "Before I start stabbing things."

The Spider didn't move, didn't say a word, long enough that Gus thought Milo would indeed stab his pencil into a tender spot.

"You could just hit him," Gus suggested, one corner of his mouth hooking upward to reveal his missing teeth.

Milo looked at him. "What?"

"Or break a finger. Plenty of ways to get him talking."

"Hear that?" Milo directed at the Spider. "The man knows the business."

That got the Spider chuckling, which put frowns on both their faces.

"The *business*?" the Spider smiled and, as God was his witness, Gus thought the rotten teeth in the guy's head were ready to fall out onto his chest. "That what you call it? Yes. You might know something about the *business*. Maybe even a few things. But don't think you're an expert. You're not."

Gus bopped him on the bare head with the shotgun barrel. The connection caused the Spider to shrivel up on the spot.

"Next time, I use this," Milo brandished the pointed pencil.

The Spider sucked in breath through those clenched nubs called teeth, and Gus thought they would break right there. "We were hit," the prisoner said. "Just after midnight."

"Yeah?" Milo asked. "Lose many?"

The Spider wavered. "Maybe. I don't know."

"Know who did it?"

"Maybe. A soldier."

That caused Milo and Gus to trade looks.

"Wearing a mask?" Gus asked.

"Yes."

Gus couldn't contain the relief that broke out across his face.

"How many soldiers?" Milo wanted to know.

"Just one."

"All right. And why did you come here?"

The Spider slumped. "Reinforcements."

"And we took care of them," Gus said.

That got the Spider's attention. "Did you?"

The men quieted.

"I know this is a Leather town," Milo said. "How many are here?"

The Spider smiled again, the sight damn near stomach turning. "In Winnipeg?"

"*Here*. This place. This *shack*."

"I don't know. Maybe a baker's dozen. Or close to that."

It seemed strange for such an individual to use an old expression like "baker's dozen", at least to Gus.

"A guard post?" Milo continued.

The Spider tucked away his horrible smile. "Yes."

"Guard post?" Gus asked a second time, to make sure he'd heard right.

"Go count up the bodies," Milo said.

"What for?"

"Just do it. I'll stay here and watch him."

Gus regarded the soldier and then the Leather tied to the chair. He gripped the bullpup in both hands and went out into the corridor.

Four dead. He went to the entrance and stuck his head out.

Six more out there.

But then he heard the engines, paralyzing him to the spot. Several engines in fact, racing, ripping up the streets and heading in their direction. It was the sound of a motorized army, pushing, buzzing its way through the city, becoming louder. Gus stood there for seconds, listening in growing terror, while his mind fabricated all sorts of imaginary fiberglass frights and four-wheel-drive abominations. And the figures that drove them.

He backed into the doorway, and the connection rattled him enough to get his act together. He closed the door, hesitated, and ran to the office area, where Milo and the Spider glanced up.

"Milo," Gus blurted. "Cars are coming. A lot of cars are coming."

The soldier grabbed the prisoner by the throat. "Guess we missed one."

The Spider didn't squirm in his grip. "Maybe you did," he strained.

"One got away?" Gus asked, the panic rising, and with it, the need to act.

"Hey, look at me," Milo ordered, and got Gus's attention. "Relax."

"We gotta get outta here."

"No time. Besides, he can't go anywhere like that," Milo gestured at the Spider. "And we can't carry him."

Gus swallowed, but the dread welling up in his chest and gullet urged him to run. "Milo, I… I can't get caught. Not again."

That knotted up the soldier's expression. "We're not getting caught. We're staying right here. They got cars, we don't. We got nowhere to go, anyway. Our backs are against a river. They'd run us down on the bridge or chase us into a corner."

The sound of approaching engines grew louder.

"Oh Jesus Christ," Gus swore. "What do we do?"

"Go lock the doors," Milo ordered.

"Go lock them doors," the Spider smiled. "Go lock them, son. And do it fast. As fast—"

Milo punched him, cracking the man's head back and quivering him against his bonds, which was the only thing keeping him in his chair. Blood gushed from a shattered nose in choking spurts, like air being expelled from water pipes. The Spider lurched forward to better let it flow.

But the reddening smile on his ugly French-fried face was sly and unchecked.

"Not another goddamn word outta you," Milo warned him. "Not another goddamn word. Gus. Go lock the doors and get your ass back here pronto. Now."

Gus ran off, hearing the threatening collection of eight-cylinder might penetrate the walls, coming for them. Memories of Carson, the mechanic and all-round handy guy, filled his mind then, and the mutilations he'd suffered at the hands of the Leather. Josh Rogan had outfitted the guy with a motorized wheelchair, taken from Whitecap's vast stores, as well as potent painkillers, but even then, the physical pain Carson had suffered was the clinging stuff of nightmares from which there was no waking.

Gus went to the front door. There was no window and it was already closed. He secured two sliding bolt locks above and below, and the doorknob's deadbolt. That done, he checked on the other rooms, his anxiety spiking when he saw the windows.

Oh Jesus, Jesus.

Ever since the pack of killers had shot him off the highway and strung him up by the tow truck boom, Gus swore he would never be caught and held at the whim of anyone ever again. The absolute horror of being at another's mercy had stabbed his psyche deep, leaving wounds that he hadn't even shared with Collie. Nightmares where he was once again a human piñata, marked by ribbons of dried blood and swinging from a boom. Helpless. Suffering. Pissing down his leg when he had to. But in his dreams, Wallace didn't come to his rescue. In his dreams, dead things surrounded and reached for him, pulling at his skin, devouring him in great gushing bites until his screams freed him from the nightmare. And sometimes, Comeau and his gang were there instead of the undead. Smiling and joking as they punched, cut, or simply broke things still a part of Gus, trapped within that *second* nightmare.

Being torn apart by decomposing corpses was one thing, but hanging like a slab of meat while those savages worked him over was another.

And the deeper the sleep, the more difficult it was to pull himself back.

He didn't have the nightmares all the time. When they did seize him, however, they held on hard, held on tight, their terrors sinking gray fingers into his arms or shoulders, right up to the white knuckles.

Not ever again, Gus swore on those nights when he woke up alone, his sheets soaked with sweat, and wished for a drink of something at least forty percent alcohol.

The engines were much louder now. In fact, he believed they were right outside the building.

Shit oh shit oh SHIT. Gus hurried through the central hall, back into the reception area, where Milo was already closing the north wall door.

"All done?" the soldier asked

"Only one door in," Gus answered. "The one we came through. What's out there?"

"Warehouse. Filled with building supplies. Wood mostly, but also two large tankers."

"Tankers? *Gas* tankers?"

"Or whatever they put in their machines. There's two big doors out there but they're closed."

They stopped talking, suddenly uninterested with anything the other guy had to say.

Because all had become quiet.

"They're here," the Spider whispered, his nose squished to an ugly pulp and still dribbling fluids into his lap.

Milo held up a fist, warning the Spider. He moved over to a desk where he'd left the bat. He picked it up and shared another cautious look with Gus. Everything was dead silent.

Someone pounded on the outer door.

25

Three pickups stopped outside the building.

Leather-clad figures spilled from the cabs and from the box beds. They brandished spiked clubs and metal bats. High-tech crossbows and compound bows. Scratched axes, crude maces, and impish spears with charcoaled points. They circled the rides in a clatter of boot heels and the hiss of gloves and skin on dusty fiberglass, the early winter air unable to pierce the stylish outwear covering their frames.

One leather-draped individual emerged from a king cab. He wore a skull cap the color of an oil slick, while a set of steampunk goggles covered his eyes. High boots—broken-in, dirty and eager for a row of sizeable asses to tee off on—clicked off the asphalt in a saunter of *weeell, what do we have here?* A leather duster—so very favored amongst the Leather—covered him. The coat's collar, sharp and spectacularly wide, was flicked up in a full cobra spread. He carried an honest-to-god mace. A prickly cannonball studded with one-inch nails that shone in the daylight. If the sight of that weapon didn't draw an individual's taint tight, then the very thought of the strength required to *use* such a weapon should have.

Steampunk studied the dead Leather in front of the building. The Leather had bled out on the pavement, where the rivulets had pooled in gutters and trickled into storm grates. Steampunk lingered on the last corpse, his head cocked in grim consideration, taking in every morbid detail, every ugly implication. All the while, the dozen other members of his patrol stood and waited for his commands. They'd all heard the shotgun blasts two blocks over and had saddled up to investigate.

They didn't expect their watch post on the river to be attacked.

Certainly didn't expect to see their fellow clan members wiped out.

No one killed the Leather. To do so meant a sentence of being captured and converted into one of the mindless, for all eternity. Or at least until your head was shot off. Steampunk promised himself to teach someone those lessons.

Not a breeze blew by that corner of the city, and only the pings of cooling engines disturbed the peace. Steampunk studied the outer façade of the building, noting the closed front door. With all the snap and poise of a drill sergeant, he snapped a gun finger at the door.

The Leather rushed up the stairs to the entrance.

The steps and landing weren't very wide, so only three could stand before the door. The others gathered at the base like a misplaced crew needing a battering ram. The lead Leather, one particular individual that wore a rivet-studded mask resembling a Roman god, tried the knob. It would not open, so he pounded on the door and waited.

No response.

The Roman god pounded again, a good solid thrashing that no doubt left a sting. The remaining Leather stood behind and below him like a hot and seething oil slick.

Again no answer to the summons.

The Roman god looked over at Steampunk, whose goggles stared back with mechanical indifference, until he nodded with all the curtness of a sitting warlord.

The Roman god knocked again.

And the window—the darkened window ten feet to the right of the door—erupted with the killing cadence of a twelve-gauge shotgun, sending glass flying outwards.

The blast savagely bent the Roman god backwards—and would've shoved him clear entirely if not for the iron railing surrounding the platform—which took the Leather across the waist and flipped him.

Designer boots flashed through the air as the figure was blown away.

But the gunfire didn't just hit the one target, nor did it end. Shots ripped into the other figures on the landing. A head blew apart in a meaty geyser and a split-second jiggle of nerves before the whole body slumped like a discarded tube sock. Another was spun around in a dandelion burst of maroon before a follow-up shot splattered him over the railing. The blast brutally hung the Leather over the bar, where he wavered as if on a boat enduring harsh seas.

Just before a parting shotgun blast utterly *wrecked* the Leather's upturned ass.

In a span of two heartbeats, a thick drizzle of shredded fabric and body bits covered the remaining Leather poised upon the stairs. Blood splattered everything as if a five-gallon bucket had been dumped over their frames.

The abrupt show of violence drove Steampunk into a goggly-eyed crouch.

One of the Leather in the rear leaped for the smashed window, realizing where the gunfire had come from. He swung a red fire axe into the sill, slamming the blade into the wood some two feet over his head. He was about to yank it free when a shotgun blast tore through his upper chest. The Leather flew ten feet across the pavement as if stomped on by a giant, where he stopped in a broken heap.

"JESUS *CHRIST!*" someone shrieked at the display of firepower.

The remainder broke and fled for cover.

Steampunk would not blame them.

He was already behind his jacked-up pickup, wide-eyed and staring.

26

Gus slammed himself back against the wall and stared, listening for an armed response. He'd just gunned down four of those little costumed fuckheads, and he didn't think he blinked once. The bullpup shotgun smoked just a little, but he held it close to his cheek and thanked God above for having it.

Ram Fist!

"What was that?" Milo whispered-screamed from outside the conference room.

Gus heard him, but the shooting was still with him, still energizing him, and leaving him at a loss as to what to say.

"Gus?"

"Yeah?" he finally said.

Milo stood in the doorway, clearly divided by leaving the Spider wired and scotch-taped to a chair, and the shotgunner in the conference room. "How many you get?" he asked.

"Uh… three or four."

"Jesus Christ," Milo swore and withdrew again.

Gus glanced at the smashed window. He edged towards the opening until he saw the trucks. He jerked back on impulse, and an arrow slashed through the space before skewering the far wall with a frightening clap.

Then things got quiet. Until the motors started up.

"Great," Gus said and hazarded a peek outside.

Leather. Taking cover behind their vehicles. Two aiming arrows—Gus pulled back again as the twin missiles flew. One razored through the spot where he'd only just stuck his face out, while another bounced off the window frame itself with all the force of a hammer hitting an anvil. The archers were good. Perhaps even *real* good. Just waiting for him to show his face again, so they could stick one of those broadheads right through his brain.

Boots clattered outside, which got his attention. Gus did a quick mental recollection of the building's layout. Only one entrance, which he'd covered. Otherwise, the place stood on a cement foundation about six feet high. Another four feet from floor to windows, for a total of ten. That would need a ladder.

There were other windows, however.

Gus scooted back to the hall. He checked on the front door before continuing to the office reception area. The Spider's bloody face lifted as he entered.

Milo stood next to the open door to the manager's office, where a square window could be seen behind a desk. That window also overlooked the road, and like the conference room, it was a ten-foot climb to reach.

"So what do we do?" Gus asked.

Milo stared back, processing the question. "We gotta get out of here," he said, changing his earlier stance.

The smile spreading across the Spider's busted features was a nasty, blood-laced cut of smugness.

"We can't go the way we came in," Gus reported. "They're covering it."

"Shit."

"What about that way?" Gus pointed at the warehouse door.

"There are outside doors, but they're closed."

Gus decided to check for himself, glancing at the prisoner as he went past. "The fuck you smiling about?" he demanded.

The Spider kept quiet and lowered his head, but watched Gus from the corner of his eye.

"Gus," Milo called out.

He stopped with his hand on the doorknob. "What?"

"Give me the Glock."

Give me the Glock?

Gus's face twisted into a disapproving *fuck that* as he pulled open the door. He'd just as soon as shoot his own nuts off than do that.

The door opened to a landing and a short flight of steps that led down to the main floor. The only light spilling into the warehouse came from the office area behind him and a few boarded-up windows, so the entire area was pretty much an early winter cave. Wood dust wafted, cold but still sweet to the nose. Tall square stacks of lumber covered the area, some bare, others covered in protective plastic that shone in the scant light. The far walls were divided into sections filled with more wood, roof trusses, and even ready-to-install windows. A pair of fuel trucks were barely visible at the far end of the warehouse. An assortment of trolleys and forklifts were parked everywhere in between Gus and those tanker twins.

He went down the flight of steps, boots hard on the wood, and chugged through the easy maze of untouched building supplies. He reached the tankers and moved past them, seeing the main warehouse doors outlined by daylight.

The nearby sound of a starting engine spun him around. Then another engine joined in, revving as if ready to race.

Gus stopped and listened, sizing up the doors. Multiple bars secured them, the sliding kind, reinforced by a knot of formidable chains. He sighed at the sight but then realized they didn't have to worry about the Leather entering that way. What was worse, there was no way of escaping out the back.

The vehicles pumping their engines began to move. One rig surged alongside the warehouse until it turned the corner. Gus stared, listening, as the unseen machine stopped directly before the warehouse's closed doors. There it idled, warning him to stay clear.

"The fuck you doing?" he muttered, feeling the tension again in his guts and his lower legs.

Gears shifted and the machine seemed to huff back and forth a few places, until perhaps one corner of the vehicle scraped against the outer door.

"The fuck are you doing?" Gus asked again in nervous puzzlement.

A part of him knew, however. A part of him realized it the very moment he heard the machine turn the corner.

The Leather was blocking a potential escape route, parking as close as possible to the warehouse doors.

And sealing Gus and Milo within.

27

Steampunk wasn't the kind of person to fuck around.

The Leather's job was to patrol the closed-off sections of the city, watching for trouble while guarding the one avenue cleared all the way to the Royal Bentley downtown.

Which happened to be the local base of operations for the Leather.

He had enough lessers to help him with his duties, but when he heard the shotgun going off, he knew trouble had come to town. When he discovered the bodies splayed across the asphalt *outside* the warehouse, Steampunk knew *a lot* of trouble had come to town. But that was fine.

That was okay.

The Leather was the worst trouble around.

So even though he ran for the rear of his pickup when the shooting started, he didn't really lose control. In fact, he was already assessing the situation and making plans.

First thing he did was signal his lessers to cover the entrance, to make sure no one escaped that way. He knew the general layout of the warehouse, but couldn't remember if the loading bay doors were secured, so he dispatched a team to watch the back as well. More to the point, to block them with a truck, to ensure that whoever was inside didn't slip out that way.

Next, Steampunk grabbed a minion and ordered him to return to the hotel and bring back reinforcements. To alert the Bear Trap and muster the troops if they hadn't already heard the shotgun's thundering. All that would take no more than twenty minutes, or so he figured, and in that time, Steampunk would ensure whoever was inside the warehouse would not be leaving. Whoever was doing the shooting might've damn well walked into the city, but they sure as hell would not be walking out.

The pickups roared to life and sped off like smokey missiles homing in on their targets.

Steampunk flipped down the tailgate and searched through the weapons and gear tossed into the back. He pulled out a crossbow case and flipped it open. Therein was a jungle-camouflaged crossbow and attached scope in the lower section of the case, while a rack of silvery broadheads were on top. The words *"Black Scorpion"* were stamped on the crossbow's shoulder stock. He extracted the weapon and three bolts and readied the crossbow without missing a beat. A single bolt fitted into the flight groove. Once that was done, Steampunk left the weapon on the lower tailgate. He located two smaller handheld crossbows and their bolts and loaded them as well.

Five other minions were nearby, including the two archers already firing upon the shattered window. Kevlar vests were pulled on and adjusted and spare weapons readied.

"No one gets away," Steampunk said in a frayed voice to his nearby lessers. "No one escapes. Wounding them is preferable… but kill them if you have to."

Believing himself to be under cover, Steampunk put aside the smaller crossbows and picked up the Black Scorpion. Rated at close to five hundred feet per second, the crossbow was surprisingly powerful, powerful enough to punch a broadhead through an armored vest at close range. At medium range, it would still pierce a vest and wound, but not kill.

Steampunk hefted his crossbow onto the lowered tail gate, aimed at the one window belonging to the office, and let his breath out with a hunter's patience.

If anyone showed their face, he would nail the whole head to a wall.

28

"Get back here!" Milo insisted, his voice an angry whisper.

Gus was already doing just that, running from the warehouse doors when he heard the soldier. The order only made him move faster. He chugged back to the stairs and stopped at the base to catch his breath.

"Get up here and help me!" Milo snapped. "This is a two-man job up here. Fucking five-man job, really."

"Checked the doors," Gus huffed, pulling himself up the railing. "Locked up."

"Locked?"

"Chained. You should see it. Like… like ten pounds of steel. All in a knot. Along with the regular shit. And that's not all."

Milo backed away so that the man could enter the office area.

"They parked a pickup against the doors," Gus panted. "Just before I started running."

That silenced the soldier. He waited until Gus was inside before he closed the door and locked it, twisting one deadlock and sliding two bolts into place.

"They parked a truck against the doors?" Milo asked.

"Yeah."

"They don't want us to leave."

"They don't?"

"Yeah," Milo said. "Like that. They deal in skin, man. Skin and bones. And we're just their type. Matter of fact, I'm guessing they're gonna make an example of us. They fuckin' *love* to break hard asses."

"I ain't getting caught."

"I don't blame you. Not by those fuckers."

"Not by them, not by anyone. Been there, done that, and almost fuckin' died because of it."

"That's usually the way it goes, but not with the Leather. They'll make use of us if they can. Like the meat puppets. Gag us with those plastic balls and then put a Halloween mask on us. And that's just for starters. And *that's* if we don't die first."

Gus glanced over at the Spider, slumped over in his chair like a sulky man-child attempting to take a dump. The troubling thing was the sly smile covering the guy's deep-fried face.

"We gotta get outta here," Gus finally said. "I think I heard a car or truck driving away."

"Getting backup," Milo said and pointed. "You better give me that gun."

"Like fuck. You ain't gettin' a gun so stop asking me about it."

"Don't be stupid here. You got the shotgun. I can use the Glock. We watch each other's backs."

"I don't give a shit. Last fuckin' thing I'm doing is *arming* you. Keep your bat. You seem to get by with it."

His mouth becoming a frustrated button, Milo exhaled. "All right," he finally said. "Fine. We make a run for it. Take our chances."

Gus liked that idea. "What about him?"

They looked at the Spider, who felt it was time to speak.

"You're fucked," the prisoner said, smiling, dribbling blood as he said the words. "So, very, very fucked."

Milo crossed the floor and clocked that gore-dripping face with a right hook, rocking the head back like a warped punching bag. More blood flew. The Spider quivered before slumping again, and this time, he was unconscious.

Milo, however, stood ready to drive home another if needed. He remained that way for a few beats before eyeing Gus. "You ready?"

"Oh, fuck yeah," Gus nodded. He was ready to get out of Dodge ten minutes ago.

"Come on, then."

They crept into the nearby office manager room, where, behind a desk, was the intact window facing the street.

"Get on that side," Milo ordered Gus. "And do as I do."

They rounded the big desk in the center of the room, and when Milo reached the window, he stayed low and pressed himself up against the wall, staying out of sight.

Gus did the same on the left, shotgun clutched to his chest.

Milo slowly peeked out from the window at an angle, keeping his head behind a wall while widening his view and taking in everything in the street. Gus mirrored him, seeing the situation below from the opposite angle.

"Okay," Milo whispered. "I see three guys down there on your side. Bows and arrows. See anything behind me?"

"Three. Wait…" he leaned out a little more, drawing a look of warning from Milo. "Yeah, three."

Gus drew back.

"What are they doing?" Milo asked.

"Just watching."

"Yeah. They're watching, all right."

"I saw scopes."

"Yeah, some of those things are pretty high-tech." Milo paused before inspecting the drop outside the window. A frown crossed his features. "This way."

He circled the wall back out into the reception area. Gus did the same on the other side.

The Spider remained knocked out.

"There's a drop to street level," Milo explained. "That means if we go *out* a window, we drop and then run."

"What about upstairs?" Gus asked.

"That's higher. We ain't getting out of here by running along on the roof. Sooner or later, we gotta get down. We stay down here. The windows in the washrooms are too small for anyone to come through. This way…"

Milo hurried into the hall with the dead Leather and looked up the stairs to the landing. A much too narrow window allowed light inside.

"Ain't getting out that way," Milo said and went into the conference room. Through the windows, the railbed and trees could be seen. Crouching and hugging the wall, he moved around until he reached the glass and carefully peered outside.

"Well," Milo said. "Whoever's out there is parked in the best spot. Covers the front door and this side. If we drop here—and it's a nine- or ten-foot drop—we have about two seconds to recover and run for it. That's a lot of time for them to shoot at us. If we reach the river, there's another problem. Crossing that fucker. It's wide open with no cover. And we can't swim it."

"Fuck no," Gus agreed.

"And if we run *that* way," Milo pointed in the direction of the bridge, "across open ground, they have trucks. They'd run us down and laugh all the way."

"We should've taken the vests."

The soldier didn't say anything.

"We're fucked," Gus whispered. "So what do we do?"

Milo scratched at his temple. "The one thing we can do."

*

Back in the chair, the Spider woke.

He was aware of voices, then realized his eyes were closed. Then he remembered telling the two shitheads their fate, just before one of them sucker-punched him. That truly angered the Spider—being hit while he was tied down. Striking him like he was a common meat puppet.

He was so much more than that.

Power cords across his chest held him in place. Staying limp, the Spider cracked open an eye.

There, near a wall, tossed aside like a piece of garbage was his face. His *true* face. The sight of his mask lifted his spirits enough to clear his head. It wasn't just a means to hide his scarred features, it was his totem. His talisman. His goddamn good luck voodoo mojo. His captors were in the next room talking, no doubt panicking over what was going to happen to them. Lord above, the Spider was going to be there when the Leather took them. For what they did to him. Not since the Dog Tongue had anyone hurt the Spider in such a way. He intended to tie them both up, for his version of a carnival's strongman competition, where he'd be swinging a sledgehammer. Or a rubber mallet. He'd start at their feet and work his way up. He'd even make a new set of bladed gloves for the occasion, for when he ran out of legs.

He could hear their screams already.

That would be his reward. For escaping.

Careful so not to arouse suspicion, he inspected himself. The cords would be a challenge, but not the Scotch tape. Even better, the one who had searched him missed the secret blade in his belt buckle. A one-pull, one-fist knife resembling half of a stubby set of scissors. The Spider knew his knives, knew how to use them, and he could whip out his belt knife in an instant. One hard punch to the throat was all it took. Or several stabs to the gut.

But first he had to escape the power cords.

Aware of the two men nearby, the Spider kept his head down and worked his right hand, testing the tightness there.

*

"We *what?*" Gus blurted, not sure he heard correctly.

"We go for the nearest truck," Milo repeated. "That one parked on the corner there, pointed for the river. We go for that, like, *now*."

"How the hell we do that?"

Milo straightened. "We rush that bastard. You got the shotgun. You cover me. Shoot anything that moves."

"There's only ten rounds in this."

"You got an extra magazine?"

Gus nodded. The last one.

"Any more?"

"Only loose shells."

"Then load them up," Milo said and went for the main hall. Gus followed him, swapping out one magazine for the other.

In the hallway, they studied the locks of the main entrance. Once the magazine was readied and inserted, Gus considered the nearly empty one.

"Here," he said and handed it over to Milo. Holding the shotgun in one hand, he fished spare shells from a pocket and passed them along as well.

Milo frowned. "You want me to reload this thing."

"Yeah, I do."

"You know I could've jumped you a couple of times now. If I really wanted to. Just then, for example."

"Maybe," Gus admitted and aimed at him. "Get to it."

Annoyed, Milo made short work of reloading the magazine.

"Now give it," Gus held out a hand and got what he asked for.

"You're an idiot," Milo said.

Gus ignored that. "Unlock those things." He nodded at the door.

"We do this fast, okay?" Milo said. "They'll be shooting at us, but it takes time to reload a crossbow. Or just a bow. You scare the shit out of them with the shotgun and I'll go for the truck. Pin these dickheads down, especially the ones nearest the pickup. Those are the ones with the keys." Milo stared at Gus. "This will go smoother if you give me that Glock. Or the shotgun."

Gus shook his head.

Milo's shoulders slumped. "Ready then?" he asked.

"What about the fuckwit in the chair?"

"Go back and kill him if you want."

Gus shook his head.

"All right, then," Milo said, giving up. He faced the door. "Here we go."

He started undoing the locks in a flurry of movement. The freed bolts cracked in the hall, and Milo was done in seconds.

He opened the door.

A bottle exploded to the right of his face, spraying him with its contents.

He threw himself against the wall. A split second later, he reached out and pulled the door shut.

"The fuck was that?" Gus demanded as a cringing Milo wiped at his face. Then they both remembered and started sniffing.

It wasn't old man piss, however, that had splashed Milo.

It was ethanol.

29

His fingers flexing on the crossbow, Steampunk locked his sights on the smashed window next to the front door. All the while, he was thinking. There were people in there with guns. They hadn't tried to escape yet, or they were *about* to try to escape. So if they were trying to escape, how would they do it? How would *he* do it?

The foundation was high, and to drop down from one of the windows would be risky. Easy to twist an ankle.

They could try and flee through the main door, but Steampunk and his remaining minions were aiming at the entrance. If they did come out, they would come out firing their guns—if they had ammunition to spare. And once out, what might they do to escape?

On foot?

That seemed foolish to the leader.

To the nearest pickup, he realized. If they had guns, they could provide cover fire while rushing for the trucks. It would be costly, definitely bloody, with a fair to reasonable chance of success.

As long as whoever was in *there* killed the Leather out *here*, thus obtaining their keys.

Steampunk didn't like that conclusion, which informed him his thinking was right.

He didn't need to storm the building. That would come later, when the reinforcements arrived. All he needed to do was keep the attackers in place.

He signaled to a nearby minion, asking for cover. Once done, he leaned into his pickup bed and rooted around, locating five whiskey bottles plugged with cloth wicks and filled with a very flammable ethanol blend. Steampunk extracted all the bottles. He then whispered instructions to a lesser and sent him scampering off to the pickup on the corner facing the river. No one fired upon the running man, which surprised Steampunk.

Nodding at the nearby Leather, Steampunk stood back from the tailgate and threw a bottle at the main entrance.

And a split second before the bottle crashed to the right of the door, the door *opened*.

Only to slam shut again.

Elated, Steampunk chucked two more bottles at the building, smashing the contents along the base. One of his minions did the same from behind the other truck. Together, they coated the areas below the windows.

Feeling bold, Steampunk threw his remaining bottles, breaking them against the stairs and splashing the concrete foundation.

Heart hammering, Steampunk returned to the rear of his pickup.

Where his minion already had a flare gun.

30

Gus was still sniffing when he heard the other bottles smashing against the walls. Milo stopped clearing his eyes, but still suffered from watery vision.

"The fuck was that?" Gus asked in alarm.

"Glass bottles," Milo cringed. "A piece of it clipped me right above the eye."

"You bleeding?"

"No." Milo dropped his hands and squinted. "But I sure as hell ain't happy. See what that shit is, in the conference room. I'm all burning and blurry here."

As he said it, the soldier turned to the door and pawed at the upper lock, sliding the bolt back in place.

"We're not leaving, then?" Gus asked

"No, we're not," a half-blind Milo growled. "Not if they're dousing us with ethanol. Those bastards outside will light us up if we run for it. God*damn* that shit stings."

Gus wavered, but then decided to do as told and check out the conference room. He hurried into the room and followed the inner wall to the window. There he stopped and peeked outside, trying to see the extent of the splash.

What might've been lightning flashed towards him.

Gus recoiled a split second before a bolt slammed into the frame and ricocheted upwards, rendering its lethal five-hundred-feet-per-second thrust useless. The bolt bounced off the ceiling and clattered along the conference room table, before coming to a stop at the far edge.

Not happy at having his head nearly perforated, Gus spun into the window and fired three quick shots at the pickup parked across the road. A roof light shattered and a section of the windshield crumpled in a salty spray of laminated glass. He whipped himself back behind the wall and waited. No one returned fire, so he hobbled over to the other window facing the railway tracks. Careful not to expose himself, Gus peeked out and saw and smelled that evil mystery blend of the Leather's ethanol.

He returned to Milo.

"See anything?" the soldier asked, part of his face red, but he wasn't squinting so bad anymore.

"They splashed everything."

"Yeah. Figured." Milo pointed at the door. "I locked it up. We ain't going anywhere now."

"So... what do we do?"

"Only thing we can do. We fortify."

"Fortify?"

"Fuckers don't want us to leave," Milo explained. "They want us right here. And we can't go anywhere until night at least. Which means they'll be coming before then. They'll try to get in. We can't let them. Got it?"

Feeling his balls draw up in a cold clutch, Gus nodded.

Milo waved at the room. "Start flipping shit."

He went for the conference room table and, staying low, started pulling out chairs. Those he overturned and positioned directly underneath the window facing the railbed. When that was done, he motioned for Gus to help him with the table. They flipped the huge piece of furniture onto its side and slammed it up against the window facing the trucks in the street.

"Peek out from the sides," Milo said. "That'll give us some protection from their arrows. If they come in, they get tangled in the chairs for a few seconds. This way."

They returned to the office reception area, where the Spider was still strapped down and slumped over.

Milo spared him only a glance.

Gus slowed down, however, taking a second more to examine the prisoner. The posture was relaxed, the chest leaning against the cords, his hands bound to the armrests.

"Watch him," Milo ordered before going into the manager's office.

Gus did, hearing furniture being flipped and moved.

A minute later, the soldier returned, breathing much harder. "Fuck me gently," he softly exclaimed. "Never thought I'd be in this position."

Gus never thought it himself.

"You see any way into the basement?" Milo asked.

"No."

"There's nothing on this level, but there's gotta be a basement. Foundation's too damn high." Milo went to the door to the warehouse and unlocked it. "Stay here and listen. And watch *that* piece of shit over there. Don't be shy about smacking him one, either."

"Hey," Gus called out. "What about the tankers?"

"What about them?"

"They might be full."

"You know how to unload them?" Milo asked.

"No."

"You got any explosives?"

Gus shook his head. That was something else he should've taken from the limo.

"Then we're S.O.L," Milo reported.

Shit outta luck.

That's when they heard the sound of more approaching engines.

31

The two men rushed into the conference room and took positions on either side of the table.

"That didn't take long," Gus said, holding onto his bullpup.

Milo didn't answer. He moved around, getting the best peek from an angle.

"Two pickups," he reported. "Fuck. Looks like a half dozen more of them."

"That all?" Gus asked.

"You want more?"

"Just figured there would be more."

"Don't worry, you'll get your wish," Milo warned.

And he was right.

The ball-hitching racket of additional vehicles reached them. An angry, fearless chuffing and surging reminiscent of a midnight street race just getting underway, where hordes of onlookers cheered from the sidelines. In this case, the hordes would be riding shotgun in box beds and war-prepped school buses or simply popping wheelies while waving machetes over their heads.

The image unnerved Gus.

"Hey," he said to Milo.

"What?"

"We didn't check the upstairs."

"You wanna go *now*?"

"There might be an attic."

"The fuck you interested in an attic for?"

"We could hide up there."

Milo shook his head. "That might work with mindless, but not with the Leather."

More trucks rolled to a stop outside the building, plugging up the streets. Dozens of Leather emerged, jumping down from box beds or springing from crew cabs. There were Leather with rhinestones studded into their coats. Leather with two-inch nails festooning their shoulders. Leather with only half-masks that covered either the lower or upper parts of their faces. They carried axes and bats and a few even wielded, of all things, goddamn machetes. Some of them even held one in each fist.

The reinforcements joined their companions at the front. Gus could see the main entrance stairs, but another pickup stopped out there, across the street. Three masked bastards stood upright in the box bed, leveling crossbows at the building.

"Christ almighty," Gus said.

Milo glanced over. "More?"

"Yeah."

"You okay?"

"No."

Milo inspected him for a heartbeat. "Go check on our prisoner."

Grateful for the distraction, Gus left the conference room while the small army outside continued to rev their engines, charging the air with a palpable eagerness for violence. That disturbing racket stopped him just inside the office doorway, where he lifted his head and simply listened, remembering the motorized armada that rolled up to the island bridge of Camp Red Wolf.

Oh shit, he thought then, wondering if the group outside had their own mindless stashed away somewhere, just for such an occasion.

"They'll take you," the Spider spoke then, grabbing Gus's attention.

The hunched over man looked up as if he'd just finished a round of retching blood. He smiled, and the sight of that alone was enough to turn stomachs.

"They'll take you," he said again, his long arms flexing and fingers twitching. "And when they do, I'll be there, looking over their shoulders, waiting for my chance to get at you. And I'll get it. I'll get it. I'll *demand* it. And when I do…"

The Spider's scorched and scarred mouth twisted into a war face, where he snapped black teeth.

Milo burst into the room then and charged for the manager's office. He stopped upon noticing Gus's unmoving posture and the Spider chittering his teeth. Milo crossed the floor, grabbed the Spider by the throat and pistoned three punches into that contorted face. It was a startling, heavy-handed pounding that put the prisoner under once again. Once finished, Milo shoved the unconscious man back in his chair.

"I said don't be shy about smacking him," Milo told Gus. "Remember? That's rule number one. Rule number two, if he starts talking shit, consult rule number one. Got it?"

Gus nodded.

"All right. On guard now. We're going to be busy here, soon."

He hurried into the office and stopped at the side of the window. Gus went to the other side. They peeked out at the force gathering against them. The Leather wasn't attacking, but more vehicles blocked off sections of the road, and where there once was only a handful, there were dozens more.

"They can't get in through the washroom windows," Milo said. "Too small. That leaves only this one, and the two in the conference room. We'll have to watch both. When they come up the steps, you open fire with that thing."

He gestured at the shotgun.

"You think they're going to charge us?" Gus asked.

"Yeah. The warehouse is blocked off on the outside and locked up on the inside, right? So they can't get in there. That leaves here and the conference room. But we're going to stop them."

Milo looked right at Gus.

"Look. Think for a second. If I was going to backstab you, I had plenty of fucking chances already. If I was going to club you with this?" he held up the bat, "I could've done it long ago. *Long* ago. And then gotten the hell out. Or made peace with the Leather. Not that I think they would let me. Not after they finished questioning me. And they would. Big time. Think about that."

More vehicles arrived outside, distracting Gus from Milo's penetrating glare.

And the mob's numbers swelled once again.

32

It was becoming a full-blown automotive show in the streets, where the patrons were extras from a bad slasher horror movie from the eighties. Vehicles blocked every road leading to the building, creating a bumper-to-bumper blockade. Multitudes of Leather formed up behind those lines, their heads and shoulders bobbing. Archers and crossbow men aimed at the windows, waiting for targets. The dead bodies lying on the pavement remained there, as did the corpses at the building's front doorstep. A grim reminder of what had happened with the first frontal assault.

"Maybe I should check upstairs," Gus said again.

Milo rolled his eyes. "Go on then. But if you hear me hollering, get your ass back down like you got the chocolate squirts."

They glared at each other then, while the streets teemed with the Leather and their vehicles.

Gus knew what the soldier was waiting for, and goddammit if he wasn't considering it. He screwed up his face as if tasting liquid shit. "You better not shoot me."

"I'm not going to shoot you," Milo said.

"'Cause if you shoot me, Collie will be pissed."

"I know she'll be pissed."

"She'll fucking hunt you down."

"You gonna give me that gun or not?" Milo finally snapped.

Gus continued to glare, knowing he was fucked one way or the other.

One of those ways, however, would be by the Leather.

"God*dammit*," he released softly and switched his shotgun over so that he could fish out his Glock. Even then, he hesitated, hating himself, knowing the next few seconds would be life or death. The thing was, he grudgingly admitted that the gurgling shit bucket across from him was right. Milo could have turned on him anytime. That didn't make it an easier choice for Gus, however.

Not pleased in the least with his options, Gus lowered himself until his arm was underneath the windowsill. He stretched and offered Milo the sidearm.

Who took the weapon.

There was a moment of reckoning then, of what would happen next. Milo released the magazine and checked the load. Then he moved the gun's slide back and quickly inspected that.

"Loaded, too," Milo said as he lifted the gun to his cheek. "Thanks."

"'Course it's loaded," Gus sighed in annoyance. "Wouldn't be much fucking use if it wasn't. Not to mention awkward."

Neither man said anything then, waiting for the other.

Milo went back to peeking out the window. "See?" he eventually said. "You're still alive. Wasn't so bad, was it?"

Gus watched the soldier for long torturous seconds.

Milo glanced over at him. "What?"

"Nothing."

"Oh, there's something. Out with it."

"Just waiting is all."

"Jesus Christ, Gus, we still on that? I could've shot you the second you handed this thing over."

"Still... you could be thinking 'I need this guy. If I'm going to live through this shit, I'll need him. Once it's all over, for better or worse, *then* I can shoot him.'"

"Holy shit. I should shoot you *now*, just for even going there."

Gus watched him.

"You stubborn, untrusting bastard," Milo said. "You've seen too many fucking movies."

"Kept me alive up to now."

"I'm not going to shoot you," Milo insisted. "Now eyes on those dickheads out there, okay?"

Reluctantly, Gus did just that.

*

Minutes passed, and more of the Leather arrived, rolling up to the building like a tide of effluent filth. They parked their vehicles far back up the street, filling one lane completely before getting out and running to the front.

Steampunk approached the fresh troops, careful to keep his head down. The new Leather followed his example. One figure in particular strode forward, with nearly two dozen minions accompanying him. The leader wore a long duster with a shiny golden vest underneath. He held onto the hilts of a pair of katanas, hanging from his waist and parting the folds of his heavy coat.

A golden, unsmiling mask and helmet of a Samurai covered his head.

"Where's the Bear Trap?" Steampunk asked, meeting the figure midway and crouching behind a truck.

"Coming," the Samurai answered.

"They have guns," Steampunk reported, nodding at the surrounded building.

"Your lesser said so," said the Samurai.

"We already tried the front door."

The Samurai sized up the landing, some sixty feet away.

"We go again?" Steampunk asked.

The Samurai shook his head. At that time, the huff and hiss of a much larger vehicle drew closer.

A transit bus drove down the street, shielded from the gunmen hunkered down in the building. Sunlight gleamed along the windshield of the bus as it motored to the front. Before it got any farther, however, a Leather stepped into its path and signaled the machine to stop. Other black-clad individuals swarmed the doors before creating a channel. The side doors opened, and figures spilled out.

Meat puppets.

Half of them coming off the bus wore hockey or football helmets. Some wore hockey masks, the old seventies kind associated with serial killers. Some carried riot shields. The meat puppets wore vests and other various padding, perhaps stripped from the dead. About three dozen or so gushed into the street, ready for battle but contained by their Leather handlers. The meat puppets milled about, some looking to the sunny sky while others glanced around anxiously. A few of them shouted—harsh, wild-man expulsions of air meant to stir up their juices.

The Samurai walked past Steampunk without a word. The leader stopped behind a truck with his hands on the hilts of his katanas and fearlessly faced the building.

*

"Something going on out there," Gus said, looking up the street.

"What?" Milo asked from the other side.

Gus stared. "Looks like..." he shook his head, "looks like a football team is forming up."

Milo frowned. He got low, came around to Gus's side, and immediately pulled him back.

"Shit," the soldier finally said.

"What?"

"Get ready."

"Get ready for what?"

"You know about the meat puppets, right?"

"Yeah, sorta. They're slaves, right?"

"Yeah, they're slaves. The Leather use them for the shittiest jobs around, for as long as they can. Until they die or they're promoted."

"What?"

"Yeah," Milo said. "That's right. And I'm telling you, after a few months living like they do, getting shit and stomped on like they do, they're *ready* for a promotion. They're ready to wreck a little ass on their own. They'll fuck up anyone and anything to get into the Leather's clubhouse. Any-fucking-*thing*. You understand?"

"So, they're gonna come at us?"

"They're gonna come at us *hard*."

"What if they get in?"

Milo locked eyes with him. "Then we fuckin' kick those numpties back *out*. Understand?"

Gus clutched his shotgun to his chest. He understood. They both went back to watching the events outside. A line of pickups appeared farther up the street. Leather surrounded them, and the meat puppets were loaded into the box beds. They didn't just climb into the rears, they hauled and pushed themselves aboard with a rabid vigor that was unsettling to see.

"They're getting into trucks, Milo," Gus said.

"I see that."

"The hell they up to?"

"You can be sure it involves getting in here."

Tailgates were slammed. Engines revved. And the meat puppets, their padded torsos visible over the pickup cabs, *screamed*, an anger-fueled yodeling that was frightening and carried across the cold cityscape. Blades were brandished, as were bats and those makeshift *Lord of the Flies* spears, with their pointed tips tempered by fire and scorched black.

Horns sounded in the distance.

The Leather crouched behind the trucks joined in, smacking the metallic hides and creating an even greater noise. And even though Gus had stared down entire armies of undead, all that noisemaking summoned an almost primal fear within him, one that started in his calves and spread to his chest in a clutch of icicles. He remembered the shitstorm that was *Camp Red Wolf* and glanced about nervously, dearly wanting to run, to just put boots to floor and leap out a window on the other side of the building. Maybe if he left now, they'd be preoccupied with Milo and saving the little freak bastard they had wired to a chair in the other room.

A hand on his shoulder almost broke him.

Holding his Glock at high guard, Milo shook his head, his message clear. *Don't you do it. Don't you break on me.*

Gus did not shake off the hand.

And some sixty feet back, the oddest thing happened.

A freak in a leather duster climbed into the rear of one of the parked pickups, just off to the side of the revving, screaming, yelling spectacle of meat, machine, and body-armored fabric. The Leather wore a mask, and it practically glowed with sunshine. The figure threw back one side of its coat and pulled a sword free, whipping it high overhead and holding it there as if about to start a race. Or lop the head off whatever poor bastard was nearby.

Daylight lit up the edge of that blade.

The revving of engines became impossibly louder.

The figure chopped at the building, signaling the leashes were off.

The pickups and their meat puppet cargo sped forward, rushing the windows while the Leather and their armed slaves not only continued making a racket, but somehow *amplified* it.

Milo stayed low and darted to the other side of the window. He met Gus's eyes, but didn't say a word.

The lead pickup swung to the right of the building and immediately slowed. Rusty brake pads shrieked. Three other pickups sped by, their boxes filled with rancid cheerleading squads. They ripped by the window, fast enough for Gus to hope the meat puppets would tumble onto the asphalt. There were dead bodies down there, but that didn't slow down the machines, as one charging truck bucked and jumped as if rolling over an unseen speed bump.

Gus took aim when a flurry of arrows rushed through the window, driving him back.

"*Jesus Christ*," he yelled, his voice drowned out by the crazed, earsplitting vocals and the brazen, open-hand drumming on rooftops. He was about to rush to the conference room when a pickup reversed at ninety degrees into the building, mashing tail gate against iron railing in a single, harsh note.

The first wave of masked freaks jumped for the window, holding up police shields.

Milo fired first.

*

When the Spider heard the crash of metal and glimpsed the teeming black figures attempting to jam themselves through the window, he began pulling on his bonds in earnest.

He had to free himself.

He had to free himself *now*.

*

The first black visor that appeared in the office window had two shots perfectly grouped within its face, violently perforating the polycarbonate, and not only kicking the head back, but heaving the entire meat puppet into his fellow companions.

Then all hell attempted to force its way into the building in a great, uncoordinated mass.

A bristling barrage of spears, machetes, and crowbars stabbed, chopped, and pawed around their shields while the meat puppets squealed with piggish glee. Eager to please their Leather overlords, that armored length of human train smashed against the opening, attempting to cram themselves into the room. Milo fired into legs and limbs, the Glock flaring, the shots booming in the close confines. He stuck the weapon over the shields, around, or under. Wherever there was a crack. The meat puppets' screaming reached new heights—until Gus entered the fray.

That initial frantic rush of invaders caused him to take a step back, to avoid the stabbing and swiping weapons. The window was only so big, but the meat puppets pushed forward in an oily surge, backing Milo up while they attempted to stab him. The scene was something out of a horror flick, where a multi-limbed alien mass attempted to shove its way through the window.

Some of those masked heads saw Gus, and that unlocked him. He unleashed the full might of the Ram Fist, halting the charge right at the threshold that was the windowsill. Rounds didn't just hit that fiendish, bloated mass of limbs and torsos, they *bashed* invaders backwards with bone-shivering violence. Two of the puppets were forcefully shoved back, becoming unwilling battering rams that smashed whoever was behind them. The charge stalled, freeze-framing for a split second upon a contested threshold before being kicked back. The Ram Fist shotgun didn't care about their crude body armor. It cared less about their numbers. It *heel-stomped* the armored slaves as if they were shocked ants. One shield twisted under the opening shots, the power too great to withstand, and that slanted opening was all Gus needed. He fired and blood erupted in thick drizzles. A hockey-masked head blew apart. A severed arm boomeranged over a shoulder. One round blew straight through two meat puppets at once in an explosion of grisly ribbons. Another flew backwards, ass over tits, and his legs kicked up in time for a full, unobstructed blast that removed *everything* below the puppet's knees in a gruesome erasing of limbs. Those that weren't hit by the same blast were speckled by grainy bits.

The shotgun's devastating salvo cleared the pickup's box bed, but the battle had a hold of Gus. He fired when he saw the cab. The blast punched a salty hole through the rear windshield and slammed the driver chest-first into the steering wheel, half-lifting him out of the seat.

The shotgun clicked empty then, forcing Gus to reload.

But with the can cracked open, Milo kept up the punishment, firing out the window when he abruptly spun and directed fire at the doorway *behind* him, nailing black garbed invaders from that quarter. The unexpected turning startled Gus, and he fumbled with his last magazine, while Milo divided his attention between the window and the doorway.

A meat puppet screamed gibberish outside; only the upper shoulders of the figure were visible above the windowsill. Another darted into view at ground level and pitched a javelin at the soldier—who magically ducked, rose, and put a round through the hockey mask of the thrower, torqueing that bone melon around in a spurt of coffee grounds. The puppet behind the falling corpse did a double take of the kill—a murderous beat before Milo lit him up with two rounds to the chest. The soldier crossed the floor as he fired, the impacts killing a meat puppet attempting to rise from the box bed.

Gus reloaded, wavered, waiting for instructions.

Milo didn't give any.

So Gus went for the doorway—just as a shape materialized within the frame, carrying a riot shield.

Gus didn't shoot the shield. He shot the forward boot underneath the shield, practically disintegrating that size eleven up to the ankle and causing a yowling of white-hot agony. The meat puppet pitched backward, falling near the office desk. Gus fired at more figures behind the crippled lead. The door frame exploded in thunderous puffs. Heads and torsos retreated from the overwhelming firepower.

Gus pursued them into the hall and fired.

One puppet flew *forwards* as if his ass were strapped to a jet engine taking off.

Another got mashed into a wall, where he quivered for a split second before falling.

Yet another got his shield up, but the tremendous impact of the shotgun still sent him airborne, back into the conference room.

Gus reached the conference room's doorway, where more meat puppets struggled to clear the overturned chairs and tables. Gus unloaded, spattering one puppet into a corner. Another figure was plastered against the window frame. Yet another tried to take Gus's head off with an axe but missed by a half foot—before the shotgun destroyed his chest and flayed him to the bone.

Then Milo was in the room, shooting exposed feet and knees, causing shields to drop before the finishing bullet, all the while pressing for the nearest window.

There were pickups parked outside, one on the railbed side and the other on the street side. Milo sank two rounds into the metal rump of the first and that got the driver anxious. The driver stomped on the pedal, choosing self-preservation above the collective, and peeled away in a screech of rubber. Milo crossed the floor to the other window facing the street. He slammed a shoulder to the wall and put his last round into the rear windshield. The shot prompted the driver to peal rubber and drive for parts unknown. The sudden acceleration yanked the three individuals still standing in the box bed off their feet and sent them flying. Two fell to the pavement, while the third managed to stay inside as the vehicle whipped past the concrete stairs to the main entrance.

Then they were gone.

The invaders repelled.

Broadheads sizzled through the space where Milo had extended his arms, missing his limbs by a hair. He pulled back, getting behind cover.

A shotgun blast whipped his head up.

Gus was nowhere to be seen.

"Gus?" Milo shouted. Aware of the open window and the shooters outside, he hurried over the mess on the floor, toward the hallway.

Gus stood over a corpse before the upstairs doorway. He turned at Milo's approach and visibly relaxed upon spotting him.

Milo inspected the human ruins coating the hallway.

"Jesus," he muttered.

"Packs a punch, don't it?" Gus asked.

"I'll say."

"This one," Gus pointed the smoking barrel at a carcass on the floor, "tried playing possum. Didn't work."

"They get you?" Milo asked.

"No. You?"

"No."

"What now?"

"Now?" Milo said. "We regroup and reload."

Licking the space where his front teeth used to be, Gus pawed at a coat pocket and extracted an extra magazine for the Glock.

Milo grabbed it on the fly.

They entered the office reception area, where Milo made a wide turn to check on their prisoner, still tied down to the chair.

"Wakey, *wakey*," Milo grunted as he clocked him—*hard*—across the jaw. The impact rattled the slumped-over figure.

If the Leather had been pretending before, he was pulling off a Shakespearean *performance* after that unexpected jaw-breaker. If the guy woke up in time for Christmas, Gus figured it would be too soon.

They stopped in the office, mindful of the bodies and the damage therein. Milo dropped to a knee, loading the fresh magazine into the Glock. The brutal repelling of the Leather siege resembled the aftermath of a particularly nasty house party which would require a shitload of screen doors and windows. The size and scope of it wasn't lost on Gus, and he zeroed in on the open window and the body hanging over the sill. He went to the corpse, mindful of staying out of sight. He lowered the shotgun long enough to grab a leg by the ankle and heave that impeding carcass all the way out the window.

Where it landed with a sandbag thud on the pavement.

"*Yeah!*" Gus shouted from behind cover. "*Yeah!* You all-weather chicken *fuckers*! That's *right*! First wave fuckin' *down* and we're still *here*! We're still fucking *here*, y'salty cocksucking tongue *flickers*. You open-mouth, tapioca puddin' jizzim junkies! Send more over if you got 'em. Send more over *when* you got 'em. Send 'em right on fuckin' *over!*"

Releasing that energy lightened Gus's mental load considerably. He glanced over at Milo, crouching and watching him with an expression of amused disbelief.

"What?" Gus asked. "Too much?"

"Y'know," Milo said after a long considering second, "I don't think it was." He crossed over to the other window.

Gus watched the soldier. "You okay?"

Milo glanced over again and did a curious thing. He *smiled*. Just a little one, but it was there, for all of two seconds before he got control of it. "Just the one spare for the Glock?"

"What you got is what I had," Gus replied.

"How many of those you got?" Milo asked, meaning shotgun rounds.

"This is it. Plus a few loose shells."

"Okay, well, we got plenty of pointy things here now, if we run out." He gestured at the tangle of bodies and the various arms scattered among them. "I'll keep an eye on those bastards out there. They'll think twice now before coming in here again. Thing is, if they have any mindless? We'll be overrun in no time. And if that happens…"

Milo shrugged and looked Gus in the eye. "You have my permission to shoot me."

That quieted the two men.

"Hey, listen," Gus started. "Back there, when we first came in here. You saved me. When I got clipped upside the head. You started swinging your bat there. Bought me a few seconds. So…" he almost hated saying it, but the truth was like that sometimes. "So… thanks. For saving my ass."

Milo absorbed that. "You're welcome. But, you sorta saved mine as well. Back when that Leather was pulling a knife in the hall. The asshole with the teeth. I saw him coming, while I was still wrestling with shithead back there. Not saying I couldn't have taken two of them, but thanks all the same."

Gus nodded. "All right. We're two thankful asshats."

Milo smiled again.

Gus was about to say *But I still hate your guts for shooting Collie*. What came out of his mouth, however, was, "I'm gonna check upstairs. It's bugging the shit outta me. Might be something up there to help."

"Give the whole place another go around," Milo said. "Maybe you'll find something to start a fire."

"Gonna burn something?"

Milo frowned. "I haven't been thinking here. They doused us in a few places with that ethanol-smelling shit. They did that to keep us inside, until reinforcements came, but it wasn't smart on their part. We can use that same shit to keep them out. You find something to start a fire, we'll light up the whole damn works."

"We still got the tankers out back," Gus pointed out.

"Yeah," Milo agreed. "It might come down to setting those off. Get moving. And hurry. Find something we can light up and toss outside. Just to keep them thinking."

Keeping out of sight of any snipers outside, Gus went on the hunt for fire.

33

Steampunk watched in black goggled dismay when the shooting started. His jaw dropped when the meat puppets were blasted back out of the windows, and he was mortified to see the building's defenders open fire upon the trucks. That ignited an unexpected frenzy, as the drivers weren't expecting to be shot at. Tires screeched as they bolted away as fast as possible while still maintaining control over their vehicles. A few of the meat puppets fell from the box beds onto the pavement, where they rolled over and either crawled or limped back to the Leather lines.

Steampunk glanced over at the Samurai, standing behind his pickup. The Leather didn't even flinch at the carnage.

A dry thud seized all attention then, as a body was flung out of a window and onto the sidewalk below. Then the yelling began. A foul, obscenity-laced blast that taunted the Leather surrounding the building.

When the yelling stopped, Steampunk glanced over at the Samurai again.

The Leather officer was still as stone, but there was a tightness about the figure, a spring-loaded tension, that wasn't present before.

Steampunk knew what it was.

It was anger.

*

As told, Gus decided to check the main floor again. The reception desk had nothing except office supplies and stationery. There were no secret stashes of cigarettes. No hidden lighters. Gus searched all the filing cabinets, opened drawers, and pawed through everything he could find. A *Mighty Hunter* magazine was in one drawer, with a smiling couple riding their four wheeled, all-terrain vehicle off into a rising sun, but nothing else. Gus stopped and pondered where to search next, his eyes lingering on the slumped form of the Spider in the room.

Gus had his shotgun. He knew what he should do, just for peace of mind, but he could not bring himself to execute a senseless dickwad of a prisoner. That made him think for a second, which got him moving for the storage room located adjacent to the reception area. There was a literal *ton* of combustibles inside—old furniture, cabinets full of folders and paper, but nothing else.

"Should've grabbed some of those grenades," Gus said, cursing himself for the oversight. Collie would chew him out for that. He looked at a windowless wall, in the direction of Fort Jay, and sent a silent message to her to be well… and to drive up in the limo and save their trapped asses.

Nothing answered him, however. Not even a single yodel from the masked derpwads laying siege to the place.

Fire. His old shifty friend. Gus needed to find fire. He searched through a pair of old lockers that should've been in a school somewhere.

Nothing.

"God*dammit*," he swore aloud. "You think they'd have a fucking match at least."

But they didn't.

He hurried back, giving Milo a curt headshake as he ran into the hallway. He skipped over the bodies lying about and hoofed it upstairs. He discovered another, much bigger office, with daylight from three windows lighting up the interior.

"Oh my," Gus whispered, sizing up the lordly space.

A sofa lay to his right, gray and massive and ideal for an afternoon siesta if the boss so desired. There was a coffee table covered in magazines before the sofa, and a couple of chairs just after that, facing what could only be the owner's desk—a grand chunk of wood with one of those world maps covering the majority of the surface. The wood was thick cut and heavy, scuffed by elbows and stained by hot coffee cups, and the sight of the desk made him glad he didn't have to carry the damn thing up the stairs. He gave it a nudge with his hip. No give at all. No movement. As thick as he was in the head at times, he wasn't an expert on wood, but this particular pyramid building-block of a desk definitely wasn't made of beaver barf shit like the receptionist one downstairs.

His eyes locked onto the matching cabinet behind the desk.

Nothing of use was inside, however. A framed picture of a family of four, all grinning as if the photographer had ripped a monster fart at the most perfect time. A pair of winter gloves belonging to a woman and still smelling faintly of strawberries. A dozen or so pocket novels as well as several technical textbooks. The prize was an unopened box of cigars, Cuban, but not a match or lighter in sight.

The desk also contained nothing of use.

"I mean, you got the *cigars*," Gus whispered. "How the hell do you light them? I mean… seriously?"

Bewildered by the lack of igniters, he drifted to the window behind the desk. He pressed himself against the wall and leaned in to peek, presenting no target at all. The sun warmed the clear glass. He tried to see what was below, and discovered he was situated above the main entrance and the stairs. Across that two-lane highway, the trucks remained like watchful Dobermans, and the Leather stood behind them, at the ready.

That sight lured him perhaps a little too much out into a sniper's sights.

A broadhead pierced the window, transforming the glass into a perfect doily of lightning before his face. Gus did a frenetic jig on the spot while reversing his ass full-speed backwards. He felt his cheeks, nose, and mouth, checking for blood, and exhaled a gust of relief.

"Fuck me," he whispered and sized up the bolt still stuck at an angle in the ceiling.

The sound of more engines distracted him.

And as much as he hated to admit it, they sounded *bigger*.

Gus turned and ran, almost clipping himself on the corner of the desk. He raced down the stairs, the light hitting the landing before him, and turned sharply while holding onto the railing.

With his three-fingered hand.

His grip faltered, and Gus sailed shoulder-first into the opposite wall, where he rebounded hard, leading with his chin. His good foot came down three-quarters of the way on the stair's edge and went over. His bad foot, unwilling and refusing to take the weight, immediately buckled.

Gus skidded headfirst down the stairs and into the hall. He got his right arm under his forehead so that the stairs only clipped the tip of his nose, which fluttered like a playing card in a bicycle wheel.

And all the while as he slid towards the hall, his mind screamed *RAM FIST!*

Still in his left hand, thank the Lord. Until the barrel jammed *into* the floor and wrenched it from his grip. At the same time, Gus rammed his head into what felt like an overfilled bag of grapes.

He came to a stop.

"Jesus," he whispered, feeling the rattling effects of the stairs on his nose and body. He lifted his head, seeing his arm draped over a mound. He still had a hold of the bullpup, aimed towards the main entrance.

Gus grimaced and pulled back enough to see that he'd landed right in the center of a dead man's crotch. A *damp* crotch.

Mouth-first.

"Oh Jesus, Jesus," he whispered when the smell hit him.

With a disgusted whimper, he untangled himself from the bloody corpse, trying hard not to look at the dead man. He glanced around, not seeing Milo anywhere, and thanking the Lord again for that small mercy. All he needed was the soldier reminding him of the time he practically gobbled a dead man's knob.

Gus's hand grazed the front pocket of the body.

And felt something.

He stopped and patted it down, feeling just a touch of metal within. He plunged his fingers into the pocket, and his eyes popped wide at the discovery.

*

Steampunk turned at the noise. The Samurai did the same.

Coming up the street was a pickup escorting a Mack transport truck, its pipes puffing blackness. The huge truck halted farther back, but the pickup proceeded a little more before stopping.

The Inflictor was the first to get out, dressed and outfitted in raw highway savagery. Even from a distance, Steampunk had no problem seeing the wiry thickets of man-moss coating those intimidating shoulders. Leather straps parted that human fur, connected to what looked like a set of leather overalls. Scorched dressings covered the Inflictor's face, while a set of aviator's goggles sized up the situation ahead.

Only for seconds, before the Bear Trap emerged from the same truck.

The leader of this particular war party wasn't the physical specimen that was the Inflictor. Not many were. But the Bear Trap radiated menace all the same. Covered in a studded leather duster common within the road clan, Bear Trap's features were hidden beneath a black and white bee-bottom ski mask. The one distinguishing characteristic, however, the one thing that let Steampunk know that this was the one and only Bear Trap, was the oversized set of aluminum jaws taking up most of his face. Fanged and serrated and twinkling in the sunlight, the low jaw actually *moved* when the Bear Trap moved his head, like a bare-assed skeleton having a quick chuckle. There were straps that kept that horrific piece of dentistry in place, and though Steampunk knew those oversized teeth were more theatre than practical, he also heard rumors the Bear Trap wanted to find someone who could rig up a *real* set of jaws, which would indeed bite.

And bite hard enough to sever.

The Bear Trap got out, assumed a gunfighter's stance, and stared at the siege before him. Sunglasses shielded his eyes. A black, felt cowboy hat with one squished side topped off his head, crowning his ski mask. Sunlight glinted off a fire axe he carried in one hand, just behind its red head.

The leader stood that way for a short time, before glancing over at the obedient Inflictor—who turned and cut a knife-hand across his throat.

The rumblings of all those engines stopped.

In the awesome silence that followed, the Bear Trap watched the office building. No one moved. Motors *pinged* as they cooled, and the barest of breezes swept over the scene.

The Samurai watched the Bear Trap.

Steampunk watched the Bear Trap.

The Bear Trap allowed his hand to slide to the mid-point of his axe. He lifted the red weapon into the air and waved.

Three lessers came forth, bearing a green cooler. Inside that cooler was a number of scent bags, the ones the mindless would follow into hell if need be.

Steampunk looked from the lessers to the Bear Trap and the Samurai, who drew close and exchanged words. Steampunk waited until he was summoned to give his reports.

When a voice shouted from *within* the building.

"*They're leaving out the back! Out the back!*"

34

The first tanker smashed through the chained doors in a brutal burst of metal and wood. Heavy slabs of debris rained down on the pickup parked in front of the door an instant before the tanker's greater mass slammed into the vehicle and shoved it broadside. The Leather minion in the box bed didn't have time to scream before he was pitched into the air. The tanker plowed the pickup a good twenty feet forward, clipping a power pole which ripped the bumper asunder with a steely squeal, and rammed the truck into the front of a nearby house. The windshield sprang free in a pebbly pop of glass. There was a stunned pause, and then the tanker, smashed hood and all, reversed with a shaky death rattle of gears. The thing backed up, shuddering on its chassis, and then drove forward at an angle.

Where it up and died in hacking chugs of black smoke.

The driver's side opened, and Milo dropped down to the street.

Engines were coming to life on the other side of the tanker. Gus knew he and Milo had very little time. The last five minutes seemed like seconds. So concerned with being captured and igniting the contents of the tankers as a last resort, neither Milo nor Gus had stopped to consider the more obvious way of escape, practically smacking their foreheads it was so obvious. One that only presented itself when Gus lay face-first in the balls and stink of a dead man. The corpse had two key fobs in his pockets, belonging to the tankers, and that set into motion the two men's last-ditch effort for escape.

That was all after Milo smoked the Spider one last time—a hard uppercut that would leave the Leather spitting chicklets all the way into next week.

From there, it was a sprint to the warehouse. They unlocked the bolts barring the main doors and unwrapped that knot of chains in a rattling rush. Milo ordered Gus into one tanker while he climbed into the first. The soldier then rammed the doors and smashed everything away, creating the opening for Gus to drive the second tanker through.

Milo hurried around the front of the intact tanker, going for the passenger side. Past the smoking wreck of the dying tanker, Gus saw shapes moving.

"Come on!" he shouted as Milo's head bobbed past the hood.

Two seconds later, the soldier was pulling himself into the cab.

Gus hit the gas pedal and the world turned until the tanker was facing a glorious open road. The wrecked tanker behind them only partially blocked the street, and already the surviving Leather were swarming the machine.

Didn't matter.

Milo slammed the door shut and let out a cowboy's peal of delight.

The tanker was an automatic, so Gus didn't have to worry about shifting gears. All he had to worry about was driving.

"Limo?" Gus asked.

"Limo," Milo replied.

"You know how to get to it?"

"Hell no."

Gus did a double take of the soldier before focusing on the road. "Fuck it, then."

Houses and small buildings whipped by. They headed north, then were forced to veer left, along the snaky Red River. Through gaps in between the houses, a bridge appeared in the distance. A new bridge that spanned the waterway.

"I see it," Gus said a second after Milo pointed.

"We cross that and then loop back for the limo."

"Got it." Gus checked his sidemirror. "Nothing yet."

Milo held onto an overhead grip and peered into the passenger mirror.

The few houses disappeared, replaced by an aging industrial section of the city. Filled parking lots whizzed by, along with on-site trailers for workers, and a collection of heavy equipment. Gus wheeled in and out of the few cars on the road, keeping the bridge in sight, all under a sunny November day.

"Well shit," he let loose, when the road straightened and darkened under an overpass, which sloped towards the bridge they wanted to take.

A spent avalanche of traffic choked the ramps, blocking any attempts to cross.

"That way," Milo pointed at the relatively empty road ahead. "There's other crossings."

Gus accelerated, ignoring the signage that recommended fifty kilometers.

Faded billboards and the odd mural sped past. *No Exit*, one sign said.

Watch us, Gus mentally projected and asked, "Where we goin'?"

"Just keep driving. That's north, and the river curves back and forth. Plenty of bridges. We just gotta find the one *not* blocked off."

"Maybe we came across the only one."

A pensive Milo glanced over but kept his mouth shut. Then his side mirror got his attention.

Gus looked into his.

"That didn't take long," he said before turning back to the road.

*

A dozen pickups closed the gap upon the speeding tanker.

Steampunk leaned forward, holding a length of pipe with the lower end bound in duct tape. The sound of straining rpms filled the interior of the vehicle, as the driver, wearing a cheap clown mask, concentrated on pursuit. Lessers stood hunched over in the box bed, holding onto the roof rack while carrying bats and axes with their free hands. Steampunk checked on his support and saw that he was the spearhead of the pursuing Leather. The Samurai was back there somewhere, as was the Inflictor and the Bear Trap. All the important people were present and involved, and Steampunk knew whoever captured the tanker would be held in high regard. Especially by the Dog Tongue.

The city streaked by in an early winter blur and the rising growls of horsepower. The tanker drew closer.

Steampunk adjusted his goggles and took a deep breath.

*

Gus swerved left and right, feeling the tanker's considerable ass swing, as if the machine were warning him not to get too crazy.

"Watch them," Milo cautioned, his attention divided between the road ahead and the trucks behind.

Gus kept glancing into his mirror.

Milo lowered the window, flooding the interior with cold air. He held the Glock between his legs. Knots of vehicles loomed in the road, creating a linear maze spaced out enough to easily navigate at a lesser speed, but driving at twice that gave Gus the cold sweats. He whipped by a small delivery truck, missing its corner by a foot. A red sedan zipped past, missing his left by the same margin. He shifted from one lane to the next, hearing the tires scrub against the concrete median dividing the road.

The lead pursuing pickup avoided the delivery truck and the sedan as well. It bounced over the low median, leaving the pavement in a rumble of horsepower before crashing down and fishtailing. The driver applied brakes to regain control and was left behind.

Two more pickups sped up to replace him.

"Don't let them get a bead on the tires," Milo yelled.

Gus knew that. He'd seen plenty of chase sequences in movies to know how things were done. Thing was, those were carefully choreographed maneuvers performed by professionals, designed to deliver maximum thrills, and usually done with a green screen or some other trickery. Gus was pretty much making shit up on the fly, and one wrong turn would have him clotheslined by his own seatbelt an instant before the tanker crashed into another car or a wall.

Colonial buildings stood tall on the corners of a large intersection. What might've been a shopping mall materialized on the far side. Vehicular blockades dotted the roads, some with their doors left wide open.

"Go right!" Milo shouted and pointed. "Up here! Turn *right*! *RIGHT!*"

Gus turned and felt one ass cheek leave the cushion. Both men leaned into that ominous tilt, flashing by a sign that said *Main Street*. The tanker clipped the open car door of a blue Camaro, sending it flying into the air in a loud and frightening reminder of the dangers of high speed on a crowded roadway.

Another overpass crossed the skyline ahead. The tanker charged it. The road sloped downwards into two lanes. Gus positioned the tanker's hood ornament right over the faded white line dividing the lanes. Daylight winked out as they charged through the tunnel. Support pillars flashed by.

Gus lost sight of the nearest trucks behind them, but he glimpsed what was coming behind those pickups.

A goddamn parade.

Sunlight flooded the cabin as the tanker emerged from the other side, charging by storefronts and various signage. The median on the left became a dangerous rise studded with decorative rocks, bare-naked trees, and the occasional power pole. The streets became four-lane obstacle courses on either side, littered with enough derelict vehicles to cause Gus's heartrate to red-line.

*

Speeding past a Leather truck to again take the lead, Steampunk saw the fleeing tanker drift back and forth over the dangerous road, attempting to block its pursuers. The driver was good, avoiding collisions with the abandoned traffic—with the exception of that one car door which dropped from the sky and bounced along the pavement. Steampunk believed his own driver superior to most. The clown straightened out his arms while gripping the steering wheel, concentrating on navigating the automotive graveyard.

What was farther up ahead got Steampunk's attention, however.

A rare drag strip of open road.

Banging on the ceiling, Steampunk alerted his crew in back to get ready. He was about to make his move.

When the fleeing tanker drifted left and then right, Steampunk gave the command.

And the clown hit the gas.

*

The pickup in Gus's side mirror suddenly swelled as it attempted to surge past him.

"Ram him!" Milo yelled.

Any other time, Gus might've told the soldier to fuck off.

Now wasn't one of those times.

He turned the tanker into the oncoming pickup's lane.

*

Unprepared for the tanker veering into him, Steampunk's driver swerved and lost control of the pickup. Moving at eighty, the pickup was redirected into the lethal speed bump that was the median. The machine's front wheels bronco-bucked over the concrete edge, salad-tossing bodies from the box bed. Steampunk cringed as brakes were applied.

The clown screamed. The truck's left tire hit a boulder, and the world went into a punishing tailspin that threw and thrashed an unbuckled Steampunk around as if caught in a savage spin cycle. Bones snapped and arms flopped.

The last thing Steampunk saw was a pickup truck charging his grill, and the split-instant glimpse of the Leather *inside* the opposing rig...

Then the collision, and the irresistible force of two large masses mashing into each other.

*

The pickup made a vicious whirl before being slammed grill-first by another speeding truck, where both vehicles did a spectacular demolition *doh-si-doh* curtsy in the street. Gus glimpsed bodies being ejected from the impact as crooked parts scattered in all directions. A leather figure skidded across the pavement like a human torpedo doing at least a hundred… before vanishing from sight.

Then Gus was back concentrating on his own driving.

Milo jerked one way then the other, trying to ascertain what was happening behind him.

"They crash?" he asked.

"Yeah."

Milo watched his mirror. "There's more coming. The river's over there. Just keep doing what you're doing. You're doing great."

Several side roads streaked eastward between the main street buildings. Signage whipped by, too fast to read. A clutter of cars formed a roadblock up ahead, and Gus braked to give himself enough time to get around them.

"*Oh shit!*" Milo screamed, scaring the unsweetened chocolate out of Gus before an unseen juggernaut slammed into the tanker's rear with a boom of popping metal. The force jerked both men around, but their seatbelts kept them grounded as pieces rattled off the asphalt. The rear wheels skidded three feet to the left. A pickup bounced to a stop behind the tanker, its chrome pipe fixtures hanging off its grill.

The tanker's tires got traction and kept moving, but there was a new sound now, one of steel grinding relentlessly against rubber sidewall.

"The fuck was that?" Gus yelled as he eyed the gauges.

"Pickup rammed us," Milo reported, trying to keep sight of his mirror. "Shot right out from one of those side streets like a fucking missile, the sneaky cock-knuckle."

"*Fuckin'* cock-knuckle. Give me a heads-up next time."

"I'll try. Must be another road running parallel with the river. One without all this shit."

Great, Gus thought.

Within his side mirror, the shaky image of another pickup surged forward, growing within the frame. The driver saw an opening and decided to go for it.

Gus pulled to the left, cutting off the lane.

The pickup driver suddenly didn't want anything to do with the tanker and swerved to avoid.

Straight across the street and into a metal lamp post.

The boom was startlingly loud and hollow, as if someone had just burst a metallic paper bag. The lamp post buckled at the halfway point, its upper mast falling and karate-chopping a storefront. A leather-clad body shot out from behind the truck's windshield and spattered the large window. Gus wasn't even sure what he saw was a person at first until he saw the fluttering arms and the boots.

Then he was back, focusing on the road.

Two lanes over, a pickup sped into sight. Gus saw him, the driver wary of the aggressive tanker. The figure in the passenger seat stared at him. The golden face and helmet were that of a samurai, with an expression of unhappiness that Gus thought just a touch surreal.

"There! *There!*" Milo yelled.

Gus saw the turn and didn't check his mirror. He braked, the grinding from the rear diminishing as he put his foot down. A metro bus flashed by. Then a pawn shop that bought gold and a liquor mart. Then the intersection and a pile-up of vehicles that might've been the result of God just upending a toy box upon the street and pawing through it all, looking for the rare hot-rod edition.

But there was an opening before that mound of scintillating metal heaped underneath the sun. An improvised endzone that consisted of one corner of a brick building, a collapsed wire mesh fence covering the grass like a crude electrical grid, and the towering ass of a dead transport truck which formed the other corner. The front of the transport was mashed into the automotive heap dumped into the heart of the intersection.

There wasn't much room.

Hell, Gus figured his fucking *pee-hole* was wider.

Out of time and options, he aimed the tanker for the opening. It would be a tight fit—tighter than a rusty catheter threading an old man's pisser.

The sight of all that potential mayhem robbed Milo of words, and he jammed himself into his seat as far back as the cushion would allow.

The tanker jumped the curb with a crash and rattle that might've ripped the entire chassis from underneath. The world bounced. A sun visor flopped down, dropping an assortment of pamphlets into the cab. Ass cheeks left their indented cushions as seatbelts locked in place. The front tires rolled over the fallen fence in a monstrous snap, pop, and crackle that ripped up the length of Gus's spine before ringing his brain and putting vibrations to his teeth. The corner of the building slapped away the passenger side mirror in an explosion of metal and glass, causing Milo to flinch from his window.

Both men were screaming, shrieking those final *we're gonna die* pipe-organ notes that signaled the final fleeting moments they would ever know…

Then they were through.

A panting Gus stopped screaming and straightened out the wheel. His throat hurt after singing those high death notes he never thought possible. His boot located the gas as his hands reaffirmed their grip on the steering wheel. The tanker responded, but there were new sounds over the relentless grinding of sidewalls. Fire appeared in Gus's mirror.

Not fire. *Sparks.*

"What is that?" a recovering Milo wanted to know.

"We're dragging a section of the fence."

That dumbfounded the soldier.

A section of mesh and the support piping stuck out from beneath the fuel tanks and strummed the streets like a flattened bird's nest of live wires. Gus almost barked a laugh until he realized what he was driving.

And the hundreds—perhaps *thousands*—of liters of fuel the tanker was potentially carrying.

He and Milo shared a *holy shit* moment, before they both got back to the business at hand.

A straight two-way strip, right up to a steel truss bridge much like the one they'd crossed on foot. The tires' screaming increased, as did that labored grinding that slowed them down. Gus accelerated all the same, ignoring the red-lining of important gauges along the instrument panel, ignoring the sparkling mesh underneath the chassis. His pursuers came into view, spreading out as wide as they could on the two-lane road. Gus kept the tanker straight, hogging the ghostly yellow line.

A snack truck appeared just ahead, stopped in the middle of the road. Signage and lettering on the truck's side offered chili-cheese dogs and three-patty meat (or *non-meat!*) burgers.

"Speed up," Milo ordered. "And ram that fucker."

"What?"

"Right on the corner there. Speed up, power through, and bitch slap that thing's ass."

Gus did as ordered, hearing the sickly groan of the machine giving everything it had left, but weakening with every passing second. An unhealthy chuffing erupted from under the hood, the sound horrifying. He floored the gas, demanding whatever the tanker had left. The machine responded, impossibly sped up, and the snack truck, the size of a small RV, rushed forward. Gus braced for impact, focusing on the very spot where the two machines would meet.

The tanker clipped the rear of the snack truck doing a hundred and *ten* kilometers an hour, and that was more than enough to send the unmoving vehicle into a destructive tailspin. There was a nerve-peeling *bang* of metal as the tanker's hood crumpled and launched over the roof in a colon-clutching moment. A headlight burst apart. The tanker's left fender leapt up and did a cartwheel over the hood, punching a section of the windshield and leaving a mark. The grill was ripped off like weak wallpaper and whipped out of sight, while the snack truck spun around *behind* the forward-charging machine mass.

Where it rolled to a stop a few feet behind.

Effectively blocking the road.

Which left Gus with a clear path all the way across, to the other side.

"Straight?" Gus yelled.

"*Straight*," Milo replied, no longer distracted by his side mirror.

Gus looked into his and saw the shredded rhombus that was the section of wire fence once hanging off their ass, but now jutting out from underneath the wreck of the snack truck.

Problem solved.

Except for the gray-black, intestinal coils of smoke issuing from the tanker's hoodless engine block. The tanker was noticeably losing power, as if gut shot and running on fumes alone.

Gus pumped the gas, but his speed slid down to forty as they reached the other side of the bridge. "Losing speed here. Something got wrecked."

Milo looked around. They were driving through a residential zone. Brick houses behind wild hedges went by, along with the occasional two-story apartment building.

"Funeral home," Gus said.

On the corner of the next intersection, big balloon letters on a sign said, *Safe Journey*.

"Right!" Milo demanded. "Go *right*."

Gus saw the side road. "There?"

"*There!*"

The tanker rolled onto the road, and Milo checked on the whereabouts of the Leather.

"See them?" Gus asked.

"Yeah," Milo said.

*

Brakes squealed as the lead pickup stopped before a roadway covered in debris. The Bear Trap stuck his head out the window and stared at the wrecked snack truck blocking the way. The tanker had gotten through but had taken a steel fist to the face for its efforts. The pickups would not fare any better, and the Bear Trap wasn't about to damage his rides without reason or reward.

And the black smoke fuming from the tanker informed him that there would be reward, very soon indeed.

The Leather still had to deal with the roadblock that was the snack truck.

The rest of his war party stopped behind him, their engines rumbling in his ears. Several minions were already jumping out, going for box beds to gather up chains or ropes. The Samurai leaned out a window, staring on impassively.

The Bear Trap shouted and all movement paused.

The Bear Trap then gave orders to the Inflictor, riding in the backseat of the crew cab, looking like an ogre that had survived a burning at the stake.

The pickup truck bounced as the enormous bruiser dropped down to the pavement. He straightened, and as he did, he made a show of rolling his massive shoulders. The Bear Trap didn't care for such theatrics, and he let the enforcer know. The blowtorched dressings hiding the Inflictor's face made the day all the gloomier. The Inflictor's goggles stared ahead at the snack truck, and he strode forward with purpose, all the while throwing those spine-snapping arms of his wide in a warm-up stretch. He stopped at the front of the machine, which had been turned around upon colliding with the tanker. The Inflictor sized up the situation while the Bear Trap and the remainder of the Leather watched and waited.

Without warning, the big man dropped into a half squat and hooked those nail-studded calloused hands underneath the front of the vehicle. He huffed, and then actually growled, which caused the Bear Trap's driver to glance over at his leader.

The Bear Trap stared on, ignoring the lesser.

The Inflictor growled one last time as his hairy shoulders flexed and rippled. His legs tensed with the enormous weight of the snack truck. Then, as slowly as a mountain freeing itself of the earth, the Inflictor straightened.

Lifting the front of the truck in a groan of metal.

If it wasn't for those rotten dressings covering his face, arteries the size of tree roots would be seen bulging from the Inflictor's neck.

There was another lung-clearing snort of air, a refueling then, and the big man slowly tip-toed backwards, *pulling* the snack truck out of the way of the Leather.

*

The thickening smoke from the engine rendered the road visible for a couple of seconds at a time. A viscous smear coated the windshield as well. Gus tried using the wipers, but only the one on Milo's side responded, and that only worsened matters. Not that it mattered. The tanker was chugging along at a shaky thirty kilometers an hour, and every nine or ten seconds, the engine would cough and shake as if stricken with deathly pneumonia.

Milo lowered his window and checked on their bearings.

"All right," he said. "The river's on the right. We stay on this road, or any other heading east. With luck, we can reach the limo."

"I like that," Gus said, straining to see through the growing mess of his windshield. "Anyone after us?"

Milo leaned out the window and twisted his head around. He grimaced and pulled himself back in after a moment. "Can't see shit. But they'll find us."

Gus figured they would. The tanker was smoking like an incinerator choking down a meal of rubber tires.

"We could run," Milo suggested. "On foot."

Gus shook his head. "I'm getting thirty klicks out of this thing now. You ain't getting thirty klicks outta me if we get out and run. Ain't no way."

Right at that instant, the tanker hit a pothole that left both men weightless for all of a micro-second. Then the tanker bounced, *hard*, thumping both men around in their seats. Gus's jaw clacked off his chest and he hit the brakes out of reflex. The tanker slowed but kept running.

"Jesus Christ and shit on rye," Gus muttered and hunkered low over his steering wheel.

"Watch where you're going," Milo warned.

"I am watching."

"Like just then?"

"Well, stop talking to me while I'm driving."

"Just watch the fuckin' road."

Gus shot him a glare, but Milo was already divided between gazing ahead and trying to see what was behind.

"Yeah," Milo said, whipping his head back and forth and up and down. "We're close."

"Close to what?"

"The river. Turn here."

Gus hauled the tanker onto a southerly route.

"Work it," Milo urged. "Everything you got."

The last word he said was nearly drowned out by a loud popping from the engine.

The road became a four-lane highway running north and south. Gus didn't recognize any of the city features.

"We're close," Milo informed him as the tanker chugged past a section of parkland. "Bridge up ahead and I'll bet you this is the one we couldn't cross."

"Which means?"

"There! Take the ramp right *there*. On your left."

A sign that read *Talbot Avenue* passed Gus's line of sight. He turned, and silently prayed for the tanker to last a little longer. They rumbled along the residential street with the odometer's needle wavering at the twenty-five kilometer per hour mark. Apartment buildings huddled along the road, but between them were empty parks with faded yellow grass.

And every now and again, Gus thought he could see an opening past it all, which had to be the banks of the river.

"Just a little more," Milo urged, growing more excited. "We're almost there."

Which was when the tanker up and died.

35

The tanker came to a stop with a cancerous chuffing and a belch of smoke. With its last remaining gigs of power, it sent up an alarming SOS across its dashboard display, informing the men that it pretty much had the goddamn equivalent of a massive heart attack.

Whereupon the machine up and died on the spot.

Gus pumped the gas anyway, trying to resuscitate the battered thing, and failing miserably.

"Forget about it!" Milo shouted and opened his door. He got out and reached back for his bat. "We hoof it from here."

Gus released the steering wheel, knowing the situation and what lay ahead. His foot was already dreading the run, and his ass wasn't happy about it either. He got out, dragging his shotgun along with him.

Milo was already bolting away from the dead tanker.

With one final pat of good-bye on the door, Gus lumbered into a run after him.

And while he ran, the growing sounds of motorized hunters filled his ears.

*

The Leather reached the smoking carcass of the tanker. The Bear Trap led the way, leaning forward in his seat as his driver slowed the pickup down. Black coils enveloped the front of the tanker, but there was enough room for the pickup to get around. The big machine had the living shit kicked out of it, but the storage tank itself looked intact, which was good. The fuel stored there would be later salvaged and transferred to another container.

But first, the Bear Trap wanted the person who had taken the tanker in the first place, and who had caused so much excitement this day. The Bear

Trap wanted to capture that person and show him what excitement was all about. Some *real* excitement.

The driver steered the pickup through the smoky veil, and when the smoke cleared, he pointed.

The Bear Trap saw.

Not half a klick away, stupidly running down the middle of the street, were two fleeing fugitives.

The Bear Trap reached over and slammed his palm down on the horn.

*

The truck horn goosed the very air, causing an overheated Gus to glance over his shoulder.

There, speeding down the road, was a pickup. And as Gus continued to slap pavement, his fucked-up foot sounding the alarm with every step, *more* trucks charged into view and picked up steam.

"This way!" Milo shouted, jerking Gus's head around.

The soldier ducked into a driveway, cut across a backyard, and pounded through the neighbor's driveway, which faced an adjacent street.

"River's right there!" Milo pointed with the bat. He cut across an urban strip of prairie dotted with a few trees, leaving Gus some twenty feet behind.

The guy was right, however. The river was right there.

And as a red-faced Gus hurried at failing speed, he saw what Milo saw.

Looping chains hung from knee-high posts, sectioning off a riverside park of sorts, where the grass grew high around a few benches facing the river. The river itself was just beyond that. A green sign said "NAIRN AVENUE" and pointed at the four-lane road with a helpful white arrow, but that didn't lift Gus's spirits any.

It was all open ground, and nowhere to hide.

Across the road was an apartment building of sorts, but there was no way either one of them would make it. Not at the rate the Leather were gaining.

And to make matters worse, the parking lot of abandoned cars was visible, merely a minute's run away, on either side of the same arched truss bridge he and Milo had crossed earlier that day.

Gus knew the limo was close.

Just when the limo crept into view, sliding out from behind the far side of the apartment building, rolling into full sight.

Gus staggered to a stop and stared goggle-eyed at the approaching vehicle. The long-assed SUV glided along like a smiling automotive crocodile eyeing a couple of wildebeests hanging out by the river.

Milo skidded to a halt.

The SUV stopped with a lurch, the engine loud and rumbling.

No, Gus corrected himself, he wasn't hearing the limo. That thing's electric motor barely made any noise at all.

He looked over his shoulder.

A wedge of pickup trucks spread themselves out through the street and parkland behind him, slowing down because of a few roadblocks.

*

The Bear Trap spotted the limo first.

But his driver was the one who said it.

"Is that a fuckin' *limo*?"

No sooner were the words uttered when the limousine's roof both lifted and extended, hoisting itself upwards a foot and revealing an ominous deck that sported a pair of holes.

The Bear Trap stared at those menacing open ports in narrow-eyed disbelief.

When the limo opened fire.

*

The blasts prompted Milo and Gus to drop and kiss asphalt. Unseen projectiles screamed past them and left smoke trails a microsecond before the explosions kicked in. The lead pickup took a missile straight to the engine block. For an instant, the machine looked like it had its face forcefully driven back, as if refusing to taste something, before the entire vehicle blew apart in a burst of chunks, flames, and rolling smoke.

The blast left Gus lying on his side, slack-jawed.

More explosions erupted, a series of bubbly fireballs that swept through the Leather's motorcade and bounced trucks off the earth like toy vehicles upon a flaming trampoline. Truck doors flew off and thudded to a stop some twenty feet away. Freed tires rolled away. One pickup attempted a standing somersault in the very place it stopped, only to be grabbed by gravity and pile-driven, face-first, into the parkland. Leather-clad figures partially obscured by haze did lazy loop-de-loos before being swallowed up by the smoke. The other pickups drove through the billowing clouds and rampant destruction and swerved left and right in ear-ripping peals of rubber on pavement. Unable to hold on, figures tumbled from box beds and fell, skittering across the hard asphalt, getting much more than just a road rash.

But the limo no longer fired directly at the trucks.

That long-bodied mechanical titan of destructive energy launched explosive rounds into the air, which didn't simply rain down, but fell with hammering blows. Chunks of earth and pavement erupted in blooming geysers of matter. One pickup flipped ass-over-tits as if it had rammed grill-first into a fire hydrant—before blowing apart in mid-toss. Another rig did the exact opposite, flipping *backwards* from an unseen force detonating in its box bed, which came apart as if made of tissue. Debris pitter-pattered over everything, reaching out and quickly peppering Gus, while a billowing blob of smoke obscured the land. A length of chain clattered off the road. Then a golden mask. Half a charred torso splattered not ten feet away from where Gus lay, scaring the bejesus out of him. He lifted a hand to shield himself not only from the parts and pieces raining down, but from the incredible wall of heat that enveloped him a split second later. A moisture-evaporating, hateful furnace belch that sizzled his sweat and skin and dried out his eyes against the insides of his closed lids.

Through the smoke and the cascading bits of earth, metal, and meat, the explosions continued to rip through the street, the park area, and the houses just beyond. The one or two trucks that avoided the initial destruction from above were eventually tossed into the air. Whoever was unleashing that killer salvo had cast a wide net, ensuring that there was no escape. Seconds after it seemed all life had been destroyed, *more* explosions ripped into the earth, pummeling the world and sending shockwaves through the ground.

Gus blinked, forcing water to his eyes, watching the thundering dust and flare-ups of flame through the shifting smoke.

Goddamn.

It was Collie, of course. There was no one else. She'd made her way to the city, somehow located the limo, and come looking for them. Her timing was ungodly good, if not a touch cliché after the fact, but goddamn cliché, too. If cliché meant saving his ass, then give Gus a fucking cliché every day of the week and twice on Sunday.

His ears ringing, he reached up to cover them when movement caught his attention. A figure appeared through all that carnage then, striding forward through the thick charcoal gauze of smoke, coming into focus. Maybe Gus was shell-shocked from the overwhelming bombardment, but he thought the thing walking out of that hellfire and smoke moved in cinematic slow motion.

And the sight of it chilled him right down to his nuggets.

A man, an impossibly *huge* man, waded through that storm squall of falling debris. Leather-clad, of course, but what got Gus's attention, what truly horrified and mystified him, was that the towering sonnavabitch was holding a truck *door* over his head, using it as a shield against the killer tempest. That imposing figure strode through the dreamy destruction all around him, coming into greater clarity with every step.

Until the final, game-ending shell fell from the sky with a high pitched-whistle.

It was a stage-exiting encore of *fuck you, you're dead and I'm not*, where all the chunks and parts strewn across the killing field were lifted into the air and flipped yet again.

And one of those blasts blew the advancing goliath apart in a spray of hot tar.

The truck door clattered to the street, where it rattled about for a second before becoming still.

When everything became silent.

"Christ almighty," Gus whispered and collapsed, bopping the back of his head off the pavement. That hurt, but pain meant he was still alive. So there he stayed, too wasted to move, too overwhelmed to think. There he lay, waiting, for that one parting shot which would remind him that, yes, his bacon had been flicked off the fire yet again, but there would be some charring around the edges.

All he heard was the crackling of fire.

Fire that was coming closer.

He turned his head to see the limo creeping along the road, its stretched-out bulk as sleek as a great white shark just after a very bloody feeding. The fire wasn't fire at all, but rather the crackling of pebbles underneath the great machine's multiple tires. Gus tried to sit up, but his body wanted none of that. His limbs failed him, seemingly boneless, thrumming with spent energy. *Shell-shocked*, he figured. Sensory overload by the shock and awe of the limo's weapons systems. He squeezed his eyes shut for a resetting moment and that helped. He rolled over onto his side and barfed, the puke bursting from him in a rancid jet. A beans and baloney gravy that wanted out. There wasn't much—he didn't remember eating much, really—but he had the sense enough to move away from that awful stream and wait for rescue.

The tires continued to roll toward him.

Maybe it wasn't Collie.

Maybe it was someone else. Someone who managed to gain access to the limo, because he couldn't, not for the life of him, remember if he'd locked the doors or not.

That little thought distracted him more than he knew, because boots magically appeared not five feet away from him. Right in front of an imposing tire. Gus flinched and wondered where the last few seconds had gone.

"You okay down there?" Collie asked.

Gus looked up at her and took his time answering. "Yeah."

"Yeah, you look okay. Still got all your parts."

"Yeah." Seemed so, and he gently moved some of the more important pieces. Everything responded.

"You kids," Collie continued after a beat, shaking her head. "See, this is why we can't go anywhere. Or have nice things. And especially why I can't leave you by yourselves at night. Lock the doors, I said. Get to bed, I said. And the minute my back is turned…"

His senses still a touch scrambled, Gus just lay there and took it.

"Well, you're both in one piece," she sighed with a shrug. "Can't complain, I guess. Thank the Lord for 'B and E' explosives, s'all I can say. I know they left the paint business behind, but I swear I smell a touch of turpentine coming from somewhere. God*damn*. I thought for sure I'd hit a gas line but nope. Good thing I didn't. That shit would've gotten the stadium a rockin'. Mm-hm. Yippee-ki-yay and all that shit."

She stopped talking and stood over Gus. Only then did he notice the assault rifle in her arms.

He cleared his throat. "How'd you…"

"Find you?" Collie finished after it became clear Gus wasn't operating at maximum efficiency. "Not hard. After I finished up at Fort Jay, I headed back to get you guys, only you guys were gone. Not even a note on the kitchen table, fuck you very much. Anyway, after a minute of deduction, I figured you took off after the same dickweasel I was after. Only one road down to the city, and I knew the Leather were camped out at the hotel. So, I hit the highway and drove on down. Not like the traffic was bad or anything. Found the limo back there. And found a banged-up Mustang I recognized right after that. Didn't find you guys, though."

Gus blinked as a ringing in his ears came and went. When it finally left him, he grimaced, wiped his mouth, and tried to sit up.

"Take it easy now," Collie told him. "Nothing's moving around here besides you, me, and Milo."

Gus questioned her with a look, then he remembered who Milo was. He took another couple of seconds before asking, "You killed them all?"

"Oh fuck yeah. Just listen. Hear that? Nothing, right? No dipshit Leather driving away, right? Goddamn right there's not. I unloaded everything in the missile system, seeing as you had a small army on your ass. *Then* I unloaded the grenade launchers. For dessert. Wide-spread. Forward and aft. Dropped a ton of boom-boom on anyone thinking they could play dead. I hate them phony-assed bitches. And the stragglers. I'd say I got 'em all. And one or two gophers besides."

Gus stared at her. "How'd you get in the limo?"

"The limo?" Collie lifted her mask to reveal her mouth. "I just rained sulfur down on these fuckin' heretics and you're wondering how I got into the car? Man oh man. Well, if you *must* know I got a second set of keys, okay?"

Gus hardly heard any of that, because he was staring at Collie's lower face. A cadaver shade of gray-black, streaked with dark lines that could only be veins and arteries. Her carotids were especially visible, resembling engorged worms stretched from chin to collarbone, against a background of charred webbing.

And as if realizing her mistake, Collie pulled her mask back down over her face. She didn't say anything. Didn't have to. Gus had seen enough, and something inside him sank.

"Don't worry about that," she said, cutting off whatever he might say, but in truth, what he'd just seen robbed him of all speech.

"Don't you worry," Collie repeated in a much gentler tone. She bent to help him. "C'mon. Can you stand?"

36

The three of them later gathered around the front of the vehicle, eyeing the craters of the warzone while the smoke dissipated. Collie was right. If she'd hit a gas line, any residual fumes would have finished off the place entirely. As it was, Gus felt like he was in downtown Annapolis, just after he'd lit up the place. Wreckage covered the street and park area with shiny garnishes of shredded metal. There were bodies amongst that mess as well, the closest being that one Leather that had been cut in two and was currently decorating the middle of the road.

Gus didn't stare at that mess for too long, but he figured he'd still have nightmares.

"So, the survivors, they're back there?" Milo asked.

"At the fort, yeah," Collie said, lifting one butt cheek off the front of the limo. "Why does this thing smell like dead ass? Jesus. You guys hit a skunk or something?"

Neither man answered her.

"What're you going to do with them?" Milo asked.

"I gave them directions to Whitecap," she said. "They got the rigs the Leather had. No big deal to get the fuel outta those tanks. And they said they had extra stored nearby. They'll make it."

"And that's it?"

"That's it."

"No interviews?" Gus asked, turning away from the battleground.

"No time."

"You just sent them on to Whitecap? I mean, I thought…" he trailed off.

"I gotta sense about these things," Collie told him. "You should know. And hope. They're good people. Might be one or two assholes in there, but overall, good people."

Gus cleared his throat. "Just wondering, s'all."

"Wonder away. And I found Sandy's aunt with those prisoners. Guess what? Her name? Collette. Yeah, Collette Garber. And *she* goes by the name of Collie."

"Freaky," Gus muttered.

"I know, right? So, anyway, I thought that was good karma. Which helped in the decision to send them on to Whitecap. Reunite what's left of that family, anyway. Maybe we'll reunite a few more on this run."

No one said a word to that.

"One thing's bothering me," Gus said. "Uh… while my dinner bell was ringing and I was on my back there, did I see… a *giant* walking out of that smoke?"

"Big guy carrying a car door?" Collie asked. "Using the thing like an umbrella? Yeah, you did. Before I sank his battleship-sized ass. Stupid bastard. Bringing a car door to a missile fight. Oh my. Hope they're all as smart as that."

They quieted then, thinking.

"Maybe they are as smart as that," Milo said.

That got him looks.

"No, really," he said. "The Leather… I never once heard any of them talk shop. No army or police lingo was dropped—anything that might indicate that they had training of some kind. None of that shit. I think I said they sometimes *move* like they have training, but that's it. All they have is numbers, really. And the leather get-ups."

"And the mindless," Collie said.

"But no training. Nothing. Except that willingness to put the hurt on others."

"Truth is," Collie said, "these days, that's all anyone really needs."

Another round of quiet.

"All right," Gus declared and slap-wiped his hands. "What now?"

"Getting on in the day," Collie said. "I think we reload and ride on to the hotel. See what's up."

"To the hotel?" Milo asked.

"Yeah. See if there are any leftovers. Hard to believe we caught them all here."

"Well, nothing moving out there," Gus said, gesturing at the graveyard before them.

The black mask turned to him. "Exactly. So we go to the hotel. We make sure. Just so we're clear, this is the mission. We're killing every last one of those leather-wearing fuckers. We're not leaving anything unturned. We're especially going to kill any of the *leaders*, that being Dog Chops."

Gus lowered his head at that. She was getting good at screwing around with the Dog Tongue's name.

"Who drove down here?" she asked. "You do that, Milo?"

The soldier nodded.

"Then you take the wheel again." With that she fished out the key fob and waved it at the limo. Doors chirped. "Go on. Get in."

Milo did exactly that.

Collie waited until he was gone then, "Anything else on your mind?" she put to Gus.

He saw his reflection in her sunglasses. "No. Thanks."

"You sure?"

Gus nodded, taking care not to look at her neck.

"How was Milo?" she asked.

That was a stinger, and he took a while to answer, making sure the soldier was out of earshot. "He… was good. Yeah. He did all right."

"Yeah? Excellent. See? Intuition. Same vibe I got from Collie Garber."

Gus didn't tell her about how Milo had saved him back in the office hallway, when he got touched up by a bat. A part of him just didn't want to put any more of a shine on the guy.

Another part of him didn't want to admit he might have been wrong about Milo.

"Okay," She said. "Let's hit that hotel."

"Wait," Gus said. "We better check out something first…"

"What's that?"

"The warehouse."

"All right. We go back the way they came, in case someone's on the road wondering what all the smoke and noise was about."

Gus didn't care. All he wanted was to be inside the armored comfort of the limo.

They got aboard and got moving, with Milo driving around that bit of scorched earth and the deceased Leather. And just beyond the worst of it, struck by the farthest reaching of the launched missiles and grenades… was a transport truck. The Leather's transport truck. The rig had been in the rear of the pursuing Leather, and had taken an explosive right on the chin. The engine resembled a crushed beer can that had been tossed into a campfire, while the cab remained intact. The windshield, however, had been blown out, and the two ragged figures inside were bloodied and dead.

The transport's cargo trailer was untouched, however.

"Well, shit," Gus let out, peering between the head rests.

"What do you think?" Milo asked.

"We gotta check it out," Collie said. "Gotta make sure. Could be people in there. Ball-gagged and squatting in the corners. And it could be crammed full of MBs."

Gus sighed. "I'll go."

"No," Collie said and opened the door. "I'm going, just back me up."

Without another word, she got out and took her assault rifle with her.

"No fear in that one," Milo said under his breath as Collie walked to the front of the limo.

"None," Gus agreed.

The operator took her time sauntering over to the truck's cab, bracing her rifle against her shoulder and taking a firing stance at the warped door. She got in close then, pulling herself up a short set of steps to the cab. After a quick inspection, she dropped back to the pavement, gave a thumbs-up at the limo, and continued walking, sizing up the trailer as she went.

The doors were chained and padlocked.

The limo pulled up alongside the rear just as Collie rattled the chains. She took a step back after that.

Gus lowered his window and leaned out to better see and hear.

"Anything?" he called out.

Then he heard it. The maddening beat of dozens, no *hundreds*, of hands slapping against the container walls. A concert-sized mob jam-packed into an eighteen-wheel cage with no windows. There was even a smell, faint, but, if those doors were open, Gus figured it would be the equal of tear gas for sheer debilitating power.

Collie cocked her head as if smiling.

"Still think they're people?" he asked.

"Nope," she answered. "But there's one way to find out for sure."

Gus thought she was going to open the doors. She didn't, though. Instead, she got close to the rear of the transport.

"Anyone in there?" she called out.

More hammering, like hundreds of amateur drummers warming up and each one doing their own thing. All those hands banged on the walls as if they were steel drum bongos. Then came the wailing, and the sound of that caused Gus to be very attentive indeed.

"I said, anyone in there?" Collie asked again, though the noise overpowered her weakened voice.

Fuck it, Gus thought, and with a warning glance at Milo, he got out.

Collie turned and squared up as if ready to fire upon the limo if Milo decided to drive away. Gus left the door open, but that meant little. If the soldier wanted to go, he could do so, and there wasn't a damn thing either one of them could do about it. Worse, the mistake would be on Gus's shoulders.

Milo, however, did nothing of the sort. He kept the motor running.

"Shouldn't you be in the car?" Collie asked, after a few seconds.

"Huh?" Gus asked back.

"You heard me."

"You can't yell worth shit anymore."

"That's not what I meant."

"I know what you meant and… look. He's still there."

And he was, but for all her talk, Collie still drifted over to the passenger side and opened the door wider.

Milo took his hands off the wheel and shook his head in disdain. "I should drive off just for spite. Just because you shits were thinking it."

"We appreciate you not doing that," Collie said.

"Just get this done and over with," he grumped.

Gus stopped at the trailer doors, still surprised himself that Milo was around. His getting out to help was an impulse thing. A spur of the moment call. Now that he was out, however, he realized just how big a risk he'd taken leaving Milo in that rolling fortress.

Yet the soldier stayed.

Gus regarded the trailer doors and flinched at a renewed hammering from within. *Fuck me gently*, he thought, and sighed. Memories of what the gimps would do to their poor hands came back to him in a flood. No pain. No fear.

No fear.

He glanced over at Collie.

"What?" she asked.

Gus didn't answer. He looked at the doors again. "Hey. *Hey*! Calm the fuck down in there."

He slammed a hand against the door. A little too hard, causing him to shake out his fingers. "Goddammit. Hey! *Shut the fuck up so I can ask some questions!*"

Wailing perked his ears then, along with that cringeworthy battering of meat on steel doors.

"Look," Gus tried again. "If you're people, quiet down. If not, we'll assume you're mindless? All right? We'll assume you're fucking *zombies*, and…

and we'll leave you. All right? Got all that?"

Scratching from within then, a sound that horrified Gus, as he didn't know what could be making that noise. The wailing and hammering continued, however, and intensified, drowning out the unsettling scratching.

"I said quiet down!" he yelled, but with less heat.

"Honey?" Collie asked. "You're going to wake up the neighbors."

Gus studied her while the ruckus continued.

Milo leaned into sight. "Those aren't people, man."

Collie shook her head as if it was the most obvious thing on the road.

"No," Gus said after a few heartbeats. "I guess not. So now what?"

Collie sized up the trailer. "First thought? Hang a 'Do Not Open' sign off the doors. This rig ain't going anywhere, ever. But just in case someone comes along and they're looking to open up a full can of dead ass, I say… give me ten minutes."

And perhaps twenty minutes later, Collie sat in the front seat of the limo. They had backed up and were safely out of range of the distant transport… and the explosives rigged to its girth.

She held up a remote detonator. "Everyone ready for this?"

They were.

"Just so you know… this bang is using up all our heavy stuff."

Neither man said a word.

"Okay, then. Brace yourselves."

They did.

And Collie pushed the button.

37

The drive back to the warehouse took longer than expected, as Collie insisted on stopping and checking out the wrecked pickups belonging to the Leather. Bodies were accounted for, and more importantly, no one tried jumping them. During that time, she ordered the men to strap on their armored vests, which they did.

All the while, Gus watched her move.

Careful. Precise. Slow.

That last word stuck in his mind. She was moving slower. Much slower.

He kept that nugget to himself while they rode to the warehouse. Seeing the building and the dead piled up and crushed on the road did nothing to lift Gus's spirits. He had hoped that the guy with the spider mask had gotten free before the chase, and that he was aboard one of the Leather's pickups. He'd really hoped the Spider was dead—killed in Collie's bombardment.

But it was hard to confirm that.

Collie went inside the building to check.

"You think he's in there?" Milo asked Gus.

"No."

"Yeah. Me, too."

After a long thirty minutes or so, Collie returned, wavering as if she'd downed a dozen beers and trying hard not to show it. Gus recognized the act. Knew it for what it was.

"Nothing," she declared as she climbed aboard. "He's gone."

"You check upstairs?" Gus asked.

"Everywhere. Even out in the warehouse. Nada. Spider-guy has fled the scene. Hopefully, I got him with the 'death from above' like the others back there. If it's the same guy I missed from the fort, and from your description sounds like it is, then he's a grade-A freak. Terrorized the people back at Fort Jay. If he *did* die back at the bridge with the rest of the Leather, then he got off easy."

She closed the door and got comfortable. "That tanker you used to bash through the warehouse doors? That thing's wrecked, but the tank itself is good. You should keep that in mind for when you come back here."

"What do you mean?" Milo asked. "Don't you mean, 'we'?"

"I ain't coming back," Collie said matter-of-factly, and a grim silence settled in. She realized it immediately and slapped the dashboard. "Hey, smiles everyone, smiles. I'm here now. For a good time, not a long time. So let's check out that hotel. You know where that is, cowboy?"

Milo nodded. "Not exactly, but I'll follow the signs."

"Pitter-patter." And she twirled a finger.

Ten minutes later, the limo pulled up in front of the Royal Bentley.

Gus couldn't believe his eyes.

All through the last three city blocks, flipped cars and stacked tires filled the north and south streets, blocking them off completely. Every space in between the buildings appeared to have something crammed into them, sealing off all access. A tall wooden fence had been started at the northeast end, the construction shoddy. The Leather had perhaps taken the timber from the warehouse and built it against the barrier in an effort to reinforce it. In two streets, metro buses were parallel parked with crude stairs leading up to a roof, where what appeared to be a castle's battlements had been built. Coils of wire draped the top.

The east-west avenue, however, had been cleared of vehicles as far as Gus could see.

But the thing that jumped out at them all, was the crucifix.

"What the hell is that?" Gus let out slowly, not quite sure what he was seeing.

A body wearing only a few rags had been nailed to the cross. The head rolled because of a huge missing section in the neck. Graying flesh stretched graphically over an exposed rib cage, while the pants had been ripped away at the knees. The legs below were withered and as thin as sticks, as were the arms.

Milo stopped the car in front of the gruesome display, so that they could all get a good look.

"Seen this before," he said in a toneless voice. "Might be seeing more of it. That's the Dog Tongue's mark."

"Christ Almighty," Gus whispered.

Collie sat and stared at the corpse.

"They stick them up wherever. Mostly places that the Dog Tongue calls his. This is a fresh one, though. Eventually, it'll just be the head. The skull. Not that I've seen those, but I've heard Jake talk about them."

"That someone who pissed him off?" Collie asked.

"No idea," Milo replied. "Maybe. Though from what I've seen? They probably just stuck up the nearest unlucky bastard. Because it was Wednesday. Who knows."

"Drive on, Milo," she said.

Which he did.

They drove underneath a pedway that crossed the six lanes of the street. On the next intersection, the Royal Bentley hotel loomed, towering over the city block and the three smaller buildings on each corner. Huge white letters hung across the third story, proudly displaying the establishment's name. Sunlight sparkled off the hotel heights but down on the street level, shadows darkened the block. Regular shopfronts ringed the area and made up the ground floors of the nearby buildings. There was signage for Tim's, Subway, even a Mary Brown's. To his right and down the street was a sign for Staples, next to the entrance for the pedway that connected two buildings. A department store stood across from the hotel on the opposite corner. Gus focused on the hotel's main entrance. The bottom floor was barricaded with treated wood, but above that was all glass for four floors. Dusty granite in need of a scrubbing framed all that glass. The smooth rock probably sparkled like obsidian back in the day. Bare trees, four to either side of the main entrance, grew up along the sidewalk. There were crude bastions made of tires, wooden planks, and barbed wire—all along both sides of the street, and in front of the hotel.

Cracks split the pavement underfoot, and it would be a long time indeed before anyone got around to patching or replacing it.

And there were skulls, perched here and there, decorating the tops of stacked tires or posts, having the opposite effect of house ferns.

"Those look older," Collie noted.

"Plenty around if you know where to look," Milo said. "They like their skulls."

"Watch those bastions," she ordered. "Just in case someone decides to pop up."

No one did, however, and the place grew all the more eerie because of it.

The main entrance of the hotel was an unmoving revolving door, jammed in place, with its glass smashed out.

"You know something," Collie said. "That hotel? If you were at the top, you'd have a good view of almost everything."

"No one taking any shots at us yet," Milo said.

"Probably waiting for us to get out of the rig," Collie pointed out. "If they're there at all. I'm thinking they had all hands on-deck when you guys rolled into town. Still. We'll check it out."

"Me too?" said Milo.

"You too, cowboy."

"Yes ma'am."

Collie opened her door and got out.

Gus struggled to get out, the weight of his vest complicating matters. The thing was heavy. An extra twenty pounds of shit he didn't really need. The weight didn't seem to bother Collie or Milo, so he didn't complain, not wanting to be reminded he was a *civvie*.

The temperature had dropped, leaving them cold and the wind cutting. Nothing moved around those crude bastions or inside the hotel, yet Gus's warning tingles continued all the same.

"I expect a few rats around here somewhere," Collie explained. "Probably even spider-dick. If I escaped the warehouse, I'd make a beeline for headquarters. Warn the others and all that shit."

"What do we do?" Milo asked.

"Go in anyway," Collie said. "I'm not in the mood to hunt, so it's best to draw them out. Just like the poison they are."

Milo shared a look with Gus.

"You got your bat there, Milo?"

"Yeah, but I was hoping—"

"No gun for you, though you did well last time. Gus? Got your shotgun?"

Gus held up the weapon.

"All right, then." The limo chirped as Collie locked the doors with the key fob. "On my flanks, boys. Watch my six. Eyes sharp and stay low. No shooting until I shoot first and that means no swinging that bat, okay Milo?"

"Got it."

"One last thing. When I go down, you guys go down immediately. And I mean drop. Got it?"

That puzzled Gus, but before he could ask questions she was walking for the hotel, her assault rifle at the ready. The two men hurried after her, three steps back and hunched over. Gus was a little in awe of the size and scope of the roughshod fortifications around the Bentley.

Collie marched for the wrecked revolving door. Gus and Milo followed. She slowed as she approached the entrance. Whoever had done the job on the doors hadn't bothered to root out the teeth-like shards ringing the edges. A wave of crystal sprinkles lay across the red carpet, dull in the deep shadows that doused the foyer. Another wide carpet split the interior right up to the front desk. Luxurious furniture filled the ground level on either side, but the right extended around a wall and out of sight, perhaps to a dining area or a gift shop. The second level was open and overlooking the main foyer. Cloudy glass partitions encircled the edges up there, and Gus thought he saw tables flipped onto their sides and pressed right up to those pale barriers.

His paranoia really started to sing.

Collie's boots crinkled on glass pebbles, and she stopped on the threshold. She held up, head cocking left and right. Deeming all was fine, she entered, walking straight up the middle.

Milo exchanged looks with Gus, who shrugged and followed her lead into the dark interior.

Collie walked toward the front desk, which would be a great place to hide—and Gus realized that was the trouble. There were *too many* great places to hide in here. Too many nooks and crannies and too much oversized furniture, and that was only on the ground floor. The second floor was a perch for lookouts, and Gus wondered how many floors were in the place. Twenty? Thirty?

And it was quiet. The worst kind of quiet. A forced silence that thrummed in one's ears, where whoever was waiting, waited with their breaths held. Waiting for a signal of their own.

That's when it hit Gus. Collie was walking into a nest. They were *all* walking into a nest.

Which was when two leather-wearing fuckheads with loaded crossbows popped up from behind the front desk.

And shot Collie practically at point-blank.

38

Collie collapsed on her back with a pair of feathered shafts sticking out of her armored torso.

Gus didn't dive, instead he took aim at the Leather behind the front desk. He spotted another rising from behind one of the big sofas to his right.

Another popped up from behind a plush chair on the left.

While two more sprang into existence on the second level.

Milo sprinted for the door.

One of the crossbowmen fired, nailing the soldier in the back. He dropped with a grunt and rolled about the glitter covering the red carpet. Gus tensed and met the eyes of one of the archers on the second level. There were two of them up there, and both had the drop on him.

Could he dodge an arrow?

Judging by the way Milo was moaning, he didn't think he could.

So he lifted a hand and slowly placed the shotgun on the carpeted floor, hearing his knees pop as he did so.

Another Leather appeared up top, to the left of the archers. He gripped the railing and leaned out, his posture positively brimming with evil delight that the ambush worked. He wore a mask Gus recognized right away.

The Spider gazed down at them, drumming his fingers as if puzzling what to do, what to do. Seconds passed and Gus waited for the dickhead to start talking. Something like, *well, well, well, what do we have here?* Or, *you made a mistake not killing me.* Or the top tier of quality fromage, *Prepare… to die.* Any of that prime B-movie shit which would make a person's eyes roll.

Which was when Collie opened fired.

Lying on her back, she drew her prized sidearm and shot the top off one archer's head. Collie smoothly cupped her right hand with her much steadier left and snapped off two rounds at the remaining archer. One bullet straightened his spine, while the second removed him from the picture. A bow and arrow dropped to the floor.

Those unexpected killings caused the Spider to have a split-second seizure of fright. Then he turned and bolted.

Gus dove for his shotgun.

Collie straightened out her arm and fired, sinking a round into a crossbow man.

Gus scooped up the shotgun and looked to his left.

A Leather aimed a bolt at Gus's face—when a flying baseball bat crashed into the masked man's head. The bolt snapped free and rebounded off a stone pillar with an amplified crack.

Gus looked for Milo, who fell back into the wrecked revolving door, overcome from the effort of throwing the bat. Gus remembered himself then and shot the stunned Leather, blasting the man into a sofa chair and flipping him over the back, where only feet and ankles were visible.

Collie's Sig boomed. Splinters flew from the front desk and the panel wood behind it as she drew a ragged line across the top.

Gus hurried around her, charging the front desk. He jumped behind it and leveled his shotgun at the two Leather crossbowmen cocking their weapons. Their black studded masks jerked up in surprise whereupon Gus opened fire. Shells slammed into the Leather, skidding them back a good ten feet or so. They crashed into a computer station at the far end like a pair of wobbly bowling pins. Office items rained down on the dead men as Gus pumped more rounds into that tangle of meat, just to make sure.

He backed away and saw Collie attempting to sit up, with a pair of bolts sticking out of her chest. An unhappy Milo was already retrieving his bat, but a feathered shaft protruded from his back.

"Get them all?" Collie asked in a strained voice.

Gus nodded. "But Spider-dick got away."

"Then go get him."

It took a beat for the order to sink in, but when it did Gus ran out from behind the desk and huffed it around the corner. There was, of all things, a cigar shop back there, as well as a little place selling wines and liquor.

There was also a brown door with a single window.

Gus pulled that open and stepped inside.

Stairwell. Unlit and creepy. A railing was on his right, along with battery power emergency lighting that had died long ago. His boots scuffed on the floor tiles, and when he stopped to figure out which way to go, he heard it.

The ghostly squeal of a closing door. Far below.

Gus hurried down two flights of steps, taking the pain, and nearly crashing into a wall at the bottom. He yanked open the door there and charged through.

And had his foot hooked out from under him, whereupon he sailed into an underground parking garage. Gus landed with a clatter, his shotgun skittering across concrete. He drew his legs up to stand when a boot smashed him across the lower back, driving him down. The body armor absorbed much of the force, and the Spider knew it the instant he struck Gus.

Because he switched targets and kicked for the head.

He partially connected, just as Gus's hand jerked up to shield his face. The boot mashed his hand into his head and flipped him onto his back. Gus's senses went loopy, penetrated by a far-off ceiling light.

The Spider drove a boot heel into his guts. Then into a hip. The Leather stomped on a kidney and then a man-boob. Everything was the heel, and everything landed like a pointed rock. All the while the Spider attacked, a frenetic, hate-fuel breathing wheezed loud and clear from behind his mask. At the end of the Spider's temper-tantrum fueled boot mashing, he stopped, gasped, and reloaded on air. Once he got fresh wind in him, he moved in, seeking to stomp on his enemy's exposed face and flatten Gus's skull.

Gus knew what was coming.

So as the boot came up, the house painter from Annapolis lashed out with all the last-second desperation of a man about to get his head crushed.

He made the only move available to him.

His fist snapped upwards and nailed the Spider square in the balls.

It's amazing... how... one, reflex-fueled, straight-armed punch to the nuts will cripple an opponent and take all the steam out of him, but it does.

The Spider crumpled to his knees, cupping his chicken tenders all the way down. He landed in a crackle of bone, incredibly tried to rise, only to fall forward again. This repeated itself for seconds. Gus rolled onto his side, couldn't stop himself, and landed on his stomach, in full view of how the Spider was trying to get away while dealing with his screaming testicles. A high-pitched whimpering came from the Leather, salted with a few bewildered squeaks of rage.

Gus knew the feeling. A part of him marveled at how the Leather, as hurt as he was, managed to keep his wits while drowning in that sinkhole of nauseating agony. Gus was positive he hit a protective cup, but he'd nailed the bastard dead-on, getting more than enough force through to the pickle and onions, as evident by the Spider's pain-stricken, stand-and-stumble escape. The Leather staggered away at his best, floundering speed, driving his shoulder up against parked vehicles and cement pillars for support.

Gus got to his knees. His feet. His world tilted and righted itself with sickening clarity. His shotgun was left somewhere behind him, in the opposite direction of the escaping Spider. Gus couldn't do shit without it, however, so he got to the weapon at best speed and picked it up.

"All right," he groaned. "Guess who's got his thunderstick back."

To his surprise, the Spider answered with a squawk of pain.

Gus started after the fleeing man, recovering strength with every step, but still not operating at optimum level. A broad beam of light lay across the pavement on the far side of the parking lot, and the Spider skittered in that direction, his black outline easily seen.

Gus fired from the hip.

The Spider screamed and darted in among the maze of parked vehicles. Gus saw that he'd just blew the tin ass off a little import model. One of those green cars that could go for years on a single tank of gas.

The Spider's hunched-over form bobbed into sight, some five or six cars over.

Gus brought up his shotgun and put two rounds into the rear windshield of a sedan, sending glass onto the cement floor.

The Spider dropped from sight, but Gus was certain he'd got him that time.

"Gotcha," he said under his breath, hurrying between a pair of cars. "I gotcha. I *know* I gotcha. Saw ya go down. Like you were hooked by your nutsack. I gotcha."

He reached the spot where he shot the Leather, felt crystal bits roll under his boots, but no Spider. Gus whirled, realizing the little nine-lifed sonnavabitch might have crawled up under a car. He bent over, much too fast, and his brain reeled because of it. He staggered against a machine and stayed there, feeling his face go cold with sweat.

The shriek and echo of tires pealing across the cement jerked his head up.

Pickup truck. Making a smoking charge for the underground exit. Even as Gus watched, the machine made a hard right and raced up a ramp, disappearing from sight. There was a distant screech of brake pads, then the accelerated roar of victory as the Spider sped away.

Gus stopped and stared, listening, realizing he'd just been given the slip.

"Piece of..." he stopped, the hate pinching off his words. He glanced around and knew he didn't have the time to search every ride until he found one that could move. Everyone else was upstairs, and he was damn well sure they heard Spiderdick drive away. Maybe Collie was on her feet. Maybe Milo was...

Gus stopped.

Milo was alone with Collie.

That realization made him think. Maybe Milo was being good because he knew Collie was an operator. Maybe that scared him enough to be good, until he saw his chance, saw his chance to put her down. Once she was gone, he could then try and kill Gus and that would be that. The soldier could go back to Whitecap with whatever story he wanted.

Bringing along whomever he wanted.

Well, shit.

Gus ran.

He returned to the lobby and saw Milo and Collie both on their feet. Milo was leaning against an overturned sofa. Collie was across from him.

They looked Gus's way as he charged into sight, whereupon he immediately slowed to a stop.

"You need to take a leak or something?" Milo groaned, but then he saw the unwavering shotgun.

And where it was pointed.

"See?" Milo said to Collie after an awkward silence. "Told you."

Feeling heat rise in his cheeks, Gus lowered his weapon.

"He's fine," Collie said, her masked features aimed at the plucked arrows at her feet.

"Y'know," Milo said, glowering at the floor. "I'm gonna let that one slide. Just because it's important to me."

"You sure you're okay?" Collie asked the soldier, changing the subject. "You sound like that last one got through."

"Just tender is all. Goddamn vest."

"Goddamn vest saved your life." She looked at Gus. "Get him?"

"Got away." He answered, thankful for the change of subject. "I punched him in the balls, though."

"You did?" she asked, soft delight in her voice.

"I did. Pretty sure I got part of his dick, too."

"Yeah? You did?"

Gus frowned. "C'mon, Collie. All you been showing me is how to dick punch people. No problem dick punching a guy, if I get in close enough. Which I was."

"See? All that training did you good."

"Yeah," Gus said drily.

"Hey, now," she cautioned. "Don't ruin it. Besides. You wanna be the dick puncher or get dick punched? Or just upright dead?"

"How'd he get away?" Milo asked, changing the subject.

Gus didn't meet his gaze. "Got to a pickup. He was doing the funky chicken, mind you, but he still got to a rig. Drove off before I could get a shot at him. I was woozy. He was stomping on me pretty good before I managed to get one back."

"In the dick," Collie finished.

"Yeah. Well. Partial dick. Mostly balls."

"Shouldn't we be going after him?" Milo asked.

Collie considered it. "I'm too sore to go after him. Let him go. If we're lucky, he'll bring back a pack of buddies with him and save us the trouble of hunting him down."

"And if he doesn't?" Milo asked.

"He's a fuckin' civvie wearing a Halloween suit. They're *all* fuckin' civvies in Halloween suits. And he's probably shittin' himself. We missed him twice now."

"Three times," Gus corrected.

"Three times," Collie conceded. "Chances are he's long gone. You say the next Leather town is Regina?"

Milo nodded.

"Then that's where he's headed. At full speed. We'll go there in the morning. Maybe we'll catch him rallying whatever Dog Dick has holding the city. You get guard duty. I'll relieve you later in the morning. Don't come get me otherwise, and I mean that. I don't wanna accidently shoot you in the middle of the night."

Milo nodded but didn't look too happy with his orders.

"So what do we do now?" Gus asked.

"Right now, I want to rig up some surprises. In case someone comes a'calling during the night. Then I want to check out the hotel. I gotta feeling with a name like the Royal Bentley, there should be some pretty sweet rooms here."

"It's a tall hotel," Milo pointed out.

"It is a tall hotel, Collie," Gus said.

"Lotta floors," Milo added.

"Lotta walkin'," Gus tacked on.

The two men regarded each other, not entirely pleased with their agreement on the matter.

"Yeah, well," Collie said, glancing at the imaginary watch on her wrist, "let's get busy."

39

Collie parked the limo in the garage, a little ways from the ramp and out of sight. The open garage door would spook most people, she said, but if any of the Leather did come around, they weren't going to steal their ride. She explained all that while loading up a pair of backpacks. She also revealed to Gus that one of the Leather she shot in the lobby wasn't completely dead, and that with a little prodding, he revealed that the hotel was empty. Collie asked about the Dog Tongue's whereabouts, but the Leather died as an answer.

Once finished loading up the backpacks, she punched in an unseen code in the limo's dashboard interface, where the lights changed from green to red. She shooed them all outside and exited the vehicle herself. The limo was an armored dream in the shadows of the garage, the paint and polish marred by the last few days of travel. Collie held up the key fob and flicked her wrist as if cracking a whip. The limo chirped, and Collie faced the two men.

"Armed and dangerous. Do *not* touch those door handles. Not unless you feel a chill coming on."

"What if they try and take the tires?" Gus asked with a smirk.

"They who?"

"The Leather. Or anyone."

"Honey, if the electrified doors don't sizzle 'em, the other surprises will. I didn't mention it before, but there's an AI in that thing and I activated it for the night. I don't do that while we're aboard, because it's kinda spooky. Thing's wide awake, now, and it has no issue with defending itself against unauthorized personnel outside of you and me. You, on the other hand," she aimed at Milo, "are not authorized. Not yet, anyway, so don't give up hope."

"Thanks," Milo said.

"Don't worry," Collie said, picking up on his disappointed vibe. "I got a good feeling about you. And that's coming from the person you shot."

Milo winced.

Collie led the men back to the stairwell, and once through the doors, she stopped and went to work. She stuck a small grenade-sized explosive against the wall, pulled a wire from the top, and attached the end to the door. She fiddled with the device, whereupon a red light no bigger than a freckle flashed for second before going dead.

"That a booby trap?" Gus asked.

"Yeah," Collie answered.

"Got any more of those?"

"Oh yeah."

They returned to the lobby, where she trapped the main doors with two more of the explosives, and a fourth and fifth door they discovered in the rear.

"How big a boom will that make?" Milo asked her at one point.

"Enough to make it rain body parts. So keep your watchful ass up on the second floor there."

By the time they finished securing the place, the sun was going down, and long shadows filled the lobby.

"We're good," Collie remarked and headed for the stairwell. When she pulled the door open, she stared and shook her head.

"You okay?" Gus asked.

"Yeah. Well, no. It's just… it's a chore to climb these things."

"Want me to carry you?"

"Y'know, I know you would, but no. Thanks all the same."

Milo didn't appear happy with the situation.

"Something on your mind, cowboy?" Collie asked.

He didn't sugarcoat. "This is tactically a bad decision. I don't like it. We should've gone after him."

"Yeah, well, here? You answer to me and him," Collie said. "Just stay awake until I relieve you, all right? Camp out someplace that gives you a view of the street, but don't engage if anyone does come creeping up on the place. I truly don't expect anyone tonight. It's what? Six, seven hours to Regina?"

"Seven or eight," Milo said. "Depending on road conditions and how fast you're driving."

"Let's say six then, if the guy is really driving hard. So six hours to get there, another thirty minutes to rally the troops, if they're so inclined, and then six—no eight hours to get back. At night. You might even see their headlights in the distance if they're stupid, and they might be. Based on what I saw at Red Wolf."

"Camp Red Wolf," Gus clarified.

Collie pointed at him. "That's the place. They rolled right up to the front gate there, dicks out and just a'swinging. And in broad daylight. They like to make an entrance. As big and flashy as possible. Get people scared and all. So by all that reasoning, by the time any of those cow fuckers roll up here I'll have already relieved you. Okay? All right, then. We're heading upstairs. Third floor. Someplace westerly. And Milo? Don't come knocking unless you spot an army out there. I'm knackered, as the British would say. Aren't you?"

The receding light of the day made Milo's face a little more haggard. He shrugged but it was clear he could use the sleep.

"And last warning, don't wander around the lobby," Collie advised. "In case someone does come poking around here. Wouldn't want to have to dig you out from below if they set off those explosives."

"What are they anyway?" Gus asked.

"Mag-mines," Collie answered. "We call them *Maggies*. Love child of the limpets, except new and improved. And the best thing about them? If no one sets them off, you can disarm and reuse them somewhere else."

They started climbing the stairs. There was even less light in the stairwell, but they made their way up. Milo stopped at the second-floor door.

"I'll be down later," Collie told him again.

"Yeah." Milo opened the door.

"Hey. You did good here today. Real good."

Milo nodded. He met Gus's dark gaze.

"Yeah," Gus grudgingly admitted. "You did good. I'll give you that."

"You did all right yourself. For a civvie."

Gus frowned.

"That man's a survivor," Collie corrected and started hiking up the stairs. "That's what I keep telling him. Dick punches or not."

They left the soldier then and wound their way up a couple of dark landings to the third. Gus noticed the visible drag in Collie's steps. He kept his mouth shut.

"Y'know," she said, pawing at the door, "I'm starting to like him. Especially the part about the tactically bad decision."

"What did he mean by that?"

"That we're still here. And that we should've gone after the Spider instead of letting him reach friendly lines."

"So why don't we go after him?"

"I like my way better."

She cracked open the door. The corridor stretched east and west, with two nearby elevators stopped and closed. Dusty beige carpet lined the floor, while the walls looked clean and marked at intervals by unlit lamps. Evening light marked the far westerly end, spilling through a large window. An assortment of vending machines filled a nearby nook, all of them pried open and emptied. Torn wrappers littered the floor.

"Rats," Gus said. "The two-legged kind."

"Some people's children," Collie agreed and walked towards the distant window.

"Hey, did you get a key card or something to get into any of these rooms?"

Collie shook her head. "We just keep right on walking until—here we go."

A door was open. Inside was a maid's cart, with cleaning supplies and about half a load of sheets, towels, and face cloths. The dark cave that was the bathroom was across from that. Collie made her way for the pair of twin beds inside the room while Gus did a quick sweep of the facilities. There was no power, and the only light came from the wide window which offered a limited view of the downtown area and the street below.

"No like this one," Collie muttered, and retreated back into the hall, coming close to colliding with Gus as he came back out of the bathroom.

"How you like my meatbag impersonation?" she asked.

"I didn't."

"Too soon?"

"Yeah, it is, matter of fact."

She stopped and faced him, the sunglasses reflecting only a bulbous caricature of Gus's battered features. "Sorry," she said, and made tracks up the corridor. "My mistake. Won't happen again."

They reached the end and Collie zeroed in on one door. It was locked, so she motioned for Gus to back up. Once he was clear, she stood back at an angle and leveled her assault rifle at the lock.

She fired, the tracers bright in the enclosed space, causing Gus to reach for his ears. Dust whirled while splinters and shards fell to the carpet. Collie inspected the holes she made before hoisting one boot and kicking in the door. The door clattered off the inner wall and Collie, for her effort, toppled over. Gus grabbed for her but hooked only air.

She landed on her side, her rifle barrel drawing a line in the corridor's paint all the way down.

"Jesus Christ," Collie swore a second later.

"You okay?" Gus asked, holding her shoulder.

"Yeah, I'm okay. Except for the part where I'm becoming a fucking walking corpse."

That smacked all the wind out of Gus.

She regarded him, shook her head, and attempted to rise. He helped without saying a word.

"Christ," Collie said, leaning against the wall and looking to her boots. "I'm…"

Gus waited. "You're what?"

No answer. She picked up her rifle instead, bending over as if afflicted by some very cranky arthritis. The door was partially open, so she shoulder-checked it, banging it off the inner wall again.

Gus let her go as she stalked inside, searching for threats.

"Clear," she eventually reported.

"Safe to enter?" Gus asked, checking on the hallway.

"That's what 'clear' means."

Note to self, he said to himself.

"Everything good down there?" Milo bawled out from the stairwell entrance.

Gus backed up and spotted the soldier's head. "You heard that?"

"The gunfire? Yeah, I did."

"Collie was just opening a door."

That deflated Milo. "Opening a door," he repeated, and withdrew back into the stairwell.

Gus watched him disappear before he turned and followed Collie inside.

Dust motes rode sunbeams in a room a little bigger than the previous one. The southwest corner was a meeting of windows and offered a much better picture of the downtown area, as well as the evening sun. Collie walked over to the south window and slammed her rifle down on a round table. A gloved hand came up and plastered the glass as she looked down on the street.

Gus walked to the edge of the nearest twin bed and inspected the blankets, very much aware of where Collie stood.

He cleared his throat. "Not a bad place."

She didn't say a word.

"Even smells decent," he went on. "And them duvets look like they cost a couple of car payments at least."

No reaction.

Gus shut up and quietly sat down on a corner of one bed. He remembered Milo talking about hotel duvets, and he screwed up his face only to relax a second later.

Collie turned away from the window with a bored swagger that struck him as odd. But then he realized it wasn't odd at all. She was having trouble moving.

She pulled away a chair from the table, turned it around, and sat down as if it hurt to do so. Once sitting, she placed elbows to knees, clasped her hands, and hung her head.

Gus waited, very much wanting to reach out and touch her, just a hand on her shoulder, some measure of comfort.

He did not, however.

"You know something," he eventually said. "I think a lot about missed opportunities. Like, school and shit. Painting was okay and I liked it, but, honestly? I wasn't ever gonna get rich doing it. If I had my time back, I would've gone back to school. Studied something interesting. Get a degree, and maybe, like, be the guy who invents new ice cream flavors. Get a job with *Ben and Jerry's*."

Collie didn't move, but after a while, she said. "Yeah?"

"Yeah."

"Any flavors in particular?"

"Oh yeah. Already had the next big thing."

"Yeah? What's that?"

"Fruity Baloney."

Collie let out a chuckle. "Fruity Baloney."

"See? Got best seller all over it, don't it?"

"Oh, it's got something all right. Any more like that?"

"That's the main one, but with training and funding, I could come up with others."

They shared a little laugh then, and it was good. The tension in the room eased off.

"This…" Collie finally said, "isn't going according to plan."

Gus stayed quiet.

"I mean, at first," she continued, "… I didn't feel a thing. And that was cool. Actually really cool, considering. No pain in the least. No discomfort. Just a tugging here and there. Like a wet rope being pulled tight into a knot or something, and then… the tension. No pain, you understand, but a sensation like a rubber band being stretched out to the point of breaking. The smell doesn't bother me anymore."

The smell? Gus asked himself, and then he got a whiff of her in that enclosed space. Just a whiff, but it was there, under the deodorant. A faint tease of spoiling meat.

"And the cold doesn't bother me, either. Never did, really, since I'm on the subject, but the slowing down sucks. It fucking *sucks*, man. You don't know how much it sucks. I mean, I used to… used to be…"

Gus remembered, remembered Wallace talking about her.

Collie leaned back as if gut shot. She turned her attention on him. "It's hard to take. My legs feel fifty pounds heavier and that's just like, over*night*. And you saw me kick that door in. That shouldn't have happened. Should've been able to bring the leg up and snap it out, all in one beat… not fucking fall *over* like I was eighty. Like I'm the fucking bionic old woman."

Between a pair of high rises, red sunlight filled the western horizon and colored the room. Gus edged a little closer to her.

"Is there anything I can do?" he asked.

Collie shook her head. Then, "No, wait. There is something you can do. What I need you to do."

"Better not be massaging your feet."

"Ha. No. Something worse."

Gus didn't like the sound of that.

She straightened and nodded. "Bring over the backpack."

Gus did so and placed it on the table where she wanted it.

"Get out the duct tape," she said.

He did that as well, the zipper loud in the room.

Collie became very still then, and for a moment Gus wasn't sure what was about to happen. Then she started, like someone working her way out of a deep thaw. She peeled off the Velcro straps and buckles of her armored vest, clawing at them until Gus helped her. When that came off, she unbuttoned her camouflage jacket underneath and shrugged that off as well. A black t-shirt covered her torso, but the sight of her bare arms shocked Gus to the core.

Gray black. The musculature sagging in places and rotten with veins swollen with trapped dead blood. Several of those passed through her grim reaper tattoo on her right bicep. The coloring of her skin and veins wasn't the only disturbing thing, however. The crossbow bolts had penetrated the vest, just enough to let a person know they'd been tagged. The missiles left jagged little entry holes in her t-shirt, surrounded by ominous wet patches. And the smell was that of rancid milk that someone had shat in.

Gus swallowed and heard his own throat click.

"Yeah," she whispered. "Sorry. Forgot about that. I stink. Especially when I lose those layers."

"S'okay," Gus said, but not sounding okay in the least.

"It's awkward for me to do my own field dressings, okay?" Collie said. "I need you to help."

"That's what the duct tape is for?"

"Yeah."

Gus took a breath to steady himself. "Okay. Let's do it."

She pulled up her t-shirt, and a chill enveloped Gus right down to his boys.

Perhaps it was her still walking and talking that had convinced him that she was still alive, still okay, but what he saw when she took off her undershirt reduced his mind to a soft crashing of static. Like her arms, her midriff, right up to a wet sports bra, was a cadaverous gray black. The skin appeared as translucent as the membrane-webbing of a bat's wings, and underneath it, a tracery of poisoned veins. When she lifted her arms, her skin stretched over her ribs to the point of breaking. Then there were the cloth wads marked by X's of duct tape, creating a pirate's trail around her torso.

Collie tossed the shirt over her rifle.

"Getting a good look?" she asked.

Gus couldn't talk.

"S'okay," Collie said. "Take it easy. Breathe. Okay? Now, I need you to tape this shit up, here and here."

She touched the spot, one of which was just over her left bra strap, just below her collarbone.

"I don't have any bandages," Gus whispered.

"We don't need no stinking bandages," Collie said. "Just tape me up. Double layer it if you got to. There's not a lot of fluid to come out. I've already bled out everything that's going to come out, I think. The only thing left over now is keeping shit out of the wounds. Doubt if they'll get infected but probably a good idea to patch them up, just in case."

"Yeah," Gus said, only half-listening. He ripped off the necessary pieces of tape and stuck them to the table edge. Once that was done, he lifted one bra strap and threaded a piece across the puckered wound left by the killer dart. One piece went on without a hitch, so he got another and repeated. It only took a few minutes, but once he was finished, he stood back and inspected his work.

"That's it," Collie said. "Thanks."

"Yeah."

"You don't sound too happy."

"What's... that?" He pointed at her chest, and the obvious plastic lid above her sternum.

"That's where they got me," Collie said and drummed her fingers on the lid.

Where Milo shot you, he thought. Gus hadn't seen the raw damage until then, and the sight of it horrified him to chills. "Jesus, Collie."

"I'm over it. I mean, Milo was being whipped by the Leather at the time. And, frankly, after today, I think you should get over it, too. Sounds like he had plenty of opportunity to put you down. Especially after you handed him a gun. He could've shot you, returned to Whitecap, and, knowing my condition, he could've made up any story he wanted. But he didn't. He *didn't*. That counts for something."

Gus lifted a hand. "May I?"

"What?"

"Touch it?"

"You want to touch this?"

He nodded.

"Weird. Real weird. But fuck it. Go ahead. Just lay off my boobs. Now is *not* the time to find out you're into necrophilia."

Mortified that she would even suggest such a thing, Gus wondered if he should touch that killing wound at all. He did, however, in the end. He reached out and slowly tapped on the plastic container lid, confirming its existence.

"Oh my fuck," he whispered, and reality rushed in, making him woozy.

He backed off until his legs bumped against the bed and tripped him into sitting down. There he stayed until he got his senses back.

"Holy shit," he released in a stunned voice.

Collie inspected herself. "Not bad. I could've used you when I was taping up my back. The bullet went all the way through. Good thing I didn't, though. Judging by your reaction now, I made the right call."

"You taped... up your back?"

"Yeah. Wasn't easy. I had Josh help. He seemed the best choice given the circumstances. No surprises for him."

Gus's mind had returned to a state of numbness, where no thoughts entered.

"And, by the way," Collie said. "The Tupperware? I stashed explosives in there."

He ogled her chest as if he were exposed to a nuclear core.

"Relax," she chuckled. "Jesus, what a face. Oh my. I needed that. What do you think? I'm going to blow apart if I sneeze or something? Relax, I said."

Gus smiled weakly but was very aware of the tremor in his knees. "You got a grenade in there?"

"Yeah," she told him. "Kept in place with some foam. I had a couple sticks of old school plastique in there too, just in case, but I used that to break out the prisoners at Fort Jay."

"Forgot all about that place."

"I'll tell you about it later. But first…" she reached for the backpack and pulled out, of all things, a stick of deodorant. "Ocean Mist," she said, and popped the lid.

Gus braced himself.

"What?" Collie asked, seeing him cringe.

"You gonna eat that?"

The question stopped her cold for all of two seconds, then Collie laughed, cool and pure and oh-so needed. She slumped back in the chair, the bar of *Ocean Mist* dropping into her lap.

Gus smiled in spite of himself.

"*No*," she finally unloaded with a giddy chortle. "I'm not gonna *eat* this. Holy shit, Gus. I'm not gone that far. I mean, you saw me load a case of this shit into the limo back at Whitecap and you actually *thought* I was gonna eat them?"

Stupid smile at half mast, Gus shrugged.

"Well, I'm not."

But then she hesitated. "Then again, maybe I should. I mean, Josh got by on the shit. Can't be all bad, right? Better this than the alternative."

She popped the lid, extended the stick, and lifted it to her masked face. "Smells okay. Not my brand. I sorta liked *Old Spice*, myself. Reminds me of my grandfather."

"You're not… really," Gus got out, unable to look away.

And as an answer, Collie lifted one arm, rubbed the stick underneath, and repeated with the other arm.

Gus relaxed.

She then applied the deodorant over every patch of exposed skin, right down to her waist. She painted herself, stopped, considered something, and then looked at Gus.

"Okay, look," she said. "I'm going to take my mask off. Just because I need to. Fair warning. What you're about to see isn't pretty. Okay?"

He was going to see her without the mask sooner or later, so he nodded, and braced himself for the worst.

Collie removed her sunglasses, and her eyes, once an electric blue, were clouded over by a milky white. The pupils were still visible, but not by much.

"That bad?" she asked, seeing his reaction.

"It's… different."

"Ha. Smooth."

"You can still see?" Gus whispered while cupping his beard.

"Yeah. Just fine." She looked over the room. "I see better at night, though. For some reason. Anyway. I need you to help me with my boots and pants so I can grease up my legs, too."

That slapped any further talk from Gus.

With that she removed the mask, her short brown hair dry and lifeless. As with the rest of her, those rotten veins extended to her missing ear. Her bitten-off nose, a souvenir of some long-ago fight, was crisscrossed with lines, right up to her facial tattoo of thorny vines, which actually matched. She was still Collie, dare he say *his* Collie, but her face had become more skull-like. The skin, thinner, tighter.

And it stunned him. "Christ Almighty."

"Yeah," she said solemnly. "I know. I think I'll stay away from mirrors for the next little while. Outta sight, outta mind, and all that."

Gus's throat tightened. The emotion reached his eyes. He wavered, not knowing what to do, and in the end did nothing except button up his mouth and batten down on the sadness.

"Sorry," Collie said. "Maybe… you should sleep in another room tonight. Might be—"

He crossed the space between them and wrapped both arms around her, smothering her, willing some of his warmth to flow into her, and hiding his face the only way he knew. She let him get it out of his system, stoically standing there, feeling the shudders going through him. In time, however, she lifted her arms and hugged him back, burying her face against his neck.

"Thank you," she whispered, the sound muffled.

Gus held onto her even tighter.

Daylight receded and the evening crept in, and while it did, Gus did the only thing he could think of doing. He dried his eyes, trying not to let Collie see, but she did anyway, and that only made things worse for both of them. He closed the door and swung a bolt lock into place, the thing undamaged from the earlier rifle burst. He also put a chair against the door, just for reinforcement. There was very little chance of anyone finding them, let alone getting the jump on them, but he did it anyway.

Then he returned to bed, where Collie lay underneath the blankets and sheets, undressed as much as she cared to be, and stinking of deodorant. He took off his coat and tossed it onto the floor. His shirt came next, but he left his jeans, socks and undershirt on.

"Not having anything to eat?" she asked him when he got in next to her.

"No."

"You should."

She was right, of course, but after the events of the day, after what he'd seen, eating was the absolute last thing on his mind.

"I just want to sleep," he said, and rolled an arm over her.

His coat was off, and the coldness radiating off her was a terrible thing. She was ice. A chunk of glacier ice. Gus rested his forehead against the nape of her neck, and even that contact was cold.

"Something wrong?" Collie asked.

"You're... really cold."

She didn't say anything to that.

"Wait," he said.

He got out from underneath the blankets, peeled two away, and crawled back in between. With at least a pair of sheets and a blanket as a barrier, Collie's lack of body heat was bearable.

They faced the south window and didn't move. Collie lay on her side.

"Not like Lazy Lou's mattress place, is it?" she asked in the stillness.

"No," he said, and smiled in spite of himself. "That was probably the best bedroom I'd ever crashed in."

"Showroom."

"That, too."

Quiet then, and Gus was more than aware of Collie's lack of breathing. That little detail caused him to squeeze her tight.

"Jesus," she let out. "You're gonna break me."

"Sorry."

"You know something?"

"No."

"When... Wallace was changing, I would do the same thing at night. So...

I know a little of what you're going through."

Gus closed his eyes.

"I know," she said. "Really. I do. It's going to get harder. I know. But I'm going to do what I can. Right up until the end. Understand?"

"Yeah."

"Just needed you to know that."

Gus already knew it. Never expected anything less. And he really didn't want to hear about it now. So, he did the only thing left to him. Like the fucking wuss that he was, he changed the subject.

"Can you remember…" he asked, "the last thing you had for takeout?"

That quieted her. "Before everything went to shit?"

"Yeah."

"A tub of Fruity Baloney."

"I don't think so."

"All right." She thought about it. "Italian."

"Ohhhh, that sounds ravioli."

"Cheesy spaghetti, actually. It was really good. What about you?"

"Can't remember. Might've been spaghetti. No. Wait. That's something else. Nope. Too long ago. Can't remember."

"Can you remember the last TV show you were into before it all went to shit?" she asked back.

"*The Office.*"

"Classic. Dwight's the man."

Gus smiled into the back of her head, breathing in that fabricated smell. He nestled in closer, settling down for sleep.

"Don't stop," she whispered.

"Hm?"

"Keep talking to me."

Gus cracked open an eye, his vision adjusting to the darkening room. Over the outline of her head, a tall building on the other side of the street loomed, the windows a wall of black squares.

"What about?" he asked.

"Anything. You were doing good there a few seconds ago."

"Those just popped into my head."

"Then pop some more. Please."

Gus thought about it, then, "What would you buy for groceries?"

"For groceries?"

"Yeah. At *Sobeys*. Or wherever."

Collie talked. Gus listened. Then he talked, and she listened. And back and forth they went, in that dark hotel room, where the wind would sharpen itself on the glass. They did that for a long time, until all the light was gone from the room. To them, it only seemed like minutes.

And some time before midnight, the snow started to fall.

40

A scratching at the windows woke Gus up first. He realized it was *warm* underneath the blankets and turned to see that Collie wasn't beside him. That's when he realized gray light was filtering into the room, and that it was snowing outside. Great flakes stuck fast to the western window, creating patterns on the surface. Gus sat up, realizing the cold was the drop in temperature, and went for his shirt and coat. Even as he pulled the clothes on, he knew he'd need more.

"Just fuckin' great," he whispered, dressing while watching the snow continue to fall. Early winters weren't unheard of, and he'd even been around long enough to remember a freak snowstorm on Halloween, of all times.

This snow, however, felt like it was going to be a problem, in ways he knew would be a pain in the ass.

His thoughts drifted back to Halloween and the clan of masked nutjobs creeping across the country. The image of the guy using a truck door as an umbrella came to him then, where the monster walked through the smoke and carnage of Collie's bombardment. *Civvies*, he thought, but they weren't ordinary civvies. They had pretty much shed their civilian-ness. It was easier to think of them as simply insane.

"Collie?" he asked, looking towards the hallway, and the door he'd braced the night before.

Her clothing was gone, as was her gear. There was a bottle of water on the table, as well as a pre-made sandwich in a sealed plastic slip, and a handful of bite-sized *Crunchie* bars. She'd gotten up, set breakfast for him, and moved on.

Christ, he thought. He slept through all that? You think he would've heard something.

The falling snow held his attention for a few more seconds as he finished tying his boots, then he wandered over to the south window and sized up the streets below.

"Well, shit," he muttered, shaking his head at the ongoing avalanche. Snow covered the pavement as far as the eye could see, at least up to the gray fog that swallowed up the city. The sun was up there somewhere, but it couldn't punch through the cloud cover. It wasn't a blizzard, but it was steadily coming down, and had been coming down for quite some time.

He wondered if the limo could cut through all that shit.

His stomach yanked on his chain, and he remembered he hadn't eaten since yesterday. The sandwich was processed turkey and ham, with a slab of processed cheese and a dab of salad dressing. It went down like it was a medium-rare steak, though he wondered what had happened to the cheeseburgers and calzone. The candy bars followed, and they were a little stale, but still mighty fine. The snow continued to fall as he ate, and when he was done, he wandered into the washroom. It was too dark to take aim at the toilet, so he dropped his drawers and sat.

A row of unused toilet paper was on a rack overhead. Gus noticed them and, after finishing his business, grabbed all three rolls, because you never knew. There was nothing left in the room besides his own personal gear, so he picked up his things and left the room.

"Collie?" he asked and looked both ways in the corridor.

No answer.

He proceeded to the first room they had checked out and she wasn't there either. Growing a little pissed, he went to the stairwell and stuck his head in. Darkness, and forbidding silence that he didn't want to disturb. So he descended the stairwell, cringing at his boots echoing off the floor tiles. Gus would've been just as quiet if he had nailed a pair of dinner gongs off his boot heels.

He opened the second-floor door and listened. Collie was talking.

"—I've used that. Piece of goddamn work, really. Minimal recoil. Very easy to shoot. I put a modified can on the barrel to relax the neighbors."

"You didn't mind the barrel weight?" Milo asked.

"That's what the foregrip is for."

"Duh. Right. You mentioned that."

They paused then, which drew Gus over, and he tentatively peered over the glass partition to look down into the lobby.

The two of them were sitting in a furniture set while the morning brightened the interior.

"Morning, Sunshine," Collie said, looking up at him. She was back in her mask and army camos. Milo sat across from her, a bottle of water in his hands. He took a drink and Gus noticed the soldier had a blanket wrapped around his shoulders.

"Morning," Gus said after a few seconds. "You heard me?"

"Yep," Collie said and adjusted her sunglasses. "You move quiet, though."

"I heard him, too," Milo said, taking interest in the bottle's label.

Gus frowned at that.

"You get the breakfast I left for you?" Collie asked.

"Yes, I did. Thanks."

"Don't mention it. Lookin' mighty white out there. You pack your long johns?"

"No."

"Just jeans?"

"Yeah."

"And your coat?" Collie asked.

"Just what I got on."

"Thought so. Well, guess what? I thought this might happen while we were out here, but it happened a month early. So this morning, we're going shopping."

"Yay," Milo said with a touch of surliness.

"Don't mind him," Collie said, waving a hand to dismiss the lack of enthusiasm. "He's cranky about staying down here while we got to snuggle."

"It got fucking cold down here last night, man," Milo pointed out. "I had to hunt up whatever blankets I could find."

"Cold?" She asked and gestured at the wrecked entrance. "With the open door? I wonder why? I came down early, though. You said you got some sleep."

Milo didn't comment.

"Grumpy. It's practically winter. Temps drop. Unfortunately, the ass dropped out of her last night. Didn't figure on the snow. Which brings us back to this morning's job. You both are dressed for the fall. As of this morning, 'the fall' up and left our asses. We get some coats at least, then we're on our way."

"You think the limo is going to get through the snow?"

Collie shrugged. "Let's find out."

In hindsight, parking the monster in the underground garage had been a good thing to do. Collie had already retrieved her booby traps from the night before and returned them to her backpack to reuse at a later time. Gus expected to find perhaps a dozen of the leather lying around the limousine, as dead as cockroaches around an exterminator's trap. There weren't, however, and the only sound came from the open garage entrance, where the wind continued to pile up into a snowdrift.

"Pay attention now," Collie said to Gus. She deactivated the car's defenses before entering on the passenger side. Milo climbed in behind the wheel.

She waited until Gus was aboard and looking between the seats. Once he was in place, she went over the functions before tapping on an interface, bringing up various screens. Gus watched as best as he could, but before long his mind began to jam with the influx of information.

"Remember now," she said to Gus. "There's gonna be a test later."

He didn't like the sound of that.

Collie signaled Milo to drive, and they rolled up the snow-covered ramp and into daylight without a hitch. The machine intuitively switched over into all-wheel drive mode, to give it the extra pull it needed to leave the underground garage.

"Whoa," Collie said.

As Gus had seen from above, a good six or seven inches of snow covered the road, forcing Milo to reduce his speed. Drifts blanketed the street, and in some cases Milo had to swing out around them to bypass those wind-sculpted mounds.

"Whelp," the soldier said from behind the wheel. "It's official."

"What's that?" Collie asked.

"The fucker that got away? He's gonna stay got away."

"Pessimist."

"I'm a realist."

"That's the name pessimists give themselves because they don't like being called pessimists."

That shut Milo up.

"We'll get him eventually," Collie continued. "And whoever he reaches."

"That's bad for us," Milo said.

"Does sound bad, Collie," Gus agreed.

"Doesn't matter. Maybe he'll reach friendly lines. Maybe he won't. If he does, he'll tell his buddies we're coming. He'll tell them about Fort Jay. He'll tell them about the blow-out back around the bridge. And he'll tell them about the hotel back there. Two of those are some major league scalps. Pro-level ass-kicking. *Then* he'll tell them we're coming this way, which I'm sorta hoping he does. Put a little shit-liquifying fear into them all. They've all gotten used to scaring people, so we're gonna change that. We're gonna scare them back a bit before we kill them. Don't you worry. I've been putting down little bastards like the Leather my whole life. Spiderdick might've gotten a head start, but we're not at a disadvantage here. Even better if they come looking for us. Save me some time."

Milo glanced over at her but didn't say anything. Gus saw that he wanted to, but in the end, he kept his mouth shut.

"There," Collie pointed. "Pull over right there."

Big red letters displayed the name *DUFFET'S & WIND* clothing store, and a series of faded signs advised people to *"Get ready for winter!"*

Milo stopped before the storefront, lining up Collie's door with the wrecked doors of the shop.

"Your one-stop shop for all winter shit!" Collie said and cracked open the door, allowing a blast of wind inside that might've shot straight out of old man Winter's ass crack. The cold air repelled Gus and made him appreciate the warmth of the limo.

"Get out," Collie said to them. "Find some winter clothes in there, and that includes long johns if they got them. Looks like the place has already been ripped through, but maybe you'll luck out."

She took her rifle and made tracks through snowdrifts nearly a foot deep. Gus and Milo got out as well, and by the time they reached the front doors, their heads and shoulders were white.

"Coming down hard," Gus noted.

"Then hurry the fuck up," Collie said. "If your pocket pearls aren't swinging, you're not moving fast enough."

The two men left her at the door.

Perhaps half of the shop had been cleared out, but there was plenty left over to go through. Winter coats, vests, even thick shirts any lumberjack would snatch up. There were wool caps, scarves, and gloves, and Gus actually stopped and tried on a pair while Milo continued for the coats.

He glanced over the store shelves, back to the entrance.

A relaxed Collie stood on guard there, rifle lowered, watching the street and the falling snow. She was dark against all that white, and for some reason, that image struck a chord within him. He stopped and sighed, watching her watch the storm.

Then he glanced to his right.

Milo was watching him with one eyebrow cocked in deep reckoning.

Fuck off, Gus silently mouthed at the soldier. He fired off one last unappreciative look and then grabbed a couple of winter caps. He walked over to the men's coats section. Milo was already in a black coat when he noticed Gus approaching, and immediately looked away. They stood not five feet apart.

"You taking that one?" Gus asked, deciding to change the subject.

"Yeah."

"Thought you military guys would go for the white ones. Y'know for winter camouflage."

"This ain't that kinda store," Milo said, and started moving off. "Besides. All the white coats got reflective shit on them."

Gus saw that. He checked the size of the nearest gray coat. Large. It would do him fine.

He wandered over another aisle and located the thermal underwear. He grabbed two and realized he should've taken a basket with him.

Fuck it, Gus thought, and shucked off his boots and jeans right there in the aisle. The cold nipped at his exposed bits, making him go faster.

"What are you doing over there?" Milo asked.

"Putting on some long underwear."

"You found some?"

"Yeah. Why? Want some?"

"Yeah, sure."

"What size?" he asked Milo.

"Large."

Gus found the size and took them off the rack. He fired both over at Milo, who caught them.

"Thanks," Milo said.

"Don't mention it."

"Any undershirts over there?"

There were, actually. *Fruit of the Loom* long-sleeve thermal undershirts. His brand of choice.

"Yeah," Gus said, and started searching for his size.

"Toss me over a couple large."

"Come over and get your own large. I'm not shopping for you."

"We're not shopping here. We're looting. Shopping implies we're spending money."

Gus let that one go. He tugged on his snug thermal under bits. The tight fit made him feel better. He got on his jeans and then his boots. Not five minutes later, he was decked out underneath and feeling fine. He pulled on his winter coat, picked up everything else, and started back for Collie.

She turned toward him, the falling snow now freckling her front. "All done?" she asked.

"Yeah," Gus waved at the coat. "Just my size and color. Lucky, lucky."

"Looks good. As long as it's warm."

"It's warm. My junk's already happy."

Collie's head gently rocked at that before she looked to the street. "Snow's steady, but it's not getting any thicker. The roads will be bad. We're going to have to go slow."

"Let me guess. The limo only has all-seasonals."

"Yup."

"Christ," Gus released in disgust. "You think they have some winter tires for that thing."

"You think the snow would've held off another month," Collie said, and noticed the coating of white on her front. "I wonder if they're getting this back at…"

She trailed off.

Gus waited.

And waited.

"Collie?" he finally asked.

"Yeah?" she asked back, facing him.

"You okay?"

"Yeah, well no. I… forgot where we came from, is all."

The chills returned to Gus, despite his insulated underwear.

"That place," she struggled to remember. "Where we came from. You know the one. Where we fought the Leather. Underground. In that government place."

"Whitecap," Gus supplied gently, not believing what he was hearing.

She stared at him, her sunglasses dappled with snow. "Whitecap. Yeah. That's it."

"You forgot."

"Yeah, I did."

They didn't talk for a while then, hearing only Milo going through the clothing section.

"S'okay," Gus said, reaching out to touch her shoulder while trying to sound confident. "Don't worry about it. No big deal. You're going through a lot."

She nodded.

"And it's morning," Gus explained, gently dusting off the flakes covering her. "Hell, I forget shit all the time in the morning. Even after I have some coffee. One time, I was on the crapper? I sat there for almost an hour—I forgot I'd already unloaded."

She kept on nodding.

That worried him even more. "You okay?" he asked.

"Yeah," she said, and looked to the street. "I'm going back to the car."

She stepped out into the weather, walking through her own tracks.

"Hey, I found woolly socks!" Milo exclaimed from an aisle, holding up the bundles in a victorious 'V'.

"Fuck off, Milo," Gus said under his breath, watching her go.

A short time later, they returned to the limo with their newly appropriated winter clothing and took a few minutes to store everything away. Milo got behind the wheel again while Gus landed in the back. Collie rode shotgun, staring at the dismal conditions ahead. The city was slowly being buried. Gus's concern for her intensified, but he didn't want to say anything in front of Milo.

"This is going to be shitty driving, Collie," Milo finally said, pointing out the obvious.

"I know."

"Really shitty driving."

"Just go slow, Milo," she ordered, sounding like herself once more. "Stay in the center as much as you can. I mean, goddamn, you know how to drive in winter."

"Yeah, I know how," the soldier said as if thinking of other things. "Where to?"

"You said Regina?"

"Yeah."

"Regina it is. Our work is done here." Collie chopped a hand at the road. "All ahead full."

41

They got out of Winnipeg's city limits roughly an hour later.

Not that Gus minded, as it was comfortably warm inside the limo. The kind of heat that would eventually put you to sleep. As it was the beginning of the prairies, the land flattened and disappeared completely about a kilometer out, swallowed up by the curtain of falling snow. The few buildings that scrolled past the limousine's windows were coated frosty white, as were the derelict vehicles dotting the TransCanada highway. Beyond that was a winter wonderland. No sooner did Gus think it when Dean Martin's version of *"Marshmallow World"* started up in his head. That summoned a smirk, and he kept that scratchy needle tune playing in his head as it kept him distracted.

Gus blinked wearily, still hearing Dean Martin as the limo cut through the snow. Milo kept them as close to the center of the road as possible. The all-wheel drive provided traction, but occasionally Milo had to brake to avoid drifting too far left or right due to the snow-covered cars blocking the road.

The sun seared itself against the thinner points of the clouds, hoping to punch through, but falling just short.

"Goddamn," Milo released at one point. "Must be a foot of snow down."

"Go slower then," Collie said.

"I'll go slower, just remember that when we get to Regina next week sometime."

"How long to Regina?" Gus asked.

"Seven or eight, usually," Milo answered. "That's a straight run, doing the speed limit. In this?" he rattled his head. "Maybe a day and a half. If we're lucky."

"Time is ten twenty-three." Collie tapped on the clock. "What day is it, anyway?"

That silenced them all. No one knew.

"Feels like Wednesday," Gus said.

"It does feel like Wednesday," Collie agreed.

"Hate Wednesdays," Milo grumped.

"Tuesdays and Thursdays were my favorites," Gus said. "Tuesday because it's not Monday, and Monday was over and done with. And Thursday was before Friday, which was the beginning of the weekend. If you were in a good mood, it was almost like you got off work on Thursday evening."

The wind scraped up enough of that wintry dust-up and lashed it at the limo, straight into the windshield.

"Life's been nothing but a string of Wednesdays for me," Milo said wearily, adjusting the wiper speed. "Ever since everything went to shit. Been falling in with the wrong groups, time after fucking time."

"You're with a good crew now," Collie said.

"Am I?"

She looked his way.

"Even Jolly Jake was good in the beginning," Milo said, meeting her stare. "I would've had to put him down, too, at some point. I knew I would. He was infected with crazy. You couldn't tell at first, but it was there. Spreading. It was the killing kind, too. Worse, the sadistic kind. Sooner or later, I would've had to shoot him."

"You were taking your time on that," Gus pointed out.

"My fault," Milo said, eyes back on that featureless land. It was becoming difficult to find the road. "I'm paying for it now. Making payments at least. God knows if I'll ever pay it all."

In the back of the limo, Gus thought about those words.

The world became a white plain.

Snow covered the asphalt in most places, but there were curls of gray pavement still visible, leaving enough of a hint as to where the road was. The very sight of it worried Gus a little. Unmoving vehicles were strung out along the highway, but were spread apart in white camouflaged lumps.

The highway was a divided one, or so Milo said, but those eastbound lanes had been buried by the weather. Snow and frost clung to the road signs, partially hiding their messages.

"Not a track," Milo observed at one point, meaning that no traffic had passed through overnight.

"He probably got ahead of this shit," Collie said. "Lucky bastard."

"If he even came this way. Plenty of highways leading to Regina."

Gus didn't need to hear that.

"Good news is," Milo pointed at a gauge, "we're good for power."

"I wonder how much it'll reclaim in these conditions?" Collie said.

Milo didn't comment. That was one thing about the man, Gus noticed. There was very little bullshit. He could appreciate that. In a way, Milo sorta reminded him of Gord, his old painter buddy. That soured his mood. He didn't want to taint Gord's memory by associating him with fucking Milo.

Collie switched on a rearview camera, asking Gus to pay attention when she did. She then instructed him how to do that very thing on his own, much to his distaste. Gus wanted to ask why she was going through the trouble. She was there and Milo was driving, but he realized where the conversation would likely go and didn't want any part of it.

The dashboard screen showed the limo's considerable tracks in the deepening snow, flowing away from the vehicle. Two great grooves that cut the white depths into two distinct lines. He found the creation of those lines soothing, hypnotizing, trailing away into a gray white. He didn't realize it until Collie switched the view off.

At which point he went back to looking out the window.

There weren't any distinct clouds, only a perpetual gloom that swallowed up the land some fifty meters out. The tint on the glass made the day darker. Lines of trees decorated by white fluff came into sight at times, only to ravel out and disappear. Lines. Life became a line. And as they drove straight for the next city, Gus's mind wandered, dulled by the snow, the dimness of the limo's interior, and the seductive heat.

Until, scrolling by the window, was the dark silhouette of a man, his outline ink-stamp bold against the dreary day, some twenty feet off the highway. He stood as if he were waiting for a traffic light to turn red for him. And for a speeding fragment of time, Gus thought he saw the person *smoking*. A cigarette, a cigar, or even a blunt. Gus was certain the person was puffing on something.

Then the figure was gone past the window and out of sight.

That jerked Gus awake, and he lurched to the window, angling to see outside.

Nothing. Just the same bleak emptiness from before.

"See something?" Collie asked.

That whipped his head around, totally thrown by the question. He hesitated, realizing he was indeed awake and in the now. *Had* he seen something? Because, at a glance, and damn his eyes, he *thought* the apparition was the same individual that had lured him into the liquor store the other day, when he had picked up the smiling display of the Captain.

Collie stared at him, waiting for an answer, showing no indication of having seen anything. Milo wasn't driving that fast, and there weren't any snowed-over cars around.

Essentially, there was nowhere to hide.

"Gus?" Collie asked again.

"Just dreaming," he eventually replied and wiped at his mouth. It came away wet.

"Drool much?" Collie asked, watching him from the front seat.

Gus cleaned his hand on his coat. It was evening outside, and the soft interior lighting gave the cabin a space-age ambience. Nothing was outside his window, convincing him that he had in fact been dreaming. A creepy follow-up of a dream that he didn't need.

Was it the same person he'd seen back at the liquor store?

"Good news," Collie said, light playing across her sunglasses. "It's stopped snowing. The low's behind us. And the roads are clear."

Gus smiled, grateful for the distraction, and hoping she didn't sense how rattled he was feeling. "Good. That's good. And the bad news?"

"We're still a ways outside of Regina."

Gus realized they weren't moving. "We've stopped?"

"Overpass ahead," Collie said. "Less than a klick out. Milo spotted it."

"There anyone up there?" Gus asked, coming to his senses completely.

"We'll find out soon enough."

"So, you're gonna creep up there and kill them all?"

"Nope. Not me. Figured we'd drive on through."

That got Milo's attention.

"You heard me," Collie said. "Drive on through. They try something, *anything*, and I release the monster. We're out of missiles and grenades, but this tank's got plenty of bite left in her."

"They might have IEDs up there," Milo said.

"They might," Collie admitted. "They just might have a tank up there themselves. Except they don't. After the last ass-whupping we gave them, I'm thinking they don't have a lot left. I'm thinking all they got are firebombs, maybe a truck full of expired meatbags, and condoms filled up with their own piss. Not much, is it? I'm thinking all their forward elements had the heavy stuff, and we chewed through all that and shat it out. They can't have a lot left. They can't. Not after Whitecap and Fort Jay and that pack back in Winnipeg."

Milo put his foot to the accelerator, and the limo moved ahead.

The sky remained overcast and darker because of the lateness of the day. The overpass loomed about a kilometer away, give or take a hundred meters. The crossing didn't look like much. A skinny concrete ramp bridging the two raised sections of the north-south highway.

The very sight of it, however, uneased Gus. Badness radiated off that thing. The land appeared empty all around the construction, except for the ramps leading to the overpass on either side. The north-south road had nothing on it except a few derelict cars, but those were commonplace.

Gus checked on his shotgun, ready and waiting. He pulled it closer to him.

"Cars on that thing," Milo said.

"Cars all around," Collie said. "Drive on. The way's clear."

And so it was. Nothing lay underneath the overpass, except four lanes of highway, separated by concrete columns and an open space of about twenty feet. The grass was an autumn yellow, and thus far untouched by winter. A sign warned of the clearance being only 5.3 meters, but Gus didn't mind that. His brain was buzzing. Memories were percolating, harassing him, trying to recall but failing.

"They could have lookouts," he whispered.

"What's that?" Collie asked as the overpass drew closer.

"Lookouts."

"Doesn't matter."

Milo glanced over at her again.

"Stop doing that, cowboy," she told him. "And just drive. It'll work out for the best, you'll see."

Potholes frosted around the edges dotted the highway, but Milo avoided the worst of them. The bridge became a hardened slab of fabricated steel and concrete, filling up the windshield, until the limo sailed into the thing's shadow. The overpass walls were clear of graffiti. On the far left, behind the structure and drifting into view, a collection of pickups and cars were crammed into and spilled over the ramp.

The limo emerged from the other side and Gus was just about to let his breath go when multiple thumps landed on the roof. Just then, from the collection of dead vehicles, a pair of pickups—one black, one blue—blasted onto the highway and veered hard towards the limo.

Milo stepped on the electricity.

The pickups closed in on either side of the limo, easily outpacing the vehicle.

Collie was already working the touchscreen. Words and symbols went from green to red.

Something hard crashed down upon the limo's roof. The pickups—what might've been off-road Dodge rams—sped past the luxury vehicle's hood before swinging in, attempting to tap the engine with their rears. Leather-clad individuals filled the box beds, holding on to metal railings and assorted weaponry.

Milo braked, releasing a grunt of pain that sounded like he was deadlifting five hundred kilos.

In the sudden deceleration, the three wisemen making the racket on the roof tumbled off, slamming and rolling off the hood before disappearing over the edge. Gus winced as the limo rolled over those meaty bumps in the road, rising and dropping hard onto the pavement.

The pickups ahead of them slowed as well, their tailgates studded with spikes. A third pickup came up behind the limo, ensuring that the big car didn't try a hard reverse.

"Goddamn hitchhikers," Collie said and tapped the screen. A firing controller lifted from the armrest, which she gripped. On the dashboard screen, red crosshairs popped into existence dead center of the two rigs blocking their path.

The Leather in the rear of the trucks shook their weapons. A couple had axes, while one of them reared up another crossbow.

But then a curious thing happened.

The Leather in both trucks stopped dead in mid-pose, as if seized by a mysterious forcefield.

Which was right about when Collie fired.

What looked like laser beams lanced out from the limousine. A devastating line of holes and craters ripped across the trucks, crumpling tailgates and blowing apart brake lights. That same murderous stream punched *through* the tailgates and mowed down the Leather at the ankles in stunning gouts of meat and maroon. Figures dropped into the box bed, where the unrelenting hosing of bullets pulverized them into chum.

It only took two seconds.

Collie didn't stop there. She swung that joystick left and right, leveling both driver cabs to shreds in squeals and pops that barely penetrated the limo's interior. Neither pickup attempted to drive away, so she ceased fire and inspected the smoking, bleeding wreckages of both man and machine.

A force slammed into the limo from behind, driving them forward. Gus lurched into his seat and rebounded, ending up on the floor.

"Goddamnit," Collie blurted and switched views to the rearview camera.

Where the chrome grimace of the third pickup prodded the limo's behind.

"Oh, you bastard," Collie said.

"Shoot him!" Milo yelled back.

Collie's fingers stumbled across the screen and froze as if forgetting a step.

The angry surge of an engine reached Gus's ears an instant before the pickup rammed them again, and that time, the driver *floored* the gas. Amazingly, the limo lurched forward, shoved into the smoking wreckage of the blue pickup. There the limo pressed up solid in a pop, crinkle, and groan of metal hides. The pickup behind them increased power, the engine singing angrily as it pushed the trapped limo.

Collie still wasn't moving.

"Collie?" Gus asked anxiously.

"I forgot the code."

Another love tap, rocking the limo, but unable to push it any further.

Gus grabbed for his shotgun and then his door, the cold air energizing. He got out, smelling that burning stink only a spinning tire could make. He fell to the pavement as the limo actually shuddered forward an inch, but he quickly regained his feet.

Pickup. The glass tinted, but there were three masked individuals in the rear, holding onto a metal bar for balance.

Gus brought up his shotgun and fired.

The windshield imploded under the onslaught. The gunshots silenced the screaming engine. The driver jumped and jiggled in his seat as the passenger door flew open. The Leather in the rear dove for cover, so Gus walked toward them, firing away, hoping to nail one or two more.

An assault rifle opened up, cutting down figures emerging from the pickup's passenger side. Collie had exited the limo.

One of the Leather tumbled from the rear of the pickup and landed on a knee. The masked asshole tried to stand but his leg failed and he crumpled to the road. Another Leather stood in the box bed, and Gus put a shot through his chest, rudely shoving the target over the far side.

Gus stopped not five feet away from the immobile Leather on one knee and aimed.

That one froze, hands up, palms bleeding from being cheese-grated across asphalt. The minion wore a steel-studded leather muzzle and sported pigtails.

"Like the ponytails," Gus said, keeping the shotgun aimed between the Leather's eyes.

"Fuck you," the woman shot back.

That surprised him. He supposed there would be women among the Leather, but he hadn't actually paid attention to each individual target. This one, however, was bulked up with perhaps winter clothing underneath her coat.

She got to her feet and cocked back one leg, as if gauging the distance to sweep one of Gus's own.

"Get down," he warned, aiming at her head. "And stay still."

She did so, lowering herself to sit back on her calves.

There were three short bursts from the other side of the truck, then all was smoking and steaming.

"You okay over there?" Collie asked.

"Yeah," Gus answered. "I got a live one."

"You do?"

"Yeah."

Collie came around the truck, rifle at the ready.

"You bagged a girly one," Collie said, inspecting the prisoner. "I bet she's mean, too."

The Leather looked from one to the other before taking a second to size up her frayed hands. The hard landing on the pavement had shredded her gloves and palms,

"Bet that stings," Collie said, getting the Leather's attention. She tried to make fists, which only caused them to bleed more.

"They're all dead, honey," Collie informed the prisoner. "In case you're wondering. You're the last."

The Leather peered up at the operator for a few reckoning seconds, and actually appeared to be gauging her chances. If she could, Gus knew right then the woman would spit acid at them both.

"You do anything and I'll put a bullet in your knee," Collie warned. "Or your shoulder. I'm not picky."

The Leather became very still.

"I count a dozen of you demented fuckers," Collie said. "Including you, still kicking. You feel like answering some questions?"

"You're so dead," the woman said.

"Sure we are."

"So goddamn dead."

"Heard you the first time."

"The Dog Tongue will bite off your lips. Your tongue. He'll make you beg for death."

Amongst the steaming, hissing background noise of wrecked pickups, Gus looked to Collie. "Didn't she just say we were dead?"

"Don't mind her," Collie said. "Having your ass kicked rattles a person."

The Leather lunged.

Surprisingly *fast* and caught Collie across the thighs. The operator staggered under the weight, before hammering a fist into the ear of the attacking woman.

Who released a feral bitch-growl of fury.

Collie hit her three more times. The first one caused her attacker to go limp. The two follow-up strikes put her on her back and left her groaning.

"You're quick," Collie said, taking hold of her rifle once again and aiming at her. "For all the good it did you."

Gus reset himself, cursing for allowing the Leather to get between him and Collie in the first place. Collie had knocked her down, however…

Gus's eyes narrowed.

There was a knife sticking out of Collie's left thigh.

Noticing his stare or perhaps feeling the blade, the operator assessed the damage. She reached down and pulled the knife free, one of those short three-inch jobs which were easy to hide.

Collie dropped the blade, and the steel tinkled off the pavement.

"All right," she said, backing up a step while maintaining her aim. "Now that *that's* over with, I got questions."

The Leather watched her, wondering how she was still able to stand. She got to her knees.

"Stand down," Collie warned softly.

The woman released another one of those brutish grunts, so Collie shot her dead, putting a three-round burst into the Leather's chest. The dead woman flew back and bounced off the highway.

In the smoking aftermath, Collie lowered her weapon. "This way," she said to Gus, and walked back to the other side of the pickup. There was no limp, which probably meant the blade hadn't severed anything major. Ahead of her, the two other machines continued to smoke.

"You okay?" Gus asked as he hurried to catch up.

"Never better."

He was going to ask about her leg when, there, propped up against the front tire and holding onto his side, a still-breathing Leather came into sight.

"Winged this one as he tried to take flight," Collie explained, stepping around the man.

A red skull mask covered the Leather's features. Sunglasses lay nearby, as if they'd flown off the guy's face as he went down. Dark shadows colored the flesh around his eyes.

"You still with us?"

Red Skull listed to one side as an answer.

"That mean yes?"

"Yes, fuck yes," the Leather groaned.

"Don't look good, though," Collie said, holding her rifle steady. "I say, without medical attention, you're a goner."

"You think?" Red Skull said, sounding as if the shock of being gunned down was wearing away.

"Where's the rest of your buddies?" she asked, changing the subject.

"In the city."

"Regina?"

"Yes. Regina. You dumb twat."

"Where in Regina?"

The dying man gave directions. He ended with, "Just follow the skulls."

"Skulls," Gus whispered in quiet distaste.

"How many?" Collie asked Red Skull.

"Huh?"

"How many of you Leather dorks are *in* Regina?"

Red Skull didn't answer right away. He studied Collie, smoldering with a loathing that Gus could not only see, but feel.

"Enough," he answered.

"Give me a number," Collie said.

"Two dozen."

"Yeah? You're not lying to me now."

"Two dozen," he insisted, apparently sensitive to her implication that he might be telling a few falsehoods. "Waiting. For you. They'll be ready. You'll see."

"You see a squirrelly fucknut roll through here?" Gus cut in. "One of your cock-knuckles, wearing a spider mask?"

Red Skull looked to Collie to Gus and back again.

"Answer the question," Collie ordered.

The dying Leather hesitated, and that little bit of defiance seemed to lend him strength, if only for a few scant heartbeats. He went limp then, and Gus thought the man had died right there, taking his secrets to the grave.

But then, "Yeah," Red Skull got out, sounding tired. "He came through. Warned us. You might. Be coming."

No one spoke.

"Anything else you want to share?" Collie prodded.

Red Skull's head drooped. "No," he whispered.

Collie shot him, one round straight through the chest. The Leather rattled against the tire before rolling onto his side. Collie loomed over him, inspected the shot, and for a moment Gus thought she was going to plug the dead guy again.

She didn't, however. She turned her sunglasses upon him. "What a day, huh?"

"Whatta day," Gus agreed.

He realized then that Milo was still aboard the limo, and he hadn't gone anywhere.

"Nothing that we didn't already know," Collie said.

"Two dozen more," Gus reminded her, and he got a dismissive shake of the head.

"About that. I figure there's about a one percent chance there might be more, but I don't think so. Dog Dick's all in. I'm surprised he's not riding with his gang, but maybe he thinks all this shit is beneath him. God, I hope he's not religious. The crazies give religion a bad name."

"Collie?"

"Hm?"

"Your leg?"

"Oh, that. Didn't feel a thing. She was quick, 'eh?"

Gus thought about it. "I don't think she was that quick. I think… you're slowing down."

The operator didn't comment. She hefted her rifle and took in the vast emptiness of the land around them, as if either smelling something or just pondering the mysteries of the universe.

"Yeah," was all she finally said. "Point taken. You wanna get the duct tape out?"

"What for?"

"Best to tape that off now than later. Don't want my shit to be leaking into the limo's seat. That'll gross you both out. And I don't know if it'll wash out."

They went back to the driver's side of the limo. Milo lowered the window and squinted. A part of Gus wasn't surprised to see him sticking around, and that surprised him even more than Milo actually staying.

"Get 'em all?" Milo asked.

"Yeah," Collie said.

"You get cut?"

"Nothing a little tape won't solve."

Gus entered the limo and located the duct tape. When he got back out, Collie was leaning against the side and motioning for him to come closer.

"Right there," she said and pointed.

"You don't want to drop your pants?"

"At this point? No."

"Might be easier later on."

"Later on?" she asked and chuckled. "All right. Milo, you mind?"

"You gonna strip?"

"A little."

"Go ahead. Ain't nothing I haven't seen before."

"I think we both know the truth to that," Collie said to Gus as she started to undo her gear. "Keep a lookout, cowboy."

Which Milo did.

It took ten minutes, but Gus taped up the knife wound—an ugly little slit of a mouth that gave a peek as to what was going on *inside* her body, which wasn't pretty. The edged steel missed the bone entirely, so that was good. It entered on the side, inserting itself in the muscle underneath instead of slashing it. The Leather didn't get a chance to *twist* the blade, which was a good thing. He bound the cut several times before tearing the strip off and securing it.

"You did good there," she said to him. "Getting out when you did. When I forgot the codes. I remember them now, by the way. Won't happen again."

Gus wasn't sure about that, and Milo was smart enough to stay quiet. Gus finished what he was doing and stepped back.

"Collie?" he asked, as she pulled her gear back on.

"Yeah."

"What happens if you break a leg?"

"Probably nothing."

"I'm serious."

"I was being serious," Collie said as she tightened her belt. "Nothing will happen. Well, I won't be able to walk, like anyone, and the leg won't heal at all. That's a given."

Gus massaged his neck.

"Don't you worry," she said, reaching out and gripping his shoulder. "About anything. I'm not going to break a leg. And if I did, just for argument's sake, remember, I don't feel a thing right now. So there's that. Only hope it's the left leg and not the right. I can still drive then."

Gus smiled thinly, unsure if she was trying to be funny.

"And I won't forget how to operate the weapons systems again," she added.

Silence to that.

"Gonna be dark soon," she noted, changing the subject.

"You want to keep going?" Gus asked.

"You heard the man. Said they were waiting for us. Ready and waiting. So what say we find a place to hide. Get some shut eye. And then we'll creep up on them in the morning. When we're rested and they're sleeping."

"What if they're waiting for these guys to come back?" Gus asked, indicating the dead Leather.

"Fuck 'em. We'll still sleep better than them."

"What if they come looking for them?"

"Fuck 'em again. We'll kill anyone they send out. I don't mind that, actually. Let them come one at a time for all I care."

"You think Spiderdick is with them?" he asked. "In Regina?"

"We can hope so," Collie answered, looking past the darkening highway, toward the horizon beyond.

"But that one has the luck of the Irish with him. Sorta like you. I bet the little pocket weasel is already heading for Dog Dick. To report to him directly. That's my guess, anyway."

Gus thought it was a good guess. Milo was in the driver's seat, watching the horizon and listening all the while. He didn't say a thing, which made Gus think he was in agreement with everything Collie just said.

And very much aware of her worsening condition.

"I'm gonna check on those dumb fucks who jumped on the roof and then fell off," Collie said. "Make sure they're dead."

She turned to Gus. "And if they're not, I'll take care of them."

42

It was nearly midnight by the time the Spider reached Regina.

The TCH was a straight run to the city core, with one stop at a guard post, where the Spider got one of the watchmen at the overpass to top off his fuel tank. The Spider didn't waste much time with the dozen or so Leather there. He told them to be vigilant, that there were soldiers coming, that they had guns. Honest-to-Christ weaponry that the soldiers were very much proficient with. He told them that Winnipeg had fallen, as far as he knew, based on the series of bomb blasts coming from across the river. The Bear Trap, the Samurai, all of them had been wiped out.

Then their killers had taken over the Leather's hotel and the Spider had only just escaped.

The overpass Leather listened with the usual masked indifference. The Spider sensed they weren't taking his warnings seriously enough. The Spider himself didn't feel invincible anymore. He felt… hunted. Hunted with extreme prejudice. He'd done bad things, *very* bad things, and now someone out there with the skills, strength, and righteous sense of justice aimed to punish him for his actions. Aimed to punish them all.

That thought pushed him to warn the Dog Tongue. At this point, despite his plans to separate himself from the clan, he didn't think he could do so until this latest threat had been removed. And he would need help. That meant sucking up to the Dog Tongue one last time. The Spider didn't think his ambitions were suspect, so it would be an easy request.

The soldiers pursuing him were formidable, but even evil had its champions.

He'd let the Dog Tongue deal with the soldiers.

The Spider informed the overpass watch that he would be traveling to the

Four Towers. Once there, he would talk to their commander to send reinforcements. The overpass watch didn't say anything to that. Surprisingly, the vibe he sensed was one of excitement, the kind that broke up an otherwise boring assignment. Though the Spider warned of how dangerous these new adversaries were, he understood the Leather's mindset completely. The clan valued scalps and stories of blood and spectacle. Get enough of those, earn a reputation, and the Dog Tongue would hear of it. Get enough and the Dog Tongue would summon you to an audience.

Impress him, and the Dog Tongue might reward you with a pack, which might one day lead to a full command.

"We'll take care of them," the leader of the overpass watch said.

Like fuck you will, the Spider thought, knowing what the lessers were all thinking.

Kill the soldiers. Earn the favor of the Dog Tongue.

The Spider drove away after that, leaving them to whatever surprises they might devise. He didn't think they would kill the soldiers. Not after what he'd seen. Even the pair that had captured him had managed to do well against the Leather. The one that truly worried him was the black masked soldier. That one was… special. He needed to find a way to kill that one. Or get someone else to do it. Based on all that, the choice was clear.

The Dog Tongue.

The Spider thought about the Leather's rock star overlord. How he came into existence. Legend had it that the Dog Tongue was—of all things—a singer in a boy band group back in the old world. That the inflictors were his steroid-injected bodyguards. And that, the one reason why the whole clan maintained silence when invading new territory was because the Dog Tongue preferred the sound of his own voice.

Or something like that.

The Spider didn't know if that was true or not, but he knew one thing— the Dog Tongue *did* have a nice voice. Not deep, not high, but… *melodious* was the word. Which was weird, but then again, the world was weird, which was the new normal. The Dog Tongue might have a sweet set of pipes, but the Spider knew their overlord. Knew firsthand what the Dog Tongue was capable of. Saw bones being broken.

The signs were all around. Skulls on posts dotting the roadsides like grim warnings, reminding whoever traveled these highways who owned them. The further east the Dog Tongue invaded, the more signage he would leave in his wake, marking his territory.

The Spider drove west on the TransCanada, taking that straight runway to the Four Towers. He saw the turnoff that would keep him on the main highway, but ignored it, staying on the current strip and seeing the sign for Victoria Avenue.

Ghost town. Like all the great cities, Regina's downtown hub was a haunted sprawl of streets, alleys, and empty buildings. The road was clear, as ordered by the Dog Tongue. He wanted Highway One to be cleared of all obstructions, and his minions had done his bidding. The truck's headlights lit up Victoria Avenue, forcing back the deep, deep dark, as if the whole city had sunk into a near bottomless trench. Streetlamps were lightless, bowed, and some even bent. Business signs were unlit. Cars were shoved aside, up onto sidewalks to form a cracked pavement channel straight to the Four Towers.

And as the Spider drove along, in that moonless, urban graveyard of a city, the headlights uncovered more signage belonging to the Dog Tongue.

Skulls, fixed atop crude posts cut and nailed together, lined the avenue. Human skulls had become as commonplace as the leftover automobiles packed into the streets. The Dog Tongue preferred canine skulls, but he made use of the more readily available source. There were all shapes and sizes. Whatever was available, really. Some had holes drilled into them to avoid cracking the bone when nailed to the wood. Some were missing their jaws. Some were staked through the eye socket. Some were smiling.

All were screaming. Or trying to.

Skulls.

And the road was decorated on both sides with them.

The word was that the Dog Tongue intended to create what he called *Skull Road* from the west coast all the way to the east. The Spider knew that the TCH was already marked from Vancouver, right up to Regina's prairie-dusted ass. Sort of like a nationwide connect-the-dots in a horror book of adult activities. The rest of the country would follow.

The pickup moved past the skulls, the empty eye cavities downcast, but the faces crazy upbeat, as if knowing that, someday soon, a celebrity warlord would be passing by them. And that was something to scream about. Just behind those haunting expressions stood the dead buildings with their own secrets. Some of the places had been looted, some barricaded, but all had been searched. Still, the Spider didn't appreciate that feeling of rolling through a place he most certainly was not supposed to be.

The Spider braked, slowing to sixty. The skulls were placed closer together now, spiked on poles not ten feet apart. The commercial zone stopped at an intersection and a wall of cars blocked off the streets to the north and south. A deserted residential section began after that. Wild lawns grown to hip-height had been hobbled by cold weather. The pickup's engine droned on, but inside the cab, the Spider was very much aware of the absence of life.

The residential area whisked by. The dashboard clock said 12:33 am. The skies remained clear overhead but the moon was nowhere in sight. Star fields lit up the heavens. On ahead, however, the Spider sighted two towering blocks stamping out the night, one that resembled a gigantic 'H'. In the day, the Four Towers—four hotels which crowned the central downtown intersection—were easily seen against the night sky. Now, their combined girth cast the blackest of shadows across the cityscape.

And the Spider scurried towards them.

The road ended at an intersection, where two large dump trucks parked nose-to-ass blocked any further progress. A streetlight post ripped off at its midway point rose from the center of the street. Hanging off the top of the thing was an honest-to-Christ buffalo skull, with the horns snapped off at the base. The skull was a little out of the ordinary, considering the regular heads the Dog Tongue had marked the highway with, but that was the overlord's decision. Or the Vampire's.

The Spider remembered the commander of Regina a split second before he rolled to a stop before the intersection.

And the world exploded in light.

Headlights blinded him from the left and right. Machines on either side shot out from the walls of trashed cars like missiles flying free from silos. The trucks screeched to a stop within five feet of the Spider's own pickup, while two more rigs pulled up behind him, ensuring no escape.

Putting his machine in park, the Spider lowered his window and yelled, "Where's the Vampire?"

Silence answered him. The headlights didn't relent, but figures moved just behind them, aiming weapons. The Spider covered his eyes to better see. "I want to see the Vampire! I've got news. Winnipeg's gone. The Bear Trap's dead. The Vulture's dead."

That calmed things down.

The headlights switched off, and the figures moved forward. A handful of Leather stepped up to the driver's side of the Spider's truck. The closest one wore an outlaw's mask that only covered the lower half of his face, while his shorn head appeared blue black in the night. His eyes were narrowed and fierce.

He opened the Spider's door and, stepping back, beckoned him to exit.

The Four Towers were special.

They were each upscale hotels, Marlot, SeeBot, Chorus, and Anchor Bay. Their lobbies were palatial, filled with posh furniture of unstainable whites and grays, all underneath grandiose chandeliers. Gold railing and trim complemented paneled wood walls, and artificial plants stood in almost every corner, seeping putrid decadence as dusty as the surroundings. The four-tower cluster of hotels was an exceptionally rare find in the larger cities, and an even rarer example of corporate teamwork amongst its owners. Each tower was connected by skyways on the ninth floor, creating a considerable lounge circuit for their well-paying guests. One could have a drink and choose to stroll, sprint, or stagger through the stormproof skyways—nine floors above the downtown core.

Not only were the hotels connected, they were entirely disconnected and separate from the existing power grid, drawing their power from advanced solar and geothermal technologies. Tech that had been years away from being affordable for residential owners, but readily sold to the wealthy corporate sector as being the next step in clean and plentiful energy systems. From the streets looking up, however, there weren't many lights, and what *was* on was barely seen. And the leader of this rare outpost didn't inhabit the lower levels.

He resided at the very top.

Each hotel had its own elevator, and the Spider was escorted to one of these by four of the Leather. One of the lessers, a thick-set animal with broad shoulders standing in front of the controls, carried, of all things, a rechargeable chainsaw. Classic guitar tunes played through hidden speakers as the elevator lifted them to the thirteenth floor. As they rose, the Spider's eyes wandered over a once-lavish interior now coated in dirt and grime.

The elevator doors opened to black and white tiles laid out in a narrow chessboard pattern leading up to the entrance of Vampire Joe's abode.

Vampire Joe wasn't just a Leather. He was a real, living, self-*declared* vampire, professing a genuine taste for human blood, and willing to slowly drain a person over a period of days before swapping out the old for the new. The Spider wasn't surprised that a freak like Vampire Joe managed to survive the zombie outbreak. Only the hardest made it through the apocalypse, the craziest, and the Dog Tongue gathered them all under his grisly banner. What really uneased the Spider, however, was that Vampire Joe was, at one point before the zombies, part of an online group who actually, *actively,* drank each other's blood, without any safety measures in place for testing of diseases.

Which was totally fucked up, in the Spider's opinion.

In any case, Vampire Joe survived like the rest of them, and the Dog Tongue somehow recruited him. In time, the real-life bloodsucker actually got promoted.

That was life in the new world, especially in the Dog Tongue's ranks.

The more fucked up you were, the better.

The penthouse suite's double doors might have been pulled off a castle. Varnish glossed up the surface with a killer shine, while fine lines of gold embossed the angles and edges. The lesser with the chainsaw glanced at the Spider while another stepped up to a doorbell and rang.

Chimes sounded from within.

Seconds later, one door cracked open and a woman peeked out. She wore red contact lenses and a half-ninja mask that covered everything below her eyes. At a glance, she looked like a Japanese Tengu, a demonic figure fancying herself as part-assassin.

Words were spoken between the two Leather, and the woman closed the door.

The lesser who had spoken to the door guard glanced at his chainsaw-toting companion, then at the Spider, then back to the entrance.

Seconds later, the woman pulled open the doors and waved them all inside.

"Welcome… to *Regina,*" Vampire Joe greeted, speaking with an English accent and stressing the final word. The trouble was… Vampire Joe wasn't English. He was from British Columbia, and the accent mysteriously disappeared when the bloodsucking bastard truly lost his shit. Or was high out of his gourd. No one—not even the Dog Tongue—demanded that the man dispense with the fake accent. The freak actually functioned much better in his fantasy.

With feigned grace, Vampire Joe tipped a pewter goblet toward his visitor. The leader stood at a bar, and was decked out in an outfit that might've come from a masochist's fashion show—a black leather vest with stylish red trim, ruffled sleeves peeking out of an overcoat that might've been taken from a rock 'n' roll buccaneer. Its high collar covered his neck as though to protect against garrotes and stranglers.

Vampire Joe had colored his face a deep disturbing pink, and his hair was shorn to his gleaming, grease-slicked white skull.

The Vampiric One also wore diamond-studded dentures, and Lord only knew where he appropriated them. And when he lifted his goblet and smiled, power chords of trepidation ripped through the fibers of the kingdomless Spider.

Serving the bloodsucking bastard was another female, and she wasn't wearing a mask. She wore aviator sunglasses, however, which only accentuated the stark black and white make-up that divided her face straight down the middle. Her elbow was flat against the countertop of the penthouse suite's bar as she leaned forward to check out the visitors. The Spider remembered seeing the woman doing the same thing once before, but a person's throat had been underneath it at the time.

Nowhere did the Spider see an Inflictor, and that was a nod to the Dog Tongue's complete trust in the loyalty and competence of Regina's overlord. The Vulture had been the same, although he did have the Bronze following him around.

Vampire Joe held his pose until the Spider remembered his manners.

"Vampire," he greeted. No one dared use the Vampire's given name in his presence, and though the Spider had as much use for the psycho as a preserved bottle of dog shit, he wasn't going to unintentionally provoke him. Not in his kingdom, and certainly not in front of his people.

"Greetings," the Spider added as an afterthought.

"I'm surprised to see you here," Vampire Joe said.

"I bring bad news."

"Oh? I see. That's troubling. Very bad?"

"The worst."

"Oh dear. Distressing, indeed. Well, then. Let's have it."

So the Spider started talking, careful not to exclude Vampire Joe's two companions. As he related the recent events of Winnipeg and Fort Jay, the blood guzzler stopped drinking and listened with an increasingly pensive face.

Which was fucking disturbing to say the least.

It took roughly ten minutes to get all the details out, but no one attempted to rush the narrative, right up until the Spider finished.

Vampire Joe was silent in the aftermath, swishing his goblet as if trying to summon a whiff of whatever he was drinking. His brooding features had become even more pinched, bordering on insulted, as he reflected on the report.

"Well," he finally whispered, still holding onto his accent. "Holy shit."

Indeed, the Spider thought.

"Apologies. Poor manners," Vampire Joe said as an afterthought. He snapped his fingers at the woman behind the bar. "Scotch for the man. My Lord Spider. Ah, these people after you. After us. Are they truly soldiers? You're certain of that?"

"Fairly certain."

"And they decimated Fort Jay?"

The Spider nodded.

"And only you managed to survive?" Vampire Joe asked with a glimmer of amusement.

"I had to warn the others," the Spider explained with the barest touch of heat.

"Of course, of course. And in this army, the commanding officer is everything. The head of the serpent and all that. I don't question your decision. Not at all. I would've done the very same if they'd gotten the better of me."

The Spider didn't respond to that, but once again he was grateful for having his mask, to hide the blood rising in his cheeks. They hadn't gotten the better of the Spider, they'd only won a skirmish. The Spider would win the war.

At that moment, the bartender completed the Spider's drink and placed a small, delicate glass upon a serving tray. She handed the tray over to someone just out of sight behind the bar, and twiddled her fingers then for that person to get moving.

A little person walked around the bar, carrying the tray. A plain white gimp mask with dangling hoop rings covered the person's face. The little person was a child perhaps only nine or ten, decked out in a knee-length leather skirt and coat that seemed cold for the season. White high socks stopped at the knee, and on the child's feet were shoes which again seemed entirely wrong for the weather.

That little Leather person marched over to the Spider and presented the drink to him, the glass tumbler carefully placed upon a cocktail napkin. Scotch whiskey of a brand unknown filled the glass, and a handful of what appeared to be dice rested at the bottom.

The Spider took the drink without thanks, and the little servant returned to her place behind the bar.

The Spider watched her go.

"How many did you say again?" Vampire Joe asked. "Three?"

That brought the Spider back. "At least, yes."

"But you say only one sacked Fort Jay?"

The Spider hesitated. "Yes."

"Formidable. And armed? Full 'battle rattle', as they say?"

"To the teeth."

"God help us," Vampire Joe said and sipped, staring off into space. "God help us all." He sipped again, smacking thin lips as if the drink needed something more. "And you say they're on their way here?"

"I'd assume so."

"I'd *suggest* we assume so, so there are no surprises. And, forgive me, you say they're traveling in a *limousine*?"

"Yes. One of the big ones. Like a stretched-out SUV."

"A stretched-out SUV. Dear oh dear. That does sound… snazzy."

No one moved in the room. The Spider considered his drink again. He wasn't a Scotch fan, and there were at least four fingers of booze in the glass, even with the funky dice.

"Well," Vampire Joe finally said. "The first question that comes to my mind is… not so much who they are or what they intend on doing. It's clear their intent is to kill the Leather. That much is obvious. But where did they come from? And where did they come into such weaponry? And is there more? More to the point, do they have more ammunition? And are their others?"

The Spider lifted the drink to his face and sniffed.

"They obviously come from somewhere," Vampire Joe rambled on. "Perhaps seeking to stop the Dog Tongue's advance. And you say they've already killed the Vulture?"

"They didn't name him, exactly. They said they killed 'every last one of my buddies back east.' Or so they said."

Vampire Joe looked to the huge window facing the west. "They had to have help with that. The Vulture spearheaded the bulk of the Dog Tongue's *army*. Which might mean that the Vulture discovered something back east. A community of some sort. One with at least a handful of soldiers perhaps, and the weapons to arm themselves with. Perhaps a great *deal* of weapons. And ammunition. Considering the size of the Dog Tongue's forces, it stands to reason that they must have *stores* of munitions."

The Spider nodded again, following the thread of logic.

"Fascinating," Vampire Joe said and drank once more. When he finished, he glanced over at the Spider, who hadn't tasted a single drop.

"Something wrong with the Scotch?" Vampire Joe inquired.

"No."

"You haven't tried it."

"Ah…" The Spider looked around. "You have anything to mix it with? I take cola but I figure you don't have any. Maybe some water?"

The bartender straightened, her posture on the defensive, if not outright insulted.

The other woman, the one with the contact lenses, looked directly at Vampire Joe.

Vampire Joe stared down the length of his nose at the Spider, as if deciding upon a verdict of death or simply life imprisonment.

"That's *Scotch* in your tumbler," the Vampiric One said in a frosty tone of warning. "Back in the old world I've publicly slapped people for asking for mix. If I'd known you wanted *swill*, Lord Spider, I would've poured you a glass of common *rye* or rum or any of the other pig piss squeezed out of a common swish barrel."

Silence then, between the two.

"Suppose so," the Spider eventually said, absorbing the rebuke. He lifted his mask just enough to sip. He stifled the shiver and dropped the mask to hide the curl of his lip. *Acquired taste,* his ass. A chipmunk's fuzzy ball sack steeped in ethanol probably had more flavor.

"Well?" Vampire Joe asked.

"Good."

And like that, the storm clouds gathering behind the vampire's eyes dissipated. He went back to thinking. "You were right in coming here, to warn me."

"I was…" The Spider swallowed, still affected by the septic heat of the goddamn Scotch. "*Am*…only passing through. I'm heading for the Dog Tongue."

"Lord Dog Tongue?"

"To warn him."

"Of the soldiers?"

"Yes."

"But there are only three of them."

"I think."

Vampire Joe shrugged. "Well, then, we'll dispatch them."

The Spider forgot about the Scotch sizzling through the lining of his guts. "You'll what?"

"We'll assume they're coming here. A more than fair guess, since they're waging a private war against the clan. Hence, we'll prepare a trap for them."

That was the stupidest thing the Spider had ever heard out of this fake fuck's pink face, but what he said was, "They've taken out the Vulture."

"Yes."

"And my own forces."

"So you've said."

"And the Bear Trap and *his* forces."

Vampire Joe sipped his drink and nodded in understanding. "Yes. Quite."

"That's well over six *hundred* Leather. Maybe even seven."

"Yes. And their mindless."

The Spider nodded as well. "And their mindless. How many Leather do you have here?"

Vampire Joe exchanged looks with his companions. "Roughly two dozen."

"Including the Chemist?"

"Not including the Chemist. She's a non-combatant."

There was no such distinction in the coming fight, or so the Spider thought. The Leather had committed crimes against humanity, he knew, and the soldiers were seeking to punish them all.

He also realized it wasn't his decision. "I'm going to the Dog Tongue. To warn him. To tell him the same thing I've told you."

"Then tell him my plans as well. To trap the soldiers. I'll keep them alive if I can, so that he can amuse himself when he arrives."

Vampire Joe stopped talking then, and though he shut up, what he'd left unspoken still reached the Spider. Old Vampire Joe was hooked on his Bloody Mary's and Marty's like an old-fashioned junkie (or a modern-day leech), and he was already looking forward to his next plasma hit. Vampire Joe didn't drink his followers, but the Spider suspected the self-styled, blood-slurping connoisseur sampled one or two of the meat puppets if the need *really* got bad. The very image of the pink-faced metro-goth cutting into an unshaven neck and showering in its arterial flood curled and twisted the Spider's already tortured stomach.

Fucking Scotch. Never was a Scotch drinker. Never would be.

"I'll ask that you give me enough fuel to reach Vancouver then," the Spider asked.

"Vancouver? Lord Dog Tongue's not in Vancouver anymore, my eensy-weensy fellow."

Again, the Spider was grateful for his mask. The condescending prick before him might be one of the Dog Tongue's prized lieutenants, but the Spider was beginning to want to outfit his truck tires with winter chains and drive over the fake bastard's spine.

"Oh, goodness no," Vampire Joe continued. "Lord Dog Tongue is on the move. He's left Vancouver's rotten heart and is on his way here," Vampire Joe said. "Left there a week ago, I believe. Scouring the countryside as he travels, no doubt. When the dust settles, the mice creep out of their holes, so he might just catch a few stragglers. Should be here in a day or two at least, I expect. If there are no distractions. Though I'm sure he stopped in Banff. The mountain air will surely agree with him."

That stopped the Spider. "Why is he coming here?"

Vampire Joe shrugged. "I don't question the Dog Tongue."

No one does, the Spider thought. "Who's with him?"

"Everybody, I suppose. Who's left, that is. And if these soldiers have killed all you've said they've killed, then... there's nothing between them and him. Except... us."

"I'll go on ahead, anyway," the Spider said. "Meet him on the highway. Tell him what's coming."

At that point, an evil scratch of a smile hooked one corner of Vampire Joe's pink face.

"I'll be leaving then," the Spider said, ignoring the smirk, and moved to place his drink on a nearby table. When he turned around, the Leather who had escorted him blocked the way.

"You'll leave when I grant you permission to leave," Vampire Joe said.

The Spider faced the Regina overlord.

"Drink that," Vampire Joe commanded, meaning the Scotch.

The Spider didn't move.

"Drink. That," Vampire Joe repeated.

"I'm not a Scotch drinker."

"I don't care. That was poured for *you*. In my home. Taken from my private and very much prized stock. No one here is going to drink it, and, frankly, I want *you* to drink it. Seriously. And remember, we both know I could do a *lot* more than command you to drink a glass of fine Scotch. Now then. Drink. And be on your way, tarnished knight, before the snow falls."

No one in the room moved, and it occurred to the Spider that if he *didn't* drink the whiskey, Vampire Joe might not wait until the soldiers arrive. Vampire Joe might just drink him instead and fabricate any story he pleased to give to the Dog Tongue. He was just fucked-in-the head enough to try it.

The Spider picked up his glass again. He lifted his mask and, slipping a hand up under to pinch his nose, gulped down everything in the tumbler without pause.

When it was empty, he exhaled, put the glass down, and shivered in spite of himself.

A smiling Vampire Joe dismissed him with a hand.

And the four Leather escorted him back to his truck.

43

The Spider drove along that fat ribbon of highway called the TransCanada One, west of Regina. He wondered if he'd had to turn the wheel once in the hours since leaving Vampire Joe. He didn't think he did. *Flat.* The world was flat out here. A white, frozen grass plain periodically pricked with lonely-looking houses, and even those were few and far between.

The grass grew tall out this way, right up to the edge of the crumbling pavement, creating a channel some four feet tall. Frost crippled that vegetation, grass or wheat or whatever, hinting that snow wasn't far away. The prairie winters were legendary, where the temperatures could easily plummet to minus thirty, minus forty or even fifty. Those were the days you stayed inside all day and brought in the dog. The Spider wasn't sure if that temperature was with a wind or not, but it didn't matter. He wasn't going to spend his winter out here. It was too empty for him. Too much of nothing. And those frost-stricken fields of whatever-the-fuck-was-growing didn't lift his morale. In his truck, riding high, he could see the upper bits of cars shoved off the highway, slowly being smothered by the prairie. There were plenty of vehicles, in fact, all pushed aside to clear the road. He had to give it to the Dog Tongue. The guy wasn't just another goon. He had a vision, and one of the items in that vision was a singular road cleared of shit, so that if anyone needed support of any kind, they could jet along those runways at full raging speed.

Deer be damned.

Deer was, in fact, good eating, if you were lucky enough to strike one, and had the ram plate fixed to your front.

The Spider drove through the remnants of Belle Plaine, which was the first place he actually had to turn the wheel. Then it was skirting the boundaries of long-pillaged Moose Jaw, which he did not enter. The Spider stopped and refueled when he could. The minions of Vampire Joe had supplied him with seven gas cans of Dog Piss Premium—the spiced-up ethanol blend that the Chemist had formulated during these days of expansion. The red fuel containers were stowed away out back, and when the Spider emptied one, he didn't throw them away. He *almost* whipped one out into the endless prairie, just out of spite for being in such a predicament.

Mindless. The Dog Tongue wasn't mindless. The Spider had to remind himself of that, but he was also confident in his acting abilities. He'd successfully hidden his ambitions to break away from the Dog Tongue for some time now, and though he loathed to meet the leader of the road clan, he knew he had to.

The soldiers that hunted him, hunted them all, were beyond his ability to take on alone. He was intelligent enough to realize that. Where he possessed a willingness to inflict terror and pain and had experience in doing so, these self-righteous soldiers were actually trained professionals capable of doing so much more. And to a greater degree. Or at least in the Spider's mind. They were vengeful paladins roused to the actions of the Dog Tongue, and were moving against him and his minions. They would be beyond Vampire Joe's abilities as well. If Vampire Joe *did* manage to kill them, then no harm no foul. The Spider would simply apologize to the Dog Tongue and take on whatever task the leader deemed fit.

But he had to alert the Leather's overlord.

A feeling of dread spread throughout the Spider.

A month or two among the slaves, the meat puppets, seemed a reality, something he did *not* want to think about.

He didn't think about running, however.

The Dog Tongue would find him. The Dog Tongue would make it a *mission* to find him. And he *would*. Like all the others. If that happened, a month among the meat puppets would be nothing.

No, there was no running, only meeting the leader, reporting, and facing the consequences. If the Spider was lucky, the Dog Tongue and the soldiers would kill each other, thus creating a void within the ranks of the Leather.

That might be the best scenario for the Spider, and his spirits lifted at the thought.

Sometime just before dawn, the need to sleep caught up with the Spider. The road became only a headlight-whitened thread, where the dark pressed in on either side. There was no light around the horizon, suggesting it would be an overcast morning. The darkness made the edge of the highway all the creepier, as the frost crinkled the tall grass growing there. The Spider continued to drive, however, even playing a few tunes on the stereo. He preferred talk radio, but copies of those shows were impossible to obtain. Audiobooks were out there, and he had listened to a few, but there were no such entertainment options aboard this particular rig.

But not even the music could keep him awake.

Sometime into the late morning, the Spider jerked his head up as his foot landed hard on the brake.

A deer stood in the road.

He slowed the truck, rebooting from the scare of almost falling asleep and crashing into the animal. The deer didn't move, seemingly transfixed by the nearing headlights. The closer the pickup got, the more of a cardboard cut-out the animal appeared to be.

Until it decided enough was enough and bolted off the highway to disappear in the grass.

The Spider stopped the truck. He lowered the window and fresh air rushed into the cab. If the deer was a shock, that frigid breeze woke him right up.

A set of headlights appeared in the distance.

Getting closer.

The Spider watched them approach. With the slow conviction of a man knowing it was time to get his game face on, he placed the vehicle in park and waited.

As expected, it was the Leather.

A convoy of pickups, tankers, and one tractor trailer that brought up the rear. Exhaust whorled about the wheels, partially obscuring them at times, but there was no mistaking the road clan. There was no one else who traveled the highway in such force. With such a total lack of fear.

They surrounded him, and when the lead elements recognized who he was, a handful of them escorted him from his pickup to the Dog Tongue's command RV. There they stopped and waited, not speaking to the Spider at all.

Once again, he was grateful for his mask.

The driver's side of the RV slammed shut. Seconds later, a figure sauntered in from the side and stopped directly before the Spider, looming over the smaller man. An Inflictor, the personal guard of the man he'd come to see. High-heel cowboy boots elevated the tall frame another two inches at least. The brute wore a rubber pig mask, while a regular hood covered the rest of his head. A bulky leather jacket protected him from the cold, but the Spider suspected he had layers underneath.

The piggish Inflictor stooped and sniffed at the Spider, who didn't dare budge. The Pig sniffed down one side of the Spider's profile and then up the other. When he stopped, he studied the visitor once again before reaching out to the RV door.

"What's your business?" the Pig asked.

"Winnipeg's fallen. Everyone there's dead."

That stopped the Pig. After a moment's pause, all the while keeping his mask aimed at the Spider, he rapped on the door with solemn respect, as if awakening some ancient, slumbering power.

And perhaps he was.

The Pig opened the door and held it wide.

It was gloomy outside, but it was pitch black within, and a whiff of some unknown incense drifted upon the air current. The Spider hesitated, but an uncertain glance around informed him that there was no turning back. The Leather surrounding him were as solid as a fence.

The Pig watched him.

So the Spider pulled himself up two steps and entered the RV. He checked on the rear of that cavernous domicile and then the driver's seat. The driver's seat was empty, and a sun visor, to keep the interior from getting too hot, was pulled across the windshield. The receding light marked the closing of the door, and the Spider turned around in time to glimpse the last glowing line being pinched off. All light was extinguished, then, leaving it surprisingly dark for the morning. Nothing penetrated the RV's interior.

He fought down the impulse to speak first, then fought down the need to clear his throat. His eyes couldn't quite adjust to the darkness at the back of the RV, as if every window had been spray-painted black and then boarded up. A chill overtook him, and he couldn't dismiss the notion that he'd done a very bad thing.

"Lord Dog Tongue?" he finally said, his voice sounding tiny in the dark. He couldn't see a thing, as whoever had covered the windows had taped the ends as well. He was practically standing within a tomb. There wasn't even a telltale sliver marking the doorway.

"Lord Dog Tongue?"

The words hummed in his ears, and still no reply. So he stood there, in that oppressive unlit shell, and waited.

In time, he sensed a presence near the rear of the RV, but he dared not go deeper.

"What is it?" the Dog Tongue asked, his singer's voice peeling and frayed around the edges. The kind of voice where a microphone would transform his words into a rumble.

"I have bad news," the Spider said, turning in the direction of that striking voice. He became very still at the sight of a shadow. An exceptionally large shadow that could easily touch the ceiling if it reached for it. That dark outline stood directly before him.

"From the front," the Spider said in a small voice.

Silence. Then, "All right. Speak of it."

So the Spider controlled his breathing, attempted to ignore the hammering in his chest, and reported in. He retold the savage night attack upon Fort Jay, and his capture and escape in Winnipeg. He elaborated how he managed to escape the firefight at the hotel, and how he single-handedly put down a soldier in an underground parking garage before making yet another escape, to warn Vampire Joe in Regina. Once that was done, he went on to explain how he felt it was his duty to report to the Dog Tongue personally, to inform him of how… deadly serious these soldiers were. And to warn him that they were coming for him.

At points, the Spider closed his eyes while he talked. His personal darkness was far more preferable to that of the RV.

When he finished, he swallowed, the click loud in the trailer.

"Soldiers," the Dog Tongue said, mostly to himself.

"They're coming," the Spider said, attempting to nudge the leader into action.

The Dog Tongue did not nudge. "I'll deal with them."

The Spider didn't quite like that answer.

"Where will you go now?" the Dog Tongue asked.

That question chilled the Spider's innards, rendering him at a loss. "I'm sorry?"

The Dog Tongue didn't repeat himself.

"I'll… stay here with you."

"Here."

"Yes here, if you'll have me."

"With the Leather."

The Spider didn't like the sound of that.

The shadow moved closer, coming within a foot of the smaller man, the presence alarming. And still, the Spider didn't move. Didn't budge.

"The Leather…" said the Dog Tongue from above, "…have no need of you."

That set the other man to blinking. "I can…"

"The Leather…" the Dog Tongue quietly insisted, shutting up his follower, "…are conquerors. You… are *not*. You… are a cowardly little shit of a man."

The Spider didn't like the sound of that. "That's not—"

A paw of a hand seized his throat. A second paw grabbed him by his crotch—the contact breath-stealing—and a terrible strength lifted the Spider off the floor. He didn't resist, couldn't, as his screaming testicles and collapsing windpipe rendered him all but helpless. His head cracked off a hard edge, ripping the mask from his face. He clawed at the ceiling. His boots kicked and struck and crunched in a cupboard door. He flailed and grabbed for the hands around his balls, out of reflex, nowhere near reaching them…

When the Dog Tongue broke the Spider's back across his knee.

That sudden, vicious wrecking of vertebrae, muscle, and spinal cord did two things.

One, it cut off all pain from the Spider's crotch.

Two, it cut off all *feeling* entirely below his chin.

The Spider gasped, struggling to breathe, the sound a ragged, wheezy noise…when a studded boot pressed down on his upper chest.

"You ran," came the accusing whisper from above, "when all others stayed at their stations. You ran. You call yourself the Spider."

A scrape of metal then, and the slap of a heavy tool fitted to the hand.

"You're really just a worm."

The Spider was still attempting to draw breath when the sharpened prong stabbed him.

The first of about a dozen thrusts.

44

Sometime well past midnight, well before Gus, Collie, and Milo left the highway overpass, the men took time to eat. Not a lot, but just enough to get something on the fire so that their stomachs wouldn't be nagging them later. Collie refrained from eating anything, content to lean against the limo and watch the road. Then they geared up, checked their weapons, and climbed aboard the machine. Milo drove, which was now the usual, while Collie and Gus took up their regular seats. The only change was in Gus, who no longer felt the need to take aim at the soldier's somewhat hippy profile.

Not long after, they were rolling towards Regina.

Five minutes into the drive, however, Gus smelled it. A rancid, decomposing stink of meat and things best not thought about, even worse than before. He cleared his throat and glanced at the back of Milo's head. The soldier kept discipline and didn't react. If he was smelling the same thing, he was hiding it much better.

Ten minutes in, and Gus cleared his throat again. "Ah… you guys smell anything?"

Collie looked at him. "No, why? Do I stink?"

Gus didn't reply right away.

"Well, shit," Collie snapped off. "Milo, you smell anything?"

"Yeah, I do."

"Me?"

The soldier shrugged. "Maybe. Yeah. Sorry."

"Goddammit," she let off, and opened the glove compartment. "I've gone fucking nose-blind. Gus, I can't find the no-stink out here. I must've packed it into a backpack. Look for it and pass it out here, please. Can't drive all the way to fucking Regina smelling like bloody ass."

"Not that bad," Gus lied, as he fetched the deodorant.

"Yeah, that's why you were sounding like you had a cock jammed down your throat a few seconds ago. *Fuck*, guys—do yourselves a favor and tell me about this shit. Give it here. Thanks."

She took the stick, popped the lid, and lifted what clothing she could. When she did, a wave of stink practically stole Gus's breath. He looked out the window.

Milo was already pushing the button for the air exchanger.

Gus couldn't wait that long. He reached for the armrest controls and lowered his window halfway. Fresh air rushed in and permitted him to breathe again. Hearing the breaking of the seal, Milo did the same.

Collie was applying the stick to herself, both underneath and over her clothing.

"Wallace was like this," she said. "Really bad at times."

"I don't remember," Gus said.

"Sure you do, you just don't wanna say. I don't mind. I'm glad you finally said something, though. I can't be creeping around the city smelling like the shitty-ass off a barbequed skunk. The bad guys will smell me before they see me. Jesus Christ. What a thing to happen. And the *time*. Christ. Well, adapt and overcome. Sorry, guys."

Gus didn't know what to say, so he stayed silent. Milo did the same.

After a while, they rolled their windows back up. The smell was still present, but nowhere near as ferocious as before, lessened by the generous layers of *Ocean Mist*.

Wallace, Gus thought. Thinking back to the man. He was forgetting things, about the soldier's final transformation. He remembered the man's burial, however, and that turned his mood just a little more miserable. Gus sighed and tried to think of other things.

They reached the outskirts of the city in short time. Collie instructed Milo to pull off the main drag and park behind a two-story house. She activated the defensive measures upon the car, told them to hit *enable all* if and when they needed it, then announced there was no place safer than in the limo. So there they stayed, stayed until two hours before dawn, when the limo crept out from behind the house like an oversized river croc taking to water. With only the sound of tires crackling softly over pavement, the vehicle slunk deeper towards the empty heart of the city. The directions Red Skull provided were easy enough to follow.

Just follow the skulls.

Just follow the skulls.

Just so happened Victoria Avenue was *filled* with skulls. On either side of the road.

Milo killed the headlights. The night vision provided by the limo's cameras showed them everything in an eerie, LSD-shade of green and black right across the windshield. Perhaps every ten feet or so there was a post, just a length of fence nailed to a wooden base for stability. On every post was a skull. A screaming, very-much-looking-like-they're-in-pain, skull. At least, those with lower jaws looked like they were screaming. There were others without a jaw, and they just looked frightening.

Those fleshless heads drifted by the limo, one right after the other.

His head between the seats, Gus stared at the frightful decorations passing by. "Holy… Jesus."

Collie glanced over her shoulder at him. "Could be worse. Could be straight-up heads. Decomposing ones, I mean."

"This doesn't bother me," Gus said. "Not that much, anyway. Saw my share back in Annapolis. And they were still moving."

Milo's fingers tapped the steering wheel. "You get nightmares?"

"No."

"Never?"

"Not as many as I should."

"I get nightmares."

"Even now?" Collie asked.

Milo kept his eyes on the road. "You know something? I haven't. Used to get them plenty when I was with Jake and the Jipman and fucking O'Leary. O'Leary was probably the one who gave me nightmares."

"When do you think they stopped?" Collie pressed.

Milo let his breath out and thought about it. "Maybe… as far back as Whitecap? After you put me in that room? I think I was sleeping pretty good after the first night. I still wake up every now and again, but no bad dreams."

"Sounds like a clearing of conscience," Collie agreed.

Milo didn't say anything to that, but Gus supposed she was right. He went back to watching the road and the parade of skulls. At any time he expected to see a person out there, either strung up to one of those posts or hanging from a streetlight.

"All right," Collie said, as they rolled through what appeared to be a residential area. Cars clogged the intersections, forcing the limo down a four-lane street divided by a raised median of dirt and dead leaves.

Rising above it all were the Four Towers, easily visible in the distance.

Red Skull spoke briefly about the hotels before he died, supplying directions on which one to target.

"Now," Collie said, "you let me out here."

Here was roughly four blocks out from the Towers. The limo's electric engine was almost soundless except for that soft, warp drive hum filling the interior.

Milo stopped the car. Collie gripped her rifle and regarded them both.

"Stay here, okay? Until this," she tapped the dashboard clock, "turns six-forty-five, upon which you drive up this street. Cautious, but you go. Drive right to these four towers and take what they got. Draw their fire, and I'll start taking them out."

"You think you can do that?" Milo asked.

Collie didn't hesitate. "Course I can."

"Because if you can't, maybe it's better you stay with us."

"You're bait. You distract them, and I'll kill them. Got it?"

Milo nodded and looked to the road.

Gus and Collie shared a look. She took her sunglasses off and placed them in her breast pocket. Her eyes were unpleasant to look upon.

"Later, Sunshine," she said.

"Later, Moonbeam," he answered and wished there *would* be a later.

Then she was gone, closing the door after she was clear of the limo.

She did not look back.

Collie didn't *want* to look back, because as soon as she got to her feet, she was instantly reminded of that growing cement-like weight in her limbs. She hoped that she would air-out before she made contact with the enemy, but if she didn't, that was fine. Gus and Milo would be safe inside the limo, unless the civvies had a front-loader or a tank. And if they did, Collie had roughly twenty-five minutes to reach the Four Towers and do a little quiet head-hunting before the shitstorm descended.

She marched across someone's driveway, where a black four-door sedan remained parked. The windows of the bungalow were rectangular sheets of darkness, and the overgrown backyard was no different. There were fences, but someone had busted them down in places, and, judging by the size of the opening, that someone had been in a hurry.

Moving quietly with her eyesight and her hearing fully amped, Collie hefted her rifle, keeping it at the ready. She assumed the Leather would have sentries this far out, but judging by the lack of interest in the limousine quietly idling in the middle of the road, no one had detected them. No alarms had been raised. They just might be sleeping.

If that was the case, they would never wake up.

She stopped behind a house, listened, and decided she was very much alone. A small wooden table stood on a deck, tucked in close to the rear wall, and unattended flower beds lay to her right. Collie crept past, through tall grass, and sided up against a garage. There, she peered into the next lot over.

Nothing moved. Not a sound.

She moved to the back fence of the next lot, where a sizeable hole had been bashed through. Mindful of the angle, she checked out one side of the backyard and then the other. The house ahead had a rear porch with a propane grill, as well as a big old parasol that somehow had bent over and resembled a bashed-up satellite dish.

Collie approached the house, wary of the windows, and went past the deck and the grill. She stepped around fifty feet of garden hose left in the empty driveway, and aimed at a basement entrance where concrete steps led down to an open doorway.

She reached the end of the house and peeked around the corner.

A small residential area, the lots perhaps all neatly measured out at one time, but now a bomb blast of disarray. Blown over signage and cars were driven up onto lawns. Overturned furniture rested against fire hydrants while wrecked bird houses hung from tree limbs. Garbage bags either close to bursting or broken with their dried-out refuse were strewn along the gutters.

Collie watched, listened, and decided upon her line of approach. She snuck past the rear of the house, a wraith drifting across the steps, aiming at the windows as she went. When she was clear, she moved into the driveway and crossed the road. She wanted to be at least one lane over from the main street, and come up behind the enemy if possible. As long as the landscape cooperated—which it usually didn't. Hedges were as black and forbidding as granite barriers. Chain mesh fences surrounded a few houses, which she avoided like the oversized noise makers they were. Apartment buildings scrolled by, three of them in fact, but only one faced her, forcing her to be extra careful while going by. The other two were side-on to her, their walls windowless. All three buildings were only two- or three-floor affairs. Large garbage cans marked driveways, some were tipped over, and Collie absently wondered if Regina ever had a raccoon problem.

She stopped at a white fence—or what she thought was white—and dropped to one knee before peeking out at the intersecting road ahead.

Empty, except for a few cars. Not even a rat, which was a good thing, she supposed, remembering a couple of Gus's stories.

Across the street was a two-story brick building, and the back road she followed continued straight on from the other side. *All clear*, she saw, and got up to scoot across when the unexpected urge to puke overcame her. The disturbing thing was… the sensation didn't originate in her guts, but at the back of her skull. Worse, that inescapable impulse surged forward, without warning, like a warm jet of polluted water fired from a pressurized garden hose.

Where the inside of her head became a fishbowl filling up in a violent rush.

And before she could react… Collie's mind went blank.

45

"You think she's okay for this?" Milo asked thirty seconds after Collie had disappeared behind the house.

Gus stared in that direction, half-expecting her to come back for whatever reason. Maybe she'd forgotten something. She didn't come back, however, and Milo's question interrupted his thoughts.

"She's fine," Gus replied.

Milo glanced around, sizing up matters. He took a firmer grip on the steering wheel before relaxing and allowing his hands to fall to his lap.

"She smelled bad," he said, so low Gus wasn't sure if it was a private conversation with himself.

"I know," he agreed anyway.

"Real bad," Milo quietly stressed. "Like… zombies left—"

"I know," Gus said, cutting him off. He didn't need to hear the rest of that comparison. Didn't want to hear it. "She's not in good shape, I'll give you that, but… she's still Collie."

Milo mulled that over. "Because, if she's not okay, then she's placing this whole operation at risk. You understand that, right?"

"She's fucking *fine*. Enough about it, all right? If she wasn't fine, she would've said so."

"You think?"

"Yeah, I goddamn think, because she's like you. She's fucking military, and she knows best, right? She certainly knows what's going on with herself. You think she'd go out there if she *wasn't* feeling right?"

"You don't know these operators."

"You do?"

Milo went silent then, his head swinging one way then another, chewing on a comeback.

"No," he finally admitted. "Not really. Never served with any. Never *met* any. Not like we grow them off trees or anything."

"No?" Gus asked. "Because that's the vibe I'm getting from you now. That they're grown on trees and fall off when they're ripe and ready. Just before the peel goes bad."

More silence from the soldier. "All right."

"All right what?"

"She's fine."

"Goddamn right she's fine. You don't know her like I do. That woman is…"

Death walking, he thought but didn't say, remembering only whispers of Wallace's original sermon the first time Collie went off on her own. At that motel where they'd freed those people, where Jimbo, poor old Jimbo, was on a ledge, trying to stay awake, to keep from falling over into a pit of decomposing but reanimated heads.

Jimbo's luck. The shittiest kind.

She's still Collie, Gus told himself, but even that sounded… wrong… to him, like an infection lurking underneath a line of healthy-looking stitches. She's still Collie, his treacherous mind repeated, as if waiting for him to wise up to something. To some little detail that was right before his eyes but he was missing, or simply refused to see.

She's still… herself, he rambled internally, and then came the killer, *because if she's not, then who is she? Because she's becoming more and more like Wallace every day.*

Despite the comfortable temperature in the limo, Gus's innards went cold at that thought.

She's becoming like Wallace. And Wallace, he remembered, was sticking knives in himself—biting *pieces* off himself, just to stay focused. Just to stay Wallace, and not become a fucking undead thing still walking around.

Gus exhaled. He was suddenly glad that he was sitting behind Milo, so the soldier didn't see his face filling up with doubt.

He looked over at the dashboard clock. No longer did he feel like it was a countdown on an operation, on a mission. Now it felt like the seconds were dripping away to something much more ominous.

"You okay back there?" Milo asked.

"Huh?"

"Look, I'm not a goddamn parrot up here, so I'm not repeating myself. I said it loud enough the first time."

"I was thinking about other shit."

"What other shit?"

"You're fucking nosy, you know that?"

"I'm not nosy. I'm just picking up something from the backseat, like there's something going on back there and you don't want to tell me."

"Just nerves, is all," Gus said, feeling that was close to the truth. "We don't know what's out there."

"We'll find out soon enough."

"Yeah."

"We're in a tank, here. Like she said, they haveta have something serious up there to crack this thing's hide."

"Maybe they do," Gus said, the floodgates of doubt opening now.

"Like I said, we'll find out."

"Guess so."

"Okay then."

"All right so shut up."

"I will," Milo shot back. "Why don't you?"

"Maybe I will if you stop yakkin' at me."

"Yakkin' at you? I'll solve that right now."

"Good. Fuckin' glad to hear it."

"Fuckin' glad to help."

Gus sighed in annoyance. "You like getting in the last word, you know that?"

"Yeah? Well here's a couple of last words for you—Fuck off."

A fuming Gus shut up and decided to give that round to Milo. He didn't need to get his dander up with the soldier, because now he *did* have a shit-ton on his mind.

After about ten seconds, Milo asked, "You getting up front?"

"Huh?"

"Jesus Christ, Gus. Either pay attention or just drop that fucking annoying habit of getting me to say things twice for you. And not because you didn't hear me the first time."

"No," Gus grumbled, not wanting to argue anymore. "I'm staying back here."

"Good idea," Milo grumped right back.

So they sat again, in a simmering silence.

The clock showed 6:26. The sky was dark, but a generous dash of stars was spread out across it.

At 6:30, Milo shifted in his seat and started checking the clock much more often.

At 6:43, the soldier sighed. "You ready?"

"Yeah."

Milo put the limo in gear. "I better not die today. I better not fucking die."

Gus heard him but didn't know if the man wanted his input or not, so he kept his mouth shut. The great machine lurched forward, and the houses started to drift out of sight. At one point a tree branch lay across the street, but Milo drove over the thing anyway. The limb latched onto something underneath the limo, and got dragged along.

"Christ," Gus muttered. "Sounds like a snake dragging its balls over the pavement."

Milo didn't comment.

"Shake that thing loose, willya?"

"It'll fall off," Milo said.

"It would've done that already."

"Give it time."

"What do you mean give it time?" Gus said. "We're moving here."

"Listen. There. It's gone."

And it was. Just like that.

So Gus shut up about it.

Milo watched the dashboard, keeping his speed at forty kilometers an hour. "This thing handles like a Honda Civic. Which says a lot about the engineers who put it together. They did a good job."

Gus let out a deep nervous breath and tried to look out of all windows at once. The night sky was fading, and the horizon was a red wire of light.

"Red sky at morning," he muttered.

"What's that?"

"Sailors take warning."

"You talking to me?"

"No," Gus said. "Just an old saying. You must've heard that before. Red sky at morning, sailors take warning."

"First time hearing it."

"Popular back our way."

"Probably with old guys."

"...Fuck off."

Through the windshield, the line of skulls drifted by. Any moment, for some strange reason, Gus expected the empty eye sockets of one of those things to light up red. They passed by a small intersection, and the houses were replaced by more commercial buildings. A post office went by. There was a pet store with an empty parking lot. A larger building that had a government look about it scrolled past.

And the skulls kept going by.

"Jee-zus," Gus whispered. "Dog Dick got a major chubby for skulls."

"Dog Dick's a sick fuck," Milo said back. "And that's coming from a guy who worked with sick fucks."

"I've come across my share of sick fucks."

"Yeah. I guess you have."

They quieted then, but Gus pulled his shotgun closer. He had plenty of shells. Every pocket was full, and he had three magazines on him.

"Gus?"

"Yeah?"

"The skulls are closer together."

Gus studied those grim street ornaments. "Yeah. They are." Then he noticed the cars. "The streets are blocked off, too."

"Yeah. Get ready."

"You see something?" Gus asked.

"No, I feel something. As in something's gonna drop."

Gus felt it, too. He was on one knee and looking out the side windows until the windshield got his attention.

"The hell is that up ahead?"

"No idea."

"You see that, right?"

"That big 'H'?"

"Yeah, that big fucking 'H'. But the part that goes across is up awfully high, like an old guy with his belt hoisted up to his nipples."

Then he saw the dog skull with what looked like snapped-off horns, on a post in the middle of the street.

Even with the headlights off, there was no mistaking that ominous portent.

"That's a big one," Gus said in a low voice.

"That's not a dog," Milo said. "That's a bull or something."

"What kind of fucked up person does this?"

"What kind of fucked up people follow him?"

"You said it," Gus replied, stooping just a little to better see the thing roll by.

"Something's up ahead," Milo said and pointed.

And there was.

Like that enormous 'H' that blotted out the fading night sky, a barrier of some sort came into sight. A low barrier of angular metal that the limo's cameras revealed in shades of green. A barrier directly across the road blocked it off.

Then Gus saw the tires, and the shape fell into place for him.

"Dump trucks," he said.

Milo stepped on the brakes, not a hundred feet away from them, where the street finished.

A second after the limousine stopped, the side streets came alive with light.

Headlights.

The peal of tire rubber penetrated the limo's armored shell as multiple shapes launched themselves from the walls of vehicles. The dashboard screen broke into four different picture frames, each showing a charging set of white eyes that quickly grew.

Gus saw the screen and then saw the real thing rushing the limo.

The first hit came from the rear, tossing Gus into the upper part of the seats and the partition. While he rattled to the floor, the left side of the limo shuddered from the impact, and one of the headlights of the attacking truck (it was too high to be a car) winked out.

Gus screamed.

Milo worked the gears, stomped on the accelerator, and the limo propelled itself backwards in a one-inch punch of force, shoving its armored bulk into the mass behind it. That demolition-derby collision launched Gus into the base of the seats where he lost his grip on his shotgun. He slapped the weapon away from his head in a panic-fueled patty-cake, just as a third collision, this time from the right, rocked the limo on its reinforced chassis.

"*Jesus Christ,*" Gus ejected over the roar of red-lining engines.

The limo didn't move, but Milo was trying. He shifted gears and shot forward in a screaming crescendo of armor-plating along the limo's sides, before halting with a lurch and a jaw-snapping crunch. Gus's entire frame log-rolled, still very aware that an exceptionally powerful shotgun was on the floor with him, and its barrel was presently jammed up hard against his left shoulder. He clutched at it, scooted the barrel above his head, as whatever had hit them from behind decided to smash all two tons against them once more.

"We're hemmed in," Milo yelled out.

Gus heard but responded with only a pained grunt, now knowing firsthand what going over Niagara Falls in a barrel must feel like. He was shoved left, right, then forward and back. The Ram Fist's barrel got lodged into something above his head, and he wondered briefly if the interior was bulletproof. An unexpected shove jammed his nose into the weapon, just before he rolled again and got a snoot-full of new car smell from the carpet.

Then the grinding started.

The limo's engine hummed as Milo sought to work against the forces trapping the monster, pressing it from all sides. There was little give, however, and Gus righted himself, leaving his shotgun on the floor. Headlights flooded the interior with sunny intensity. Eight-cylinder engines strained and heaved as they shoved steel bars into the limousine's sides. Through the windshield, one of the dump truck's tires was stopping the limo from going any further.

Gus couldn't believe his eyes.

They were rammed up against that wall of heavy industrial equipment.

Milo was gripping the steering wheel with one hand, shifting with the other, going from drive to reverse, trying to make space. The problem was, as soon as he went ahead, the machine pressing him from behind went with him, until the limo was where it was going to stay.

Nose-first into the sidewall of one exceptionally meaty tire.

The warp drive engine spiked with every heel crush of the accelerator, then a pause as Milo shifted, and a split-second lurch in the opposing direction that was halted even before it got going.

"Use the turbo boost!" Gus urged

"I don't know where it is!" Milo shouted.

The touchscreen was to the right of the soldier's knee. Red buttons glowed, but Gus didn't see anything that would give them the mule kick they could use to get free. And the trucks pinning them in didn't budge from the rubber-burning effort of the limo.

Outside, figures moved between the vehicles.

There was the unmistakable sound of a chainsaw starting up.

Gus and Milo exchanged incredulous looks of horror just before a lightning strike of a cut clawed at the limo's shell. That lasted for all of two seconds before it paused with an enthusiastic revving from the chainsaw as if eager to try again. The operator did so.

Multiple figures landed on the roof, their shapes obscuring the starry night overhead as seen by the limo's exterior cameras. One of those figures reared back and cranked a sledgehammer into the limo. There was a frightening, metallic drumbeat of a noise, where the sledgehammer bounced off the armored shell. Like an ice-fisherman seeking that sweet spot, the figure moved down the roof, adjusted his stance, and swung again.

Just then, one of the Leather stood practically ten feet away from Gus's window. The Leather hefted a crossbow, and before Gus's martini-shaken mind realized what the weapon was, the Leather loosed.

A bolt bounced off the limo's hide with a whipcrack, leaving the slightest chip in the outer layer.

Just as the chainsaw attempted another cut.

The noise was ear-ripping. Mind-shredding. And Gus had to concentrate to keep his shit both in and together. Milo was pressed back into the driver's seat as a wrecking crew of Leather worked over their vehicle. The chainsaw continued cutting, but a collection of pounding sledgehammers and squealing crowbars added to the mounting racket. The Leather punished the monster, hammering, cutting, needling the great machine to the best of their ability. A threesome of Leather stepped up to Gus's door in the rear, as if inspecting the entry point.

One of them reached out for the handle and shivered as if gripped in a brain-blasting seizure. The Leather dropped out of sight, as good as shot, leaving Gus crouched on a seat and staring in awe.

Then he remembered.

Electrified door handles.

What could this armored bitch do? What was it that Collie said?

"The fuck was that?" Milo wanted to know.

"Shocked him," Gus replied, lurching to the partition opening and pointing at the touchscreen. "It shocked him!"

Milo regarded the screen as if it were a treasure map. Then he started tapping.

Defensive measures.

A list of available armaments flashed into existence, just as the Leather overhead launched into a five-dude-long mamba across the limo's roof—complete with more sledgehammers and other heavy tools. A pickup engine roared, and the trapped vehicle rocked to the right just a fragment.

Gus blinked at the steady red-lettered list.

Smoke Bombs.

Gas Bombs.

Spikespitters.

Machine Guns.

Flamers.

And the Vegas lottery winner of them all, outlined by a double thick line of alarm klaxon red.

Enable All.

Milo's forefinger trembled above the glowing red rectangle, vacillating on whether or not to apply pressure.

Gus didn't understand the hesitation, and with at least *three* two-ton trucks shoving them from various points, while a pack of mask-wearing wannabe construction fucks tried to forcefully can-open the limo....

Well.

A second seemed like an hour.

Gus launched himself at that touchscreen and mashed his thumb on that glowing red rectangle, which sent the screen into flashes of *all-ahead-full.*

That was all the limo needed.

All its defensive *AI* needed.

And after being poked, prodded, shoved, and rocked for what seemed like a goddamn eternity, the limo, the *monster*, revealed exactly what it was capable of.

The flamethrowers engaged first, and the world outside the limo became a blazing backwash of fire that leapt up from underneath. Screams erupted, bursts of skin-crisping agony that was god-awful to hear. A hand slammed against the window before yanking away. One of the masked bastards on the roof ignited like a candlewick caught in a blowtorch. The rest of the pack leaped off en masse, clearing the surface entirely before raining down upon the pavement. An immolating ghost trailing smoke rushed off between a pair of pickup trucks. The chainsaw ceased grinding at the armored shell and the hammering stopped as well. More screams, blistering, pitiful notes of searing that frazzled the ends of Gus's nerves.

Then came the smoke. Appearing not two seconds after that solar flare-up of flame that purified the entire vehicle. The smoke engulfed the limo, creating a gauzy ghost world that the exterior cameras could not penetrate. The flame throwers still flared, the AI either sensing the vehicle remained under attack, or just too pissed-off to stop from the earlier drubbing. The limo was pinned in place by the other trucks, but the human element had pretty much been torched to ash in one colon-cleansing rush of fiery badassery.

The machine guns didn't go off, and Gus didn't know why—but he suspected the front of the limo being mashed up against the dump truck had something to do with it. The AI was smart to realize the proximity to its target and elected not to unload whatever it had. Which was a shame.

That same factor might have prevented the limo from launching the gas bombs, if they launched at all. Perhaps they simply oozed. Or ejected to parachute in from above.

But the spikes, or more accurately, triangular pyramids, fired away—bouncing and rattling off the roof like a shower of razor-sharp cake sprinkles.

"Holy shit," Milo said, utterly amazed, his gaze alternating from what was going on outside his windows to the touchscreen.

"What else is there?" Gus said, stretching through the partition and struggling to right himself.

"That's it. As far as I can see."

"The flamethrowers are still going."

And so they were, in great orange chuffs that flared up in precise intervals, perhaps provoked by the machines keeping the limo in place. They scrubbed away the human filth from ass-to-nose and back again, leaving nothing untouched, nothing unscorched. The wrecking crew assaulting them had fled, retreating beyond the limo's reach, or they were simply dead and charred. Gus couldn't tell for sure. Between the smoke and the flamers, he couldn't see *shit* out there. Shadows came and went, but he didn't know if he was looking at actual people, or some scene depicting hell.

"There must be more," Gus said, trying to take it all in at once.

But there wasn't.

"How do you go back?" he asked in a huff, trying to make sense of the controls and hating himself for not paying greater attention when Collie was at the helm. But then, he didn't think he'd ever be at the helm. Replacing the ENABLE button was now a DISABLE.

He jammed his thumb across the touchpad, repeatedly, and when that had no effect, he swiped at it, to no avail.

Nothing moved beyond the windshield, at least not to Gus's eye.

"You see anything out there?" he asked, on his elbows.

Milo glanced around. "No. Nothing."

"Help me."

So Milo helped Gus pull himself through the partition window and settle down in the passenger seat. It was no small task, requiring legs and arms to go places they were not meant to go, not up front. All was fine after a minute, but Gus was breathing hard as he checked on the surroundings.

Nothing moved out there. Not one damn thing.

The flamers still fired in raging sweeps resembling passes in a car wash, and that distressed Gus. He studied the touchscreen and, with a steadier thumb, applied even pressure to the disable button.

The flamer died out in a final puff of fire.

Then all was still.

"Fuckin' touchscreens," he muttered.

"I hate the things, too," Milo added.

"And then the fucking fingerprints…" Gus tacked on.

They quieted, aware of the three pickups trapping the limo against the dump truck tire. The trucks were either partially or completely obscured from the rear camera. Through one of the side cameras, Gus noticed something in the rear that made his heart sink.

"What's that?" he asked, pointing at the screen.

Milo leaned in.

There, behind the pickup, attempting to doggy-style the limo, was *another* pickup parked broadside, to reinforce the first.

"Another truck," Milo said. "More weight to push."

"We got power?"

Milo checked on the gauge. "Plenty of power at forty-six percent, but I don't know how we can move that."

"What about the turbo boost?"

"Fuck if I know."

Gus didn't particularly want to use the boost standing still, or with a pair of trucks jammed up his ass. In his mind's eye, he envisioned the limo backing up and *over* the two blocking machines, only to land atop the pair and stay there. It was a comical picture, but the reality was he didn't know what might happen.

"Probably in one of these sub-folders," Milo said, aiming a finger at the interface. "Just give me a minute."

"Take your time."

As Milo worked, things became even more quiet outside. Gus watched the camera screens for movement, wondering where the lions were, but nothing showed as the smoke slowly cleared.

"Something's going on," he said. "Nothing's moving out there."

Milo straightened and looked around. "Maybe the thing scared the chocolate outta them."

"It did me," Gus admitted.

"Me too."

They sat, unsure of what to do next, as the short but fierce confrontation replayed itself in their heads. Gus's nerves were on edge, however, from fingertips to toes and everything in between. His hands trembled, and he made fists to control them. And to make sure that Milo wouldn't see.

"All right," Milo said, finally opening a screen with the outlined button called TURBO BOOST.

"Wait," Gus cautioned, remembering. "Collie was driving when she did that. She pushed something on the steering wheel."

Milo moved his thumb. "Must be this. Another 'enable'."

"Great. Well. Fuck it. Try it."

Milo thought about it, then scrambled for his seatbelt. Gus clawed for his, and a snap and click of the locks filled the interior.

"You set?" the soldier asked.

"Yeah. Wait. You don't think we'll go up and over those trucks, do you?"

"And land on the roofs?"

"Yeah."

Milo shrugged. "Fuck if I know."

They shared a thoughtful moment.

"Your call," Milo said.

"Why is it my call? You're military."

"All right, then sit back. I'll put it in reverse and let God sort this shit out."

Even though he didn't like the sound of that, Gus got ready for that rocket-burst shove of love he'd experienced only once before, and God help him, *enjoyed*.

Milo put the limo into reverse and put pressure on the accelerator. The engine flared up and pushed, raging against its cage. Tires began to spin, the roar matching the engine's rising pitch. The rear pressed and screamed against the pickup behind it, the force rising, intensifying with every second.

Milo hit the ENABLE button on the steering wheel.

A red message flashed across the dashboard.

BOOST UNAVAILABLE IN REVERSE.

"Well, shit," Gus muttered. "That's disappointing. I was all ready for a backward flip alley-oop."

"Followed by the upside-down shit fest," Milo said. He took his foot off the accelerator while everything started shutting down. "That's that."

"We could go forward."

"And mash ourselves against that?" Milo asked, gesturing at the dump trucks.

Gus glanced around. "So we're stuck here."

"Until Collie gives us the okay to get out. Maybe she's out there now?"

"And killed them all?" Gus continued and nodded. "Something to hope for."

They sat. And hoped.

Nothing moved. Nothing approached the limo. No sight of Collie.

The sky started to lighten, and the horizon glowed.

"This ain't right," Gus muttered. "She should've been here by now."

"Maybe she got sidetracked?"

Gus supposed so, but something else got his attention.

As the sky got brighter, it was easier to see the Leather corpses collapsed on the pavement in various poses. There were others beyond that, untouched by the flamers.

"Hey, look," Gus pointed.

Milo did. "How about that."

"Maybe the gas bombs worked."

"I think that's obvious."

"You think they're dead?" Gus asked.

Milo shrugged.

Minutes passed. The clock showed 7:07.

Some of the Leather surrounding the limo came to life. They rolled over and lay on their backs, while others pushed themselves to their hands and knees.

"So much for that," Gus remarked, watching the figures rise. "Fuckin' gas. You think they'd load up on the good stuff."

As the Leather regained their senses, they retreated from the trapped vehicle.

"The game's afoot," Gus said. "They'll be back."

"We stay inside," Milo said. "After that face-scrubbing, inside this shit-kicker is the safest place to be."

"Roger that."

"So we wait for Collie."

"Yeah. Okay." But Gus wasn't so sure. Something had gone down, and he couldn't think what.

The sun rose, glaring down on the street.

The clock said 7:22.

And still no Collie.

Inside the limo, Gus and Milo kept an eye on their surroundings, catching glimpses of the Leather behind their trucks and maintaining a safe distance. They lurked back there, lifting only their heads above the hoods, or peeking out from behind corners. The Leather studied them from one angle before withdrawing for minutes, only to reappear from another quarter.

"Jesus Christ," Milo eventually ejected. "Feels like we fucking parked over a prairie dog colony."

Gus actually smiled at that. He was thinking the same thing, oddly enough. No one attacked.

That was all fine and good. As good as cursed gold.

Until *she* appeared. Above, standing on something to lift her above the rim of the dump truck body. She stood in the rear, the dumpster part. It was a Leather, and Gus thought she was a woman. Dressed out in a black duster and wearing a cowboy hat. Underneath that, long hair flowed. A half-mask hid her face.

"Someone's got balls," Gus said.

"We can't touch her," Milo said. "Unless we get out."

"Or they want us out."

Milo nodded. *You got it.*

As if knowing that herself, the figure stood there and watched the limo.

"Look all you want, bitch," Milo said, watching her right back.

But then the Leather's plan became clear after the woman hauled up what appeared to be a child, wearing only a t-shirt with a green dragon upon it, and a knee-length leather skirt. A little girl, perhaps only nine or ten. Red-faced and quivering, her cheeks slick from crying.

"Oh no," Milo whispered in unchecked horror.

It wasn't little Monica, or little Sandy, which was her real name, but in that morning light, her shape was pretty much the same. Small and scrawny and squirming to free herself from her captor. The Leather hauled on the little girl's arm, hard enough to pull it out it seemed—and brought the little girl under control.

Then the Leather produced the cleaver.

"Oh… my… gentle Jesus," Gus whispered.

The Leather placed the cleaver's edge underneath the child's hitching chin, where the broad slab of steel hid her throat entirely. The little girl's face was in shadow, but Gus's mind filled in the details. Dirty, soot-stained cheeks, where fearful tears made tracks down to her chin. It was enough to rip his heart out.

"Get out of the car!" the female Leather screamed. "Or I'll shave her face off."

The very thought of that happening stunned Gus and left him staring.

"She won't do it," Milo said, shaking his head. "She won't. She *can't*."

"Why not?" Gus asked in a rush.

"Get out of the car in five seconds or I start cutting!" the woman blared. "*FIVE.*"

The little girl's mouth, an upside-down smile, opened in a wheezy intake of pure terror. She didn't dare pull away from her captor now, for fear of cutting that tender place under her chin, and releasing the stuff of nightmares.

"*FOUR.*"

"Oh Jesus," Gus said. "Oh Jesus, oh Jesus."

"She won't do it," Milo said.

"You sure about that?"

"*THREE.*"

Milo didn't answer.

"*You sure?*" Gus demanded, and when Milo couldn't answer, Gus knew he couldn't—he *wouldn't* take the chance. Not with the Leather.

The armored limo was a tank, make no mistake, but the masked crazies, goddamn them, knew *precisely* how to breach it. How to break the resolve of the hardest of hard asses.

Start slaughtering innocents.

"*TWO!*"

Gus let his breath out in a hiss. "Fuck this," he said.

And cracked open the door. He kicked it free and, leaving his shotgun on the seat, scooted out as fast as a second would allow. Winter air hit his face and his breath came out in a puff.

The female Leather watched him from high above, her fingers tight on that butcher's tool.

"Anyone else in there?" she blared.

Gus didn't answer right away, and that was his downfall.

"I meant *everyone out of the car. ONE!*"

She never got the whole word out when the driver's door popped open. Milo emerged, frowning as if he'd just lost his life savings at an illegal poker table. He exchanged that troubled look with Gus, who read it instantly.

I couldn't do it, either... and now we're fucked.

The female Leather didn't release the girl. Didn't move the cleaver. She held on to the kitchen weapon and the child as boots hit the pavement.

A frightful pitter-patter of heels caused Gus to glance over his shoulder, just in time to glimpse *something* before it crashed into the side of his face. He was aware of rebounding off the side of the limo, and then he was falling.

But he was long out before he hit the ground.

46

A red brick building slowly materialized up ahead as the blizzard scrambling her mind rapidly lost strength. With a drunken lurch, Collie realized she was on her side, in the middle of the street, facing the structure. There was no sound until she tested an arm, and the rasp of clothing and padding on pavement assured her that her hearing was fine.

Just everything else was fucked up.

Or she suspected was fucked up.

She rolled over onto her belly with all the grace of an eighty-year-old turning over in bed. It was then she saw her arm. Her left arm.

Cuts, three of them, through the combat camouflages she wore. Ichor stained the cuts, and she assessed the damage with newfound dread, remembering dearly departed Wallace.

Oh shit, she thought. *Did I do that?*

Joints creaked, popped, and strained as she pushed herself up at a speed that both horrified and amazed her. Once upon a time, she could do thirty push-ups in thirty seconds, but it took her almost a minute to get her torso off the ground, and that was just on her knees.

Collie glanced around and saw two things.

One, that she was out in the open, in the back street she'd been following.

Two, her knife lay to her right, covered in a creosote slime.

She sat up and clawed for the knife, and even that required effort.

Jesus Christ, she thought. *Wallace, was it this bad for you? Was it always this bad for you and you kept it all to yourself?*

She suspected it was, and that he did. With one last show of strength, she got one foot under her and then the other, and stood, forcing dead blood into dead meat. She wavered after straightening, and actually let loose with a half moan, which she clamped off mighty fast.

"Christ," she whispered.

Behind her was the white fence where she'd stopped before the attack, whatever that attack had been. Her rifle was there, lying on the ground where'd she dropped it. From there, though she had no memory of what had happened after—she apparently had made her way to the middle of the street all the while managing to pull her knife and give her arm a few good whacks. She didn't feel any cravings, but Wallace had talked of them, so she figured they weren't far off.

She staggered toward the fence, actually concentrating on walking a line, and stopped over her rifle. When she bent at the knees to pick it up, her back played a troubling tune of popping bone, but thankfully nothing came apart.

The weapon was heavy, far heavier than before, and she realized she was losing strength fast. That set off another anger-fueled string of whispered expletives, which didn't help in the least.

With a grunt, she hefted her rifle into her arms and groaned at its tripled weight. It was becoming a log. Unless she was on her belly with something to rest the thing on, there was no way she was shooting bad guys. Not from the shoulder. No way. Even going from the hip seemed improbable. She couldn't leave the HK in the road, however, so she took it with her and almost collapsed against the fence. She leaned the rifle against one board and left it there, which was when her sliced-up arm got her attention again. Poking and moving cloth around, Collie didn't have the capacity to gasp.

She'd carved up her arm pretty damn good, from just below her wrist to mid-forearm. The flesh and muscle resembled a filleted salmon marinating in thick tar, but that wasn't the worst. The worst was the stab wounds, straight through the meat of her forearm and out the other side. Two stabs, before she switched up and started hacking away at her arm.

There'd been no pain, very little blood, and while the damage was bad, she could still move the limb, still flex her fingers. Collie stared at the mess, not remembering a damn thing, but wondering if, during her whiteout period, on some unconscious level, she attempted to inflict pain as an ignitor, or a grappling hook, to bring herself—to *pull* herself—back to the present.

Maybe it worked. Maybe it didn't.

It was daylight. Morning. The sun poured into those gray city channels, lighting up the empty houses and buildings. Then a ripple of horror went through her. She was supposed to reach the Four Towers to back up her boys. To *save* her boys.

"Oh shit," she whispered, and pulled the rifle into her arms. "Oh *shit*."

She struggled with the weapon but eventually marched at best speed across the back street. The world was quiet, just like it had been before her episode. Maybe thirty minutes lost? Forty? An hour? Not quite an hour, but almost. Collie hurried past the red brick building, through a deserted parking lot, and sighted the Four Towers—a lot closer than expected. She hoofed it past a string of parked cars and stopped at a corner. The nearest tower rose up across the street, but the main road to her left, the same strip Milo and Gus would've continued on, had been cut off by a wall of cars. Also across the street was what appeared to be an oversized parking garage connected to the first tower.

There was no sign of the Leather, but she knew they were there. She also had the terrible feeling of missing something important.

Collie walked into the open, crossing the street. She forced her limbs to do her bidding and focused on the garage entrance. Any second she expected to hear a shout from a missed lookout. She stayed the course, however, eyes fixed on the opening to that concrete cavern.

I'll make it, she told herself, zeroing in on the opening as the distance shrank.

I'll make it. I'll make it.

She entered the garage and made a straight line through the half-empty level. On the opposite side was an exit sign over a door leading to a coffee shop. She stopped there. Collie reassessed her prized German-made HK. It was too heavy to lift. Felt like she was toting around a howitzer instead of an assault rifle. Hating to admit it, it was just about as useful in a firefight now as a missile without its launcher. She looked at the nearest car, a small Honda Civic, and tried the rear door. It opened. Collie dropped the rifle on the vehicle's floor and left it there. She then stripped the extra magazines off herself and dumped them beside the weapon. A few other items got tossed into the car, and once she'd lightened her load considerably, she closed the door.

Then she pulled out her sidearm, readied the Sig, and checked her spare magazines.

She had three.

She also had a suppressor, which she screwed onto the weapon.

God bless you, Collie mentally sighed. Even though the Sig felt like it was double its weight, she could whip that lethal stinger around faster than the rifle. Adapt and Overcome.

Lord above, she was adapting… and *would* overcome.

The military had taught her many things, but the one thing her instructors had drilled into her, cemented by experience, was that mindset was a weapon in itself, and that the body was merely a sheath.

She opened the coffee shop door and stepped inside. Long dried-up pastries lay behind spore-blotched glass. Collie checked behind the counter and saw no one—heard no one—so she proceeded to the other side and stopped at a window. Another street, in the shadow of the first tower. A marble block identified the building as the *Anchor Bay Hotel*. The main entrance was behind that, glass doors with what appeared to be a handful of Leather on guard inside.

To her left was the same closed-off main drag, but with a sizeable gap, just big enough to drive a car through. Or a truck.

The coffee shop had a second entrance that opened onto the main drag. Collie headed for that, ducking under the dusty windows. She stayed away from the westerly exit that would have put her in view of the Leather, and peered through the shop windows that faced the main street.

There, hemmed in by four pickup trucks, was the limousine, stopped at an angle before one of two dump trucks. Figures moved around the limo. A leather-clad head popped up, near the driver's side. The Leather straightened as if stretching and turned back to the monster vehicle.

Collie watched him. She checked on the Leather inside the hotel entrance and wondered how many she wasn't seeing. There didn't seem to be any lookouts, at least none she could detect, and the Leather appeared relaxed in how they were moving about, as if all the action was over and done with. Collie sized up the puzzle ahead. It would be an easy thing to stay low, behind the wall of cars leading up to the trucks and trapped limo, but she would have to chance the gap, where the pickup appeared to have driven through.

No guts, no shit-talking, she thought.

Unlocking the coffee shop door, she waited a few seconds before cracking it open. Then she slipped outside and hugged the building's walls. At the corner, she ducked into a crouch, grimacing as she did so. She waddled—close to falling at times—behind the wall of cars, right up to the gap. Her limbs felt laced with lead, reducing her to only a quarter of her natural speed.

The Leather at the limo remained occupied with the car's secrets.

Still no sign of lookouts, Collie reached the opening in that automotive fence and peeked out at the hotel.

The Leather were still inside, but their outlines weren't easy to see, made almost invisible by the strengthening daylight. They would have no trouble spotting her, however, if they were looking in her direction. It was something of an angle, but still, she would be exposed for two seconds.

Then there was the thing with her zombie-turning ass.

Not needing to take a breath, she locked onto her first priority.

The limo.

Holding her Sig with both hands, Collie hurried across that open space…

47

At one point, in the vast, free-floating pit of unconsciousness, one that Gus was intimately familiar with, he came close to surfacing. Close. But not quite. And perhaps that was for the best.

Voices reached him, but they spoke syllables that had no meaning, like evil little musings whispered by imps. Or goblins. His arms and legs were stretched out, aching at the shoulders and hips, and he was briefly aware of swinging, as if in a hammock.

Gus heard the tiniest squeals during this black-out, or perhaps after, and what sounded like someone playing catch. Gus wasn't sure. Didn't have the capacity to determine when. But the game of catch seemed to carry on for a long time, and whoever was playing was throwing heat. Every time. Not just fastballs, but flaming, blue-red meteors that screeched across the absolute edge of the atmosphere. The kind of speed that turns those pieces of rock into falling bombs. And every now and again, one of those meteors sounded like a big one, an Everest-sized chunk of iron, and its flight almost always ended in an explosion and a gust of wind or a rattling of applause. Real honest-to-Christ planet hammers that didn't just leave a hole in the surface, but rearranged entire landscapes.

At least, that's what some part of Gus's mind thought.

It all ended with a boom, one that grabbed him by the hairy pink and chucked him back into reality.

Gus became aware of being on his back, while the distinct sound of crackling plastic perked his ears.

"Well, that was uneventful," a man spoke in an English accent.

"Just give me a few more minutes," a woman said in a breathless voice.

"No," the man dismissed. "You went too heavy this time. Look at him.

And he took it all. Just… just hook him up. The sight of that should motivate this one. And don't waste any. Remember last time?"

"Yeah."

"Get him done up and we'll get to work on this one."

This one? Gus opened his eyes.

And beheld the freak of all freaks.

Pink-faced. Sitting not five feet away, leaning in and studying him with a thoughtful expression. At this range, Gus had no trouble seeing the wrinkles and ridges of a face plastered in a thick coating of makeup. He'd slapped on enough stucco to know a good job from a shitty one, and whoever had applied the paint to the fright looming over him had royally fucked up.

Or, maybe that was the intent.

That pink face broke into a smile then, an amber tooth wreckage looking as if it might've stopped a couple of slapshots in its time.

"Ah," the man spoke. "Excellent. Good morning, Mister…"

Even though he sat a short distance away, a foul, noxious gas enveloped Gus's face, instantly repelling him. He turned his head one way and then the other, his still-rebooting mind discovering that everything below his neckline couldn't move at all.

The pink face drew back, watching Gus's discomfort, creating some much needed, life-giving space. Gus gasped in reflex, knowing he'd lost a few nose hairs in that nasty puff of carrion-stink. He sized up that horrid fuchsia-dipped catcher's mitt of a face, which was pinched off at the throat by a wicked collar clamped about the entire neck.

The pink expression stared back, switching to puzzlement, then understanding.

"Dear me." The man drew back and fumbled at his waist. "Forgot my teeth. Why didn't you tell me I had them out? Dear, dear me."

Pink Face slapped a hand to his mouth, took a moment to chew on something, then smiled again. "Howzat?"

Gus's eyes narrowed in unchecked horror.

The guy wore diamonds over his teeth. Goddamn diamonds. On his teeth. They were, in fact, Gus realized, specialized dentures, and judging by the level of detail before him, he figured it was a ten-karat gold set of choppers. The sparkly teeth might have come from a New Age disco ball that had been shattered upon an iron floor, whereupon the finer pieces were salvaged and then glued to a false palate. Except those fine disco ball fragments were, in fact, diamonds. They sparkled, glittered, the false gumline caked in some polluted residue that would repulse the strongest-of-stomach dental assistant tasked with cleaning the things.

The incisors disturbed him the most, however.

The things were long and thick and probably the envy of vampires.

Pink Face puckered up then, and those rich fangs disappeared behind an expression of smug satisfaction.

He'd gotten the reaction he'd wanted out of Gus.

But damn if he was going to get anything more from him.

"Glad to see you're awake," Pink Face said, his mouth undoing itself and parting like a worm being split and filleted. "I'm not that far gone to enjoy conversation from different quarters. From time to time. Are you feeling up to it? Conversation, that is?"

Gus stared at that horrible yet fascinating face. Towers rose up behind the man, seen through an incredible wide sheet of storm-proofed glass. A multi-million-dollar view, at least. And in between those enormous buildings was empty, sunny sky.

"I'll take that as a yes," Pink Face said. "Your… companion… is right there, by the way. In case you were wondering."

Pink Face extended an arm. From a pirate's sleeve of frilly cloth and leather, a bony, diseased-looking mottled hand with black nails pointed.

Gus turned his head and gawked.

He was in a room, what might've been a two-level penthouse suite, but that was as much detail as his mind allowed him because, not ten feet away, was Milo. The soldier was in a chair with a big piano just behind him. Dozens of leather belts lashed him to that chair, and what wasn't buckled down was… of all things, duct-taped.

But that wasn't what got to Gus.

What got to him, what *really* got to him, was the state old Milo was in, and he realized then that all those sounds he'd heard weren't just meteors pitching into the planet. Far from it.

Milo had been tortured.

To say that he'd been beaten perhaps within a testicular hair of his life might've been an understatement. The area around his eyes had swollen to grotesque proportions, reducing them to black slits. His face resembled a red plum stepped on and kicked around. Purple welts the size of golf balls bulged from his skull. Several of those had split apart, revealing bloody opaque interiors Gus didn't need to see. His hair was soaked in maroon that dribbled down his neck. Milo's right ear was hanging off his head by a shred of skin, and it fluttered like a fleshy sail every time he flinched. That happened every time the Leather moved around him, as if he were fearful of being whacked once again. The parts of the soldier that weren't bloodied were corpse pale and shone with sweat. His clothing was drenched in a mixture of fluids. Blood dripped from his left hand, from the tips of ruined fingers. The nails were scattered around his feet like blotted nips of tissue paper, and that horrified Gus only more. They had removed Milo's left boot and gone to work on his toes, much like the way they had worked over poor Carson at one time. The left foot was red, the veins engorged, and his toes were burst water balloons of meat and bone that leaked scarlet onto the floor.

Oh Jesus, Gus meant to say, but what came out of his throat was a parch dry croak of total horror at seeing Milo in such a condition.

At least he *thought* it was Milo. The person sitting across from him was so badly disfigured, so unconditionally savaged, it really could have been anyone.

Except it wasn't. It was Milo. The wretched piece-of-shit who had shot and killed Collie with professional efficiency.

And Gus didn't think he'd ever felt sorrier for anyone than he did at that moment.

His voice caused Milo to swing his head up, which shivered his nearly-detached ear. He grunted, and blood sprayed from his lips. "Didn't talk," he hitched in a tearful, shellshocked tone, his voice as hoarse and spent and pitiful to hear. His eyes swollen to the point of blindness. "Didn't talk. I didn't talk. I was good. I was good. I didn't talk. I was g—"

A Leather woman stepped in, wearing a form-fitting rawhide outfit that accentuated her figure. Aviator sunglasses covered her eyes, and black and white makeup divided her face all the way down to her neckline. She pressed a hand over Milo's mouth and rudely shoved his face back, just before she hammered three elbows off the soldier's head.

Milo stopped talking.

"Oh, *pish*," Pink Face said softly, distracting Gus. "Pay no mind to what they're doing over there. He didn't want to talk. I asked him nicely. Very nicely. And I warned him of the consequences if he didn't answer my questions. And what was it that he said to me, Dominique?"

Another Leather wandered into view, the same one who'd threatened the little girl. A black duster covered her from shoulders to boots, but she'd tossed off her cowboy hat, allowing her hair more freedom. She still wore the half mask. She orbited the rear of Milo's chair and when she glanced over at Pink Face, Gus saw red contacts in her eyes.

"Fuck you," she replied in a bored voice, and started walking past Gus.

"Fuck... you," Pink Face whispered, smiling when he said it, his lips glistening. "So, I said to him. Quite clearly... 'No sir. Fuck *you*.' At which point I bade Wanda to work her black magic upon him. To its fullest."

Pink Face turned his head towards Milo, so that an elvish tuft of hair sprouting from his ear canal was easily seen. Then the leader switched his attention back on Gus, and that evil, shit-smelling ten-karat grill blazed.

"You would be wise to mind your manners," Pink Face warned, the whites of his eyes cracked with traceries of red. "Until you no longer can, I suppose."

He straightened and slapped his hands together. "Now then. Let's begin. Quid pro quo, if you will, except for every correct answer, you'll receive absolutely nothing from Wanda."

At that, he indicated the woman with the black and white makeup dividing her face in two, who was sizing up Milo's ear as if it were a shred of dried skin needing to be peeled off.

"In fact," Pink Face continued, "she'll love you for it. Absolutely love you. Tell us nothing, however, or even a lie, which is indubitably *worse*... she'll work that dreadful black magic upon *you*."

On cue, Wanda moved away from her victim, her leather-clad ass a thing to marvel. She picked something up and returned with a high end-table of glass. She placed that beside Gus. It was the kind of table to put one's book after an evening read, or a tall glass of wine until the next sip. What covered its surface now was a wooden serving tray, with a regular hammer, and a pair of pliers. Blood and fragments of meat speckled the steel tools.

A terrified Gus looked from those items to Milo, and back again.

The rattle of glass stole Gus's attention. Wanda turned and walked away, to reposition herself just behind Milo's chair.

Gus heard a squeak of fear, barely aware that it came from him.

Someone rolled a solid glass carboy to a stop beside Milo's chair. It was an empty container with a twenty-liter capacity, with a metal spigot near the bottom. Thick tubing ran from the neck of the carboy, all the way up to the table, where it ended in a crude device that resembled a ventilator mask. What was disturbing about that was the grooved hole at the top, where a piece was missing. Wanda, in her most wicked wardrobe, stood beside it, tearing off a strip of surgical tape. She fitted the device over a section of Milo's neck, causing his dangling ear to jiggle, and Milo's eye slits to crack open a sliver in pure terror.

"Not a word," she whispered into his hanging ear. "Not a sound."

She slapped home a wide patch of tape, keeping the mask-thing in place.

The soldier's cheeks puffed out at the contact, and he seemed to sweat even more. But he stayed silent.

"Jesus Christ," Gus whispered, totally transfixed by the sight.

Wanda held up the empty roll of tape and pouted. "I gotta get more tape, Joe."

That got Pink Face—Joe's—attention. "More tape? What the fuck are you doing over there, Wanda?"

"Taping him up," Wanda protested, her hands going wide.

"You're not taping him up if you need more tape, Wanda dearest. You're fucking *mummifying* the poor bastard. Look at him. You think we were about to extract his brain through his nose. A procedural that holds no interest for me in the least, I'll have you know."

"Well, I used the other tape to tie him down," she whined in defense.

"I can see that. Bully for you. But I've told you before. Take it *easy*... with the *tape*. It's a finite resource. Once it's gone, it's fucking gone."

"You gonna tell me where you're hiding the rest of it?"

"I'm debating it."

"If you want the juice, I need the good stuff."

Joe fumed, his pink face darkening a few shades more. When he spoke, he forced his words through clenched teeth. "In the bar. Last drawer on the far right. There's a pack." He paused for effect. "Of *three*."

Wanda glared back. Obviously, the pair had navigated these waters before. She waited exactly three seconds, long enough to get her point across, whatever that might be, and then took her time as she strutted out of sight.

Gus could almost hear the drum pounding out each swing of her hips, except he was terrified of her to the point of just about ready to shit on the spot.

Joe tracked her without moving his head, until he finally gave up and looked at Gus.

"She's a good girl, really. And you seem like a very good boy. To me, anyway. A very *smart* boy. Which is why I chose him to be first. And not you."

That dreaded feeling of fear and nausea flared up within Gus once again. That sense of utter helplessness and at the whim and fancy of another, quite insane, individual. He'd been that way with the overpass gang so long ago, which had been the worst. Shovel's gang had been bad, but not like those lunatics back then. The name Comeau came to his head, but he couldn't remember the others. Or their faces. But then again, it was hard to remember anyone's face right after what old Joe just said. Except maybe Collie's

Milo struggled against his bonds.

Wanda returned at that exact moment. She saw the soldier squirm, didn't care for it in the least, and reached out and ripped off his ear in one fluid motion that sent up a drizzle of fresh blood.

It also caused Milo to shriek.

Wanda didn't like that either, so she stepped up and hammered him twice with an elbow. While he was dazed, she considered the ear before tossing it aside, having no use for the appendage. She then tore off a piece of tape and applied it to the twitching, bleeding soldier.

"Think about that," Joe said, as if nothing had just happened. The pink-faced Leather adjusted his own boys with a grimace and a pinch before crossing his legs and leaning back. His smile extended all the way up to those red-cracked eyes. Noticing his pirate sleeves were amiss, Joe took a moment to fluff up the ends.

"Now then," Joe said, unleashing the full vampiric might of those dentures. "Question period. Where did you come from?"

Gus didn't answer.

Vampire Joe frowned and looked down his nose. "I'm afraid I haven't made myself clear. If you do not answer me, I'll unleash Wanda upon your friend there. And then you."

Gus had the urge to say he wasn't his friend. Companion on the road, maybe, but not his friend. Because the little knob-gobbler had shot Collie. Because he had killed her. *No,* a little voice reminded him. Collie was gone the moment she got the TI injection from her handlers. That killed her right then. Milo might've only sped up what was already happening to her, but make no mistake, she was already gone, she just hadn't known it.

Milo was just... Milo. A guy who'd done questionable things at stressful times, but was trying to make amends, in his own way.

I didn't talk, the soldier said, just before Wanda gave him a few elbows. God as his witness, Gus believed him. Especially considering the state the man was in. And he pitied him for what the soldier had endured to keep the location of a handful of people and their home secret. *His* home, or what Milo *hoped* would be his home.

Gus saw the damage inflicted upon the man, and he knew he couldn't take a beating like that. Not now and not ever.

"What's that thing for?" Gus asked, going for time.

And surprisingly, Joe granted it. "That? You mean the IV? Ah, well, you see, I've developed something of a taste for blood. Fresh blood is a valued commodity for me. One the Dog Tongue allows me to indulge every now and again. I have two prisoners here. That one was stubborn, but he's still a great big bag of blood waiting to be cracked open. Or in this case, drained. Into the carboy there. Haven't decided if I'll keep him alive yet or not. He seems… feisty, that one. Eventually, I'll drain your companion of every last drop. I'll even wring out the meaty parts to get those last few drops. And then I'll do the same to you. Are we clear?"

Gus felt his throat click. "Clear."

"Excellent."

"Joe?" Wanda asked.

Vampire Joe's expression went dark again. "Yes, oh wicked one?"

"How many questions you gonna ask him?"

"As many as I want. Why? Do you have something else to do? Some place to be?"

She didn't answer him.

Perturbed at being interrupted, Joe regarded Gus once again. "We knew you were coming," Vampire Joe stated. "A little birdy told me so. Well, a little shit, to be truthful. But we knew. Now, what was I thinking? Yes. Let's start again. Where did you get that wonderful, wonderful, limousine?"

Gus barely heard him, because Wanda, Wicked Wanda, wasn't about to insert an IV into Milo's jugular. Nothing of the kind. That odd ventilator contraption at the end of the IV had a hole in its top, facing away from Milo. A hole which Wanda now filled with another tool that turned Gus's innards cold.

It was a metal skewer. An exceptionally *long* metal skewer, resembling a needle. But this needle would easily perforate the spot of chosen skin on Milo's neck.

Vampire Joe noticed the hesitation and was quick to act upon it. "Answer me, and I'll allow him a quick death."

"Don't… don't drain him," Gus asked. "I'll tell you everything. Just don't drain him."

Things clicked and ripped as Wanda worked over Milo. The carboy didn't move, but Gus sensed that things were about to become very bad indeed for the soldier. Then he thought of Whitecap and the people there. All the fabricated beaches and the waterfalls and the goldfish. All the amenities and creature comforts under the ground. But mostly he thought of the people.

And the fucking circus these freaks would have if they ever found out about them.

A short Leather minion appeared nearby Wicked Wanda, and Gus felt his guts sink just a little further into the floor. The kid couldn't have been any more than nine or ten. A child meat puppet. Perhaps even the very one that the cleaver-wielding woman had threatened in the dump truck.

Well, fuck.

That was as good as being dick-punched.

Duped, he thought, realizing that by leaving the safety of the limo they had, in fact, royally screwed themselves. That knowledge burned like acid and left him even more miserable.

"Everything, you say?" Vampire Joe inquired, bringing him back to the present.

Gus reluctantly nodded.

Vampire Joe regarded his silent prisoner. "*Excellent!* Well, then. By all means, please begin."

The wicked one stood poised by the slumped Milo, and when Gus started talking, he lifted his head in an admirable display of outrage.

And a squawk of protest.

Which Wanda addressed with three more savage blows across that already brutalized face.

Milo ceased moving entirely.

"Nasty," Vampire Joe smiled, flashing that mouth grill. "That's my Wanda. Oh, she knows how to break a man's balls, I shit you not. Wanda dear, if he does that again, you have my permission to use the hammer. *On* his balls."

Gus glanced over at Milo, saw the fresh blood flowing, and a new, serious gash right above his temple. Blood trickled into his ear.

"Did you cut him?" Vampire Joe asked, distracted yet again.

"Sorry," Wanda answered.

"Wanda," the Leather leader sighed. "You must control that temper. Tape that up once you finish with the IV." He focused on Gus. "Now then. Back to you. Continue, please. Don't hold anything back, and I'll remember that later."

Gus deflated, taking in points of a very high ceiling painted in eggshell white. "We got the limo from a bunker."

"Corporate? Government? Privately owned?"

"… Government."

"My, my. And you have weapons there??"

Gus swallowed. "Yeah."

"You just gave yourself a little extra piece of rope," Vampire Joe said.

The IV tubing running from the carboy to Milo's neck bothered Wanda somehow, so she reached around and flexed its plastic length.

"Don't mind her," Vampire Joe said. "She can be particular. Annoyingly so. What's the term? OCD? With the…" he twirled a finger, "…with the little things? She won't kill him unless I say so. And I won't, as long as you keep talking."

But curiosity distracted Gus. "You've done this before?"

Vampire Joe's features split into an expression of feral mirth. "What? Drain a person? Of *course* we have. Nothing like a spot of plasma. It truly hits the spot. Better than Merlot, if you can believe it. Or even a fine Pinot Noir."

"I like the coolers, myself," Wanda said.

"And you're a savage because of it," Vampire Joe softly scolded before returning to Gus. "It takes a few minutes to drain a person. As you see, we prefer to go in through the neck. Right here."

He indicated a spot on his form-fitting leather collar.

"Sometimes, if we're feeling sociable or we're pressed for supplies, we'll open up a vein here." He tapped the valley of his elbow. "They last a little longer that way."

Wanda watched Gus, aviator goggles aimed directly at him while her black and white expression was emotionless.

Vampire Joe leaned in. "Where is this bunker?"

"Back east."

"Don't be coy."

That little meat puppet moved behind Gus's chair, distracting him. Vampire Joe's rotten closeness brought him back, however. Wanda even moved a little closer to the table and the hammer upon it. That was all Gus needed. He swallowed and gave it up. "Ontario. Northern Ontario. Not near any town. Off the grid. Deep woods. You'll never find it."

"You found it."

"I knew a person. She brought me there. Led the way."

"Only you?"

Gus didn't answer.

Wanda picked up the hammer and held it at arm's length.

"There's others," Gus replied.

"Excellent. How many?"

Gus thought about it. "Not sure. About three hundred."

That silenced his interrogator.

"They all got weapons," Gus continued. "Just like us. They already wiped out a shitload of you freaks—I mean people."

"Did they?" Vampire Joe asked, letting the slip go.

Gus glanced at Milo's bleeding form. "Including a couple truckloads of undead."

"You wiped them out as well?"

"Yeah."

"Well! You certainly *sound* armed to the teeth. What prompted you to mount this massive offensive?"

Gus didn't look at the pink face. "We know about the Dog Di—the Dog Tongue." He paused, realizing how close he might've come to dying just then. Or worse. "We came out here to kill him."

Vampire Joe snorted back a laugh. "You came here to kill him. In a limo." He covered his mouth and indicated his prisoner to continue.

"Armored limo," Gus stressed, fine in revealing that detail. Not like the Leather wouldn't find that out, anyway. It was tricky, however, trying to maintain that delicate balance of untruth mixed with truth.

"An armored limo? You hear that, Wanda?"

Wanda nodded, those goggles jiggling just a little.

"You hear that, Dominique?" Vampire Joe asked.

Gus didn't see the reaction of the woman with the red contacts.

"We already figured out it was armored." Joe leaned in. "Still, the picture becomes clearer. To be honest, I've already heard reports. From a survivor of your counter-offensive."

"A fuckhead with a spider on his mask?"

The question surprised Vampire Joe. "You know about the Spider?"

"We missed him. Had him back in Winnipeg. Should've killed him then."

"But he escaped."

Gus nodded.

"Yes," Vampire Joe said. "That's him. The fuckhead with the spider mask. He's a slippery one. Should've called him 'the Eel,' really. Or something else that oozes an appalling amount of … lubricant. In any case. I needed clarification. See if your story matches with his. The who, what, and where. The why is irrelevant. The when… not so much. So there's someone else out there. To defy the Dog Tongue. Honestly, we suspected there would be someone left, but a government bunker? My oh my."

He continued to gaze at Gus. "And with weapons? Well, well. Excellent."

Vampire Joe nodded at Wanda, whose fingers flexed upon the hammer.

"We wiped you out," Gus said. "Back there."

"Did you now?"

"Two packs of you. One in Fort Jay. One in Winnipeg. Two in Winnipeg, really."

"That was you, too?"

Gus nodded and glanced over at Milo's taped-down carcass.

Vampire Joe shrugged. "Well, I have good news. When the Dog Tongue arrives, we'll all go see this bunker of yours. The one with all the marvelous toys. And all the people. Oh, yes, that's right. The Dog Tongue's coming here. On his way now, in fact, even as we speak. I expect him any time. He'll be very interested in you, dear boy. Very interested. Daresay you'll lead him all the way back to the hole from whence you sprouted. Mounted on the front of a truck, probably."

At that, Vampire Joe snorted, dislodging something significant from his nasal cavity and sucking it into the back of his throat. He swallowed, smiled, and leaned in, close enough that Gus got a whiff of his rancid breath. "You see, I smell *fear* about you. Something isn't quite right. And it's not just the knowledge of being strapped to that chair and on the cusp of experiencing excruciating pain. I know you have weapons. I know you did considerable damage to the Dog Tongue's armies. But there's something you're hiding—it's either where you say this bunker is, or its people. The number of people, I mean. You said hundreds? In northern Ontario? That's a fairly unpopulated region, I believe. An excellent site for a bunker or some other super-secret installation, but all those people living there? I doubt that. It took us about a year to consolidate our forces, all starting from a street gang of dozens, and that was in Vancouver."

Gus blinked, feeling the lie crumble, trying to maintain a poker face.

"At best," Vampire Joe thought aloud, the stink wafting from those diamond dentures eye-watering, "I'm thinking… no more than one or two dozen. Am I right?"

Vampire Joe leaned in. "Am I right?"

Gus tried very hard not to move, not to blink, not to even *breathe*, for fear of unwittingly revealing the truth.

Wicked Wanda took one deliberate step closer, the hammer at the ready.

"Yes," Vampire Joe hissed, watching his prisoner sweat. "I believe I *am* right."

Which was right about when the door crashed open.

48

Two Leather standing closest to the door were shot point blank, which got the diminutive Leather screaming. Both targets slammed up against marble columns. One of them rebounded and landed flat on his blown-out chest, spraying everywhere, with one arm pointed at the extravagant penthouse beyond the double doors.

A third Leather whirled from behind the same column and fired what might've been Gus's shotgun, before the return shot cracked the man's head backward, sending a shocking mess across the nearby wall.

Sig held in two hands, Collie dashed into the room and hid directly behind a column. There was a pink-faced individual at the far end of the suite. That same person dove for the floor when she put down the shotgunner. There were others back there as well. She peeked out to check on their whereabouts, just in time to see one Leather powering up a chainsaw. That battery-powered instrument of destruction almost drowned out the sound of the screaming kid.

Almost.

Collie edged one way and then the other, trying to widen her angle of vision.

"*KILL HIM IF YOU MUST!*" someone shouted from inside the room, in what sounded like an English accent.

Feet pounded towards her.

The bastard with the chainsaw weaved in and around the other columns leading up to the entrance. Collie leaned out and shot him through the face. The chainsaw fell to the carpet, already quiet. It bounced with a clatter and marked the center of the foyer in a startling screech of steel-linked teeth.

The kid was still wailing, however.

Collie was already behind cover. She peeked out from behind the column, hunting for targets. She glimpsed three. One of them was no bigger than a child, and that one scurried for a hallway as if its little leather ass was on fire. The screaming diminished as it ran away.

Two chairs caught her attention, situated at the edge of the main room and facing a wall of windows with a view of a skyline diminished only by the other nearby towers. In one of those chairs was the ragged looking form of Milo, duct-taped and without a doubt dead. The other chair was turned away from her, but she suspected the person there was Gus, leaning one way and then the other, trying to see who was doing the shooting.

"That you, Collie?" that familiar voice bawled out. Gussy all the way.

"Yeah."

"Oh thank Christ."

"*KILL HER, GIRLS!*" Same voice as before, but this time the accent was gone.

Fake. The one common trademark among all the evil, twisted sideshow freaks calling themselves the Leather.

The penthouse grew very quiet then. Collie leaned one way—before a shooter sprayed a short burst up the length of the column. Chalky powder dusted the air and coated Collie's side, but nothing else. The shooter had rushed the shot, spraying before aiming. She figured the weapon was from the limo. One of her favorite SMGs, which meant the vehicle's stash of firearms had been sacked.

Another long burst riddled the column, practically pollinating the space with dust.

Collie held back, letting the shooter empty her magazine, when her mind buzzed a warning about that last blast. *Cover fire.*

Collie was already sliding down the column when a hammer missed her forehead and whacked the marble surface behind. She was still sliding when her attacker's leg came into view, the knee turned inwards to get better torque behind the swing. A face painted black and white and split down the middle appeared above those leather-covered parts. Aviator goggles flicked downward and tracked Collie as she leaned away, flinging herself out along the floor, creating distance. She fired the Sig, which was practically resting on her hip, and destroyed the Leather's knee in a spurt that resembled a fat tomato being sucked into a jet engine and shat out the back.

The Leather woman went down and Collie would have put two in that evil Queen of Hearts face, except a shadow fell across her from the *other* side.

And a flat slab of edged steel came whistling down at her face.

Collie twisted, landing on her back and jerking her head, but not fast enough to avoid damage. The cleaver chopped into her right trapezoid—that large, almost skinny, sail-shaped muscle that ran from the base her skull to her shoulder. There was no pain, just a sensation of being struck and the parting of meat.

The blade quivered upon striking the floor, and there was a fleeting moment of puzzlement around the red eyes above a ninja mask.

Collie attempted to shoot the cyberpunk bitch through the knees, but having her trapezoid muscle hacked in two slowed her down. The red-eyed ninja saw that black adder of a pistol coming around, and two things happened at once.

An unseen hand clamped down around Collie's right ankle, and the Ninja dropped down onto the operator's gun arm.

The cleaver was pulled out in a grisly arc of wet soot, the Ninja already twisting, seeking to lop the sidearm off at the wrist. The Queen at Collie's ankle pulled on the limb, straightening her leg out.

Collie's left hand lashed out and fastened onto the Ninja's belt. Collie pulled with everything she had, and the Ninja fell across her chest like a rotten redwood. At the same time, the operator kicked with her other foot, missing with the first heel but hammering face with the second. A grunt came from the Queen while the Ninja released a furious—but quite girly—growl of rage.

Collie scrambled and enveloped the Ninja's neck with her two arms. She wrapped her gun-arm around the woman's throat in a choke while planting her left hand against the back of her skull.

Anyone knowing what the operator was doing might've been able to escape.

Collie was banking on the Leather *not* knowing, and knew she guessed right when the masked civvie in her clutches seized her elbow in a reflexive attempt to pull it away.

Wrong move.

Collie applied a tonnage of pressure on that chicken bone of a neck, feeling her victim tense, knowing instinctively she had the hold sunk in, but also knowing she had no time to choke the Ninja out. So she released and shoved the Ninja away, just enough to jerk her gun arm free before shoving the barrel up against the base of the Leather's skull.

One shot and a pressurized jet of head cheese erupted from the face of the would-be killer.

Scratch one—Collie thought, but then realized the dead woman was lying on top of her.

And the others were still unaccounted for.

"*Dominique? Wanda?*" that voice cried out.

Collie got an elbow underneath herself, heaving the corpse away while extracting her legs.

When she saw the Queen, far from finished, swing her hammer down like a murderous scepter.

The hammerhead struck Collie's knee with a hollow *clop* that didn't sound good. Her leg and joint buckled and bounced at the impact. Again, there was no pain, but that curious sensation of damage being taken. She tried to pull the leg away but nothing seemed to work from the knee down.

The Queen—real name either Dominique or Wanda—reared back her arm like she was about to detonate a missile perched on an anvil.

Collie swung the Sig up and shot her in the face, driving the upper body back before she fell forward, collapsing on her legs. The hammer bounced off the floor.

"Dominique?" the voice asked, surprisingly fearful. "Wanda?"

Collie got clear of the dead Queen and rolled out from behind the column.

There, standing behind a bar, was a Leather holding an HK-303, taken from the limo's arsenal. The gunman tensed upon spotting her and fired. *Wide*, the shots scalded the floor a foot about Collie's head. She stopped rolling on her belly, clasped the Sig with both hands, and lanced one round through the Leather's forehead with all the accuracy of a seamstress threading a needle.

"*Oh you bastards!*" the voice wailed. "*You fucking*, cock-sucking *bastards!*"

Past the sunken pit that was the main floor of the penthouse, next to a piano, was the speaker. Just a jump away from Gus and Milo.

Collie looked up and saw the end of a white sofa. She rolled behind it and struggled to get up. All the while, the voice continued to light up her ears with livid curses. Her knee was still out of whack, but she managed to move it a little, feeling bones click and grind.

Great, she thought, and considered the speaker.

"He's got a gun, Collie!" Gus shouted.

She sighed. 'Course he had a gun. They *all* had guns. Except for Dominique and Wanda with their permanently ventilated heads and their fucked-up hair.

She got to her knees, forcing the damaged one to bend, but it did as if stricken with twenty years of rust. 'Cranky' was the word, but she bent that fucker all the same.

"*You come any closer and I'll kill them,*" the voice warned, no longer accented.

"I'm sure you will," Collie said, getting set for the next part.

"I'll shoot, honest-to-*Christ*, I'll shoot."

The sofa wasn't one with a high back, so Collie peeked up over it and looked across a huge L-sectional, where a short set of penthouse steps parted the piece of furniture. She locked on to one of the more fucked-up individuals she'd ever laid eyes upon since starting her mission—that being the eradication of the liquid shit calling themselves the Leather.

Angry and pink-faced, with a huge choker that seemed to both hold up and squeeze his entire neck, was the next target. Insane with fear and probably standing in a pool of his own excrement, the pink-faced bastard held a gun to Gus's temple. The gun was Gus's own Glock. She also saw a glass carboy with connected tubing next to Milo's chair and resisted the wonder of what the hell was intended if she *hadn't* burst into the room a minute ago.

Laying her arms across the back of the sofa, she looked down the sights of her Sig and aimed at the angry Pink Face.

"*Put the gun down!*" he screamed at her. "*Or I'll put one in his ear.*"

Collie cocked her head.

"*Put the gun down!*" he screamed again, his pink hue boiling over into vein-bulging red. "*Put that goddamn gun* DOWN! PUT IT DOWN! I COMMAND—"

Collie shot him through the face.

The bullet flung the angry pink man back, his arms spread wide like boneless wings. The Glock dropped from dead fingers. He landed near the base of the picture window, splayed out and waiting for the vultures. One slipper—an honest-to-god *slipper*—covered a foot while the other was bare with five toes up.

All became quiet after that.

"Oh Jesus," Gus released, visibly slumping against his bonds. "Jesus, Jesus."

Milo was even looking her way, and Collie was glad she had the sense to put her mask back on, from earlier, to hide her shock. Milo had the living *shit* beaten out of him, and was probably thankful for the duct tape keeping him to the chair. A pain-weary and exhausted smile spread across his smashed, brutally swollen features, and even from where she was standing, she could see teeth were missing.

Collie stood up and swept left to right with the Sig, searching for other targets. Seeing none, she eyed the one hallway where the child dressed as a Leather had run off.

"Any more of them up here?" she asked her boys.

"Don't know," Gus said, turning his head but not able to see her. "I think you got them all."

"There's the kid," Milo said, and nodded in the direction of the hall.

Collie limped across the pit area, noticing the open second level of the penthouse. Her hammered knee was more than a little wobbly. She grabbed onto furniture where she could, and though she got by, she knew she'd be hobbling for the rest of her days.

"Sweet Jesus," Gus moaned with unchecked relief. "Am I ever glad to see you. What happened to you? Why are you walking all funny?"

Collie divided her attention on the second level and the cavernous hallway. "Got into some trouble but worked through it. Delayed me all the same. I'm here now."

As she spoke, she unsheathed her knife and sawed through the duct tape around Gus's left arm. Once he was free, she handed him the blade and staggered to the piano, where she sat down heavily upon its bench. Gus continued cutting away. He was in relatively good condition, but Milo looked like a truck had run over him. Repeatedly.

Sensing her inspection, the soldier looked up and actually cracked a smile. And though it was a wretched sight, one close to breaking her heart, Collie actually smiled back underneath her mask.

"You look like a bloody shit," she said.

His spotty smile widened. "Probably look… worse, than it really is."

Her eyes drifted from the raw destruction of his ear to his foot and hand. "Yeah," she said, forcing hope into her voice. "You'll walk it off. No trouble."

He smiled again.

"Who's the freak?" Collie asked as Gus stood up.

"No idea," Milo replied, dribbling fresh blood as he spoke.

"He didn't introduce himself." Gus stood aside and pointed with the knife. "Those two were Wanda. And Dominique. They called him Joe." He shook his head at the corpses. "You still got the moves, Collie."

She didn't comment on that.

"He said…" Milo paused for breath. "He said… the Dog Tongue. Was coming here."

"Who said?" she asked.

"That one," Gus nodded at the corpse of Vampire Joe. "Said he was on his way here. While he was torturing us."

"Was gonna... make Gus... lead them back," Milo added.

Gus became quiet then, for a moment, which Collie figured wasn't important. He stooped and got to freeing Milo from the chair. While he did that, Collie sized up the carboy.

"The fuck were they going to do with that?" She nodded at the tubing and container.

"Drink him," Gus said while cutting.

"Drink him? You mean his *blood*?"

He nodded.

"Goddamn crazy-ass leather chuggernuts," Collie marveled in disbelief.

Milo's head swayed but he didn't fall off the chair. He flexed his ruined hand. Collie tried not to look at the mess, although she could smell the blood. Smell it very well, in fact.

She shook her head, as if coming out of a daze.

"Yeah," Gus said, interpreting her reaction a different way. "Like that."

"Christ Almighty," she said. "This all of them?"

"Maybe," Gus said. "There's that little one running around."

"We'll get him in a minute. He said the Dog Dick's coming here?"

Gus looked up from his work. "Yeah."

"Arriving any time," Milo said weakly, working his arm as Gus cut it loose.

Collie wavered, considering her gimpy leg and then her companions.

"Hurry up there, Gus."

Gus inspected the tape securing the ventilator mask to the soldier's neck. "Milo?"

"Yeah?"

"I'm gonna—"

Rip.

"*Fuck*!" Milo released as he straightened with a spasmodic jerk. His good hand went to the spot on his neck, covering it before he checked for blood.

"You're good," Gus said. "Just red is all."

Still, Milo wasn't in the best shape. In fact, he was half-dead, by Collie's estimation.

"You're okay?" she asked Gus as he handed back her combat knife.

"Yeah. They were saving me for the big cheese."

"Lucky you."

"Yeah."

"Any sign of the Spider?"

"No. Nothing. I don't think he's around."

That wasn't good. "Milo, you good to hang on here for a bit?"

"Get me a gun."

That prompted Gus to go searching among the bodies. He retrieved his shotgun, as well as the HK-303 that one Leather was firing at Collie.

He handed the HK over to Milo, without any reservations, without even realizing he was doing it.

Milo cradled the weapon in his lap.

"You're good?" Collie asked him.

The soldier nodded.

"Hold the fort," she told him. "Anyone comes through the front door, you shoot 'em. And we'll come limping."

Milo, with missing ear and swollen eyes and all, smirked, and that was a horrid thing to behold. He nodded and regarded the penthouse entrance with a trembling, venomous wrath.

"You good?" she asked Gus.

"Yeah."

"All right, you come with me. Help me walk."

"Thank you, Collie. For saving us. Saving me. Again."

She draped one arm around his shoulder, which placed the shotgun awkwardly between them. "Don't mention it. You would've gotten yourself clear somehow, even if I didn't show up."

Gus didn't look so sure on that count.

They staggered towards the hallway, taking the long way around the bar. Collie checked on the entrance and upper level as they went. Abstract paintings covered the walls, lines and color that might have been people watching sunsets. They reached the hallway, and Collie motioned for silence. She let Gus go and leaned heavily against the nearest wall. Gus went to the other side, bringing up the Ram Fist.

Ceiling lights were on, and the hall went twenty feet in before banking to the right.

"They got power," Gus whispered.

"Yeah," Collie said, sizing up matters. "This place is corporate owned. Big chain. All the bells and whistles. Nothing new. Probably designed like this from day one, to take advantage of all the green initiative money and tax breaks. I'd say their power source is probably more up-to-date and efficient than Whitecap's. No wonder why the Leather like it here."

"Nothing new? You're saying there's others like this?"

"Oh yeah. No doubt. In the cities at least, where it could actually make the most sense and make a buck. Can't build one of these in the boonies. The locals wouldn't be able to afford it."

Gus flexed his brow in an answer of *suppose so*.

"Don't get me wrong. These things aren't commonplace. Just… around if you look for it." Collie stopped, standing awkwardly, her left shoulder against the wall. She aimed with both hands. Gus stopped when she did, and she placed a finger to her mouth to convey the universal signal of *shhh* before pointing ahead.

Gus braced himself, aiming at the end of the hall.

At first nothing could be heard, neither in front of them nor behind. There were doors along the hall, all open, the dark wood surfaces shining under the soft lighting. More pictures hung in between the doors, but their artwork wasn't easily seen. Then, the barest squeal of hinges from up ahead. Followed by the softest, telltale step.

Someone was shuffling along, moving towards Collie and Gus. They exchanged looks and readied themselves.

Whoever was coming down the hall stopped at the corner, hanging back just out of sight, listening, thinking.

Then, slowly peeking out, the right side of a face. A *masked* face. All in Leather.

Gus straightened his back at the sight.

Collie fired and missed, marking the corner with a ragged hole.

The head jerked back.

"Get him!" Collie yelled, and Gus chugged ahead.

He turned the corner and got the Ram Fist up in time to stop a *broadsword* from decapitating him. The sword clapped against the upraised barrel of the firearm, in a cross of medieval-meets-modern.

As startling as the attempted ambush was, that wasn't the shocking thing.

The broadsword ended in a pair of knight's metal gauntlets. The owner was a Leather decked out in what appeared to be hockey shoulder pads and a form fitting mask that covered the whole head. The mouth had been replaced by a rubber skeleton smile speckled with red paint. Rubber spikes *encircled* the fake mouth.

But, below all that, the Leather wore a frilly apron of white.

With a panicked wheeze, the Leather retreated, pulling back the sword and almost cutting Gus's hand on the Ram Fist's foregrip.

Gus withdrew, only to be replaced by Collie hobbling around him.

Seeing two attackers, the Leather backed up, pointing the blade at one then the other, as if guessing which one would come at him first.

Collie shot him through the head, dropping the morbid thing and his broadsword to the hardwood floor. Steel echoed briefly in the close confines, but no other leather-clad crazy appeared.

Gus and Collie stood there, staring at the killer lying on his back, the treaded heels of his army boots tipped up and unmoving.

"Y'know something?" Gus asked.

"What?"

"The more I'm around these fuckers, the less shocked I am."

Collie tipped him a nod of agreement. "Back up a bit. We gotta check these rooms."

They went back to the first door and proceeded to clear each room after that. There was an office. A bathroom and shower with adjoining sauna. A small exercise room with two treadmills and an impressive set of free weights. There were bedrooms and even a small library. Gus opened each door and went inside, checking out the nooks, crannies, and closets, ensuring no Leather lurked within. All the while, Collie stayed poised on the threshold, keeping an eye on the hallway.

The hallway turned right, went straight, and then turned left, opening into a corner of the building where a second living room was situated around a huge television and entertainment system. Game controllers rested on a grand coffee table of oak. White carpet covered the floor while the walls were richly paneled wood. Huge glass bubbles with twisty light filaments inside hung off tall posts that filled the corners.

But what got their attention were the toys littering the floor. All manner of toys. Dolls, action figures, building blocks, trainsets, and raceways. All the latest and the best, with even a few board games tossed in there.

"Well, well," Collie said. "The Leather do love their toys."

"I bet Saturdays are bitchin' around here," Gus added.

There was a little room further ahead with a poker table set-up, as well as a small bar at the back with a half-complement of whiskey and rum. Gus didn't see any Captain Morgan labels. In fact, he didn't see any familiar brands.

"Over here," Collie whispered.

He turned and joined her at a closed door. She held the latch and nodded at Gus to get ready. The silence in that space of time swelled to dangerous levels.

She opened the door.

And the screams lit them both up.

49

A quick count revealed eleven children, girls and boys, from ages six to perhaps thirteen. They hid behind unmade beds and peeked out from closets. Two little boys were under a bed with only their upturned faces and arms showing. There was one boy perhaps nine or ten, dressed in a pint-sized leather costume but with the mask removed. Another child, a red-headed girl of similar age, wore a green dragon t-shirt and a knee-length leather skirt. She had backed up into a corner decorated with pictures of a long-gone girl-band.

All were scared out of their minds at the two invaders.

And all continued screaming at the top of their developing lungs, fingers clawing at air, clutching at blankets, mouths open for optimum wailing, and sounding like the world's biggest set of pipe whistles in need of a boot to the brass ass.

"Be *quiet*!" Collie huffed and silenced the lot of them in one gust. They blinked at her, dribbling tears and sniveling snot. Their little frames trembled as if on the very brink of seizure. One little boy scratched his pajama-clad ass, and immediately put those fingers to his nose, all the while staring at the two invaders.

An uneasy quiet prevailed, however.

"Better," Collie said and looked around. "Much better. Now stay that way. We're not going to hurt you. So relax, okay? Just relax?"

On the other side of the entrance, Gus shook his head and stretched his jaw. "Christ, I thought I'd gone deaf."

"I don't see any grown-ups in here."

"Good, that's good," Gus said. "Great, even. And you got them to shut up."

"They're quiet for now," Collie said, not quite relaxed. "You kids with the Leather?"

"That one is," Gus said and pointed at the fully costumed one. The boy with natural brown curls shivered as if the pointed finger was a death verdict. As one, the entire pack turned their eyes on the singled-out kid, and that alone brought the boy to tears. His little shoulders quivered and his breathing quickened.

"He's not with the Leather," someone said.

"That's Marty," said another.

"He just does things for them."

"Serves them shit."

"Yeah, shit."

"Big brown turds," someone giggled.

"I do *not*," Marty bawled. He immediately shut up, remembering who was in charge, regarding both Collie and Gus with absolute terror. He got his tears under control.

"Relax," Collie said. "No one's going to hurt you, so relax."

"That one there," Gus nodded at the little girl in the green dragon t-shirt. "She's a hostage for sure."

"What's a hostage?" asked another little girl, perhaps seven, with straight black hair and brown eyes almost too big for her face.

"That's a person who's kept in a place that they don't want to be," Collie explained. "For a very long time."

That was met with a resounding moment of some serious thinking.

"Who's a hostage here?" Collie asked. "Raise your hand."

They all did, their hands shooting up like a wave of missiles.

"That was easy," the operator said.

Gus supposed it was easy, but then came the questions.

"Are you going to rescue us?" asked a boy of about seven.

"Are you going to take us away?" asked the girl in the green dragon t-shirt.

"Where are the Leather?" another kid asked, and that set off a flurry of voices.

"Did you kill them?"

"Did you?"

"Did you kill them *all*?"

"I hope you did."

"They deserved it."

"They killed my mom and dad!"

"Are you married?"

That one was asked totally without fear, and came from perhaps the youngest, a little boy of no more than six. Who, in the lull of questioning, took the time to earnestly pick his nose.

And then flick it.

Collie and Gus exchanged looks.

"All right," Collie finally said. "You wait right here. We have to talk for a bit, but we'll be back."

That was met with nervous movement and a fluttering of eyelids.

"You're going…" Collie said, trying to dampen that vibe of fear that so suddenly became airborne.

"You're going to a new home," Gus stepped in, saving her. "One that's a few days away, but a nice one. Just as nice as this one, but… with more stuff."

"More stuff?" the little nose picker inquired, wondering if such a thing was possible.

"*Better* stuff," Gus answered.

That changed their tune, and the younger ones of the bunch traded looks Gus hadn't seen for a very long time.

Hope. And *wonder*. With a shake of excitement that only young children could generate, as their imaginations ran with not only what *better* stuff might be out there, but a life without their Leather handlers.

"You just stay here," Collie said. "Just a minute."

She closed the door.

The screaming began almost immediately, as if she were sealing the whole batch of them in an oversized electric oven. The reaction was so unexpected and so jarring that Collie whipped open the door again. The kids fidgeted, red-eyed and staring, recovering from their panic attack.

"Okay," Collie said, nodding at them all. "Okay, I'll leave the door open. How's that? That good? The door's open, but stay here. Uncle Gus and I—"

Gus looked over at her, not completely sure of how to respond to the title.

"—are going down the hall here," Collie continued. "You stay right here and stay quiet."

"No one's feeling sick?" Gus asked out of worry.

Head shakes all around.

"No one needs to use the washroom?"

More head shakes.

"All right, we'll be back."

The pair of them retreated a short way from the room.

"Good thinking," Collie said under her breath. "All I need is one of them shittin' themselves."

"Same here. You're still acting mom, though."

"You kidding? My job is strictly shooting people. In case you haven't noticed, I'm completely *winging* it here."

Kids. A whole pack of kids. And not like little Becky and Chad back on the island. He remembered Shovel had a handful of kids, too, but they didn't have a pack mentality like the ones just discovered in that room. He remembered long gone Toby saying something about kids then, but couldn't quite place the conversation, lost among many.

"Okay, look," Collie said to him. "I don't know how much time we have, which is to say we probably don't have much. Dog Dick's on the way here now. Coming from god-only-knows-where. I got that from a leather head below, just before I killed him. He could be driving up the highway right now for all we know. So this is what's going to happen."

Gus listened, watching her masked face.

"You and Milo are going back to Whitecap. Okay? You take the limo and you go. You go and you don't look back. I'll stay here and make use of my time getting ready for Dog Taint when he and whoever he's got with him comes in the front door. When they do, I'll make them pay. I'll make all them bastards pay."

Gus stared at her, the words sinking in those first few layers. "I'm not going back."

"You're going back."

"I'm not going back."

"You are."

"I'm staying here with you."

"Oh no you're not."

"Oh yes I am, and there's not a damn thing you can do about it."

Collie watched him, his reflection in her sunglasses, the black wool of her balaclava unmoving.

"You gotta go, Gus," in a softer tone. "Milo won't make it on his own."

"You're kidding, right? All that shit you said to him? About his regiment and all that? And now you don't think he can drive a boatload of kids back to Whitecap?"

"That's not the point."

"Well, what is the point, then? You expect me to leave you here all alone? Huh? Just to die? That it, Collie? You want to die all by yourself here?"

That quieted her.

"Look, it's like this…" she started before checking on the children. Gus followed her gaze.

There, out in the hall, nearly a dozen pensive faces watched their discussion.

"Jesus," Gus whispered in annoyance.

"Everything's fine," Collie assured them. "Go back. Go on back. In your room there. Keep the door open. We're just talking a few things out, is all."

The children didn't all turn away at once. The one little ass-scratcher was the first, and as he went, he *again* pinched at his Scooby-Doo pajama bottoms, pulling them free from the crack of his little heiny. He was the brick that got the others moving, and in seconds, the area had cleared.

"They're listening," Gus said. "Just around that corner."

"Can you blame them?" Collie asked.

"Suppose not."

"So, like I was saying. We don't have time. None. I don't have time to argue. You go with Milo and that increases the chance of him reaching Whitecap. That's a hard road to find."

"It's an *easy* road to find," Gus countered. "Shovel's Komatsu truck flattened the damn thing out. All he has to do is follow the yellow brick road with the shit flattened out of it."

"Milo's hurt. He won't be able to drive."

Gus thought about that. "Maybe."

"Gus, you *have* to go. You know how this is going to end."

Feeling the despair rise in his gullet, Gus reached up and took Collie's sunglasses off, so he could look her straight in her own eyes.

"I'm staying here. With you. Whether you like it or not."

They stood that way for moments.

"You stubborn fuck," she said, but her eyes, the eyes of a dead person, sank.

"That's me," Gus admitted and swallowed hard.

They stayed that way for a few more seconds, knowing they shouldn't, but they did anyway.

"We better get the kids ready," he finally said.

"Yeah. You do that. The rest of this place is empty. I'll check on Milo."

With that, Collie limped away. Gus watched her until she turned a corner. He saw her walk. *How the hell is she going to face what's coming in that condition?* he asked himself. And how was he going to make a difference?

They'd find out, he supposed.

With that, Gus went to the open doorway and faced the waiting kids.

There they were, all of them, looking at him with thoughtful expressions. The little ass-scratcher piped up first.

"You *sure* you're not married?"

50

Gus rallied the children, telling them to grab their coats and their shoes or winter boots or whatever was handy and to follow them. A frenzied ten seconds later, which reminded Gus of old Looney Tunes cartoons where the Tasmanian Devil was in full spin-mode, the kids fell in line behind him. The oldest one was also the tallest, a girl named Chrissy. Chrissy had brown hair and sunken eyes, as if she'd seen a lifetime in the span of only hours. She helped marshal the other children, however, becoming his second-in-command, and for that, Gus was thankful.

"How long have you all been here?" Gus asked her at one point.

"A long time. Years. Some of these kids were younger."

"Where are your folks?"

"Dead, probably."

Probably, Gus thought and looked at the others. "Listen. I don't know how long you all been … ah, here. So, just to be clear. You're all good to leave, to go someplace better?"

She widened her eyes. "Oh, yeah. You bet. Those guys were *freaks*."

"I don't doubt it. What about the rest of you?"

A round of energetic nods and earnest *uh-huhs*.

That was all he needed, and really, none of them was going to be left behind, anyway. Gus only asked because it felt right to ask. He didn't ask about parents. From what he'd gotten from Chrissy, and from what he'd seen, the parents were either dead, undead, or broken-will servants. He just hoped he didn't kill any of them on the way in here. That would be the worst. Thoughts aside, he led the children all back to the main living area.

When he turned the corner and saw the dead Leather on his back, still dressed in an apron (which had soaked up some blood) and the broadsword nearby.

Gus stopped and stuck his arm out to halt the parade behind him.

He turned on the kids. "Uh… okay. Look, there's a dead person around the corner, okay? And he's not in the best—"

"You killed Pete?" Chrissy asked, her face lighting up for the first time.

Without waiting for an answer, she darted around Gus. That broke the formation as the others followed her in a rush.

"Ooooh *shit*!" a girl let go. "Grandpa Pete's *dead*!"

"He's not my grandpa," a boy said.

"He's the devil," declared the little girl with the green dragon t-shirt—who now wore a pink coat over it.

"Grandpa Pete?" Gus asked, looking down at the Leather's frilly apron.

"That's what he told us to call him," Chrissy said. "And he *made* us call him that. Even though he dressed like a grandmother from hell."

Without warning, Chrissy reared back and soccer-kicked the corpse in the upper arm, rattling the entire jelly-like mass. Gus waved her back from a follow-up kick. There was a mess around Pete's shot-up head, so Gus placed himself before the Leather as a screen.

"Don't worry mister," a boy said. "We won't get nightmares."

"We *hated* him," said a girl.

Gus supposed they did, figured they'd probably seen worse during their time around the Leather. Still, he remained in place until they all passed the corpse.

Back in the main living area, sitting in the chairs near the big wall-sized windows, Milo and Collie had just finished up a conversation. Probably military shit, Gus thought, and Milo would follow orders. Gus would not, however. He was just a civvie. He'd been reminded of it for so long he didn't mind it anymore. And civvies didn't have to follow orders.

"What're you two talking about?" Gus asked them.

They were sitting in the same place Gus and Milo had been taped to, and Milo was still in his own chair.

"Army shit," Collie replied.

"Figured."

"Kids, don't look at the dead people," she told the children.

"Too late for that," Gus said.

"We saw Grandpa Pete in the hallway!" someone said without a trace of remorse.

"Someone *shot* him!" exclaimed another, and that brought a flurry of *oooooo*'s from the pack.

"Grandpa Pete?" Collie asked, breaking the moment.

"The one in the apron." Gus left it at that.

"Oh. Okay, well, this is what's going to happen," she said, wasting no time. "We get everyone down below, to the limo. Milo says he's good to drive."

At that, the soldier actually nodded. The effort might've taken everything he had, but Gus was glad he didn't smile. A smile from that bloodied and swollen caricature of a face would have scared the youngsters.

"You're good?" Gus asked him.

"Yeah."

One look at Chrissy and the other children, however, suggested they *weren't* good with who was driving. In fact, they were staring hard at Milo. Grandpa Pete might've been a freak, but he wore a mask. Milo's face had pretty much *become* a mask.

"Mister, they fucked you up," Chrissy stated flatly.

Milo did smile, then, and probably couldn't help himself from doing so. It was a short grin, however, probably stopped by a stab of facial pain.

"Don't you worry," Collie said. "Wait 'til you see the car you're going to take a ride in, all the way to your new home."

That didn't brighten any faces, as they were still horrified by Milo.

"Can you even walk?" the boy named Marty said, no longer wearing his Leather uniform but rather a pair of track pants and a *Cookie Monster* sweatshirt.

Milo considered his wrecked foot, the one that might've had a two-ton safe dropped upon it. "No," he answered truthfully. "But I can drive with it. Gas pedal is the right foot."

He wiggled that one.

"And the brake."

Another wiggle.

"This one," he pointed, "is just along for the ride, for now."

"Get him up," Collie said to Gus.

Gus went over to the battered Milo, who offered his good arm. Gus wrapped that around his shoulders, and pulled him onto his feet.

"Might be better on the other side," Milo whispered, giving Gus a whiff of blood.

They switched, awkwardly, but got it done.

"All right," Collie said, taking the HK and removing its magazine. "We're going outside and down the elevator. If you see any guns, let me know first before you pick them up. Everybody good?"

A soft chorus of *yes* and *yeah* came back.

Collie didn't spare the penthouse another look. "Let's go."

She led them to the elevator. Gus struggled with Milo and the children outpaced them. He kept his eyes on the kids and Collie. There was another collective gasp of awe from the children upon seeing the dead guards posted just outside the elevator. Collie had shot them all.

There wasn't enough room to get everyone into the elevator on the first ride, so Gus and Milo waited for the second. They watched the doors close on the masked operator and all those young faces, who didn't seem convinced they were leaving the Four Towers.

The two men stood back from the closed doors, waiting their turn.

"Good," Milo groaned. "Gives us time to talk."

"About what?" Gus asked, watching the numbers light up as Collie and the kids descended.

"I heard what you said to the Leather."

Gus's mind stopped then, and it showed on his face. "Look," he said in a low tone. "I told them some things but—"

"You gave up Whitecap."

Panic clutched at Gus's core, robbing him of speech.

"I don't blame you," Milo said, quietly. "You said some shit in there as well. Probably to scare the Leather off. I could tell. Thing is. The Leather don't scare. At *all*. Hear me?"

"Yeah," Gus replied, knowing that to be true. "So what now?"

For seconds, Milo didn't speak, then, "Nothing."

"You gonna tell her?"

"Stop trying to pull away. I'll fall over if you do. Jesus, you're slippery."

"Sorry. What about the wall?"

"Yeah. Sure."

They righted themselves against the wall, where Gus stood away from the soldier and hefted the shotgun. Both men faced the elevator doors.

"So," Milo began, perhaps struggling with dizziness. "No. I'm not gonna tell. Hell no. 'Course not. What's to tell, anyway? You saw what they did to me, and you didn't want that to happen to you, so you gave them what they wanted. Despite everything, *I* wouldn't want them putting the boots to you either, y'fuckin' dummy." Milo released a tired sigh then. "Look. What I'm tryin' to say is…I don't blame you for talking. For *anything*. Besides, they're all dead. The Leather in there. They ain't… telling anyone. It all worked out. Whitecap's safe. And you? Your secret's safe. With me. I mean… it's *not* a secret. Not really. I'm not getting my words out right. Too many shots to the head. Look. What I'm tryin' to say is…We all fuck up every now and again, right? It happens. No matter who we are. Despite our best intentions. You understand?"

Gus turned his head in Milo's direction, meeting the soldier's bloodshot gaze and the black crusts of dried matter coating his battered, swollen face. There was an unspoken message in there, one meant for him alone and one that Gus did indeed understand.

Yeah… I shot Collie. But I was forced to at the time. You understand that now, right?

"Yeah," Gus finally released. "We all fuck up. Every now and again."

Milo managed a nod, one that clearly hurt him. "We're good, then?"

"We're good."

"Thanks. Means… a lot."

Gus nodded then. "Yeah. Me too. Thanks."

Milo held out a fist then.

After a moment's hesitation, Gus met it with one of his own.

With that out of the way, they stood and listened, eyes on the elevator door.

We all fuck up every now and again, Gus thought. *Despite our best intentions. Goddamn if that ain't the truth.*

When the elevator car returned, Milo surprised Gus by reaching out for his shoulder. Gus didn't mention the blood dribbles left by the soldier's ruined foot and other parts. Instead, he ensured that the soldier got aboard without trouble, and helped him to the nearest corner. Once they were aboard, Gus thumbed the ground floor button, and stood guard on the other side of the closing doors.

The lurch of the moving elevator caused Milo to grunt.

"Okay over there?" Gus asked.

"Yeah."

Quiet then.

"We got bandages on board the limo, right?" Milo asked.

"I think so."

"Gonna need more than one roll of gauze this time."

Gus nodded in agreement at that.

"And a shitload of medical tape, too," Milo added.

"They certainly fucked you up," Gus noted in a quiet voice.

"Yeah," the soldier agreed. "But I'm the one walking away."

They exchanged looks then, and the looks became spotty smiles.

"Think there's any painkiller?" Milo asked.

"Don't know. Don't think you should take any, either. You got a long drive ahead."

"Yeah. That's right. Well… damn."

"Unless that little one called Chrissy drives every once in a while."

"That the tall one?"

"Yeah."

Milo nodded, dabbing at his mouth, and wincing at the contact. "Don't worry. I'll drive the limo."

The doors opened, and Collie and the children were only ten feet away from them, in the lobby. There were dead Leather all around, spread out on the marble floor and draped over lobby sofas. One had collapsed upon the front desk, splayed over the wood and strewn stationary. Another was behind the desk, sitting on his ass and slumped over, with at least two bloody holes in his chest. Yet another Leather was dead and gone behind a huge fern, with only his two feet sticking up, filling the parted V among the greenery. Splashes of red coated sections of the floor and furniture.

Both men took in the scene with expressions of wonder.

"Christ, Collie," Gus finally said. "You feeling better or something?"

"Feeling better," she answered. "Hurry now. Who knows how much time we got."

"What time is it anyway?"

"Two forty-six!" a girl bundled up in a winter coat said and pointed to a huge wall clock.

Weapons were scattered across the floor, not far from where the dead had dropped them.

"You'll have to come back for them," Collie said, reading his mind. "Once we get the limo figured out."

The limo was a *mess*.

There were three dead Leather on the way to the trapped car, and another just outside of the driver's door. There were three more heaped inside the rear door Gus usually used, and by the looks on their faces, the blood grossed the children out.

"Just drag them outta there and dump them," Collie directed, leaning against the limo's side.

Gus helped Milo inside the driver's side first.

"You got—" he was going to ask Collie, who held out the fob. Gus took them and handed them over to Milo.

"You *can* drive, right?" Gus asked him.

"Fuck off."

Taking that as a yes, Gus backed off, but with a smirk. He dragged the bodies away, not far, and dumped them on the divider lines of the road. The last one he lugged over caught his eye. The man wore a plain mask, with black paint around his eyes, but he also had a winter scarf wrapped around his neck. A very bloody winter scarf, which puzzled him because of the twin gunshot holes in his chest.

Gus checked on the activity around the limo, then slowly dropped to a creaky knee. He pulled at the knot, tied tight at the neck, and lowered it just enough to...

"Hey, Gus."

He straightened, springing off mostly one leg, and felt his lower back as he did so.

Collie, half out of the limo, was pulling out the life-sized cardboard cutout of Captain Morgan. The good captain had, unfortunately, taken a round to the chin. Gus wavered for a moment, unsure of how to proceed, when he sighed. *First thing's first*, he decided, and realized the limo was going to be filled with children very soon. So he took the Captain out, dragged it away from the car, and placed the display in the best place possible—the street corner. When he'd done that, he patted the officer fondly on the shoulder, steadied him, and let him be.

He wasn't *the* Captain, but the figure had been his for a short time.

There was still the problem of the pickups, blocking the rear of the limo.

"Here," Collie said, and produced three more key fobs.

Gus did a double take and grabbed them all.

The next few minutes consisted of him matching up the fobs with their machines and then moving the pair trapping the limo. Gus did it all. Once finished, he spent another frantic ten minutes gathering up the excess weapons that had been taken by the Leather and brought them back to the limo. Every tick of the clock was on his mind, and he checked the surroundings often, just to make sure the Dog Tongue wasn't already there with reinforcements.

"Don't touch," he warned the children of the guns he brought back and placed inside the limo. Collie had already put Chrissy and whoever could hold a disinfectant wipe to scrub down the blood spatters on the seats. The killings had only happened in the business class section, leaving the jazzy Sci-Fi area clean.

"You got plenty to eat back there," Gus told them all. "There's cheeseburgers and calzone."

"What's a calzone?" the nose-picker asked.

"What's a cheeseburger?" asked the little girl in the green dragon t-shirt.

Gus blinked at the questions. Given their young ages, he realized, they were right in asking. They wouldn't know what those things were.

And that shit damn near made him cry.

"You'll see," he told them. "And I'll think you'll like it."

Collie had pulled herself aboard and was loading a duffel bag full of ammunition and other essential supplies. When she had what she wanted, she got back out with the help of the children and met Gus outside.

"All done?" she asked.

"Yeah."

"All right then." She limped around to face the expectant expressions inside the limo, mostly in the business class section, but with a few sticking their heads out of the lounge area. "This is where I say goodbye. Sorry we couldn't have talked more. You're going to a good place. A better place. Maybe a little scary on the outside, but you'll see. And no one is dressed up for Halloween all year round. Okay?"

A few of them nodded, while the rest said nothing. Some looked uncertain, and one looked lost, as if he hadn't been outside in a very long time. Perhaps he hadn't. Gus recognized him as the little boy who had asked if he and Collie were married. Even as he remembered, the kid started picking his nose again.

Before tucking that finger away in a coat pocket.

"Okay," Collie finished. "Good talk. You take care. Be careful. Listen to your Uncle Milo, and do what he says. He won't hurt you."

No, Gus didn't think Uncle Milo would hurt them.

There were no waves or goodbyes as Collie closed the door. She lurched over to the driver's side where Milo had lowered the window. As gruesome as his injuries were, he'd settled in just fine in the driver's seat, right hand and foot where they were supposed to be. As long as he drove carefully and was watchful of the snow, he should be fine. The soldier had the seat adjusted back just a little, to stretch out his arm while driving.

"Got a full charge?" she asked.

Milo checked. "Eighty-eight percent."

"That's a start. You hit the highway and don't look back. You clear on the systems?"

"The basics, yeah," he replied.

"No time for anything else," Collie said without apology. "You don't have any major boom-boom. I used it all. But you still got the small stuff, and the limo itself. Just be careful of snow on the roads. You *can* see the road, right?"

That cracked a smile, and because his lips were swollen and disfigured, that smile appeared mutated.

"You sure you want me driving these kids back to Whitecap?" Milo asked. "Considering my past?"

"You mean that part with Jake whasisface and the rest of the circus?"

"Yeah."

"I don't remember any of that shit. You're a different Milo now. The *real* Milo. Besides, where else you gonna go?"

His lumpy and lacerated brow shrugged in a *suppose so*, but then he got serious. "I'll get them to Whitecap. Don't you worry."

"I know you will. Get going." She turned to leave.

"Collie."

She stopped, her sunglasses meeting his gaze.

"Thanks. For everything. Especially… the second chance."

"Watch your jingle-jangle, cowboy."

She stepped back, and Gus moved in close to the driver's side. "Fuckin' hate long goodbyes," he grumped.

"Yeah." Milo's bloodshot eyes narrowed. "Y'know, you never did tell me the name of your dentist."

"You sure you want him working on you?"

"Nah."

Gus smirked. "Watch them youngsters, Milo. Get them back."

"You still got time to jump aboard."

"I very much agree with that," Collie said from behind.

Gus wouldn't have it, however. "No. I'm staying here. Hold the line and all that."

Milo appeared to want to say more, but gave up on the thought. So Gus said it for him. "You be careful, Milo. Keep out of trouble."

"Yeah. Later."

Gus then visibly struggled, because this next part was hard for him. "Ah look. I, ah, never officially…"

"I forgive you," Milo said.

That stopped Gus cold.

"For everything," the soldier added.

And damned if those words lifted an unseen weight from Gus's conscience.

Gus leaned back, sighed, and nodded. "You're all right, Milo."

Milo looked to the dash and back again. "You're all right, too. Give 'em hell when they get here."

The battered soldier smiled then and raised the window.

Seconds later, the armored giant powered up, the lights flaring to life and staying that way. Then the limo was reversing, edging past the two pickups that had previously trapped it. Milo got clear and continued to back up until he slowly swung the limo into a three-point turn. The brake lights flashed again, briefly, and then winked off as he got the machine pointed forward and drove away, picking up speed on the straight strip.

Gus and Collie watched them go until the machine was out of sight.

"Feel like we missed the bus," he said quietly.

"You had your chance," Collie said.

They looked at each other for several seconds.

"Something on your mind?" she asked.

"Yeah," he said, and pointed a thumb in the direction of that one dead Leather with the scarf around his neck. "I, ah, found something over there."

"The guy I bit into?"

That stopped him colder than Milo forgiving him.

"Figured," she said. "Thanks for not bringing it up until the kids got away."

Gus stared at her and opened his mouth to finally say something.

Collie held up a hand.

He waited, still not understanding.

She pointed to the south. "You hear that?"

51

A mechanical rumbling perked Gus's ears, pulling his attention toward the closed-off streets.

He then turned to the high steel frames of the dump trucks, hearing the approaching charge of the Dog Tongue.

"Dog Dick," he said.

Collie grabbed her weapons. She stopped and stared at him. "Last chance to get out."

He was scared. His heart rate was already racing. The sound of the approaching Leather, perhaps even the final round, frightened him. She saw that easily. He couldn't hide it. She probably smelled it off him.

But he wasn't going to leave her. "How are we gonna do this?"

"We go at them."

"What?"

"Follow me," she said, as she led him to the front dump truck. She reached up, opened the door, and gestured at the five-foot climb to the cab. Gus hauled himself up, his foot nagging at him all the way. He pulled himself into the cab, clanging his shotgun off the door frame while doing so. A quick scramble across the armrest and cup holders, and he was in the passenger side. Through the chipped windshield, there was a cleared street to the south, behind the trucks. It looked like a straight run through the city.

Collie moved up behind him and landed hard in the driver's seat. She reached up for the sun visor, and the key fob dropped down.

"Thank God for practical bad guys," she said and tossed the thing in the cupholder. She started up the truck and lashed herself in with the seatbelt. Her rifle was tucked by her door.

"You're gonna charge them?" Gus asked.

Collie checked her mirrors. "Yup."

"Jesus Christ—what about digging in somewhere around here?"

"Didn't you do that before? Back at that warehouse?"

"Yeah."

"And how'd that work out?"

"Not so good," he said.

"Yeah, well, this time? I'm driving. So hold onto your boys."

With that, Collie put the big machine in gear. It wasn't the Komatsu titan of old, but rather a brutish hog of war—fat, yet muscular, and made of steel. A ten-wheel battering ram when you thought about it. Riding high, some seven feet off the ground, Gus stared down at the street to the south.

"We can't dig in, anyway," Collie said as she eased the ten-ton truck ahead. "My superpowers are fading. Seems like taking a bite of someone? Only perks you up for a short time."

That whipped Gus's head around.

"Yeah," she said. "And a part of me thinks Wallace knew."

There was a single car below her, filling the gap between the truck's bumper and the corner of the building. She clipped the rear of the car and rudely shoved it aside in a snark of collapsing fiberglass.

"We're gonna stick and jab until we can't anymore," Collie said. "And when that happens, we do the urban warfare."

She floored the accelerator. Needles did somersaults. Lights flashed into existence. The truck cleared its mechanical throat, smelling a fight on the air and welcoming it. Even the *sound* of the thing was warthog mean. Finally, after an existence of servitude, the chance to hit things.

The machine lurched forward with a motorized chuffing that was positively eager. The jolt shoved the two occupants back in their seats.

"Right now," Collie said, sizing up the road, "we're in the best rig for that job."

"Stick and jab," Gus said, shoving the Ram Fist against the door.

"Until we can't no more."

They steamed on down the cleared highway, through a corridor of dying, flittering sunlight. The side streets to the east were blocked with cars, but not so on the west side.

Gus thought about it. The west side was already conquered. East was the front.

Collie pointed.

Speeding towards them was the lead vehicle for the Dog Tongue.

It was another big truck. A tractor trailer, with a snowplow fixed to its lower face.

And strapped to the machine's hood was what appeared to be a skull. With horns.

Not a dog skull but another buffalo skull.

"That look like a warlord's ride to you?" Collie asked.

"Yup."

"Hang on then."

Gus glanced over at her, wanting to ask, but scared to do so. He was beside her, though, riding shotgun, and there was nowhere else he wanted to be.

The tractor trailer with the buffalo skull barreled down the avenue towards them, the face of it a stern thing. Chrome and steel sprouted from the machine, and behind it, other vehicles followed.

Collie sped up.

Gus braced himself.

The space between the machines rapidly dwindled.

The dump truck trembled from the shift in gears and its increasing speed. The tractor trailer with the buffalo skull grew in size and clarity, racing up the middle of the downtown core. Smoke erupted from twin stacks, as if simultaneously rolling up its sleeves in anticipation of the blood soon to follow, and pooh-poohing the dump truck's charge. Sunlight glared off the machine's windshield. Gus pushed himself further back into his seat, unable to take his eyes off the unflinching collision course.

Collie flexed her fingers on the wheel.

"One thing about being dead," she said over the rising engine noise. "Makes it easier to play chicken."

Doing maybe a hundred klicks an hour and knowing she wasn't about to turn the wheel, Gus screamed for them both when the two brutish transports were seconds away from a very violent meeting of minds.

Then the world shifted.

The tractor trailer *pulled* to the right. A red signpost bounced off the hood then whirled and twanged off the nearest smoke stack. Gus thought he glimpsed a masked driver, bent low and gripping the steering wheel like some thirteenth-century helmsman piloting a merchant vessel through a killer storm. The tractor trailer's profile flashed by the dump truck in a savage white and silver blur. Pipes followed, then the long container unit attached to the main engine.

Gus continued to scream, because even though the tractor trailer was veering away, the *trailer* behind it was a long one and Collie was still accelerating.

The end of the trailer, the corner, clipped the side mirror, whipping it into her window hard enough to transform the entire pane into a crystal spiderweb. Gus screamed at the connection, but the dump truck's path did not change. Collie drove that hog of industrial might straight into the surprised masses following the lead truck. The steel bumper smashed the hip of a pickup truck too slow to swerve. The four Leather in its box bed flew from the machine. One of them got smacked broadside by the dump truck before twisting, falling out of sight. Gus shrieked at the connection as the last of his teeth clapped together. The pickup whirled into a gut-wringing tailspin, disappearing in a cloud of dust.

That was the one that convinced the rest of the oncoming parade.

Collie meant business.

Pickups turned hard to the left and right, escaping destruction by seconds and inches. Tires shrieked in ear-splitting notes. A mailbox exploded and blurred past a pickup truck's hood in a nose cone of debris, only to bounce in roly-poly arcs down the street. A wide storefront window exploded from unseen projectiles. The swerving trucks were the lowest of the Leather's vehicles, the jackals, and Gus could see right over their roofs. Farther back, three fuel tankers swung themselves up and onto the sidewalk, easily seeing the developing situation and wanting no part. They left the main street to reveal *more* pickups, even a bus, and even—and Gus's eyes widened at the sight of the thing—a huge recreational vehicle.

It was the Anchor Bay equivalent on eight wheels. Gray and white and scratched, with what appeared to be an actual seating area on the roof, behind a spike partition of sorts. Gus couldn't believe his eyes, because, at a glance, the crowning chair appeared to be a huge throne of bones. Right on the RV's goddamn roof.

And that rectangular juggernaut, with the responsive handling equaling that of the dump truck, wanted no part of the thing charging at its face.

Its driver decided to do something about it.

The mobile hotel swung its ponderous girth over, getting the hell out of the dump truck's wrath. It actually rear-ended a smaller pickup and sent the vehicle crashing through the front of a deserted coffee shop in an audible pop of glass and metal.

Then Gus and Collie were past them all, on a length of road that might've stretched all the way to the US border itself. The buildings on either side shrank in height as if being dosed with killer radiation. Gus remembered to breathe. He drew in several lungfuls as Collie stared ahead, fixed on the driving.

"Holy shit," he gasped, his gaze repeatedly darting between the street and her profile. "Holy shit!"

Collie bent over the wheel.

"Gus," she said in a commanding voice, shaking her head as if absorbing an electric chair's worth of current.

He waited for more, then he sensed it.

Something terribly wrong.

"Remember…the *mission*…," Collie got out, her voice straining, her shoulders twisting as if gripped by a seizure.

She slammed on the brakes, and the whole rig went into a vicious lurch as all that fabricated mass steamed forward. Only Gus's seatbelt stopped him from flying headfirst into the windshield. Collie controlled all that bulk, however, and the dump truck came to a long and screeching halt.

In his side mirror, Gus could see the lead elements of the Dog Tongue's armada turning around, intending to pursue.

"What's wrong?" Gus shouted, *pleaded*, even though he knew.

"*GET OUT!*" she raged back.

Just before the shakes overtook her.

If she was sitting in an electric chair before, then a full frying current ripped through her now.

Oh no, Gus thought. She was going over. To the other side. The mindless side. And even as he thought it, Collie reared up as if realizing she was sitting very close to him. She lunged at him across the armrest, fingers scrabbling across the dashboard, her right arm shooting out like a drunk viper.

Gus swatted aside the arm. He pressed himself against his door, hearing her feral grunts and growls. Her jaws snapped, biting at the balaclava covering her face, and the area covering her mouth became a moist patch of blackness. Staring at her, gasping, and pawing at the door, Gus's fingers hooked the handle.

The door swung open and he tumbled, ass-over-head, onto the street from a still-moving vehicle. The shotgun fell away, rattling off the steely hide. He landed on his side with a stunning crunch, the right side of his face scrubbing asphalt. The dump truck rolled on but was slowing down—no longer enraged, no longer seeking to bash any and all comers.

But he could hear her. For seconds he could hear her yowling, snarling, trapped by her seatbelt and unable to free herself. Her voice lessened as the truck continued on, becoming a haunting thing. Gus rolled onto his back, attempting to rise but still stunned from his fall. He got to his hands and knees as the dump truck finally drubbed its face against the steel column of a streetlight.

Where it actually rolled back a foot or so, parting its own plumes of exhaust.

Gus got to his feet, his hands going to his thighs, and instinctively looked behind him.

Pickup trucks.

Perhaps a half dozen of them, all bearing down on him.

With one last fleeting glance at the smoking dump truck, Gus croaked in misery and stumbled into a run for the nearest alley. His foot squeezed out angry pulses of pain with every step, but his new enemies were his knees, no longer as stable as before, as wobbly and off-kilter as dented bicycle rims. He reached the alley, missed tripping up in a pile of shattered crates, and chugged towards a 'U' of light at the alley's end. Light he hoped meant escape. There were closed doors on either side of him, red and gray, streaking past but not offering knobs or latches.

Tires screeched behind him. Boots landed on the ground.

Gus didn't look back, didn't go for his Glock which he still had. The alley ended, but a chain link fence ran on either side. Too high to climb, so he kept on running while the sounds of pursuit urged him to keep chugging.

End of the fence, where he had the choice of climbing *another* fence directly before him or going right or left. He chose left, racing between the back doorways of shops on his right, and empty parking lots on his left. There were doors, and he ran to them, his chest again warning him that it was doing overtime.

He tried the nearest door in the parking lot, a black one in the center of a wide, two-story structure. The door was locked. He ripped the Glock from its holster, aimed at the knob, and fired.

Missed. A sinewy hole appeared above the knob.

"Jesus," Gus gasped, and aimed again. He fired three times, and the last bullet ricocheted past him, close enough to make him flinch.

He grabbed the door as shadows closed in on him.

He whipped the door open and plunged through. He twisted as he went, seeking to cut down his pursuers as they came through the doorway.

A heavy mass crashed into him, plowing into his side and nearly bending him into a 'V'.

Gus went down but still held onto his sidearm. He twisted to see what appeared to be a giant glossy leech covering him. An arm, twice the size of his own, shot out and grabbed his wrist. What felt like a hundred pounds of pressure pressed down on his fingers, and that brittle, close-to-breaking sensation of pain caused him to cry out.

That crushing grip slammed Gus's mitt against the floor until he gave up the gun.

Then the leech reared up, climbing over Gus until a morbid black thing with metal studs lifted itself above his face. A huge hand seized Gus's jaw, pushing his face aside, putting ungodly tension to his neck.

But he could see what held him from the corner of his eye.

A huge man dipped in silver knobs and leather.

Then an elbow smashed across Gus's face, knocking him out cold.

*

The Dog Tongue stepped out of his pickup, boot heels clicking off the pavement. His chin was almost level with the roof of the vehicle, and for long moments he stared at the dump truck pressed up against the base of the streetlight. Leather-clad figures emerged from the pickups parked near the great machine and raced after the one trying to escape on foot. Others stayed back, however, drawn to the driver's side.

The hounds, The Dog Tongue thought. *Release the hounds.*

The Dog Tongue could hear the noise from where he stood. He rolled his shoulders, sniffed hard, and withdrew a step, past the rear door of the crew cab. The door opened. He held out a hand with spikes decorating the knuckles. A prong was placed into that waiting hand— three points filed down to deadly sharpness.

The Dog tongue snorted, swallowed snot, and strolled towards the dump truck as if he were on a beach instead of downtown Regina. The prong's sharpened tips dragged on pavement behind him. He didn't care. Wasn't worried about attracting attention. He casually glanced in the direction his hounds had gone, sparing the alley only a second of his time. As he approached the front of the machine, the Leather encircling the driver's side pulled back.

The yowling coming from the cab died away.

The Dog Tongue ignored his lessers. He focused on the driver's door and lifted his weaponized prong, striking a farmer's pose, one ready to heave a bale of hay. One of the Leather gripped the door's latch. The Dog Tongue sighed and then nodded.

The lesser pulled the door open.

An assault rifle fell to the road, startling several of the Leather, but failing to fire.

The Dog Tongue didn't flinch, sizing up the thing in the driver's seat.

There, kept in place by a seatbelt, was one of the mindless.

A woman. She wore army-issue camouflage, and she'd chewed her way through the black ski mask she wore, revealing a fine set of teeth. She stayed there, staring straight ahead as if bound in a straitjacket, before swinging her wild gaze upon the Dog Tongue. The sight of him reanimated the mindless one and she lunged.

Her fingers stopped not four inches from the Dog Tongue's unflinching face before she fell out of the cab. She clacked her face and upper torso against the truck's side, the seatbelt keeping her from falling any further. There she hung, awkwardly, twisting and clawing for the living.

The Dog Tongue stepped back, avoiding her hands. He studied her for a moment, noticing the missing nose, not that it surprised him. A missing piece of flesh was nothing these days, especially when compared to the horrors he'd seen over the years.

She was a wild one, however, continuing her attempts to grab him.

He sniffed a couple of times, however, wondering where the stink of deodorant was coming from, and realized it was the mindless.

He motioned at the Leather.

They swarmed her, taking control of her arms while they pulled her armored vest off. They retreated with their prize, which would go to one of the faithful.

The mindless still hung from the cab.

Remembering his prong, the Dog Tongue guided it past her arms. She still had her legs, and, overall, she appeared intact, so he didn't want to ruin anything that might rob her of her mobility. Wholly intact bodies were increasingly difficult to come by.

She swung at him, trying to latch onto his knee.

The Dog Tongue pressed the prong to her back, pushing, pinning her against the metal steps which led up and into the cab. The mindless stopped moving, as if wondering what was happening.

Like a bored crab fisherman, the Dog Tongue sank the prong through her back, spearing her, sinking those three individual blades all the way through the right side of her chest. It was a slow stabbing, unhurried and precise, until the tips popped out the other side. He thought he felt a brief scraping sensation as he pushed through but dismissed it as nothing of consequence. The Leather overlord flexed mighty shoulders then, and forcefully pulled her a foot more out the cab, stretching the mindless out and rendering her all but helpless.

Whereupon he glanced at the lessers around him.

Two of them came in from the sides, seizing the woman's arms. Others moved in, and duct tape was stretched out and applied. There were other firearms with her, including a pistol, which were quickly taken. When his minions secured the intact mindless, the Dog Tongue put a heavy boot to her spine and extracted his prong. When he was clear, two of the lessers hurried in with a length of shag carpet. They rolled her within, trapping her completely. She calmed down, to a twitching, near-lifeless thing, which puzzled the Dog Tongue. That, and the fact that he didn't understand how a zombie could drive a truck.

Unless she was a decoy, but even that seemed improbable.

The commotion coming from the back alley failed to distract the Dog Tongue from this puzzle, but he soon gave up trying to figure it out. It didn't really matter. Not really. He'd seen strange things during the apocalypse. A mindless behind the wheel of a dump truck would be another memory to later ponder over.

His lessers finished securing the zombie and lugged her off to the transport truck.

Once they were gone, he slowly turned in the direction of the Four Towers.

The hounds, he thought. *The hounds.*

52

A hand slapped Gus. He tried to play dead, but the hand slapped him twice more, powerful shots as if the owner were playing racquetball with his head.

Gus rolled with it, grimaced, and opened his eyes.

And immediately lowered his head in disgusted disbelief.

"Fuck me," he whispered, seeing how he was, once again, taped to a chair. It took him only a moment to realize that he was in the very same chair that Vampire Joe had used.

Boots then, strolling across the floor, coming closer. A shadow fell across him, and Gus didn't want to look up. Really didn't want to look up.

But he did.

Sitting in the same chair Milo once occupied while being prepped for an unwilling blood donation, was a man.

A big man.

Sitting before a glossy window that reflected the various light fixtures turned on in the penthouse room. The lights were dimmed to a soft orange, creating long shadows everywhere, but Gus had no trouble noticing the place where Vampire Joe had perished on the floor. The Vampiric One's carcass was missing, no doubt dragged away, but then there was another problem facing Gus.

The Dog Tongue—or the man he suspected was the Dog Tongue—sat and watched him. Draped in leather, right down to the dusty motorcycle boots, which Gus had to admit, were actually pretty cool. Dread gripped him then, as he sized up the rest of the figure, draped in layers of black. What might've been a vest was underneath all those layers, going all the way to a bearded chin. The chin and the mouth were the only things visible, as the rest of the head was covered in an executioner's mask. After seeing so many masks, this one seemed rather plain. The skin around the eyes was smeared in soot, or so it appeared, but the eyes themselves were blowtorched cavities occupied by the barest sliver of light.

Worse, the man didn't seem to breathe.

"Dog Tongue?" Gus asked, feeling how his hands were taped to the armrests again.

The big man didn't move.

But someone moved beside Gus.

He shifted, and a walking bear of a man loomed over him, wearing the same fashionable gear the Leather favored. A pig mask covered his face, the meaty snout protruding from a deep cowl. Gus couldn't see any eyes and swallowed uneasily in spite of himself.

Gus cleared his throat. "Hello," he said quietly, deciding that best behavior would be the wise thing to do.

The Pig didn't move, didn't say a word, but both hands were covered in the same armored gauntlets similar to the pair Gus once owned long ago.

"Were you driving the truck?" the Dog Tongue asked in a smoky voice, pleasing to the ears but perhaps overused from screaming. Thus far, however, the leader wasn't loud at all. In fact, he sounded oddly familiar. Beyond him, the dead city rose up beyond the glass.

"No."

"Your friend was?"

Gus sighed. "Yeah."

"And she turned?"

He nodded and looked to his knees. "Yeah."

Silence then, long and unsettling, then, "Shame."

That one word rustled free a memory and Gus looked up at the Dog Tongue.

"What did you say?" he asked, and immediately braced himself for the Pig.

The Pig did nothing, however.

"Shame," the Dog Tongue repeated.

Gus searched the corners of his mind, back when there was live television. He stared at the man sitting across from him, and realized he *knew* him. Not personally, but he knew *of* him.

"You…" Gus whispered. "I know you."

The Dog Tongue said nothing.

"Just gimme a minute to remember."

Then the most disturbing thing happened. The Dog Tongue leaned forward, hands clasped at his waist, as if taking a greater interest in his captive. His mouth opened, and this... *thing* rolled out of his face. It was a tongue, make no mistake. Long and wet and livid. It hung out of the Dog Tongue's face for seconds, before he sucked it back in.

"That help?" the Dog Tongue asked.

"Holy shit," Gus exclaimed softly and stared. "I know you. You're that one... that guy from that wrestling company. The west coast one. I see you on the sports channels all the time. Or I saw you. Used to, anyway. In advertisements, for coming events. That sorta thing. Never could afford those pay-per-views."

None of that got a reaction from the Dog Tongue.

"Yeah, what was your name?" Gus continued. "Pit Bull? Malone?"

"Murphy," corrected the Dog Tongue.

"Murphy. Right. So that's you? I mean, you're him? I never watched, you understand. A friend of mine watched you. All the time. Would quote you, too, every now and again. 'Shame,' he'd say, if, say, we fucked up on the job. Shame, shame, shame. Or if he was just joking around on them rare occasions. Shame. Yeah. Wow."

Nothing. No reaction. He might've been addressing an inanimate golem.

"Did you kill Vampire Joe?" the Dog Tongue asked.

Gus didn't answer right away, fearing the worst. "My... friend did," he finally said.

"Where is he?"

"She's... the one driving the truck."

"The mindless?"

That stuck a jagged spear of blue ice through Gus's chest. "Yeah."

"She changed while driving?"

She did indeed. "Yeah."

The Dog Tongue stared at him. "How did that happen?"

"It's a long story."

"And you jumped free. To get away from her?"

Gus nodded. Barely.

The Dog Tongue became silent for a short time, letting the moment drag out. "Did you kill the Bear Trap? And the Samurai?"

Gus blinked and fidgeted. "Yeah. We did."

"You killed all of them?"

"Yeah. I think."

The Dog Tongue leaned back, leather rustling, creaking, those cavernous holes in his face studying his prisoner.

Gus felt the need to change the subject. "I, uh, did see you once. In one of them battleground competitions. On a Saturday night freebie. I think it was two months after the event, but, whatever, right? Saw it over at my buddy's place. Thirty guys in the ring, where you were eliminated by being chucked over the top rope? That's gotta hurt, no matter how scripted it was."

The Dog Tongue cocked his head.

"I mean," Gus continued, not sensing the danger, "you were all big guys but if you were doing that for real? Fuck. Seriously. *Clothes*line? *Back*breaker? I mean, the leg locks *alone*. Someone would die or end up in the hospital every weekend. Really."

One of the Pig's hands looped around Gus's throat and squeezed, pinching off his windpipe. Gus gargled nonsense, overwhelmed by pain and the need to draw breath. His face bloomed red. Then borderline purple. The Pig kept on squeezing, squeezing as if holding an orange and looking for juice.

"It was real," the Dog Tongue explained, watching the show. "All of it. As real as the hand choking you now."

The Pig released Gus in a dismissive shove. He gasped for air, sucking it down in great gulps. He horked and spat, cleared his throat and spat again, covering himself in white gobs. His throat stung, creaked and bobbed, but air never tasted so good.

Gus leaned back and took great whooping breaths, glaring red eyes at the Dog Tongue.

"Bullshit," he finally said. "*Real* my ass. That's always the argument all you fuckers make. Sure, it's real. Get in the ring, I'll show you. Yeah. Right. Get in and suddenly thirty percent power goes up to seventy. Or more, I bet, if anyone had the balls to do it. Hell, if you *really* took a disliking to the guy, I bet you went balls—"

The Pig clamped down on his throat again, and Gus grimaced and squirmed under the pressure.

"It was all real," the Dog Tongue said, his surprisingly patient voice barely heard in that dimly lit room. "To us. Day in. Day out. All those moves. All that pain. One thing no one understood if you weren't in the business, we were legit athletes. Legit. Sure, we worked at half power, but the bones still break. As does the skin. Mistakes happen. I didn't get through six months without injuring myself somehow. Bruises. Cuts. Concussions. Torn ligaments. Blown out ACLs. Broken bones. Gouged *eyes*. Ruptured *balls*. *All* real. If it wasn't me, it was someone else in the show. If you were there, you'd know about the pain, but you weren't, so you don't know *shit*. No one watching knew, unless we *told* them. You wanna know what's real? I'll tell you. Anyone else? Any of you screaming, saggy tit sofa-shits watching from your living room? You'd be *killed* in the ring if we used fucking *five* percent power. Us? We trained for the pain. Conditioned for it. Got fucking *paid* to do it. Day-in and day-fucking-out. We were the *shit*."

The Pig released Gus, and the intake of air was loud and messy.

"But you know something?" the Dog Tongue asked. "That's not why I despise people like you. And you, I mean, people in general. Viewers. So called fans. You know the word 'fan' is short for fanatic? Never knew that until I got into the business. Fanatic. Believe you me, I know about fanatics. There's the good and the bad. The bad are the pieces of shit thinking they know better. The gut-swinging, shit crusted know-it-alls, the authorities on *everything*, who criticize everything, and how quick they jump on you if given the chance. Seen it happened all the time. Seen it happen in seconds. How a scripted good guy loses the crowd and gets shit on, or a scripted bad guy wins and the crowds suddenly love him. Loyalties switch fast. So fast. Faster than what it would take for me to stick my thumb in your eye and give your skull a good old-fashion swirl. Just like that."

Oh sweet Jesus, Gus thought, not moving a muscle.

"I was a good guy in the show," the Dog Tongue went on, "until I decided to change. Pulled a Dewy. Went from good to bad. Roughest six months I ever went through. I was spit at. Spit *on*. Drinks poured over my head. Pelted with cans and cups. Death threats. All from *fanatics*. Not real fans at all. Just little shits that didn't understand the show, but they *thought* they knew. Little out-of-shape shits who thought themselves hard in some make-believe world. Who thought they could choke out anyone's ass after watching hours of that MMA shit. Who thought the wrestlers of the day were… characters. In a book."

The Dog Tongue paused for effect. "That's why I do this. That's why I do *all* of this. Every last drop. There's a new reality, and I mean to impose it on *all* you whiney little dog shits. One by fucking one."

Gus straightened in the seat, and his mouth went off. "All while in costume, too, I suppose."

"You got it," the Dog Tongue said. "All while in costume. In our time together, you'll see. You'll understand. This thing? My uniform. You'll see. Everyone who wears one? They're *fans*. *True* fans. Drop everything and stick their thumb in their own eye and root around, right on command. Scary, huh?

But that's a fanatic. That's *loyalty*. You're going to have plenty of time to think about that. You see, just before I stuck a foot of prong through the Spider's ass, he told me everything about the 'soldiers' coming after me. Soldiers. I've met a few soldiers over the years, and I wasn't overly impressed. But then the Spider told me about Fort Jay, and how a *super* soldier took out all his Leather. Got me all worked up, to tell the truth. And now, seeing who you all are? I'm disappointed. But just a little."

At that, he held up a hand and pinched at the air.

"See, he figured you came from somewhere, and that there's others. And there's weapons. That interests me a *lot*. You're going to show me where they are."

"Like fuck," Gus got out, but a part of him remembered how he buckled with Vampire Joe.

"Shhhh," the Dog Tongue hushed. "You're just making it worse for yourself. Really. You'll see. There's roughly four or five thousand kilometers to go, and winter's coming on. Temps around zero during the day. I think you'll tell me everything I want to know. After about fifty klicks strapped to the hood of my ride. The wind burn alone should be something. You'll be pinker than a baby's dick."

Gus swallowed at that.

"Yeah," the Dog Tongue said and stood, rising well over six feet tall. "Thought that would shut you up. Strapped down to the hood. Wearing nothing more than your shitty-assed whiner drawers. Just like from those *Mad Max* movies. You'll appreciate the pain those actors went through when we hit the first pothole. Did I say fifty klicks? Nah. You'll be singing after ten, I imagine. You got that look. Breakable, I mean. *Easily* breakable. You break enough assholes, you get a sense for these things."

The towering warlord moved to the nearby piano, where he picked up a weaponized prong.

"You think about that, while you're sitting there all night. Hell, all night in that chair? Strapped down like you are? If you've never done it before, you're in for a treat. A real treat. That might be enough to break you. Especially when you shit and piss yourself. You'll be good and stiff in the morning. He—" the Dog Tongue nodded at his imposing henchman. "Might look like a pig, but I guarantee you, *you'll* squeal like a pig by tomorrow morning, when he peels you off that chair. Won't take long for you to realize that tonight? Tonight wasn't bad at all. Hell, tonight was a stay in a nice hotel. Trust me on that. I gotta sense for these things."

He walked around his prisoner.

"'Course," the Dog Tongue offered, "if you tell me what I want to know, all friendly like, in the morning, I might be inclined to change my mind. On some parts, anyway."

He left Gus with that thought, his boots clomping on the floor.

"But…" the Dog Tongue said, "just to clarify. Vampire Joe wasn't a fan. He was a *friend.* So don't get your hopes up on me changing my mind about *some* things. Payback won't be a bitch. It'll be your balls."

Which Gus understood as he was going to die.

The Pig stepped around to his front, deepening the shadow around him.

"Got something to say?" Gus asked, because, what the hell.

The Pig didn't answer.

"You an ex-wrestler, too?"

The mask didn't budge, but a voice said, "I am, actually. But these days, we're called Inflictors."

The Pig slapped Gus then, a straight-up, calloused-hand that bashed his head to the side and damn near caved in his skull. His chair toppled and he crashed onto marble.

The Pig stood over him, watching, gauging. Gus stretched his jaw, his brain feeling as if it were in loopy orbit around the point of impact. When the pain ebbed away, he realized the Pig was gone.

But he didn't think he'd gone far.

Testing his bonds, Gus knew he wasn't going anywhere. Knew he was trapped. And he knew, one way or the other, he was going back east. Tied to the hood of the Dog Dick's ride either with or without clothing. Somehow, he figured that was probably going to be the least of his worries.

Laughter roused him back to the present, a man's, coming from somewhere deep in the penthouse. Probably from that living room area with the little kitchen and bar on the side. He couldn't see, as he landed facing the window, and what lay beyond was nothing but the black outlines of buildings. Even the stars had disappeared.

Tension on his neck, as his skull touched the floor.

Well, shit. He remembered Collie, and his heart was once again slapped onto a hot grill of despair and pain while his mind choked on the fumes. He remembered her masked face just before she ordered him out of the truck. Remembered her screaming, and how she released the steering wheel to make a grab for him. Remembered her chewing through the cotton weave of her mask…

That image was going to be the newest addition to his dreams, in the last few days of his miserable life.

She was gone. Finally gone.

And he'd be joining her, soon enough.

53

When the blades stabbing Collie through the right side of her chest were pulled out, her consciousness returned. She realized she had been screaming, realized her limbs were immobilized, and that she was being, of all things, wrapped up in a fuzzy material that smelled of feet, sweat, and shit.

That alone got her squawking again, but because she knew she was in enemy hands, she continued on with the act of being a full-blown zombie. It had worked before when she'd assaulted the Four Towers, and it appeared to be working now. So she allowed her captors to whisk her off her feet, rolled up in what might've been a sleeping bag, but felt like a really long cigarette.

That just so happened to smell like feet, sweat, and shit.

The Leather, she knew. She also knew she was alone. She heard very little talk outside of her cocoon, which offered only a squished point of view just above her head.

They dumped her on the ground and shoved her about, until she was lying just so. She kicked at the material and cut loose with a scream, except it wasn't much. They had wrapped duct tape across her mouth.

Something was roped around her legs and upper body, and soon, she was hoisted upwards, dragged against a flat surface that slid along her right side. Her frame rolled over an edge, and her feet grabbed. There, she was dragged across a floor until whoever was there positioned her where they wanted her.

Metal scraped, hinges squealed, and there was a final bang that sounded like a steel drum hitting a floor. Collie stared, squirmed to keep up appearances, and wondered what the blue fuck was going on.

Just as she spun free of the material covering her.

About four Leather stood around as she unraveled from the length of carpet. She landed broadside on a metal sheet and gazed up at the foursome.

Two of the Leather quickly covered her arms and face with thick padding, while another sliced the bonds around her hands and feet.

They were *freeing* her, or so she believed, so she lay still so they could finish. The pads around her face moved. A blade stabbed through the tape covering her mouth. The tip went inside an inch before flicking up, rudely scraping teeth and cutting not only duct tape, but a quarter inch of her mouth as well. She didn't feel a thing, which wasn't quite right. She was aware of the contact, but felt no pain.

She also heard the moaning, beneath her, coming from her left.

The pads were pulled back, and for a brief moment, Collie was on her back, staring up at four figures standing against the night sky.

One of the figures was hunched over, and he pulled on the edge of what might've been a blanket.

Collie rolled away again, and as she rolled, she felt that sudden, unexpected loss of floor beneath her. Arms swinging, she fell some four or five feet and crash-landed atop a solid, stinking mass of undead.

And she lay, spread-eagled, right on top of a knobby mattress of heads and shoulders, where more than a few arms sprouted and reached for the ceiling.

Then it hit her.

She wasn't being freed.

She was being *collected*.

A decomposing face was directly to her right, another to her left. Collie's own head was wedged in between those gruesome bookends, while her back was hyperextended in a numb stretch. There were at least three or four or more underneath her, bent over and supporting her crash landing. Something was between her legs, so she pulled her head up enough to check that out, and confirmed what she suspected. Another face, rotten and dewy from where the skin had been chewed away. The smiling mouth all but hidden in the depths of her crotch.

Then everything went dark in a rusty squeal of hinges and a slap of heavy metal.

Fingers worked on a lock, while footsteps trailed off. Seconds later, whoever had sealed them inside moved away as well. There was a noise from beyond where her feet were pointed, past that dirty face peeking up from her crotch.

Well fuck me, Collie thought.

She was surrounded by functional meatbags. The smell alone informed her of that. They were in a container, which she suspected was the tractor trailer she and Gus had blown by.

Gus. She allowed herself a moment to wonder what had happened to him. Probably dead or captured, but there was a chance he'd escaped. He was a survivor, after all. The luckiest one she'd ever come across.

She had more pressing problems.

Collie tried to establish a timeline of events as they might've gone down. The Leather had discovered her and captured her, that much was clear. They'd taken her sidearm and her knife, which was understandable. They'd then moved her to the transport truck where they loaded her in from the top. Regular transports didn't have lids that could flip open on top, but this one did. Someone had done a little modifying on the ceiling. It made sense. The Leather used the mindless as shock troops. If they came across any fresh meat, it was smart to capture it and load it through the roof. The other meatbags couldn't get out that way, especially if it was barred from the top, and if and when the Leather needed to unleash the whole pack, they'd could just open up the rear doors.

Releasing the carnivorous cargo in one raving rush.

She looked around, taking in a multitude of heads and shoulders of various heights and widths. It was dark, but she could see outlines and features. Some with missing faces, and some she wished *had* missing faces. Hollow cheeks, cheeks with holes in them where teeth peeked out, and missing eyes. She saw bald heads, buzzed heads, and ones with unkempt mops of hair. There was one that might've been scalped by hand, and not with a knife. Zombies were hunched over, while a few stood straight, but there were *hundreds* in the trailer. Jammed in, squished shoulder-to-shoulder, and left marinating in their own putrefying juices. A few had managed to get their arms above their necklines, perhaps reaching for that closed portal in the ceiling, and couldn't get them back down because of the mobbish press of bodies.

The stink alone was enough to kill. If Collie thought the undead smelled bad before, she obviously hadn't considered being packed into a tin can with hundreds of them.

There she lay, upon that lumpy bed of upright carcasses. She stretched her neck to see towards one end, not knowing if she was looking at the front or the rear. There were zombies behind her, blocking her view. She moved and realized she *could* move, that her limbs were free. Which made sense, as she remembered the attack on Camp Red Wolf. Couldn't have a trailer-load of tied-up corpses. Needed them ready to move when the doors were slung open. She attempted to turn over on all those bodies, feeling how the face in her crotch probably got more than what it bargained for.

Bowed heads writhed underneath her torso. Her knees knocked the backs of skulls and sank into shoulders. She pulled at full heads of hair and they moved with her, not resisting in the least. *And why should they?* she realized. As far as they were concerned, she was one of them. Her fingers sank into hair caked with blood and sweat and a cold jelly unpleasant to the touch. She pawed at dead faces as she struggled to get situated, and in one instance, her fingers poked through an open mouth and grazed the pebbly remains of teeth. As well as a dead grub of a tongue. She jerked back at the touch but the damage was done, the memory fresh.

It was awkward, but she turned herself over and pushed up upon shifting shoulders, to lift herself to better see. The zombies beneath her weren't facing any one direction, They stood however the hell they wanted, unable to move any further because of the sheer numbers. She could vaguely make out walls on either side but couldn't locate the rear doors.

Collie lowered herself onto those dead people and placed a hand over her mouth to keep a dead woman's hair out of her face.

She thought things over.

When she remembered the hatch above her.

Holy shit, she realized. *The way out.*

Or what she hoped was the way out, replaying what had just happened.

There was a lid up there, darkly outlined, perhaps secured by a bolt and nothing more. The Leather didn't need it anymore, because they were only transporting a trailer full of dead things with no comprehension of escaping. No *inclination* for escape.

No, Collie thought, glancing around her. There wasn't much inclination of anything among this group. They were only waiting for one thing. The opening of the rear doors, where they could spill out the back. She didn't need to get to the rear doors. Chances were she couldn't unlock the things from the inside, anyway.

The one above her, however…

She reached up, stretched out her arm and fingers, and realized the ceiling was only a foot away.

Holy fucking *shit*, she thought.

She struggled to her knees, which were gouged into a separate pair of shoulders. It wasn't a level surface at all, but it was enough, and the mindless didn't move as much as *yielded* underneath her weight. She reached up and touched the barrier, just overhead, actually pressing against her shoulder blades. Being that close to the ceiling surprised her…

Which made her think of what the zombies *beneath her* were standing on.

Oh Jesus, she thought, and studied the heads and shoulders at her knees. Were the meatbags she was kneeling on standing atop a crushed bedrock of *more* zombies? Zombies simply pressed down by successive loads of corpses being chucked in on top of them, to create a *strata* of decomposing flesh? In her mind's eye, she saw ribcages and abdominal cavities collapse under the weight of feet and boots and…

Collie shut that down—didn't want to think about it. She looked up. The lid itself appeared to be just a flat sheet of irregular iron covering a sloppy rectangular cut. The latch was located on one end that looked vaguely serrated, leaving gaps wide enough for fingers, perhaps even a hand. The hinges were fastened at the straighter end, on the opposite side, crudely bolted down into the trailer itself. Night peeked in, and she could see that the bar securing the lid was something else entirely.

Just a crude gate latch, if that. Nothing more was needed, really. Only mindless were inside, and they didn't have the capacity to climb up and investigate, let alone open a latch.

The more Collie examined her cage, the more she liked her chances.

She listened for voices outside.

Nothing.

Were there guards? What time was it? Would the Leather be careful after capturing them, or would they be relaxed? Would they sleep?

Collie forced herself to wait.

54

The cab had a bunk out back. Actually, it was more than a bunk—it was an honest-to-God hotel room. There was a small closet to scoot around, which acted as a partition between the bunk and the driver's seat, but once you were back there, yeah, it was like a micro-hotel room, and a fine one at that. Polished wood finishes, a small kitchenette, closets—everything you could want.

So when the sound of metal clanging off the roof ruined the silence, it was the unlucky minion on guard in the driver's seat that got yanked to a state of alertness, and not his partner snoozing in the bunk.

The Leather, wearing a mummy mask with zippers around the mouth and eye holes, sat up and listened… and heard only the guy out back snoring.

The dashboard clock said 8:38 pm, but the short, early winter days made it feel like midnight. The Mummy looked out his side mirror then the other. The doors were locked, so he was fine.

"Lloyd?" he asked.

Nothing.

"Lloyd?"

Another snore.

The Mummy, whose real name was Karl, shot a look of disdain in Lloyd's direction. Lloyd didn't hear the noise or Karl because he had his head buried under a tangle of blankets. And it was suspected Lloyd had something of a hearing problem.

Karl sighed and sized up his mirrors again. All clear. Perhaps he imagined it? He'd been half-dozing himself. Maybe he slipped into some early REM sleep and heard the bang in a dream.

But he had to be sure.

He got up, took a hold of a hatchet, and made his way into the rear. Once in the bunk, he kicked the frame.

Lloyd's head, covered in blankets, rose like a dark contusion from the rest of the bedding.

"Heard something," Karl reported. "I'm heading outside, okay?"

"Okay."

Karl turned to go but halted midway. "I'm headed outside, okay? Now."

"Okay."

"Thought I heard a bang. Best to check it out."

Karl pulled the blankets off Lloyd's head. He wasn't wearing his mask, having discarded it while sleeping. His bald head was a rusty patchwork of faded and active psoriasis.

"I'll wait here," Lloyd said.

Karl figured the bastard would, and couldn't wait for one o' clock to come around, when it was *his* turn to sleep.

He lumbered back out into the driver's seat, unlocked the door, and stuck his head outside. The cold immediately penetrated his one layer. He'd have to break out the winter gear soon. The street looked empty, and he spied one dump truck blocking the main road. On the passenger side was the hotel where everyone was staying. It wasn't nine o'clock just yet, so most of them would be still up and moving.

Nothing to be heard.

Karl climbed out of the cab. There was a single ladder, fixed to the side of the trailer itself. He stopped before the lower rungs and looked up, shaking his hatchet as if ready to throw it, but really his hands were just freezing.

Above him, past the white wall of the trailer, was the night sky. Clouds drifted in, obscuring the lesser stars. Karl stooped and peered under the truck, one way, then the other, searching for potential lurkers. If they *were* hiding underneath, however, he would probably have only seconds to raise the alarm. He'd whack the truck, whack it like an oversized dinner bell. Sighing, Karl waited, waited, and waited a few seconds more. Nothing. So he went to the ladder and grabbed a hold. It rattled softly, but it was a familiar noise. Taking a loose grip of his hatchet, mummy-masked Karl with zippers dangling around the eyes and mouth, started climbing. He'd get to the roof, walk around it, and get a bird's eye view from up there. A safer view, too, in his mind. The mindless were of no concern. They were mindless. Packed in tight. If they had to open the rear doors they wouldn't just fall out, they would spurt as if under carbonated pressure.

He'd check on those undead dickheads all the same. Then size-up the area around the truck. It wasn't windy, so it had to have been a dream—

His head popped over the trailer's edge, and right there, looking him straight in the eye, was a mindless. A stern, black-eyed, white-faced mindless. With no nose.

"*Hey!*" Karl got out as the thing reached out and grabbed the back of his head.

Collie yanked the Leather forward with whatever strength she had, driving his throat into the steel edge of the trailer. The Leather released a pained *ack!* before falling backwards.

She didn't have the strength to hold onto him.

The Leather fell thirteen feet to the pavement, landing splat on his back. He buckled, relaxed, and finally lay still.

Collie lowered herself down the ladder, struggling with her damaged leg, sliding and hoping, and cringing at every footfall. She reached the pavement and staggered over to the Leather, who stirred, lifting a hand for his chin.

Collie collapsed beside him. She grabbed his wrist, held it, before plying it down and out of the way.

Just before chomping down on his throat.

*

Inside the cab, sleepy Lloyd *thought* he heard Karl call out, but he didn't bother to see for certain. There was no need. They were in safe territory, with roughly three dozen armed and dangerous Leather. Lloyd was probably calling out to someone in the hotel lobby. Besides, Lloyd was the one who'd gotten the shitty shift. After midnight and straight on until dawn. Oh, he'd *do* it, guaranteed, but it was just a shitty shift. A shitty *shitty* shift. One that would leave him *feeling* like a sack of shit for the rest of the day. He needed every second of sleep to get him through to tomorrow night. It was just like loudmouth Karl to try and fuck it up. *Inconsiderate.*

So he settled back down under the blankets and ignored the noise. There wasn't anything around anyway. The city was theirs.

The driver's door opened.

Lloyd heard it, but didn't budge, already halfway out like a light.

Then he felt it, a presence in the room, that tugged him back from sleep. Even worse, it was right at the bunk, or so he sensed. Frowning, Lloyd struggled with his blankets until he pulled them off his head, figuring it was Karl again making like a fucking mummy.

It wasn't Karl.

There, standing beside the bunk, was a woman. A mindless, obviously, but with her nose missing and her face looking like she'd just drunk from a fire hydrant of a jugular vein.

I'm dreaming, Lloyd thought.

He didn't even have the sense to scream when the hatchet sank three inches deep into his forehead.

*

A short time later, Collie pulled herself out of the cab, smelled the winter air, and lowered herself to the pavement.

She'd killed the two Leather assigned to the truck, but neither one of them had guns, which pissed her off. One had a hand axe, which she currently used, while the other had, of all things, a crossbow—which she left behind.

She felt rejuvenated from her feeding, charged, but not supercharged. Not quite up to speed had she been alive, but not as good as the last time she'd eaten a person. Or, rather, had eaten *parts* of a person. She suspected it would never be that way again, and that, as time wore on, she would continue to deteriorate, the energy boost from each feeding diminishing. Her muscles would atrophy to the point of her shambling around like a true mindless. No matter how many bad guys she feasted on, she would still decompose.

Until she was crawling.

Not that she intended on doing that.

But without firepower, and her limited capabilities, she had a challenge before her. She was going back into one of the Four Towers, and she guessed that Dog Dick was up above, probably in the same penthouse where she'd found Gus and Milo before. It was early at night, and she didn't think many of the Leather would be sleeping. She didn't think she would be able to get all of them before morning. Sooner or later, the alarm would go up, and she'd probably go down well before she got her hands on the Dog Dick's throat.

She looked down, expecting to see the dead Leather with the torn-out throat, left propped up against a tire, out of sight of the hotel.

He was gone.

That floored her, and she immediately scanned the area.

There, lumbering away from the truck and hotel, leaning against a building wall for support.

As Collie watched, the Leather stopped, whirled, and jerked his head about as if getting a whiff of something. Then, clearly uninterested, he lurched away.

She was of a mind to go after him, to take his head off, when she started thinking. The first person she snacked on had already been dead, shot by her, and didn't reanimate. This last one had been *alive*, and he was clearly up and about. He could be a distraction, but how big or effective of a distraction, she didn't know. Collie thought again about all the mindless in the trailer behind her and had a lightbulb moment.

All those mindless were an even bigger distraction.

Then she had an even *better* idea, one that stopped her undead ass cold.

She didn't need a distraction to take out the remaining Leather. No, what she needed was reinforcements.

And she had a fucking *trailer* full of them.

"Holy shit," she whispered, and immediately sized up the tractor trailer. It was a long shot, a very long shot, but she remembered what they'd found back at Whitecap when searching through the Leather's vehicles. There was no reason why it wouldn't be the same now.

Just above the fuel tank was the closed door to a storage compartment. Motor oil, winter chains for the tires, warning flares, and all manner of items would be placed there.

Collie stuck the hatchet down her belt and opened the compartment door.

There, before her, was a cooler. An airtight cooler.

She pulled the thing down to the road and popped the lid. The smell hit her right away, perhaps the few residual drops spattered inside the container's walls. It wasn't nearly as bad as she once thought it was, but the last time she got a whiff of it, it was dripping off Gus's beard, and she wasn't nearly along as she currently was with her affliction. Perhaps the TI shot didn't quite make her a true zombie after all, but checking on the dead Leather still staggering away, she was close. Perhaps the stink would affect her in the end, when she went into the mindless state one final time and wouldn't return.

Whatever.

There were three large pickle bottles inside the cooler, along with, of all things, some extra-large freezer bags. They were plastic and Collie knew about their purpose. Gus had taken one upside the chops and lived to talk about it.

Pickle jars. She lifted one up and examined it. There was a joke in there somewhere, maybe about squeezing pickles and juice, but she was too damn focused on future events to work out a punchline.

The Leather had used the pissbags to toss at targets, to both terrify them and to mark them for their army of mindless, who would hunt down the stink like bloodhounds.

Collie initially thought that if she opened the rear doors and released the mindless within, they might go for the Leather in the hotel lobby, but who knew how many would go? It could be a dozen zombies, could be all, or it could be none.

With the pissbags, however, she could direct them. Like a general. Turn the Leather's defining weapon against them.

Collie paused again.

She didn't need the pissbags. Not really. All she needed was what was *inside* the pissbags. Or rather inside the pickle jars.

Then, not only would she be directing the mindless, she would be *leading* them.

"Holy *fuck*," Collie whispered to herself, realizing what she potentially had in her hands.

She didn't just have reinforcements, she potentially had command of a small army.

Three jars. Collie put one down a pants pocket and hoisted the others. Sticking one in her armpit, she unscrewed the lid of the last and got a whiff of the urine within.

Nope. Still didn't do shit for her. Still smelled like rancid old man piss.

No accounting for taste, she thought.

Old man piss. Old man *donkey* piss. Collie thought about Gus then and smirked despite the situation.

She tipped the bottle and poured it onto her boots, then her knees. A stream here and there, just enough to penetrate and leave the cloth wet. She poured more on her thighs and when she got to her front, she doused that as well. Finally, she lifted the bottle to her shoulders and anointed them. She thought about her head, realizing she'd lost her balaclava at some point, but couldn't bring herself to dump that wretched foulness over herself. So, she poured the remainder down her back, the contact not bothering her as much as she thought.

Once done, she turned to chuck the bottle.

Boots on pavement got her attention then, and she looked up to see the Leather stumbling towards her, grumbling nonsense as it did so.

Holy shit, the shit works, Collie thought. She forced herself to wait, hoping there were no other lookouts.

The mindless Leather staggered right up to her and stopped less than an arm's length away. Its dead eyes examined her, but it didn't attack, and why would it? She wasn't alive and had the missing heart to prove it. To the mindless, she was just another zombie, but one that smelled like flowers repeatedly pissed on by a moose.

That put a smirk on her face.

"Follow me, boy," she said and started walking for the rear of the trailer. She tossed the empty bottle and actually kissed the air twice, as if coaxing a budgie bird to pitch on her shoulder. "C'mon, Pickles."

To her delight, the newest zombie followed her.

All right, she told herself, sliding a hand along the length of the trailer. It was showtime. The big test, and if it didn't work, things would become a lot more complicated.

She stopped at the corner of the truck and peeked out at the hotel. The lobby floor was a mass of windows, where she could see the Leather moving about. The doors all swung open, but the windows interested her. She formulated a plan and took a precious two minutes to prepare, gathering her wits and materials.

Then she turned the corner and stopped at the trailer's tall rear doors. She worked the locks, pleased at the clacking of bars, and glanced in the direction of the hotel lobby—the only one with its lights on.

Movement from inside the trailer distracted her.

They could smell her.

She swung open one door only halfway and they fell out, clipping her arm in the process. Collie jerked herself back, avoiding the first falling Moe to hit the ground with that cement bag smack she came to recognize. The others spilled out after it, piling up on top of the first as if they'd sacked a quarterback half a yard away from the endzone. Mutters and groans perked the air, and Collie immediately looked to the not-so-far-away hotel.

But only for a second, as the ones who'd fallen attempted to get up, only to be knocked forward by the push of bodies falling on *top* of *them*. The pile-up became a murderous haystack in a short time, where the animated dead tried to untangle themselves from each other. It was almost funny, watching them, until you realized what they were and what they were capable of.

Collie considered not opening the other door, in order to better control the chaos right before her. But as the bodies pulled themselves free, she made a choice and hauled the other door open. As soon as she released the handle, the door swung wide and knocked her clear.

Twice the number of bodies fell to the ground.

A mob encircled Collie, their morbid faces staring and unseeing, drawn to her and yet uninterested in her own dead flesh. She was all ketchup and no hamburger, all sauce but no barbeque, and as she realized it, her smile became all the more evil.

The ranks thickened and their nonsense banter grew. Bodies of all shapes and sizes fell from the trailer in a chunky gush. Collie pushed through the growing mob, *her* mob now, shoving aside rotten torsos and curious faces. More than a few reached out for her, but she swatted those mitts away. The ranks filled in behind her with a drunken stubbornness, in some cases teetering on barely enough ankle support.

She came out the other side and walked for the main entrance.

The zombies followed her in an ever-widening mass. They eyed her as if she were a rock star while *more* plopped out of the trailer's rear. Pickles was on her right, like a personal assistant, and glaring ahead as if sensing what was about to happen.

Goddamn, she felt dangerous.

The entrance would have been a problem, and easily locked, but Collie had something for that. Before she opened the trailer doors and freed her waiting army, she'd taken a couple of minutes to undo the front of her jacket, reach in, and unpeel the tape securing the plastic container in her chest.

Where her final grenade waited.

She *had* wanted to use that explosive bauble on herself, envisioning exactly how she'd wanted to go out, similar to Wallace. That was the plan before, but her current course of action demanded otherwise. She needed the grenade to kill the Leather.

Some thirty paces back from the hotel, she stopped, and her army stopped with her. Beyond the glass windows, figures lounged around the lobby. Some sat in furniture while others strolled around as if sizing up the hotel's features. From their lack of alertness, she could tell they were civvies. Talkin' the talk, but sure as Christ fuckin' up the walk. There would be a glare from all the light inside, hindering anyone from looking in their direction, but only for a short time.

Sure enough, one of the Leather sitting in a plush chair slowly stood up, looking in her direction. Collie knew he had spotted her growing force outside. The Leather had picked up on the movement beyond the glass and was taking the time to get a better look. His body language telegraphed everything she needed to know.

Another Leather turned, alerted by the first, who was now waving a hand, raising the alarm.

Collie pulled the pin on the grenade and lobbed it at the hotel entrance.

The explosive clacked off a padded welcome mat and wobbled to a rest not an inch from the threshold.

The blast was an ugly thing, spewing fire, glass, and smoke inside the lobby. Framework leaped and clattered. Smoke shot heavenwards in bloated, billowing coils. A glass sliver—a knife-sized shard, actually, shot out of the clouds and sank halfway into Pickles's shoulder. The Leather zombie took it like a champ, not even flinching. He was much more interested in the screams from inside the hotel.

"Stay with me," Collie said to the zombie and cocked back her arm again.

She launched the *second* jar of urine through the smoking wreckage of the entrance.

Not that she needed to, because at the sound of all that screaming, living meat, the undead mob at her back lumbered past her at an increasingly frenzied pace.

Converging on that jagged hole to the lobby.

Like a mass of shoppers smelling a Black Friday sale, the mindless stormed the entrance.

Unable to stop him, Pickles went along with the rush. Collie tried to hold the meaty bastard back, but he was freshly dead, and too fast for her. Too determined to get his share. He became part of the storm surge channeling for the entrance, but she could see his masked head, which stood out against the rest.

Gunshots then, and Collie pulled the hand axe from her belt as she marched forward, becoming one with the mob pouring into the hotel.

55

Zombies pushed and jostled her as she broke into the lobby amidst the screaming, the dying, and the feeding.

The grenade blast had not only wounded or killed some of the Leather but disoriented them as well. Mindless had swarmed several, bypassing the Leather's outerwear, pulling off material in great clumsy jerks and stabbing fingers into the red meat underneath. One zombie was bent over on its knees, shaking its head as it sank its bloody face deeper into a Leather's abdomen. Other mindless had taken down the living and were tearing them apart in sprinkler bursts of red. One of the Leather was swinging an axe, and half took the head off an attacking zombie. The collapsing dead took the axe with it, however, and the Leather couldn't fend off the other Moes tackling him from all quarters.

The Leather screamed.

Most of the Leather were screaming, in fact.

Then the death rattle of an automatic weapon, and Collie recognized her own German-made HK. Zombies flew backwards, their backs erupting in a flurry of mini-tent peaks. Pieces of meat and fluid misted the air. Artificial plants were cut down. The tops of sofas and chairs blew apart in white puffs of dust, splinters, and stuffing. A few heads burst apart, coating everything nearby in a ghastly drizzle.

The shooter was panicking, however, attempting to mow down everything.

Collie dropped to the floor, landing beside a golden luggage cart. There were at least a dozen zombies around her, the last few to escape the trailer, and they took the full brunt of that devastating gunfire. Clothing and pieces of organic matter flew from their frames as they fell. Two heads blew apart.

One zombie collapsed after his right leg left him in a black spray. Another zombie landed on top of the luggage cart. It thrashed and attempted to rise even with the gruesome purple streamers slipping from his perforated stomach. Splashes of his own juices coated his half-skeletal face as he rose.

Collie didn't need to see any of that.

She crawled underneath that deadly spray, closing the distance to the front desk, where the shooter stood and was still cutting loose. The bursts became more selective, as the shooter began picking his shots. A shotgun opened up then, and one of the mindless burst apart right above the waistline as if catching a bomb. Collie knew the weapon was the Ram Fist, because it hammered bodies for a least ten shots before going dry.

The rifle went dead as well.

Well, well, Collie thought, and used a nearby zombie already on his knees to get to her feet. She rose in time to see the two shooters frantically attempting to reload their weapons.

Collie rushed across the lobby made hazardous by all the undead. Some were down and gone, their skulls blasted apart, others were energetically crawling forward, while more still converged on the front desk.

One of the Leather brandished a spear and moved to intercept the dying operator.

Three zombies crashed into him, taking him down.

One of them was her man Pickles.

God*damn* she was starting to love that freak.

She turned the corner of the front desk, a long piece of dignified wood that glowed under the sparse light. As she went around the back, a wall of zombies reached the front desk.

The Leather with the shotgun spotted her and that meatbag charge, and in doing so, he fumbled reloading a fresh magazine. Collie cocked her arm, looking to rush ahead and bury the blade in his forehead or whatever was handy, when a body wearing a red t-shirt lunged across the front desk and grabbed the distracted shotgunner. The Leather staggered under the attack, while, behind him, the one with the HK finished loading and took aim—

When another zombie snatched the gun barrel and yanked it away.

Collie threw herself into a wall of exposed cupboards as a full burst ripped into the zombies near the end of the counter. The Leather fired his weapon while the zombie unwittingly aided him in mowing down several of his companions. The Leather fended off a second hand, saw that the lobby was lost, and released the rifle. He staggered backwards in full retreat, into what looked like a small office. The door slammed a second later.

Collie was already striding forward, mindful of the zombie—a woman in a filthy white shirt saturated in blood—held onto the rifle.

As Collie went for the office door, she hacked at the shotgunner who was still struggling with the first mindless attacker. The Leather shrieked when she saw the raised axe. Collie smashed the blade into her carotid artery. A fountain erupted. The Leather went down, all fight leaving her, and the dead thing still clinging to her took the opportunity to latch on tighter.

Collie left the axe and gathered up the Ram Fist shotgun. She finished readying the weapon and faced the closed office door.

Zombies piled in behind her, seeking a bite of the fresh kill. The bloodied she-corpse with the assault rifle slammed the weapon down on the desk and glared, as if demanding service. Collie didn't waste time on her. She braced herself five feet from the door. She took aim at the brass doorknob and fired.

Boom.

The doorknob disintegrated in a not-so-magical puff of wood and metal. The door swung open, and there, pressed up against the wall and cornered, was the last Leather.

Collie pumped a round into the figure's chest.

56

For reasons unknown, Gus opened his eyes, realizing he'd dozed off. He was still on his side, taped to the damn chair, and his neck dearly ached. He heard the occasional laugh coming from the direction of where Dog Dick, the once-professional wrestler, and his buddies had gone, but that was it.

Then his bladder got his attention.

"Hey!" he called out. "*Hey*! Need to take a piss over here."

The laughter stopped.

Then someone laughed again.

"Won't be funny when I piss all over the floor," Gus warned, mostly to himself.

Footsteps approached, and those heavy heels upon tiles worried him.

The Pig arrived, those big boots level with Gus's eyes. The Inflictor stared down, eyes twinkling with evil life.

Gus scowled back. "You still wearing that thing?" he asked, meaning the mask. "I mean, aren't you off-duty, now? It is night. Don't you take those things off when no one's around? Let your hair down? If you have any, that is, you miserable dog fuck you."

The Pig kicked him in the gut. Twice.

All the air escaped Gus, and his bladder let go, saturating his crotch with an unpleasant warmth. Even as he hitched and gasped and clawed air back into his lungs, a part of him knew he was going to regret pissing over the floor in the morning.

The Pig walked away.

Still stuck to the chair, Gus eventually started breathing again, and went right on back to suffering.

57

Collie inspected her kill, satisfied with the shot. There probably wasn't any need to shoot the bastard, since the zombies would have done the job. *Fuck it*, she thought, and leaned up against the door frame to consider the lobby.

Well.

It looked like a goddamn zombie convention out there. An honest-to-god celebration of unlife, where the open bar was perhaps two or three dozen corpses bleeding out or being pulled apart. Mindless feasted or stumbled about in an empty-eyed, chum-induced state of catatonia. One slipped and went down as if on roller skates. Another was ripping up a couch cushion for some unknown reason. Others staggered about, staring ahead as if high on their undead existence. All were dripping blood. In fact, they were positively covered, as if they'd been hosed down before entering the party.

Even as she watched, zombies continued to chow down, taking squirting, stretching mouthfuls of their victims. They chewed and swallowed, and chomped down again, at times their food spilling from their mouths. It was a Jurassic massacre. Pure bloody butchery. A gluttonous exhibition of wanton appetite and open-mouth mastication visceral enough to turn stomachs.

The sight of it stopped Collie in her tracks.

She looked away and settled upon the Leather who'd once used the shotgun. A woman zombie in red was busy gnawing upon the eyebrows. Collie averted her eyes again and settled on the unsettling zipper-jingling gaze of Pickles. Gore dripped from his face. His mouth looked like someone might've stuffed a firecracker inside a tomato and shoved it down his throat. Shreds and dangles of things Collie didn't want to think about coated the zipper's metal teeth.

"You're a savage, Pickles," Collie said. "A goddamn savage."

Pickles stared back.

"And you," she directed at the woman in the saturated t-shirt. "You're a fucking mess."

The woman-in-red watched and tracked her, all the while gnashing down on her victim.

Collie turned back to the corpse in the office and rolled her eyes. "Jesus Christ, I can't look anywhere without seeing a fucking body."

But that wasn't the thing bothering her.

Seeing her recruits eat, witnessing all that mindless *feasting*, well, that stirred something within her. A sensation she identified right away and begrudgingly hated herself for. A craving. Already, her boost of energy from eating dear old Pickles was waning. She could feel it. Perhaps it worked like a junkie, where a heavier dose was needed each successive time. She didn't know. Didn't know if Wallace was the same way, but she remembered how he'd slowed down with each passing day.

She looked back at the woman, and a name popped into her head.

Ruby.

Ruby Red.

It fit.

Ruby was currently chewing through an uncovered ear, staring ahead as if hypnotized by some unseen oddity.

Collie walked over to her. She pulled out the killing axe she left in the Leather's neck. Blood dribbled, but weakly.

That was enough for her.

"Move over, Rube," she said to the feeding corpse, and sat down on the other side.

Ruby did no such thing.

Frowning, Collie placed her hand on her face and shoved. Ruby rocked back like an off-kilter chair, and actually *growled* at the operator, speckling the Leather's profile with blood.

Collie shook her head, and then gave in. She considered the cut in the Leather's neck, deciding on where to start. And like some things, it was best to simply close one's eyes and dig in.

God help her, it hit the spot.

After a minute, she felt that familiar boost spreading throughout. She pulled back from her meal, momentarily dazed, and realized she'd really gone to town on the poor Leather bastard. Ruby sat across from her, while the rest of the unruly gang continued to monster-mash around the lobby. There was less noise of tearing fabric now, and practically no sound of stitches or seams being ripped through. For that, she was grateful.

Collie stood and swayed a little from being so unusually bloated.

"God, Ruby," she said. "You sloppy bitch. Up and move. And what are *you* looking at?"

Pickles stared at her, giving her a full blast of fish-eye.

"I know what I'm doing. Don't question my authority." Collie gathered up the shotgun, the rifle, and the hatchet. As she worked, more of the undead gathered around the front desk, perhaps drawn to the action, but probably by the smell. The whole place stank. She stopped at one point and surveyed her well-fed forces.

Two hundred at least. From what she could see, she'd lost a dozen from machine-gun fuckhead's wild-west shooting spree. Another dozen or so were still moving, but they'd lost legs or were somehow crippled. They wouldn't be of much use for the next assault.

But nearly two hundred remained.

And at least three dozen—if not *most*—of the Leather were dead.

"I don't care what anyone says," she said to the walking corpses around the front desk. "You guys… are fuckin' *awesome*. I mean that."

She looked at Ruby. "Watch the place. Holler if you need me."

And left the staring woman.

Collie limped back into the office, where she spotted her Kevlar vest shucked over the guest chair. She dropped her weapons on the desk and eased back into the armor. Once fitted and secured in place, she picked up her guns and went back to her minions.

Ruby waited, munching away on something.

Pickles stood on the other side, like a dog longing for its master.

"How do I look?" Collie asked them and got no reply. She let that go.

The axe looped into her belt, which left her with a choice. The shotgun or the assault rifle. She checked on the magazines for both and deemed them acceptable. Two guns accounted for, and the biggest ones at that. That left her Sig and Gus's Glock missing. There were probably extra magazines around here as well, but she didn't have the time or inclination to rummage through all the dead assholes.

The Dog Dick was somewhere above. Probably in the penthouse, which suited her fine. She remembered the layout of the place. She wondered if she would find Gus up there. If not, she would keep one of the Leather alive, and make him talk. She'd find him, one way or the other. Dead or alive.

And if he was dead, she'd punish whatever Leather was still alive.

Not the Dog Dick, though. She had all manner of painful delights planned for that one.

"You think you can handle this?" She held out the HK to Ruby, who made no attempt to take the weapon.

"All right," Collie said. "No gun for you." She looked over Pickles's bloodied exterior. "What about you?"

Pickles only stared as slivers of meat shivered and fell from his zippers.

"All right, all right. Stop complaining. I can see this was a mistake." Collie took both weapons. "Probably blow your feet off anyway. Or some stupid shit. Nothing positive anyway. And then *I'd* get shit for it. Just forget I said anything."

Collie pushed past Ruby, and when the operator checked to see if the she-corpse followed, she discovered the zombie was but three feet off her heels. Collie forced her way through that dripping, shifting, mass of undead indecision shuffling around the lobby. She tried very hard not to stop and examine the more brutal scenes of death involving the Leather. As far as she was concerned, the twisted fucking sisters had it coming.

She made her way through her followers, shoving where needed, close to shooting once or twice. Ruby was right behind her, and so was Pickles. The rest of those decaying meat heads fell in behind, drawn by a combination of smell and activity. Maybe even a dash of morbid curiosity.

Collie halted at the elevator.

She had a small army at her back, the element of surprise, but could only fit a dozen into the elevator. Or so she thought.

She surveyed her minions, and within seconds, headed for the hotel's main stairwell.

58

That the elevator was rising didn't really bother the four Leather guarding the outer penthouse hallway. Two sat on opposite ends of a leather sofa, positioned between a pair of miniature palm trees made of some weird synthetic but resembling the real thing. The wall behind them was wallpapered with a tropical sun, red and glowing, half sunk into a sea. When the rising elevator reached the fifth floor, one of the guards, a leatherhead armed with a Glock, used the weapon to scratch at his ear. He noticed the numbers lighting up and meandered over to the doors, boots clicking on the marble floor. He wondered what or who might be coming up. That something was wrong didn't enter his mind. They were in a secured place, with all of the Dog Tongue's personal guard in the lobby.

He exchanged glances with the other standing Leather guard, not so far from the sofa. Beyond her was the remainder of the hall, which ended in a set of double doors.

The eighth-floor light came on, stayed lit for two seconds, then winked out.

Then the ninth.

The tenth.

The guards sitting on the sofa leaned forward but didn't reach for their warclubs propped against the walls. The female Leather down the hall hefted her twin mini-crossbows, and stood like a gunslinger waiting for her opponent to make the first move.

The Leather with the Glock shook his head at the pair sitting down when he heard the pleasant dinner bell *ding* of the arriving elevator.

The doors opened.

To reveal an elevator filled with dead things.

The Leather's eyes went wide.

Collie unleashed a light burst from the HK, catching the man in the chest and launching him backward where he spattered against the wall. She stepped out, getting ahead of the dozen undead she'd packed into the elevator beforehand, and ripped a burst across the two Leather sitting on their asses.

Sofa stuffing, blood, and Leather jumped.

A crossbow bolt slammed into Collie, spinning her off-kilter. A Leather stood at the end of the hall, holding a pair of small shooters.

Pickles and Ruby ran at the Leather, along with the rest of the pack freeing themselves from the elevator.

The Leather shot Ruby in the neck, the impact staggering the charging deadhead.

But Ruby didn't stop.

Nor did Pickles, who flew past her.

Like faithful dogs, the two zombies crashed into the Leather, driving her against the penthouse doors. They hauled her down to the floor amidst her screaming. That attracted the other zombies, which piled on that thrashing logjam, clawing for whatever parts they could get.

Collie checked on her magazine and tossed it onto the sofa. She moved back to the open elevator and jammed the closing doors. She reached around and grabbed the shotgun propped in the corner. The doors started closing again, and this time she let them, slipping out between and taking aim at the penthouse entrance. The ruckus would no doubt alert whoever was inside.

The undead were massed near the door, tearing into their victim.

Collie picked up the Glock and lobbed it on the sofa's cushions. The shotgun she rested beside the armrest. She grabbed one of the dead Leather and dragged the corpse back some ten feet to the stairwell door. Resisting the urge to eat the fresh kill, she opened the door and felt the stale air sweep past her.

She glanced at the penthouse entrance.

Still closed.

Collie dumped the body against the stairwell door, keeping it open, revealing a dimly lit concrete throat with a coat of beige paint. Considering the other fine touches of the hotel, it seemed rather cheap.

Collie retrieved the Glock, checked the load, and saw that it was full. She kept that and left the heavier weapons. She hurried back to the stairwell and at the top dug out the last jar of urine.

Which she chucked against the lower landing. The jar burst apart, staining the entire platform. That would bring the horde, she knew, as she'd propped open the stairwell door in the lobby before boarding the elevator.

The question was how long it would take for them to reach the top floor.

59

The sound of gunfire widened Gus's eyes.

He lay there on his side, facing the wall-length windows and the night, and waited for more.

More came. Another burst that had him holding his breath.

Then someone screamed, a high-pitched note that was refilled and replayed, until something stopped it. Not for long, however, as the screamer let off a few more frantic shrieks. Gus waited, ears perked and listening, waiting for the Dog Tongue and Mr. Pig to come running.

All the while, the screamer ran out of breath and didn't scream again.

There was activity outside those doors, however. A disturbing rumbling and slapping of body weight, accompanied by a guttural moaning he'd often heard in nightmares.

The gunfire didn't repeat. Not yet, however.

Gus strained against the tape holding him, but whoever had done the taping had used an entire fucking roll. He strained again, pulling, rocking, attempting to twist, showing the last of his teeth and summoning engorged cords throughout his neck.

And collapsed against the chair.

Fuck was Gus's only exhausted thought, remembering a television clip with an ex-FBI guy showing how to escape being taped to a chair. *Anyone can escape*, he'd declared, standing up and pulling the torn strands from his sleeves.

Gus couldn't get free and whoever was outside wasn't shooting anymore.

Milo? Had he returned? Collie? Had she *returned?* Maybe they both had.

Gus craned his neck and couldn't see shit. So he tried moving the chair around, heaving his mass against his bonds. He got maybe two inches when he heard the Leather coming into the room. One of those was the ominous

Pig, and he was moving at a clip. In fact, a knot of them headed for the door and stopped there. Not wanting to miss anything, Gus kicked and bucked, turning the chair around in torturous slow-motion.

"Back from the door," the Dog Tongue commanded. "Get ready."

Then the leader was standing over Gus, a big boot landing right before his face, so close he could smell the faint odor of sweat socks.

"Got visitors?" Gus asked from below.

The Dog Tongue didn't answer.

"Gonna let them in?"

The Dog Tongue whipped the end of his prong off Gus's jaw, silencing him.

Gus cringed and shut up, but he wasn't out.

Spinning the prong around and holding it at low guard, the Dog Tongue forgot about the nuisance at his feet, one whom he planned to cut into pieces very slowly.

The Dog Tongue focused on the penthouse doors. His followers stood ready on either side of the entrance, waiting.

"Open it," the Dog Tongue commanded.

One of his minions did just that.

And all hell broke loose.

60

The center of a reanimated offensive line barged through, yowling, arms reaching for the living. They didn't just barge inside, but practically burst into the suite, an undead gush of torsos and heads, flailing as they fell.

Gunshots then, as a Leather with a sidearm opened fire. The shots were hurried, however, as perhaps only a pair of the charging mindless dropped, but there were others.

But then the Leather shooter—the brutish Pig—had his head violently torqued to one side before dropping out of sight.

The gunfire stopped, but the mindless had breached the penthouse.

Two of the Leather swung axes at the charging undead, smashing faces to their shoulders, showing just how horrific an axe blade to the skull could be. There was a scrimmage then, a savage tumble and pile-up, just inside the entrance.

When a figure stepped into the door frame.

Gus's mouth dropped open.

She had her mask off and looked like reanimated shit, but there was no mistaking a zombified Collie, her missing nose completing a decidedly vampire bat look.

She shot one Leather, a deft double tap that caused the man to go ankles-up and over one end of a sofa. Collie pivoted and fired again. A Leather dropped to his knees, before three zombies tackled him and bent him backwards.

The Dog Tongue tensed, gripping the prong like old Neptune himself, poised to sink those three-pointed tips into Gus.

Collie could only see the top of his head, but there was no mistaking that bald crown.

For seconds, no one said a word, and the only sound was that of the mindless feeding on fresh corpses. There were no other Leather entering the fray. They'd all perished.

"Move and you're dead," Collie warned, bringing up her sidearm in an unwavering two-handed grip.

"Shoot me and he dies," the Dog Tongue countered, leaning forward, placing a controlled weight on the prong. One tip dug into Gus's ear, while the others dimpled points on his neck. The Dog Tongue was a big man, and the gun blast might not be enough to blow all that big-man mass back. That free-falling forward weight might just sink those tips into Gus's head.

Gus's eyes narrowed as that one blade stabbed a little deeper into his ear canal.

Nothing then, as warlord and operator both thought matters over.

Collie moved further into the shadows of the dimly lit room, staring down the sights of her sidearm. Behind her, the mindless lost interest in their most recent kills.

The Dog Tongue stared back, his features masked and impassive, fists choking the length of the prong.

"Dog Dick," Collie greeted, taking a step closer, her aim unrelenting. "I thought you'd be... pinker."

Zombie mewling filled the silence then.

"One more step and I'll show you red," the Leather leader replied, increasing pressure upon the prong sticking into Gus's head, enough to widen his grimace.

Another ounce, and the threat would be reality.

"Drop the weapon," the Dog Tongue commanded.

Collie dipped her head and lowered the Glock, before firing three shots and blasting the big man backwards, jerking the prong off of Gus's face.

As the Dog Tongue fell, two of the mindless behind her rose to attack. They rushed through the room, charging towards the fallen man.

Directly in their paths, however, was an unmoving Gus.

Collie resumed her shooter's stance. She shot one mindless through the back of the head, dropping the thing onto a glass coffee table that held the weight. She shifted and shot the other mindless, twisting it around not five paces away from Gus. She fired again, tapping the dead thing once through the face.

The corpse dropped back, its arms flung wide.

Collie swung left and right and took aim at the last few zombies that had accompanied her in the elevator. Pickles was there, as was Ruby, both of them red-faced and looking like a pair of pigs snout-deep in a food trough. There was another, but Collie hadn't named that one, and she wasn't sure if it was a man or woman. Not that it mattered.

There were three zombies left, already rising, watching her every move.

She couldn't let them reach Gus.

Which was right about when she felt that vibe coming on—the prelude to the loss of self, the dangerous disconnection with reality. The last time it happened, she remembered a mosquito's buzz accompanied by a whiteout of vision. This time, it hit her with all the force of a nail being driven through the fabric of her mind. She staggered as if shot twice to the chest. And through the rising volume that attacked her from her brain stem all the way to her frontal lobe, Collie sensed movement.

She turned when a body crashed into her.

Except it wasn't the Dog Tongue.

It was the mindless she'd shot through the face.

The Dog Tongue had *thrown* it at her.

The Leather warlord surged forward, prong leveled, as Collie sought to bring up the Glock.

He stabbed her through her wrist, and she dropped the gun. The forward momentum backed her up a few steps, where she slammed into one of the penthouse pillars. The Dog Tongue punched Collie across the face, breaking her cheek in at least three places. The blow freed her from the prong, but also sent her flying over the back of a white sofa, where she landed in a tangled heap.

The Dog Tongue moved to finish her, a demonic tongue unfurled from his face and lapped evilly at the air.

When Pickles leaped at his former leader.

The undead Leather minion crashed into the bigger man, who staggered back more from fright than force. Then the Dog Tongue's mighty hand snapped out, clutching the undead, shoving that head back and holding the snapping, zipper-jingling mouth away at a single arm's length.

Which was when *Ruby* crashed into him.

The Dog Tongue wasn't a small man. He was a slimmed-down ogre, powerful of limb, but while he could hold off one mindless snapping for his face—he couldn't fend off two.

Ruby upended the bigger man, and they all staggered back onto the glass coffee table already decorated with a corpse.

The furniture collapsed under all that weight.

A scramble ensued, whereupon the third surviving zombie lumbered past Gus, throwing its carcass upon the melee, attracted to the fresh meat struggling to rise.

And rise the Dog Tongue did, not disadvantaged in the least.

The once-wrestler shoved away Pickles and Ruby as if they were all in a battle royale of old.

He lashed the prong across the face of Pickles, knocking the mindless backward, the zippers rattling as he went.

He stabbed the third, unnamed zombie through the guts and whipped him into the base of the nearest sofa.

The Dog Tongue stood, as Ruby clawed at his leather-covered shoulders. A massive backhand cracked her across the head, the force knocking her to the floor. The Dog Tongue readied his prong, set his feet, and stabbed her through the face. The entire zombie switched off with a shiver and a body-length slump. The Leather warlord ripped the prong free, spun, and stomped on the lower leg of the nameless zombie as it attempted to rise. The zombie fell face-first into the sofa cushion, where the Dog Tongue harpooned the dead thing through the back of the skull in a messy spatter of ink.

The nameless stopped moving.

The Dog Tongue held the pose for a split second and pulled the prong free, just in time to meet the onrush of Pickles. He smashed the prong's handle into Pickles's face, shattering a number of teeth, snapping back the head and stalling the charge. Pickles staggered and the Dog Tongue one-arm punched the prong through that masked face in a crunch of facial bone. Steel tips scraped the inside of the skull.

Pickles fell, finally dead and gone for real, and his weight dragged the prong down with him.

The Dog Tongue bent over, placed a boot on the corpse's head, and pulled his weapon free, when he heard her.

He whirled, rising as he spun, and stabbed a lunging Collie underneath the lower section of her body armor, halting her flight in mid-air. The prong's blades went through meat and bone and emerged from the other side in a dull pop of muscle and organic matter. Collie grasped the weapon just behind the head as the Dog Tongue, baring yellow-stained but otherwise perfect teeth, held her aloft at the end of the shaft.

Strong was the warlord, and he held her there, studying her like some fearsome insect.

"Got you," the Dog Tongue whispered.

Collie grimaced, then slowly smiled, drooping over the upraised weapon.

"Not me," she whispered, "you... should be worried about."

His black painted eyes squinted in puzzlement, but only for a second.

In that aftermath of silence, that spent, smoking charge that follows extreme violence, voices could be heard. Several voices, amplified by the near perfect acoustics of the stairwell. A collective groaning and a heavy rumbling of feet climbing, *pounding* up the stairs. An unchecked rush of animated bodies, getting closer.

In that moment of confusion, the Dog Tongue's arms trembled under Collie's weight, just enough for her to lash out and clamp both hands around the back of his head.

And pull.

She hauled herself deeper onto the prong, bringing herself and that masked face close enough for a kiss. She bit down hard on the Dog Tongue's mouth, scissoring through his lips in a searing snap of agony. He screamed, a bestial thing straight from the guts. Spewing, spitting blood, the Dog Tongue threw her away, releasing the prong as she fell.

Collie landed on the sofa and spat out a set of bitten-off lips.

A pain-livid Dog Tongue covered his mouth, repeatedly bending over and straightening. Blood poured through his fingers and colored his face. He raged, stomped, and attempted to stem the flow with his hands.

Then he stopped, straightened, and whirled upon Collie.

The executioner's mask dripped and the lipless mouth opened, and that was a sight she really didn't need to see. Then, as if remembering, the Dog Tongue turned towards an unmoving Gus lying on the floor. He took two steps and raised his boot, looking to stomp a head.

Collie grabbed the Glock from where it had landed on the sofa, and turned the weapon upon the Leather overlord.

She squeezed off five shots before it went empty.

There was no real time to aim, just point and shoot.

Three of those shots blew through the Dog Tongue's legs, crashing him to the floor.

Where he stayed.

The empty magazine slid from the weapon.

"Shit," Collie said and hauled herself up from the sofa. The Glock was empty, so she dropped it and inspected the prong still in her. Using both hands, she pulled the tool from her lower self, ignoring the thick sludge coating the blades. She dropped it on the sofa, and hobbled at best speed to Gus. His eyes were open when she knelt by his side.

"Yeah, I know," she told him, sizing up the tape around him. "Hold on, okay?"

"What's that noise?" he asked.

"That's my crew."

Gus's confused expression showed he didn't understand, and she didn't have time to answer. She spotted dead and gone Pickles, and actually felt a moment's pang of sadness. Pickles wore a knife at his waist and she grabbed it free.

"Thanks," she said. She would've had to put him down anyway. Him and Ruby. They'd served her well, however.

She returned to Gus and sawed at the duct tape.

"They use a whole fucking roll on you or what?" she asked.

"I know, right?" Gus replied wearily, getting one arm free and looking over at the Dog Tongue.

"Collie," he said. "He ain't dead."

That stopped the operator. She shoved the blade into his hand and swung herself around.

The Dog Tongue got to his knees.

Collie stood up.

The leather-masked leader swung his lipless face around, his mouth contorted into a permanent snarl of red teeth. Collie hit him hard across the jaw. He collapsed in a growing pool of his own blood once again.

But he wasn't dead. Nor could he walk, his legs destroyed.

He groaned as Collie backed away, the noise almost matching the racket from the stairwell.

She ripped off the body armor and threw it at the Dog Tongue's destroyed legs. There was enough of a scent still on the vest to bring the hounds. She undid her coat, her fingers stumbling at times, but she finished the job. She didn't take it off, however.

Gus finished freeing himself from the chair. "You're not going to kill him?" he asked.

Collie glanced at the open doorway of the penthouse. "He's already dead."

She grabbed Gus's arm, and together they staggered into a desperate step-and-shuffle, moving at best speed into the hall. They reached the shot-up sofa and the dead Leather there, where Collie slumped against the wall and jammed a finger into the controls. At the hall's end, a corpse jammed open a doorway.

The elevator doors opened.

A scream from the penthouse stopped them dead in their tracks.

"The fuck was that?" Gus asked, staring back at the entrance.

"Dog Dick," Collie answered. "Turning."

Gus stared, blinking, until the voices from the stairwell spiked in intensity.

"Get those," she said, indicating the shotgun and the HK.

Gus did so, checking on both the penthouse and the direction of the stairwell, his face filling with fright.

The sound of sneakers and shoes and all manner of things slapping steps, railings and cinderblock walls were right there, just around the corner. No need to see them to know the forward elements of that mindless rush had reached the level below and were racing around it.

Collie stripped off her jacket and threw it on the floor. She limped into the elevator with Gus a step behind.

The top button on the control panel said, "Roof. Authorized personnel only."

Collie stabbed it with her thumb.

The doors closed, just as one of the mindless ran past.

61

Gus hugged Collie and held her close as the elevator rose.

"Christ, Collie," he whispered in her ear. "You smell like shit."

She nudged her head against his, and he knew she was smiling.

"Shit," he repeated, realizing what he'd said, and held on tighter.

He was just about to ask her what they were going to do when the elevator stopped, and the doors slid open.

Winter winds blasted past them, ripping the breath from Gus's face.

"God Almighty," he winced, pulling his coat together, the same one they stopped and shopped for back in Winnipeg.

Collie leaned against the door, preventing it from closing. She lay her head back and stuck out an arm. Gus handed over the rifle, while he handled the shotgun. Once done, he stepped in close and she wrapped her free arm around his shoulders.

"You okay?" he asked, his mouth close to her ear.

"I am now."

That lifted him, immensely, but the updraft in spirit was a fleeting thing.

"Over there," Collie said.

They walked through an open area that might have, at one day, been planned to be a rooftop gathering place. Ends of canvass flapped in the wind, revealing stacked piles of unused cinderblocks. A collection of chairs had long since been blown over and flung into a corner wall, where a series of dead flowerbeds rose to waist height. There were a few tables up there, as well as several cylinder gas tanks. Gus kicked a hard hat out of the way, and it skittered much farther with the wind.

There was no light, except from the moon, which was full, pearly white, and accompanied by a sprinkling of stars. He wondered briefly then if Milo was running into snow. He hoped not.

"What about Dog Dick?" Gus asked.

"Told you," Collie cringed, looking positively frost bitten in the night. "He's turning. I infected him. He's probably crawling around on the floor down there already. Like the shit dingus he is. Or was."

She was guiding him towards a glass partition that rose waist-high. Beyond that the other hotels stood and blocked most of the view. Not a single light appeared in those dark towers, and a subtle change underfoot caused Gus to look down.

He halted immediately.

They were on clear glass, as wide as a sidewalk, and the light from the penthouse below glowed beneath. There was nothing below that, except that deep, deep drop into a city chasm. Weak light marked that distant bottom, coming from the lobby. There was very little to see in the streets, but he thought, maybe, he saw the outlines of vehicles down there.

"Scared?" Collie asked, still smiling.

Gus nodded.

Still looking positively frosty, right down to her missing nose, she pulled him to her, and they stood that way behind the protective glass barrier. The city's spires crowded around them, and the wind snaking through those heights lashed Gus's face and made his eyes water. He glanced back at the elevator.

"Don't worry about them," Collie said, slowly releasing him. "They can't operate the controls."

"They might come up the steps," Gus said. What he didn't say was, *because they smell you*.

"They might," Collie said, her smile shrinking. "They still have to get through a door. I don't think this place is open to the public just yet."

She gripped his shoulder, digging in fingers before cupping it with her hand. "I... can't hold on much longer, Gus."

That killed him. No sooner did the last word leave her mouth, his throat seized up and water moistened his eyes. He'd been preparing for this moment for a while now, lying to himself with every passing second. He clamped down on the sadness, however, and she held his shoulder fast.

"Listen, now," she said, seeing the effect on him. "You know how this'll go down. I'm not going out like that fuckhead one floor down. There's no way. But before I go, I have to ask you something, okay?"

Unable to talk, Gus nodded.

"Okay," and she smiled again, that oddly fearsome, yet totally captivating smile she'd charmed him with the first time he'd laid eyes on her.

"Don't be scared now," she said. "Not for me. Be brave. I *need* you to be brave. I'm done, but the mission *isn't*. You understand? The *original* mission. There's still people out there. Good people. Looking for *other* good people."

Gus rolled his eyes and gasped, his throat seized up so badly it was a wonder he could draw any breath at all.

"I can't, Collie," he whispered, and God above how those words pained him. "I can't. I don't know how."

"You can, you do, and you *will*."

He shook his head, but Collie held him fast, her eyes, black and piercing, stared deep into his.

"You *have* to, because there's no one else I can trust to do it. Okay? You find them, Gus. Don't give up. Don't you dare give up, because they need you to find them. So you do that. Find them and let them know you're out there. That *Whitecap's* out there. That Amy and Scott and Vick and *Tancook* are out there. All right? You do that, and *keep* doing that. Until, well… until you can't anymore. That was my job. And Wallace's. Now it's yours." At that, she smiled again. "You lucky civvie, you."

That broke him, but somehow he smiled. One great, moist, snot-hitching smile.

Then he nodded.

That pleased her, he could tell. She ran a thumb across his hairy cheek, her fingers drifting all the way back to his ear, where she traced the outer curve.

"There's no one better," she told him.

Gus sniffed, his sinuses swollen and aching and miserable.

"No one," she repeated with a slow shake of her head.

"You're better," he whispered. "You're so much better."

Suddenly looking very sad, she pulled his face in close to hers, and Collie Jones pressed her forehead against his. She kept it there for seconds.

Do the dead cry?

Gus saw up close that they did.

"You know what I miss?" she asked after a while, her whisper strained. She cleared her throat and held on to the front of his coat.

Not breaking contact, he shook his head.

"The Olympics. On TV. Miss watching them. Didn't matter where they were. What country. What time zone. I watched. Made it a point to watch. Wallace, too."

Wallace. God above. Wallace. A hot surge of sadness hit him then, leaving him absolutely stricken.

"Know what my favorite event was?"

Gus couldn't say a word, so he blinked, and committed the moment to memory. That one nudged aside another memory of her, where a relaxed-looking Collie stood on guard, outside a shop store, her rifle lowered as she watched the falling snow and the street.

Collie released him, and he was powerless to stop her.

She hoisted herself up on the top of the partition, which was wide enough for a drink. Gus reached out to steady her. She held his shoulders, until she was in place, then gently pushed him back.

There was nothing behind her except wind and a fourteen-story drop.

"You won't laugh?" she asked.

No, he shook his head.

She watched him for a few seconds. When one's time is up, it's so very, *very* short.

Diving, she finally mouthed, unable to speak. She might've wanted to say something else just then, but didn't. Instead, she smiled one last time.

And leaned back into nothing.

Collie Jones flipped over the partition and into the night.

Then she was gone.

62

A long second later, Gus fell with her.

But he only collapsed on the glass floor of that fabricated outcropping, his legs unable to hold him any longer. His back hit the unyielding wall that was the partition, and there he stayed, somewhat sheltered from the cutting wind. A moment later, he held his ears, partly because they were cold, but mostly because he didn't want to hear her scream.

She wouldn't scream, though. He realized that as soon as he thought it and hated himself for even going there. Collie Jones wouldn't scream. Not Collie Jones. Not… and right then, he remembered Wallace, telling him about her for the first time. So Gus squeezed his eyes shut, drew up his cracking knees, and held his head.

If it was below zero when he stepped out onto the roof, the temperature had to have dropped even more. The wind whistled over his head, past his shoulders, uncaring, all bitter, freezing cold.

Diving, he thought. She missed Olympic diving. He never knew that about her. Probably so much more he was never going to know. But he knew what he was going to miss. And he was going to miss it for a very long time. With that, Gus rolled over onto his back, to better stare at the moon and the stars.

He woke up some time later, cold, and feeling even more miserable. Somehow, he pulled himself up and sat there, staring at nothing in particular. The elevator was closed, and the roof was dark and full of shadows. Nothing moved and he was glad of it. Memories coursed through him as he stared on, each one bitterly painful, and yet so agonizingly wonderful to recall. Collie was in them all, but every now and again Wallace would creep in there as well. If there was another side, Gus was sure Wallace was there waiting for her.

And that thought helped the most, because Wallace loved her. As much as he did. Probably more.

"Yeah," he muttered and wiped at his nose. Grunting at what he'd freed, he dragged one sleeve across his face, twice, and that still wasn't enough.

"God… dammit," he swore quietly, and placed finger to nose and let rip. He nearly blew his head off from that, but at least he unclogged himself. For a short time, anyway. *Need some tissue*, he thought. Or maybe paper towels. A couple rolls of it, anyway.

Quit being a baby, he told himself, and wiped at his nose with a palm. But then he broke down again, the wounds fresh and running.

He mourned her for a little more, his eyes aimed at the elevator doors.

Then, at the edge of his vision, something moved.

Near the elevator doors, a shadow, he was sure of it. The sight of the figure rattled him from his grieving, and he struggled to stand. His shotgun was at his feet, so he grabbed for that, and aimed from the hip.

He scanned the dark.

"I saw you," Gus seethed, angry at being so disturbed. "Come on out and I won't hurt you."

Which was fifty-fifty. Gus was in a hurting mood, and even though he didn't want to shoot, he damn well would if it was a mindless gimp.

The wind whipping around him, Gus lurched forward, shotgun leveled, searching for threats. He eased up to the covered building materials and found no one. No one lurked behind the flowerbeds.

"Oh, you're slick," he whispered, peering into the dark. "So very fucking slick."

And he was, whoever it was. There was no one on the roof, as there was nowhere to hide.

The elevator doors opened, and Gus spun around, bringing up the shotgun as he did. He stood there, aiming at an empty interior, all lit up and waiting. In his search for his lurker, he had wandered over to the elevator and into the range of its sensors.

The doors closed again, realizing he wasn't about to get aboard.

"That's right," he said. "So fuck off."

He frowned then, one of sullen anger, and looked around. He remembered the assault rifle then, but not the name. He went back, got it, and returned to the elevator.

"All right," he announced quietly. "*Now* I'm ready."

The doors opened, and he stepped inside.

The glass partition, and the place where Collie fell—where she *dove*—to her end, was the last thing he saw in the closing gap of the elevator doors.

Gus stared at the seam for a very long time.

As an afterthought, he regarded the controls. One of the buttons said lobby. Lobby it was. There were mindless roaming the upper floors. Maybe even mindless down below. He hoped there were. He dearly hoped there were.

Down he went, way down, the lights winking on and off as he passed. He thought it had to be the loneliest ride he'd ever taken since it all began. Living on the mountain, he'd gotten used to being alone, perhaps dangerously so, so when he came into contact with other people, he realized how good it was. How good it was to talk to someone.

But there was a double edge to that sword, because when those people left, the silence didn't fill that emptiness. That chasm of loss, where poison rimmed the edges, one that a person was of half a mind to touch.

The elevator doors opened.

Gus brought up the shotgun and stepped out into the lobby.

Things moved.

Dead things.

Always dead things, Gus thought. They'd been around for so long, he wasn't really surprised to see them.

They weren't so spry, he saw, however. Some limped, impeded by leg injuries. Most crawled along the floor, either seeing or hearing him, or smelling the faint stink of urine clinging to him from hugging Collie.

Gus killed them all. Every last one that haunted the lobby. When he emptied the shotgun, he switched over to the rifle. When he emptied that, he used it as a club on whatever was left. He hunted every corpse that lurked, and when he was done, he considered going back upstairs and killing everything up there as well. The Leather had taken their weapons, and he thought if he searched the bodies, he might come up with a few extra magazines.

The ruined main entrance, blown apart by Collie, no doubt, drew his attention.

Taking a deep breath, he walked outside and sized up the situation, knew what he had to do.

He found her in a spatter of sludge, just to the right of a dark lamppost. She had hit headfirst, and at a glance, he wasn't sure it was her, except he recognized the combat fatigues. He didn't linger on the sight, because he didn't want to remember her that way. Seconds later, he found himself back in the lobby.

"Gotta bury her," he told himself. "Gotta bury her."

A part of him didn't think it would matter too much to her, but he was going to do something anyway. Wallace would have wanted him to do it.

There was an old lighter in one of the front desk drawers. There were also plenty of brochures. Gus ripped out the drawer filled with them. He ascended to the second floor, watching out for leftover mindless as he went and encountering none. The first room he found was open, so he stripped out the sheets and blankets from a double-sized bed.

Less than an hour later, he stood before Collie's funeral pyre, close enough to feel the uncomfortable heat. He'd placed her in a long flower bed in the lobby, where whatever had been growing there had long since died and gone. There were a few of those canoe-shaped, open coffins around the main floor, but Gus chose the one close to the shattered windows facing the street. He'd heaped blankets and sheets over her remains, made a fuse of sorts from the brochures, and lit it all with the lighter. A breeze blew it westerly, and Gus felt it at his back.

No mindless came around, and that was a good thing. He didn't find any ammunition for the guns, but he did find one of the Leather's medieval spears. It wasn't his weapon of choice but what the hell.

Gus cleared his throat, nodding at the fire and the remains underneath. He kept right on nodding, cheeks eventually moistened from his sad and grieving hitches.

"You were the best," he said. 'The best. I... I don't know if I can go on, Collie. I know I said I would, but I don't know how. I don't know how. You're the only one that knows. That *knew*. The only one. I mean... I don't know."

He stared at that blaze, then, shaking his head, and the fire burned on.

"I'll see what I can do," he eventually finished.

And looked to the open street to the west.

There, leaning up against the corner of a building was that dark outline again. Same one from the roof and from the liquor store shop, where he'd picked up the cardboard display of the Captain. Same one he'd spotted on the side of the highway, on the way to Regina.

"The fuck," Gus whispered, gripping his spear. "Hey. *Hey!*"

Gus moved around the funeral fire, glancing at the ground for only a second. When he looked up, the figure was gone.

"*Hey!*"

He hurried to the corner. It was a side street, dark and littered with refuse, but otherwise empty and black as pitch.

Readying his spear, Gus marched double-time down the alley to a back street. Looking back towards the Four Towers, there was nothing. Looking the other way, at an open crossroads, stood that shadow yet again.

As soon as Gus saw him, he ran after him. He reached the corner and looked around. There was an empty parking lot, the wall of what might've been a hotel parking garage, a house, and a road heading north.

The shadow went around the corner of the house and disappeared from view.

"Little—" *shit*, he was going to say, but started running instead. Whoever the hell he was, he was fast, and *quiet*, damn near soundless even, which didn't strike Gus as odd at all in that backstreet maze of darkened roads and empty lots. His foot squeezed out its familiar notes of pain, but he didn't stop, and he didn't catch up to the guy. Always, when he turned a corner, the figure was already at the next one and stepping out of sight.

It got colder, and Gus kept checking over his shoulder, believing he might be followed by leftover mindless.

None were on his trail, however.

"Gonna. Shove this spear. Up your *ass*. When I catch you," Gus panted as he pursued.

The moon was overhead, making it difficult to get his bearings, but he believed he was somewhere northwest of the Four Towers. A wire fence surrounded a parking lot, and across from that was a series of linked back doors. Crates and some unreadable signage cluttered the rear, but there was no mistaking one open door. The fence was much too high for the escaping mystery figure to climb, and flimsy enough that Gus would've heard the little bastard if he went over it.

Gus chugged to the open door, stood before it, and struggled to listen.

"If you're in there," he said between puffs, "and you're looking to knock me out or something, I'll tell you right now, you won't. And I'll be mighty pissed at you if you try it. In case you didn't notice, I lost a very special... friend back there, tonight."

He held his breath and heard no reply.

"All right, you little shit," Gus said. "All right."

Spear held before him, he entered, moving along a hallway. He kicked away a pair of plastic crates that jingled glass, and knew it was a makeshift alarm system. His eyes adjusted to the lightless interior, and he realized he was in a storeroom of such. There were shelves, plenty of shelves, but all were bare.

A door swung open ahead of him, freezing him in his tracks.

Gus hurried down an aisle, seeing the last shiver of a door as it slowed to a stop. He pushed through, realizing he was making a mistake but not knowing any better.

His boots hit broken glass that crinkled underfoot.

Gus stopped and stared. And sighed.

He stood at the back of what looked like a little convenience store. To his right were a wall of coolers that gleamed in the dark. Straight ahead were more coolers, while the center of the shop comprised about four aisles. The front door was within full view, and it looked closed yet smashed out.

Gus stepped softly into the shop and listened, hearing not a sound except that of his own breathing. He crept along the rear, passing each empty aisle, and noting that the place had been picked clean.

The checkout counter was up ahead, with all its abandoned trappings. Credit card scanner. Glass counters with scratch n' win tickets underneath. Empty boxes of kid's candies and snacks. Otherwise empty. Deserted.

"The fuck you go?" Gus asked.

Then he looked outside, along the avenue.

There the mystery runner was, standing before another shop, one that Gus recognized immediately. And there they stood, studying each other, as the wind died away into a ghost's whisper.

"Oh my," Gus said and stared, sizing up the sight before him. "Oh my oh… my…"

In a daze, he opened a broken glass door and crossed the street. Towards the closed door of the next shop over.

The phantom ahead of him let him inside.

"Sure, why not?" Gus whispered, lowering the spear and no longer concerned about his safety.

He stopped inside, right at a series of checkout counters. It was a much bigger shop, a cave really, that reached back farther than Gus could see. Not that he had to.

There was a stool right behind one of the counters, and Gus walked over to it and sat down.

There was a familiar bottle before him.

A full bottle. Unopened.

"Poof," Gus said softly and shook his head at the gift. "Drink in case of emergency, that it?"

No one answered him, and that was fine.

Gus cracked open that bottle and sniffed at the contents. It had been a while since he had partaken, remembering he'd shared a drink with Wallace when he was still around.

That seemed like a very long time ago now. And so many were dead and gone.

The sadness threatened to overtake him again, and Gus didn't want to be sad, not now, so he took a sip from that bottle, and scalded that emotion. It didn't all go in one swallow, so he doused it again, and again.

He grimaced, shivered on the stool, and nodded in approval. "Yeah, that's the stuff. Right there. Grandpa's secret sauce. Secret stash. And goddamn if this ain't an emergency."

Another sip, which almost got him coughing. Then another, not rushing, but… well, yeah, probably rushing. He didn't care. He was alone, in a cold husk of a building, and needing some company. And even the best of them fell off the wagon once or twice.

At the end of the world, the bottle would do.

So he sat and drank, listening in between swallows, the barest breeze playing a soundtrack to his ears. His throat burned, but in a good way, his gullet swishing in that witch doctor's fine brew, and sending some much needed good vibrations to his brain.

Gus sized up the bottle after yet another drink.

"I knew your brother," he said after a while, while he felt a little less sad. He still felt like shit, but not like before.

He studied the label, familiar even in the dark. "We had good times."

"Did you?"

And there he was.

The shadow that had led him to this very place.

Gus straightened, swayed just a little, and stared—all narrow-eyed—at the figure. "The fuck you come from?"

The figure shrugged. "Not important. Here I am. Ready to talk. If you are."

"That a cigar?"

The shadow nodded. "You mind?"

"No," Gus drew out, dismissing the notion with a hand. "You got another?"

"Just this one, I'm afraid."

"Save me a puff then."

The figure nodded again and looked around. He went to a corner and, lo and behold, brought over a lawn chair with a cupholder in the armrest.

"How'd I miss that?" Gus asked.

"You missed a few things," the figure said, sitting down across from him.

"And you were getting shitfaced."

Gus supposed so.

The figure produced a cigar-snipper, inserted the tip, and cut off the end. He spat a few shavings onto the floor and picked at his tongue. "Little dry, but what can you do?"

Not much, Gus half-shrugged, knowing exactly what the guy meant.

The figure patted himself down, searching for a light, when Gus remembered himself.

"Wait, I got you," he said, and reached into one pocket and then the other. "Here. Hotel lighter."

He snapped it open, producing a flame.

"Wow," the figure said. "Fancy."

He puffed on that cigar, the smoky curls lazy, and eyed Gus across the way. "So you knew my brother, you said?"

"Yeah, I did."

"Where is he now?"

A shrug. "Well, he was shot. In a kitchen. Back east."

"Hm."

Gus took the opportunity to take another drink. That one went down without a hitch, and he offered the bottle to his new friend, who shook his head.

Then the figure reconsidered with a shrug and a wave of the hand, and Gus handed it over.

"Whiskey and cigars go good together," the figure said.

"I wouldn't know. The cigar part, I mean."

"Sorry," the figure said. The cigar was offered, and Gus took it with a chin dip of thanks. He sampled a puff, then another, and handed it over.

"That's nice," Gus said, and took another drink.

His new, unexpected friend nodded that it was, and held his cigar before his face. The end of that thing burned red, but Gus could barely make out the man's features.

Then he slapped a hand to his forehead. "Sorry. Been a shitty day. Forgot my manners." He cleared his throat. "I'm Gus."

"S'all right," the figure replied softly. "No harm done. You look like you had a shitty day."

"The shittiest."

"Why don't you tell me about it?"

"Not just yet. Maybe another time."

"Will there be another time?"

Gus drew in a chest full of air then, and nodded a tad warily. "We'll see."

"Well, you look like… you could use some company. To keep you out of trouble. Watch your back. That kinda shit. If you don't mind, that is."

"I don't mind. Not at all."

"Good. That's good."

"What should I call you?"

The figure became silent for a bit. "You can call me… Jack," he finally said, before sampling the cigar again and causing the end to flare with light. "Or Uncle Jack. Whichever is easier for you."

Gus nodded, knowing, but not caring in the least. "Uncle Jack. Nice ring to it."

Jack nodded, tapping the cigar. "Lotta people think so."

"Nice to meet you, Uncle Jack. Again."

"Nice to meet you, Gus Berry."

Gus couldn't remember if he mentioned his last name or not, but he didn't really care. There were strange things afoot, but they weren't dangerous things. Jack had a friendly way about him, and Gus very much needed someone to talk to. They don't tell you this, but company, *good* company, is as addictive as any substance out there. And when it's gone, you long for more of the same.

The winter night was long and would be for several months, making it a lonely place indeed.

But Gus had a good feeling about Uncle Jack.

"To friends lost and gone, but not forgotten," Gus said, surprising himself. "And to better days ahead."

A solemn Jack tipped his cigar at the thought.

And in return, Gus raised the bottle for his old, once-forgotten friend, and took down a mouthful. *Better days ahead*, he told himself. "Lord knows we need some."

"You gonna drink all of that?" Jack asked.

"Most of it," Gus said. "It'll help me. Make it to the morning."

"What happens in the morning?"
That brought about a moment's worth of thinking.
"Ask me then," Gus replied.
Jack nodded that he would do just that.

63

He woke late the next morning.

Gus was hung over and mighty parched. There was still some whiskey left, so he drank that.

And got to a washroom in time to puke.

Only a little came up, as there wasn't much in his guts. He felt terrible, physically and emotionally, but he continued to sip on whiskey. And with every sip, he felt himself coming around, until he was well enough to walk.

All the while, Jack was nearby. Watching him.

They left the shop and returned to the hotel lobby. Gus saw the flowerbed and Collie's charred leftovers. There was plenty of dried dirt in that long open coffin and the ones nearby, so he shoveled whatever he could onto her remains, covering her as best as he could and becoming miserable once again. After that, he scratched her name into the metal side of the flowerbed, along with a crude heart. Once finished, he wiped his eyes, sized up the grave, and hoped the lobby would do. Hoped Collie—and Wallace—would approve.

He retrieved the shotgun, thinking what the hell? He even found the key fob to one of the pickup trucks parked out front. There were containers of fuel in the box, enough for nearly a couple thousand kilometers, if Gus guessed right. There was also a cooler full of dried meats, and homemade bread.

The Leather might've been savages, but it was good to see they fed themselves.

"We'll stop along the way," Gus said, peering into the morning light filling the end of the street. "When we need shit."

"Like toilet paper?" Jack asked, already aboard the chosen vehicle.

"Like that. And other shit."

"Shit's shit, in my opinion."

Gus didn't reply to that. Last thing he wanted to do in the morning was get into a debate about shit. With… him.

"So where we going?" Jack asked.

Gus thought about it. "No idea. I can't go back east, just yet. Just… can't. Need some time. Need to straighten myself out. Do some thinking. About that thing Collie wanted me to do. And that's gonna take some time. Can't go north. It'll be too fucking cold."

"Anywhere's too fucking cold now," Jack said, lighting up another cigar.

Gus squinted at him. "Where you get those anyway?"

"You really want to know?"

"Not really. So like I was saying. Not east, not yet anyway. And not North—"

"'Cause it's too fucking cold," Jack supplied, puffing life into his cigar.

Gus nodded in agreement. "South is out. Too dangerous with radiation, or so I've heard."

Jack frowned and nodded in agreement.

"So west it is," Gus said. "We go west."

"Gonna be rough," Jack pointed out. "It is winter."

"Yeah. Say… you ever see the Rockies?"

Jack thought about it and slowly shook his head.

"I hear Jasper's nice. And there's Banff, too."

"Sounds like a plan."

"Yeah," Gus agreed. "It does, don't it?"

And they said no more about it. Gus climbed aboard the truck, thinking he would stop at the nearest clothing shop and scrounge around for more winter clothes. They would need them. Certainly a new coat, one that didn't stink of piss. Maybe even pick up a bat, if he could find one, to replace the lucky one he suspected was left aboard the limo. The spear wasn't his thing. And God knew he would be looking for more whiskey. Or even rum. Whatever he could find. *All* that he could find. He didn't think Uncle Jack would mind.

He started up the rig and turned on the heat, looking forward to the warmth.

Uncle Jack sat in the passenger side, cigar smoke idling in tune with the pickup.

Gus listened to the rumbling of the machine's engine. He glanced into his side mirror, where the Four Towers shimmered. He stared at that for seconds.

Don't give up, Collie said to him then. *Don't you* dare *give up, because they need you to find them.*

Gus closed his eyes, hearing her voice in his head.

You do that, Collie's voice continued. *And keep doing that. Until, well… until you can't anymore. That was my job. And Wallace's. Now it's yours."*

Then she smiled that wonderful glorious smile. *You lucky civvie, you.*

That part brought a terrible smile to his face. *Lucky, lucky me*, Gus thought back, and felt the sadness return.

But she was with him. She *would* be with him. He had Uncle Jack riding shotgun with him as proof. If finding that bottle of whiskey wasn't a sign, Gus didn't know what was, and knowing that made the hurt a little less, and the hopelessness fade just a touch.

"You ready?" he asked Uncle Jack.

Who took his time nodding back.

"All right, then."

Gus put the truck in gear and drove away.

Westward.

About the Author

Keith C. Blackmore is the author of the Mountain Man, 131 Days, and Breeds series, among other horror, heroic fantasy, and crime novels. He lives on the island of Newfoundland in Canada. Visit his website at www.keithcblackmore.com.

DISCOVER
STORIES UNBOUND

PodiumAudio.com